Yungir's Tower
Durgrinstar

Marisko

Kallias' Skiff Wreck

Crispin Point

Sungtau Shore

Loshith Falls

Kanratu

Seal Rock

Point of the Gald

Praise for Spiritdancer: The Blade of Baresi

"Spiritdancer is a wonderful story of adventure and friendship with magicians, a shapeshifting serlcat, and a whole cast of diverse and interesting characters. What exciting exploits as they cross exotic lands to rescue the kidnapped damsel from the man determined to make her his bride, whether or not she consents. I enjoyed the romance between the main characters, as Dealla enchants the other travelers to get some "together" time with Kallias.
A delightful rewrite! I had the pleasure of reading the Blade Dancer, originally written by Luthie West with a coauthor. The new solo written version is a lovely improvement, cohesive and fun." -- **Beverly Starr**

"As Someone who reads a decent amount of Fantasy, I have to say I really enjoyed Spritdancer, which is so full of real characters with feelings. The plot hooks you in and doesn't want to let you go.
A friend recommended this book and I fully admit, I wasn't expecting such a great story with good twists, a great plot and believable characters who felt alive and jumped off the page.
Kallias is searching for his sister, who was taken from their home. He travels to an unknown land coming face to face with characters and creatures that he never knew existed including Dealla a beautiful woman with animal forms. A true bond is formed between them as they travel and face the monsters of this dangerous world.
The main antagonist stays one step ahead of them, while having believable reasons that what he is doing is for the greater good.
Over all, an engaging and lovely fantasy story 5 out of 5 experience! I look forward to more books from this gem of an author, Luthie West." -- **Robert L. Stevens**

"I thoroughly enjoyed the world building created by the author of the story Spiritdancer. It has both the familiar adventure motif as well as a new take on magic and creatures. The story has a few slow spots but overall it keeps a reader wanting to know what will happen next. It's certainly worth adding it to your reading list." -- **M. K. Barr**

Dear Reader, if you are inclined, I would appreciate your leaving an honest review with your favorite online retailers and/or other book review sites. **Thank you, the Author**

by Luthie M West

Spiritdancer:

The Blade of Baresi

Dale -
Enjoy the
adventure!
♡ — Luthie M West
LMW

ISBN: 978-1-7322514-2-7 paperback

Other available formats:
ISBN: 978-1-7322514-3-4 Kindle
ISBN: 978-1-7322514-4-1 ePub (and other eBooks)

Names: West, Luthie M, author.
Title: Spiritdancer : the blade of Baresi / by Luthie M West.
Description: Winston, OR : Luthie West as Little
    Cabbagehead Books, 2020. | Series: Spiritdancer, bk. 1.
    | Summary: The Baresian Blade Dancer effects a daring
    rescue with a small handful of friends against a
    magician and his army.
Identifiers: ISBN 978-1-7322514-2-7 (paperback) | ISBN
    978-1-7322514-3-4 (ebook : Kindle) | ISBN 978-1-
    7322514-4-1 (ebook : epub)
Subjects: LCSH: Young adult fiction. | Fantasy fiction. |
    CYAC: Magic--Fiction. | Quests (Expeditions)--Fiction.
    | Kidnapping--Fiction. | BISAC: YOUNG ADULT
    FICTION / Fantasy / Epic.
Classification: LCC PZ7.1.W47 Sp 2020 (print) | LCC
    PZ7.1.W47 (ebook) | DDC [Fic]--dc23.

Publisher's Cataloging-in-Publication Data provided by Five
Rainbows Cataloging Services

Cover design by izabeladesign along with artwork contributed
by the author. The author highly recommends the work of
izabeladesign from Fiverr.com (2020).

Previously published as The Blade Dancer.

Dedicated to Love, the strongest, most magical power in the universe-- any universe.

Acknowledgements

First, I wish to acknowledge my appreciation for my husband, Dale, who continuously encourages me to keep to my creativity and has supported me in every possible way. He always sees the extraordinary in me and my work. Thank you, Honey.

Next, my sincerest gratitude goes out to my two editors, Kali VanDusen for her hours working with me to be sure the sun was in the right place and for all the frequent revision reviews, and to M. Kari Barr, whose polish and final editing I could not have done without in order to make this rewrite not only a good story but well written.

I will always be grateful to Kane C. Huges for his part in co-creating the characters and story with me in the previously published book (however badly written it was). As a hobbist writer, his gems of ideas were invaluable to moving the story along. I am also thankful for his release of interest in The Blade Dancer to make Spiritdancer: The Blade of Baresi doable.

My thanks to the Super Tribe Mastermind group who kept me on task and gave me assitance with online information and tools for marketing (with special thanks to Lucia da Vinci, our "pocket librarian"). AND finally, my sincere thanks to Sherine Clarke for the images and the codes to bring the excerpts of this book and of my children's picture books to interactive life on my website at LittleCabbageheadBooks.com.

***

Prologue

Three men and a boy rowed toward the Baresi shore from a huge vessel with a single mast. Even from a distance the size and length of the ship called to mind stories of sea monsters. The rowboat belied its counterpart, diminishing to a quarter length smaller than the fishing dinghies of Rockscrest. A call had spread throughout the little village as soon as the ship had come into sight. The elder council consisted of four men and a woman. The three eldest, and therefore considered the wisest persons by the town, and two other men, the Boat Master and the Blade Master, son to one of the elders, gathered at the pier to await their guests. A boy and a girl stood with them.

From the ship came men bronze of skin with light brown to flaxen hair. Their eyes were powder blue like the morning sky or as gray as the overcast of cloud that usually shrouded Rockscrest. By comparison, Baresians were a dark-haired, dark-eyed and pale-skinned people. The blue of the Baresian boy's eyes was a deep cobalt. His sister's eyes were of such a dark brown as to appear almost black. How stark the strangers' icy eyes appeared to them.

The curly-topped Rockscrest boy stood beside his father, an arm loosely draped across the shoulders of his younger sister. Ordinarily, the children would be dismissed when their elders were speaking, but this time they stood with the group on the pier where the strangers came in. It was the presence of a little boy the seafarers brought with them that caused his father to call him and his sister to be with the council men. The dark-haired boy kept a wary eye on the towheaded boy as he listened to the elders.

"Welcome to the humble town of Rockscrest and to the lands of Baresi." The eldest held his hands out palms up, a gesture of peace despite the sword worn by the Blade Master.

"We're in need of supplies, the replenishment of fresh foods and water. Also of trade goods." Their spokesman, the tallest and by far cleanest looking of the men, had a long, wavy, ash-blond ponytail down his back. The small boy bore a family resemblance to the speaker, possessing not only a ponytail but a similar delicate beauty in his eyes and mouth.

The elder explained the lack of produce in this part of the country due in part to its meager water supply. "In fact, we've not seen trade here for over a generation. The last came seeking only glimmer stones." He gestured to a few younger men, who had gathered at a safe distance to satisfy their curiosity. They in turn took leave to fetch something.

"Gems?" the man asked. "Is there also ore?"

"Not that we've found. Only stones," said the eldest.

"Our children find them in the desert. They appear to have some decorative value in other parts of Iasegald." It was the Blade Master who spoke then and nudged his boy. "You have some stones, son?" The boy nodded, consternation beginning to cloud his dark blue eyes. "You can find others." He knew what his father meant. He lifted a cloth cover from a small purse at his waist and stuffed his free hand inside. He pulled it out with three stones. They had been the best he had ever found, a delicate pink, mostly clear and of large, ovate shapes, not as bumpy as usual. He looked up at his father who gestured unmistakably with his head. "*Go on*" *it said,* "*hand it over*" He held them out to the other boy. Before the youngster could take them, his tall father grasped hold of the stones.

"Indeed, a generous gift to us," he said. He pocketed them without examining them at all.

The young men returned carrying baskets. "We have little to give. But, these may provide a few days' sustenance." The elder offered a small barrel of water and bushel baskets of native tagoroot and dates to aid the visitors until they could go where food and water were more plentiful. "With the current, Olkem is only about four days southeast."

The conversation moved to a discussion of the metal work of Rockscrest, fishing hooks, tools and gate hinges, all of which would be relics if they were not continually used and sorely needed. Another of the visitors asked if anyone in Rockscrest could forge a tube and a strange mechanism, showing the elder spokesman a drawing.

"No," was the answer. The last metallurgist of the town had been dead for twenty-two years. No one had taken up the art. Rockscrest's metal work was done in Olkem now. "Someone there may be able to make this for you."

After losing his gems, there was little in the men's trade talk to interest the older boy. He turned his attention instead to his sister whose eyes were growing wide as she trembled. She was not usually shy, so her brother scrutinized the flaxen-haired boy with narrowed gaze. But he only stared at the girl until she made a face. He responded by sticking out his tongue. For that, his father turned his head towards the men.

"He had fire in his mouth," the little girl whispered.

"What?" The Baresian boy's sullen expression darkened with suspicion. "That's impossible."

The council concluded with an exchange of valuable foods and precious water. For their supplies, the Baresians were given two nets and a little sack of coins. After some small debate about the use of foreign coins, the three men and the light-haired boy sailed away and, never having made it to Olkem so far as Baresian news was spread, were forgotten—at least for sixteen years.

Chapter 1

Thousands of little suns blinked across the rippling surface of the sea. They raced toward a small skiff and pounced upon it with the harshest glare of the great yellow orb at its peak. Near the center of the fishing dory, one oar stood wedged against the forward bench seat by a utility box. Strands of rope, unwound from a fishing net, held it in place and attached a black cloak to the top. The sea breeze slapped vainly at this makeshift sail. The cloak's owner, Kallias, lay on the bottom of the boat, his long black, curly hair covering his face. Strapped to one thigh was a slender knife in its sheath, and from his belt hung a black scabbard and sword. The roar and crash of breakers against a rocky shoreline failed to awaken Kallias from his nightmarish slumber.

The flash of festival preparations, the donning of his scabbard and cloak, the smiling faces of friends and family, all rudely rent through by the report of a rifle. Baresian unfamiliarity with these new weapons held him, held them all, as the Blade Dancers wasted time wondering what the popping noise was. The alarm conch finally sounded followed by another crack and another. Only when the screams and shouts reached their ears, did the swordsmen realize the danger. Kallias leapt into action.

Suddenly he awoke as water splashed in over him, stinging parched, sunburned lips with salty water. The small boat hit a rock and began to sink. He jumped out into the shallow tide, where the waves beat upon him as he retrieved a satchel from the box and the top half of the oar to which his cloak was tied. Kallias stumbled up onto the sandy beach before his legs gave way, plummeting him face first into the sand. The taste of salt bit at the cracked ridges of his lips as he licked at them. Sand invaded his mouth. He spat. Blinking hard in the bright sunlight, he squinted to see a silhouette of sandal clad feet before him. "A—sadia," he said dimly. His head pounded while he struggled to look up. Weakness pervaded every muscle. The swordsman swept a hand through the illusion and the image vanished. Then once again fatigue overcame him.

Hours later the sound of waves hammering on volcanic rock disoriented Kallias. This was not the swoosh of water along the Rockscrest shore, nor its slap against the docks. Damp sand clung to the side of his face. Feebly he arose and gathered himself near a beached log. Kallias sat for a long moment collecting his thoughts. A partial moon hung above his head. *Almost the first quarter.* He had slept nearly the full night away. *Three days and now a third night since the raid. I may already be too late.*

A swig from his water bladder wet his palate yet barely quenched his thirst. Until he could find fresh water, that would have to do. The beach stretched both ways as far as the eye could see, an uninhabited coastline. Never before had he felt so lost, so alone. He examined a torn corner of his cloak then untied it from the oar. After which he removed his cuirass and wet, sandy shirt and laid these across the log, dropping the fisherman's supply pack beside them. Kallias prepared himself for the exercises which would help him clear his mind. He stepped onto the hard-packed sand where the tide turned and drew forth his striking curved blade. Myriads of stars joined the crescent of moonlight and blessed the beach with an eerie, dark blue, dreamlike quality. Kallias inhaled deeply, exhaled slowly with the ebb and flow of the tide. He closed his eyes, released his fatigue, and moved with exactitude, crash and rush, pull and thrust, drawing imaginary lines in space, spinning in graceful circles. The dance of the blade was as much an art as training.

Kallias felt a pair of eyes following his fluid movements. He scanned the area with each turn. If someone was there, they would not catch him unaware.

Unseen from deep shadows, Dealla watched the stranger fight the invisible with flowing slice and jab. Her curiosity piqued as she hid in the stand of trees, anxious to get a closer look as sparks of light glinted on the shimmering silver sword in the kinnir's hands. Only fear of that sword kept her in check. *What is he doing here? And where are the others?* Her thoughts, even the questions, came in feelings and pictures rather than words. Too tall to be akinn, he was obviously of the kinnir race. No kinnir came along this beach alone. *There must be a longship somewhere.* She shuddered not from the cold. *It is time to move, but which way? Where are the others?*

The soft moonlight gave his taut torso a porcelain touch as his muscles moved beneath his skin, his real skin. Kinnir and akinn alike always had removable fur. She too had been born naked except for a small top knot. But she soon learned to manifest fur when cold, and later to emulate their removable coverings so as to walk in the towns unnoticed for a little while.

He paused, scanning along the tree line. Dealla flinched. *Has he seen me? No, no, he could not have.* She slipped form and continued to watch. He was beautiful. Never had she seen kinnir nor akinn with such long, curly, blue-black hair, so dark. She crouched low hoping the animal could escape detection better. It was risky being in the first form, not knowing where the others were. She would have to go searching for them.

Dealla, now a serlcat, crept along the tree edge, remaining in the shadows. She repeatedly glanced at the kinnir as she neared a stand of trees which jutted out towards the beach. Here she would be able to see behind the rock formations to the long breakers on the other side. If the ship was there, she could easily duck back through the trees to her rough home in the thicket.

She closed in. Her keen ears picked up the dancer's breathing as it quickened from the exercise. A rock rolled from beneath her paw and caught his attention. Dealla paused as he glanced warily in her direction. His dance seemed to focus on her now.

Dealla froze not fifteen feet from him, where the rocks met the trees, and the trees were thinnest. *He did see. Would he call his companions now and go for the hunt?* She had been hunted before. She knew his kind, kill first, ask later. Oh, but he was beautiful, and she had been too long without companionship. *Where are the others?* Her body tensed. Her mind told her, *Leave, sprint, run!* But she could not turn her eyes from him.

With a flourish, he sheathed the exotic longsword. The man sat on the driftwood, his back to the sea and its star-sprinkled horizon. The sun would be up soon. After shaking out as much sand as possible from his coverings, he donned his shirt and light leather cuirass to ward off the damp chill of a mist that rose from the tide. As he fastened his cuirass, her shadowy form caught his eye. He finished buckling up, never taking his eyes from the spot. He had felt the eyes upon him. Now it was certain. To draw out whoever it might be, Kallias continued about his business, deliberately looking away. Still, he felt the presence and had seen something. Taking care not to threaten, he called, "Come out, whoever you are. I am but alone. I can defend myself if need be, stalker." With that he slowly brought his full attention back to peering into the trees.

Her ears turned forward at his strange accent. Not that she ever spoke kinnir words, but she understood most of them from her visits to villages. She understood "alone"; it had become hers. Who was he talking to? She listened for the betrayal of footfall, but heard only the night creatures she was accustomed to. As a cat she would test him and show herself, for if he lied it would be quickest to escape all but a bullet. A bullet once nicked her. It came from what the kinnir cursed as a blunderbuss. There were various shapes and sizes of these weapons. Fortunately, they were still new to the gald, not every kinnir carried one. This one did not. Slowly, half crouched, Dealla slunk out of the safety of the trees and paused a few feet from her escape route, waiting.

Kallias laughed nervously. "A big cat?" Thinking quickly, he dug around in the satchel and pulled out a chunk of cured, dry meat. It had been his good fortune to have chosen a fishing dory with emergency provisions aboard. He broke the jerked meat into chunks and threw a piece into the distance towards the strange cat. The instant the meat left his fingers, Kallias realized his error. Now the cat would view him as a source of food. His own fault if he should have to defend himself. "I am sorry. That was a thoughtless kindness." He took a bite of another piece and put the rest away. "I hope you know that's all there is. The store was meant for survival of one only. Just about gone now." The Blade Dancer spoke in order to fortify himself.

The cat sniffed cautiously at the seasoned meat, its ears moving this way and that. Finally, it crept forward stretching its belly to the sand. He kept his wary gaze upon the feline. It was large like the wild cat pictured in his great grandfather's journal. There was a newness to this cat, its sleek gray coat splotched with black markings. It appeared more delicate than the sketch he remembered. Kallias decided this one was a young lady cat. He sat as calmly as he could, watching and waiting.

She sniffed again at the meat and hesitated, letting her ears do their work once more before committing herself. She delicately lifted the jerky from the sand and ate it. She eyed him again and his pack, then pushed herself up to sit on her haunches with her tail extended out behind her, the tip curled slightly, in an unconscious pose of elegance. It was almost as if she was the mortal twin of his sword, a glinted triangle of cat against the sand. Even the color of the beast mirrored the shiny steel of his blade.

Kallias stared at her, neither his fear nor his curiosity quite gone. "You're a dangerous beauty." He offered a smile as he calmly slung his rucksack over his shoulder. "I must go now, my furry friend," he said as he stood slowly, black leather boots creaking.

The lonely coast seemed to stretch forever in either direction. So with a backwards glance at the cat, Kallias began to head south, strolling deftly through the soft sand with a practiced ease.

A different fear suddenly engulfed her. She placed one foot forward, her ears perked towards him attentively. *He is leaving me. Wait!* She could not call to him or speak in this form. But the panic did not overwhelm her survival instincts enough for her to drop form. What to do? She took a few hesitant steps. Then in her panic, she raced at him as a cat would at its prey.

Startled by the soft, padded rush of her full gallop, Kallias spun about fluidly drawing his sword, certain he would have to kill this majestic beast to save his hide.

As the shine of steel reached her eyes, the cat careened to a halt, kicking sand up at the kinnir. Her hind legs slid in under her front ones and her tail whipped forward as she managed to stop her momentum a whisker's distance from the keen edge of his blade. She froze, her head and ears drawn back, fear in her eyes. In a brief realization, she jumped to the side and ran a few steps away then turned back toward him. Again, she took up the attentive posture.

He rested his blade on his right shoulder. "I did apologize and do now. But, try that again and it will be your last." His tone was undeniable as he eyed the cat curiously. He tapped the blade idly upon his shoulder. Kallias watched the cat with a questioning gaze before heading southwards again.

Dealla twitch her tail, hoping he would understand that as acknowledgment. She felt drawn to this one; he was different. No, not just that, but he was alone, like her, abandoned. She gave little thought to the nest she had made for herself in the thicket. It was only one of countless resting places she had abandoned in her efforts to survive. She resolved to stay with him.

Cautiously, Kallias began his trek again. The blade he kept rested on his shoulder. The pack which he had dropped in an instant, he carried in his left hand. He walked on along the firm damp sand, glancing back over his shoulder frequently. She followed at a respectful distance, her foot-pads silent. After some contemplation, Kallias realized that at this distance, the cat could pounce on him before he could act. There would be no warning swoosh of sand like before.

He stopped and turned. She stopped. "Why are you following me? I told you. No more food." He lifted the sack, pointing towards the trees. "You can easily feed yourself. You live here. You hunt, probably every day. I can't, yet. I need what little I have." Having thus spoke, he stood staring at her. She stared back. Finally, when he said no more, she scanned the horizon and then into the trees before making a few bouncing steps towards the trees. However, she neither left him for the forest nor anywhere else, but skirting around him, faced him from the south. Kallias turned again. Then the cat began to lead, now looking over her shoulder to be certain he was following. "You're a strange one," he said and walked behind her. "Why not? I haven't a clue where I'm going."

Chapter 2

They had trekked on for hours with only the sound of the crashing waves and the scrunching of boots in the sand. Dealla knew of a place where the kinnir could rest. They were close. A gentle breeze blew off the sea, but it did little good against the glaring heat of the sun at its zenith.

She checked on him when the sound of his footfall slowed. She had no idea when he had put his sword back in its sheath or when he had pulled a water bladder from his bag. She waited for him to catch up to her, but moved again before he stopped. When Dealla did this for the third time, he protested. "Wait. I need to rest. Let's take a moment."

How to tell him I have a place in mind? She twitched the end of her tail. It did nothing. When he started to let himself down to sit on the sand, she ran at him. *That got his attention,* she thought. He jumped up, nearly falling over backward to grasp at the hilt of his sword. She stopped short to show he had no need of it. Dealla swayed before him, trying to convey with her body what she could not say.

"What?" he asked.

There. Do you see it? She used body and head to get him to look past her at a rocky promontory ahead. *Shelter,* she meant to say, though if she had said it, it would not have been in his language. What emanated from her throat was a soft cooing, something between a purr and the song of a dove.

"Ah a cave!" he exclaimed. "Well, why didn't you say so? Lead on." As it turned out, the cave was actually a natural tunnel through the promontory connecting two beaches. On the north side, where they entered, a steep climb was required to gain access. Then the rocky interior rose gradually a few feet more before it made a short turn to the south side exit. The formation of windswept stone just at the turn afforded a clear, almost flat surface to rest upon. The serlcat stopped and laid down at the far end of this flat area, just where the shadow and sun met.

Kallias's stomach growled. Once seated with his back to the curved, swept rock, he dumped the contents of the satchel onto the dry floor. He had counted his supplies as a daily routine since leaving his homeland. It never changed except for the diminishing food and water and the remnants of net cord he had used for his makeshift sail. It contained three packages and a water bladder with a fancy, embroidered-cloth shoulder strap. The smallest package, nearly empty, was constructed of waxed parchment. This kept dried fish, jerked mutton and hardtack, of which only pieces of jerky and biscuit were left.

Kallias lifted a piece of the jerky to his mouth but stopped short. "It's all I have," he told the cat. She stared at him. "Oh, all right." He held it out to her. "I hope you don't bite." She let her eyes rest with interest on the offer, then turned her attention to the scenery outside. "Thank you," he said, popping the morsel into his mouth.

The next package, a woolen sack with a drawstring held a simple reflecting instrument and a parchment with drawings and instructions on how to use the basic sextant. Another parchment was a little-used star chart. He folded these and returned everything to the sack.

The last package was a small box only slightly larger than the food pack. In it was all the necessary tools to keep the casting net in repair. There were also a hook and line with a handle, evidently an emergency rig, though useless in deep waters. Having cannibalized the little cast net for tie strings, Kallias had left it behind in the dory.

He finished one biscuit and another small piece of jerky. That left two more bits of jerky and the last biscuit for later. He then closed his eyes and lay his head back against the rock. A bit of rest would do him good, if only for a little while.

Dealla awoke. When had she dozed off? Because the passageway stood above the waterline, the tide would not reach. However, neither would they be able to go once it came in. She could not allow the kinnir to sleep longer. He would soon need water and food. Besides which, this was Crispin Point, where the tide was deeper and the sandy shore narrower and rock strewn. Travel would be harder.

Dealla turned to awaken her hero the only way she knew in this form to do. She licked his face, cleaning from it the dried sweat and sand. He lazily brushed her away but jumped back in panic as he awoke. She stood still until Kallias relaxed. "Alright, alright, I'm awake." He hoisted his tall, slender frame to his leather clad feet and gathered up his pack over his shoulder again.

She made a soft noise and led him down the rocky slope, keeping close to the trees along a path of slippery rocks. "It seems unnecessarily strenuous to me," said Kallias. Nevertheless, he followed, stumbling along where she stepped. His guide trotted ahead of him, her soft paws sure upon the places where his boots could not find purchase. He stopped as soon as she gained some bit of distance ahead of him. "This is ridiculous. Your animal instinct would, of course, keep you where you can bound off into the wood for escape." She was too far ahead to hear his grumblings. He picked his way down to the smooth, hard sand. "That's better." As they continued parallel to the water, Kallias traversed the sand more quickly, not catching up as fast as he expected to but keeping her in view.

The sun slipped behind the mountain peak, casting a broad shadow on the coastline. In the distance, over the shining sea of near twilight, a dark form appeared as if some small fishing vessel headed south beside the shore. Kallias stopped a moment and squinted to briefly appraise the silhouetted object far from reach. He checked to see if his leader had gotten away from him. The cat slowed and turned to sigh briefly at him, then sat to clean herself, waiting for the dark-haired kinnir to catch up.

A small fishing vessel cut through the agitated waters just beyond the tide. Its sail billowed and bent erratically as if its mast was broken. *Or,* thought Kallias, *like a makeshift sail.* This could be a fellow from his homeland. Perhaps he had not been the only one to go off madly after the men who raided Rockscrest. He glanced once at her. The cat continued to clean herself, unaware.

He ran quickly to the water's edge waving his arms and calling as loudly as his dry throat allowed. "Hallo! Hallo! Over here!" At first there was no change. He ran along the beach to keep abreast of the little boat. It sat too low in the water. Kallias feared it might sink or perhaps no one was there. "Hallo! Hail the vessel!" He picked up a rock and threw it as far out as he could.

It turned. "Here! Here!" Kallias shouted, jumping gleefully. Such a blessing it would be to have another join him on his quest to save his sister. As the skiff came toward him, Kallias noted how awkwardly it sat in the sea. The hull appeared to widen beneath the surface. Something was not quite right about the way it broke through the waves, though the dark mountain shadows made it more difficult to see. Once it acquired the tide it surfed rapidly forward upon the waves.

The boat had almost reached him when suddenly a flash of steely gray hit him in the side, knocking him off his feet and away from the tide. At first Kallias fought and struggled until the serlcat rolled off him and maniacally tugged at the shoulder of the kinnir's cuirass urging him to get up. A few yards from his feet the tide rolled in again and with it a fish, larger and uglier than any shark Kallias had ever seen, wiggled towards him. Only its weight in shallow water slowed the beast as it pushed its fins against the sand to get at him. Kallias scrambled to his feet, leaping backwards just as the huge maw of the monstrous fish snapped shut upon the air where he had been.

Dealla finally understood. This kinnir had not been here before. How foreign was he? Everyone knew the saber crispin lured kinnir to the high tide with its illusion. Every kinnir she knew anyway, those who came on longships. Was it not their blood-letting that taught this fish where to hunt?

Kallias ran with Dealla at his heels, close to the rocky shore far from the tide. After a while he paused to catch his breath. He glanced from her to the water repeatedly. "What—" The sea monster was no longer there. His visage sank. "Pakao fish!?" he exclaimed. "You mean sea monster stories are true?"

Her eyes reflected a knowing wisdom as he asked. She made herself sneeze and flicked her tail to affirm his astonishment, then placed her muzzle briefly in his hand. This one was not from a longship. He needed her. This is why she was drawn to him. The energy of the land told her he needed her. And they were both alone.

Later the shadowy image of the cat could barely be discerned in what little light remained in the sky. Kallias stood hands on hips, shaking his head. "You don't understand. People go into the forest. They never come out." She was relentless. "There are forests lining the high plains and the southern swamps all around my homeland. Death traps every one of them. It's where the war monsters and all manner of horrors live. Surely this forest is no different." Just then the tide came in high and slapped at the rocks behind him, sending a wet spray against his back. Kallias scrambled forward fearing another attack from the pakao fish. "All right! You make your point. My life is entrusted to you."

The swordsman and his odd companion wound their way through brush and trees. Kallias slowed to a near crawl in the ensuing darkness. When the serlcat looked over her shoulder, he saw two round, blue lights of her eyes. She made that small noise again, something like a cooing to encourage him to continue to follow. But, as she turned her head away to lead, she was lost to him again. He growled his frustration as he followed blindly through the brush. Though his eyes became adjusted to the dark, the vague changes to the depth of blackness created an obstacle course. He paused now and then to listen for the serlcat and then continued the pursuit. Something hit against his leg and hit again. It was snakelike as it bent across his knee then pulled away to repeat. Overcoming an initial shock that it might be some snake, he reached down with a grunt. "Is that you?" He tried to feel the presence of his friend.

The cat lifted her tail to tap his hand and looked over her shoulder again. She cooed. Kallias sighed a relief when he heard her, saw her eyes and felt the furry snake-like tail. He lost it as he clambered over a large fallen stump. Again, she slapped her tail insistently at his leg and hand until he finally caught it. "What is it?" In answer, she pulled him along to the right and then up a winding pathway. There were fewer logs, rocks, bushes and whatever else had been hitting his shins and ankles and turning beneath his boots. A light rain began sprinkling a mist of droplets through the canopy to kiss his skin. He panted, licking at the droplets as they picked up the pace along a straight away in the path. As the path turned south then down then leveled out again, the sound of waters reached them and the light rain let up as if it had only come to slake his thirst and be on its way.

The cat led him down a gentle slope and out into a small clearing where he could hear the soft crush of pebbles and sand beneath his feet. Before them a small waterfall cascaded into a pool lit with a multi-color, phosphorous glow, which clustered at the water's edge and climbed the rocks that lined it. The pool overflowed, forming a stream below it, where the phosphorescence slowly disappeared along the rocks and through the water. Just as the clouds opened upon the speckled night sky, she brought Kallias to this lower creek. In the dim gray light, the clearing appeared to be a wide river bottom barren of large rock or log, as if it had once been a pool as well. "I am saved!"

Soon they rested by a warm fire. Cool water refreshed them and a rodent, supplied by the serlcat, filled their stomachs. With his knees drawn towards him and his brawny arms hooked around them, Kallias rested his chin on top. He stared into the fire. "You have my thanks, my friend." It did not matter whether the feline understood his words. Kallias needed to talk, to feel the companionship. "I'm from a place that is arid, not like here. My father, Aurelias, said that our home once was green and rich for growing. In Rockscrest there's a saying, 'it is best to be a fisherman who can wield a sword, whereas the Blade Dancers are sword wielders who can fish'." He chuckled idly. "It isn't a compliment. We're supposed to be the guards and defenders of Rockscrest. Instead we were little more than entertainers. But, my good friend, Omarion, and I loved the sword..." His voice trailed off as he stared silently into the fire, remembering.

The sun slowly sank beneath the horizon as two young swordsmen sparred on the rocky shores of Baresi. They learned to fight under the guidance of Kallias's father.

The village of Rockscrest spread out with small stone and grass huts surrounding the few larger homes, built with precious wood by the founding families. As a fishing village, soldiers were not so much needed. Memory of the war with the Valandree, a barbarous race of pakao who had invaded from the north, kept the tradition of the martial art of the swordsmen alive. The invasion had been over for a hundred years. Consequently, there were barely more than a handful who learned the Dance of Blades, and in each generation, fewer cared to join.

The dance, which also held as tradition, formed the practice for battle and made for deadly warriors. The dancers exercised it ritualistically, every dawn and dusk. They often performed choreographed sword fights on nights when the villagers got together to revel and have festivals.

"Omarion," called a youthful maiden, bobbing her head as she passed by the training young men with a basket of fish in hand. "Asad... oof!" He winced as his sparring cohort, a youthful Kallias, caught him with the wide edge of the training sword before he could come to finish her name.

"That's my sister," Kallias said with a smirk.
"That'll make me your brother someday,"
Omarion retorted and parried a new incoming blow.
"And your older brother at that."
Kallias laughed. "Until then, watch out for me!"
"Dinner will be done soon. You two had better
finish playing your games. Omarion, you may join us.
Roselana is already here," Asadia said before
vanishing into the small house. Omarion grinned at
Kallias and followed her in for the evening meal,
ending the sparring early, much to Kallias' loathing.
"Ugh," he dropped his wooden sword and followed in
after them.

The memory faded. Kallias threw another chunk of wood on the fire and poked at it with a stick. The beautiful cat gazed at him patiently. Until then, he did not realized that he had stopped talking. He began again to tell her. "They took Asadia, my sister—men in big, long, wooden boats with strange magic sticks. It was the Season of Flowers celebration. We were dressing for the festivities. Otherwise, I might not have been armored or had my cloak." He tapped his hardened leather cuirass. "One moment we were laughing and hurrying each other along. Then the alarm sounded." In great detail his story unfolded.

"The alarm conch sounded urgently in Rockscrest. At first we presenters laughed that some child had gotten hold of it, eagerly wanting the demonstrations to begin. Then we heard the screams of women echo with the repeated blasting of the horn.

"A handful of our Baresian swordsmen charged out of their homes but stopped to gape at the people running in fear, fighting bare-fisted against armed men and being murdered savagely in cold blood before them. Never had any of the Blade Dancers including myself used our swords to defend ourselves or the people. Loud, sharp cracking sounds filled our ears, and smoke from a multitude of fires filled the air. My friend, Omarion, was first to rush at the vicious raiders, breaking the daze of disbelief for all of us. Soon all of us engaged in the fight.

"Amidst scattered pockets of skirmishes I saw my father, Aurelias, strike down a marauder, rescuing an elderly man. The invaders moved back towards the beachfront. But not in retreat, no, not running from us. They herded several of our women towards their boats. With the cry of a rampant bull, Omarion raced after them with me on his heels. An attacker appeared to our right, stampeding at Omarion with a maul held high overhead. He ducked as the man swung, then spun to his right on a heel while his blade cut a wide arc. The gleam of steel appeared like a silver crescent followed by a spray of red. The raider lay dead instantly. Just then the report of another explosion rang close past my ear. In two steps, I sliced at the one with the hateful weapon. The enemy dropped his fire stick and ran, but Omarion lay writhing on the ground behind me. Just then, I heard my sister's scream. 'Kallias!' I darted blindly in the direction of her voice. I found her being dragged away by two men. I pursued them, shouting, 'Let her go!'

"'Take her! I'll deal with this one,' the taller brute barked to his comrade and drew a blade.

"At first I fell into habit with my trained movements and with momentum that dazzled the longship man. I felt so cocky when I parried an overhead blow knocking my foe off balance. But the longship man recovered too quickly and soon pressed toward me with a strength and force I'd never experienced. My chest felt tight. I lost focus and became afraid that for all my years of training, it would not be enough. The fight for my people became a fight for my life. Then I remembered a lesson I had taken for granted to watch the eyes and body of my opponent to anticipate his strikes. With surprising swiftness, the tables turned and I dealt him a severe wound to the shoulder. It was enough to send the man fleeing towards his comrades. 'Kallias!' Asadia screamed. The men struggled with her as they pushed their dinghy back into the water.

"'Asadia!' I yelled. I thought her fight would give me time to reach her. The one I had wounded suddenly stopped and spun about. Something in the man's hand cracked loudly, emitting a puff of smoke. I felt a sharp sting on the side of my head and I fell."

"Something hit me here." Kallias indicated a cut just above his temple. "It knocked me out, though not for long. When I awoke, the village was ablaze. All around me, my people lay dead or wounded. I heard her scream in the distance. I ran to the docks. They were already hauling their dinghies aboard the big boats. I took a small boat and gave chase. I rowed and rowed and rowed—" The dancing flames flickered brightly in his eyes. After a long pause he whispered, "Too slow. How could I be so slow?"

The cat's expression became attentive as he talked, and she gave a low growl at the mention of the kinnir in the longships. So, they were his enemies, too. She twitched her tail.

"Kallias." He tapped his chest. "I'm Kallias. You probably couldn't know that. You probably don't understand. Even now, I can hear her call my name over and over. Those boats... huge... fast... disappeared. When I lost an oar, I rigged a sail with my cloak. I kept on." He stopped suddenly and sighed softly. Her body shifted forward as he said his name.

He took a long, deep breath, then smiled weakly to her in the quiet stillness of the night. "I have no idea what I'm doing. They're likely dead or worse already. It's been four days... I think." The flames gave his fair skin a warm glow. He shifted the embers to let the fire breathe.

Chapter 3

In the morning, the cat was gone. Kallias awoke slowly with a chill, arms folded, teeth chattering. He rose up and donned his cloak, checked around for the cat but only found more supplies. A pile of sticks, some moss and a much smaller rodent lay beside the cooling coals and ash. This rodent was roughly gutted and cleaned, though not skinned, as if an animal had eaten its insides. He shuffled to the stream and bent low, cupping his hands for a drink of water.

Suddenly from nowhere a gold hummingbird darted back and forth in front of his face. The gold flash backed up and rushed at him several times, giving him cause to swat. Puzzlement wrinkled his brow as he tried to focus on this blur of a tiny bird while it dodged his swings and buzzed about his head frantically. "Come on now! Shoo!" He waved his hands about. It would not shoo, but swooped down on him several more times nearly into his eyes before averting its flight. Disgruntled at the buzzing menace, he moved away from the stream with the intention of rebuilding the fire for his breakfast. This time the decidedly mad bird hit the back of his head with its sharp beak, then hovered out of reach, toward the trees away from the stream. Now thoroughly annoyed, the Baresian rubbed the back of his head and spun about. With his full attention now, the bird taunted him deliberately, darting back and forth just out of arms reach. He cursed and turned back to the pile of new supplies. *Perhaps it would be better to leave,* he reasoned. *This little flying nugget must have a nest close by.* As he gathered the sticks into his pack, the bird dove madly at him and hit him on the head again. Kallias wheeled once more to face the bird. This time though it flew to the trees and landed on a fallen log. "That'll be enough of that!" Kallias dropped the pack and stormed towards the gold flying dart.

It hovered slightly above ground on the other side of the log. Just as he reached the log, heavy footfall and a guttural sort of growl could be heard through the trees on the other side of the stream. The bird buzzed back and forth over the depression on the other side of the log as if signaling him. He paused then quickly jumped over the log, crouching low behind it as he heard the eerily strange sound.

The bird looked him over, and just as quickly as it had come, it darted back across the clearing and the stream and lost itself in the trees.

The great hulk of a creature stumbled and crashed through the brush with no care to where he stepped. It splashed across the stream and came upon Kallias' camp, where the pack lay open and the sword in its scabbard lay where he had slept. The great nearbeast with a snout for a nose and barely a visible demarcation of a neck, dug through the pack and emptied its contents. *This must be the keryplik hunters of the war stories in Baresi. Never imagined I'd have to face one,* thought Kallias. *All the monsters are here.*

It sniffed the air and eyed the uncooked, un-skinned rodent. Just as that one picked it up another, larger hunter came into the clearing. This one was obviously female as her pendulous breasts were uncovered. These creatures had at least some minor intelligence as they dressed in skin loin cloths. Besides which, they spoke in some guttural language and roared at each other.

The female approached the male aggressively and slapped the rodent from his hands. He stepped to one side as she eyed Kallias' belongings strewn upon the ground. Then the male did an odd thing. He picked up a pebble and threw it at her. She let the pebble bounce off her arm and faced him. He squatted down and brushed away some pebbles on the ground in front of him then lifted his loin cloth. His back was to the log, for which Kallias was grateful.

He eyed his sword from the safety of the log as the beasts argued distractedly. It was too far away. His only hope was that they had not caught onto his scent. If fortune held and they argued loudly enough, he might slip away undetected. He ventured another peek, then quickly ducked again and waited.

The female responded angrily in the guttural language and threw ash at the male then picked up the rodent and sat between him and Kallias' sword. She bit into the rodent in front of the now disappointed male. He stood and cursed and roared and waved his arms about, but she paid no attention. Finally, he gave up his petition and lumbered off downstream.

Kallias' heart thudded in his ears. He quickly peeked over the log and saw the male nearbeast leave. As soon as the male kervplik was out of sight, the female stood full height, threw the half rodent into the brush and shoveled the sticks and moss into Kallias' pack. With a simple regard, she turned her attention to the log behind which the stranger hid, nodded once, and disappeared back the way she had come. Kallias sank low again and exhaled silently though his open mouth. Kallias gave one final glance around, then hopped over the log back towards the campfire. He quickly belted on his sword. He wondered, *Did the large female deliberately help me? Certainly I was discovered, or she wouldn't have nodded.* It seemed all too odd when he watched the nearbeast distract the male away from his gear. He had thought his final peek at the monster was going to be the last thing he would ever see. But why would the female put everything back in his pack? He shook his head. *No. Not discovered. She knew I was here. It had to be the cat. That's why she hasn't harmed me. She must be a forest spirit.* He smiled at the idea that he could be worthy of such a guide.

Within moments, the silvery, spotted cat leapt into the clearing from the trees downstream. She approached him and stood ready to travel, attentive, foot and ears forward. He sighed a relief when his companion returned, picked up his pack and slung it over his shoulder. He regarded the cat with a different perspective, certain she possessed something about her more unique than the color of her coat. How odd. It all felt to him as if he were a child again, listening to the old ones tell frightening tales of yore. Only this time he had been cast inside the tale. The cat, the humming bird and a giant nearbeast had helped him in amazing ways. He gave her a nod that he was ready. She was cunning and intelligent in a most non animal-like way.

His people believed in the gald spirits. They hailed in the clouds, the forest, the water, even fire. The tales of Baresi's war against the pakao Valandree told of such spirits which appeared out of the north to help defend the coastal basin which was now the Glimmerbarrens. Though considered benevolent, the fight of the two powers was responsible for drying up the land, transforming it into a coastal plain which stretched inland to a desert.

Dealla led him upstream over rocks and uphill. That he needed people was clear to her. However much she distrusted them and the very idea, there was no escaping it. She knew of a place of people, the race of akinn mostly. It would be a climb and then a long walk down. It would be two days and nights and half a day through a pass, a hard trek but fast. She glanced back at him sadly. After that, he would go into the town alone and likely she would not see him again.

They hiked along silently lost in their own thoughts. Eventually, Kallias slowed. Since he had missed out on breakfast and the sun was near its zenith, Dealla looked for a good place to find a meal.

Suddenly, the thud of a falling tree and a guttural language quickly caught their attention. A large tree stump came flying at them from their right, followed by a thunderous, monstrous laugh.

Dealla disappeared into the trees at the first sound. She had let her guard drop. That kervplik male had followed them. These imbecilic creatures would kill anything and likely eat it too if hungry. If he was still alone, she could bring him down. Dealla raced through the trees to get behind it and look out for others. She had no idea if the kinnir was alive, but she could not think about that now. This thing would not stop hurling objects at him until he was smashed.

She found the lummox unearthing a boulder and pounced upon him before he could raise it above his head. Her teeth found purchase in its thick neck and she crushed through it with powerful jaws. It slumped upon the rock and grabbed at her shoulder attempting to dislodge her. Dealla let her claws out and dug in. The hunter yanked hard, dislocating her shoulder and tossing her from his back. He bled in streams from the bite. Soon enough, he would fall permanently.

Kallias had instinctively dodged the unearthed stump and quickly found refuge behind a thick tree in case another should come his way. He frowned when he saw the cat tossed. She lay winded upon the ground. The hulking beast attempted to regain its foothold while holding the neck wound. When it grabbed for a large rock with its free hand, Kallias saw his opportunity. He ran towards the mass with blade drawn. Its knees buckled, enabling the Blade Dancer to impale the creature's lower back. The kervplik dropped the rock and fell face forward with a ground-shaking crash.

The serlcat blinked as the blood of the thing splattered upon her. Then the forest reverberated with the yowl of her pained cat-cry as she failed an attempt to rise up off her shoulder.

Kallias worried. Would she attack if he tried to help? Any injured creature would. But she saved him; he couldn't just leave her like this. If forest spirits in corporeal form could be injured, could they die? Kallias would not take that chance.

The bulk of the nearbeast lay close at her feet. The creature's boar-like snout was twisted to the side of its face making it even more hideous in its death. She tried again, then stood on three legs but could not put the fourth down. She slumped to the ground only this time staying upon her belly, examining the grotesque angle of the shoulder.

Kallias inched carefully closer on all fours, reaching his right arm out slowly first to show he meant no harm to her. She lay panting, ignoring him, concentrating against the pain, allowing him to get close enough to sit next to her. "Other animals will smell the blood and come looking. We must get to safe ground," he said softly, daring to pet the top of her head. Almost as if his touch had caused more pain, she slipped from consciousness. Her head fell forward, chin upon the strong leg. Kallias wiped the blood from his blade and replaced it in its scabbard. Then swiftly but gently scooped the cat up and made his way back to the path. Limp in his arms, she was awkward to carry, necessitating that he put her across his shoulders as one would carry a calf or lamb. This was not the best for her shoulder, but there was no other way.

He exerted himself, walking along the path at the quickest pace he could for as long as he could. The sun climbed to high noon, and the heat beat down upon him before he found a defend able, rocky outcrop, which would provide some shelter. He laid the injured beast down as gently as possible. As the daylight gleamed upon her, he could see the darkened spots of her coat held small highlights of a lighter silvery white, like small snowflakes in the dark sky of a winter night.

The shoulder angled up awkwardly from its socket as her leg lay along her side, almost over her back. Kallias had seen this injury with people before, but he was no physician, and certainly knew nothing of animal anatomy. The dislocation was bad. Setting it would be the best option if the feline was to make it on its feet again. Resigning himself to the fact that there was no choice but for him to attempt to reset it, he shredded a piece of his cloak for a muzzle, just in case. There was no lore about injured spirits or how much of the animal traits they take on.

After tying the cat's jaws, he worked his fingers around the animal's coat, feeling for what might be the socket and what might be the joint. "Forgive me. This could end up worse than it is now," he confessed, for he had only a vague idea of how to set it. With a forceful shout, he pulled the leg and pushed the cat's shoulder in until it popped. Exhausted, he slumped back against the rock wall and lightly closed his eyes.

Later, the setting sun cast its orange glow upon Dealla's tied muzzle as she awoke. It took her a moment to realize her situation and to remember. With an adept claw, she ripped the cloth binding off, worked her jaw and licked her nose. Other than feeling bruised, her shoulder worked again. She heard the soft sigh of Kallias' breathing as he lay sleeping. This was a good place to camp. She set out to hunt.

By the time the serlcat returned, Kallias was awake with a strong fire going. "I knew you'd return with a catch." For a while they concentrated only on food. The prey this time consisted of a pair of rabbits, which she had carried together by their ears. Kallias noticed the appearance of singed fur around a single puncture wound on each of them, no bites. He chose not to ask where they had come from.

Once sated, Kallias again relaxed, speaking quietly to her. "In my homeland of Baresi, there are stories of mysterious beings who helped travelers. Before coming to our present land, my people were nomads, always traveling. We came to understand these benefactors to be spirits that inhabited various creatures to help lost travelers. And here I am." He chuckled. "I'm your traveler." The cat tilted her lovely head. "I will call you Spiritdancer, for your graceful moves and... you're my guide,so. Do you like that?"

She blinked and brought her ears forward. Accepting the name, she lifted the end of her tail once to let him know. Though his words were strange, Dealla understood some of what he said, because she had listened to the kinnir and akinn for many years. However she could not, would not, take the vulnerable form. It would allow her speech in her language, but was too great a risk, too deep a pain. She crawled toward him and nudged his hand with her muzzle. She was Spiritdancer and he was Kallias.

Tiredness etched his face, soon he laid down upon his ragged cloak. His eyelids dropped except when the slightest creak or crunch of a stick jolted them open. Spiritdancer walked around behind him and laid alongside of him opposite the fire. She felt certain he could not hold out much longer despite his nap. She leaned her body against his restless one and purred him to sleep.

They traveled through the mountains for two more days and nights. Kallias had no idea where she was taking him, but trusted her. She brought him food or took him to it. Kallias made fires when she did not prevent him and learned how to listen to her, how to read each twitch of her tail, movement of her body and turn of her ear. He also learned to pay attention to animals and birds that approached him urgently. As a spirit of the forest, he believed her to possess each of these creatures as needed for his protection. He called every one of them Spiritdancer.

Chapter 4

The sound of breakers and the smell of the salty sea air wafted through the trees. Soon a clear azure sky could be seen at eye level; then the traveling pair stepped out upon a ridge line along a sheer drop. Below them were more trees and the occasional appearance of a road worn by wagon wheels. Dealla turned north along the ridge and led Kallias upward again. Soon the trees below grew scattered like wayward children and spewed the road out to meander along a grassy plain and wind its way toward a village along the shore some distance ahead. The ridge began to slope downward along another set of trees as if by some agreement with road, beach and township. Dealla took Kallias back into the trees along a path not far in where glimpses of the village were rare. Finally, she jumped up upon a large rock and lay down. From behind the rock the village gate could be seen and the talk of men mixed with the squawks of gulls could be heard.

Kallias stared knowingly at the large wooden gate and then the cat. She would go no further than the rock. He nodded once to her. "I pray our paths may cross again, Spiritdancer," he said softly. From this far, the kinnir and cat could see two men standing at the sides of the gate. They looked to be half-asleep as they leaned on their pole-arms. Kallias took foot to the path nearby and headed towards the gate.

Dealla watched his slow approach until he reached the gate and one of the guards stood to greet him. Then she disappeared into the trees where she would not be seen. She felt alone again but the fear was greater. She would wait and see from the safety of the trees.

One guard stood upright. "Hold stranger." He approached non-aggressively, appraising Kallias rightly but holding to duty and an appropriate suspicion of strangers coming out of the woods. "We don't see many coming alone from that direction."

The other stood and stepped up behind the first, curiously more than dutifully. "He's got dark hair."

Kallias held as the guard commanded, though he towered head and shoulders above these men. Their facial features were rounded, almost childlike. "Greetings," he said, then paused for a moment. "I come by way of boat. It has been a long trek, and I only come as a visitor. I'm no troublemaker." He offered a reassuring smile to the guard.

The second looked seaward. "What boat?"

The first followed the eyes of the second but returned them to Kallias in short order. "Ya couldn't come by boat in that direction. It's six and twenty leagues to Kanratu and there's only sea cliff and forest between here and the Loshith Falls. If yar boat be the other side of that, ya'd be dead."

"Well, perhaps not dead..." the second started before the first elbowed him.

"Even if ya kept to the road. Far too many kervplik hunters and other nasty creatures to survive on yar own." He peered past Kallias.

"So, where'd ya come from, really?" asked the second with bright suspicious eyes.

He thought quickly and replied with a humorous tone. "Sea storm. The boat was wrecked on jutting rocks near the east of the mountain." He waited and watched the men's faces.

The second looked a moment and then burst out laughing. The first frowned and hit the second with the blunt end of his pole-arm. "Shut up, Marsk." Then he turned narrow eyes upon Kallias. "Ya telling me ya came over that mountain?" He pointed to it. "Ya want me to believe yar shipwrecked on the other side of that mountain and walked all the way here? Where's the rest of them?" He looked Kallias over again with a difference of near respect. Then he used his weapon blunt end again to touch Kallias' scabbard. "Ya can't have any weapons inside. Ye'll have to leave that out here."

Kallias appraised the interrogating guard a moment. He noted the man was out of shape. "There's no one else. I tell the truth. You may go over the mountain and see for yourself," he said as he unhooked the scabbard. "I trust you will keep it safe?"

"Yus, I'll keep it safe."

The one called Marsk interrupted. "Surely will, Stranger." He was hushed by the stern look of the first.

"There be no one I know going over that mountain by themselves. Smarter of ya to have gone around the peninsula." He points to the south. "Take ya half a month but ya might be dead anyways." He took Kallias' sword and scabbard firmly, his expression skeptical but not unkind. "Ye'll find drink and lodging at the Sailfin, midtown by the docks. Only place to get a meal too. There's a mercantile past that and up the east road. If ya need a tailor—" The guard tilted his head examining Kallias' torn cloak and general disarray. "—and a bath, there be that too. Other shops, fish market, well, ye'll see. Enjoy yar visit. Welcome to Saungtau Shore." The first signaled to the second who opened the gate.

"By-the-way, where am I?"

"Saungtau Shore like I says," replied the guard indignantly.

"No, I mean where in the gald, in Iasegald?"

"Why, ya're in Marisko."

Kallias offered a smile of thanks and a slight bow to the men. He felt naked without his sword. But the guards believed him, which was good enough for now. Kallias paused at the gate as it slammed shut with a creak, then turned to face the town.

It was much like his own, its streets filled with the daily commute and children laughing and playing. His boots scuffed against the hard dirt or made sucking noises where there was mud and hay. As he came to the square, he glanced about.

He felt odd since he stuck out a head-and-a-half taller than all the townsfolk. Their skin was as fair as his but their hair an array of blondes and reds. He pulled his ragged cowl up over his head. "Excuse me little girl," he called out to a child as she walked by with a basket of fish and bread.

The girl paused and looked at him wide eyed. "Not allowed to sell from the basket fish, mister. Fish monger be down the street." She pointed westward down a narrow street lined with sod homes.

He nodded. "Ah, thank you little one." He made his way down the alley which opened up into a busy dockside market place. He surveyed all the stands silently.

The townsfolk kept up their routines though they glanced askance at the stranger. Two boys were playing at swords with sticks near a fruit and vegetable stand until a merchant woman chased them off to play elsewhere. "Get on with ya two! Not so near the goods." She turned and looked Kallias up and down. "Can I get ya something?"

"I was simply making my way to the Sailfin Inn" he replied as he noted a scattered few taller men amongst the fishermen at the docks nearby.

She hooked a thumb over her shoulder. "Right there." She examined him again as he walked past her.

He pushed the shoddy inn door open and ducked slightly as he entered. The patrons gave slight pause and a glance in his direction then continued conversing as he shut the door behind him and stepped up to the bar. One ragged fellow hunkered over a glass of amber liquid, glanced sideways at him briefly and returned to his drink. There were only two other patrons sitting at a table and no barkeeper.

In a moment one of the men at the table put his fingers to his mouth and let out a sharp whistle. A woman's voice called from somewhere behind a door by the bar. "Reel it in Beullus! I'll be there in a tick." Soon a buxom woman in her thirties pushed out through the door, backside first and carrying a tray with several serving dishes of food on it. She turned into the room and hesitated as she saw Kallias. "Oh!

Another'un here late for the midday? Or a drink? Maybe a room?" She spoke over the steamy dishes in a friendly manner. "Sit ya self down anywhere. Canna get a room yet anyway. Might as well eat, if ya haven't already."

Kallias said nothing and took a lonely seat over in a corner. He lowered his cowl respectfully and observed the other patrons. The two men, who appeared to be fishermen, stared at him and nodded to each other. Kallias knew if anything, an inn might be the best place to start at finding a lead for his missing sister.

He eyed the steaming dishes hungrily as the woman served the locals. She placed the tray upon a table nearest to the one with the two men and then put a plate and utensils in front of each of them. One at a time she dished up some food for them, then put some on a third plate and took it to the bar to the older man. She stepped around the bar and reached behind something and pulled out another dinner set. She filled the plate and brought it to Kallias. "Here now, ya want spirits or ale?"

He perked his head up to her. "Ale, please."

She gave him a curt nod and went around to a keg behind the bar and returned just as quickly with three steins, placing one in front of each of the men at tables. "Now I'll be startin' m'wash. Don't ya be needin' anything till I gets back. None of ya!" She looked at the whistler sternly. Then she marched off behind the door without another word.

Kallias ate his meal hungrily. He was famished as the trek was long and arduous. Spiritdancer led him to tubers and berries and game on their journey here. *But nothing beats a warm home cooked meal,* he thought. He observed the other men quietly.

As Kallias came to the end of his meal the little fish girl walked in with her basket. "Shasha Murie! I has yar bread and fish!"

"She's gone to do wash, Sipsie," said one of the men at the table.

The little girl looked disappointed and a bit nervous. "What to do with the fish?"

"Put 'tin the cooling cupboard, Sipsie. If she says anything, I'll tell her it be me made ya," said Beullus, the whistler.

"Thank ya, Pom Beullus."

The older man at the bar tossed something into the basket. Sipsie put the basket down, took the shiny coin out and held it up. "Oh thank ya, Pom da Guin!"

"This last delivery?" He asked looking into his spirits now rather than at the child.

"Yus, last 'tis."

"Fares ya da's foot, lass?"

She pocketed the coin in her apron and picked the basket up. "Oh, he be walkin' on it a limpin'. Complains a lot, but it's my deliveries. He sits to mend his nets." She addressed the older man's back as if he were giving her the respect of a kind smile.

The innkeeper came through the door just then. "There ya be! I expected ya sooner. So, let me have the bread, girl."

The little girl stepped around the counter and disappeared. The woman picked up a loaf of bread and turned it over in her hand. "What's this? Why did ya let the bread soak of the fish? Look at it! Stone on top and soggy of fishy smell on the bottom! I can't use it. Ya best take it back!"

"No, please, Shasha Murie. Not my fault. Pom Drilo put it atop the fish his self, said ya wanted it. I told him..."

"I tell ya again and again, girl. Keep the parchment between." The woman scolded the little one harshly.

"But Shasha Noreem took the pappas! I had it. She tooks it for wrapping her fish. I begged her not to. She said she want to keep the fish off her cupboard clean." The little one began to cry. "Please, Shasha Murie. Pom Drilo makes me pays for it."

"And if I go to Drilo and buy more bread? He'll know ya didn't return it and then what?"

"Leave the girl alone, Murie." The older man looked up from his spirits to the woman. The other two men had taken only casual interests in the scolding of an errant child. "I'll buy bread from Drilo. Give it me."

The woman set the bread down with a thunk next to the man's untouched meal. After she scooped the fish from the basket and wrapped it in cloth, she tucked it in a cupboard under the counter. The door opened and closed with a sharp click, and that was that. "Off with ya then."

The man, Guin, raised an arm toward Murie. "Wait. Give her some milk, Murie. She's done deliveries, and I'll wager without a midday at that."

The woman put a cup on the counter and poured a bit of milk into it. "There then." She went back through the door to her wash.

The little girl noticed Kallias just then and whispered something to Guin. Then she went about the room collecting the empty dishes as if she had been asked to clean up. Little Sipsie had a round, soft face with rosy cheeks and freckles cascading down her nose. Kallias watched and listened quietly. If anything, he was an observant and patient man as the dance of steel had taught him. The man at the bar, who he first thought to be a sour old man, shook his perception of him. He was kind and defensive for the little girl. Kallias grabbed his empty dish and brought it to the bar. There he sat a stool away from Guin and gave a curt nod. Sipsie watched him walk past her and pouted. She put the empty dishes on the food tray and returned to the end of the bar, then took her cup of milk from it. She kept her eyes up, curious about the stranger.

Guin glanced at Kallias with a barely perceivable nod and took a drink. He immediately re-poured the spirits from his bottle so it remained the same level in the glass. Kallias sat with his eyes on Sipsie while she sipped from her milk. She replied to his look with a smile and a milk mustache. Kallias turned his head, thinking to introduce himself to the older man. Just then, a small weapon like the fire-sticks caught Kallias' attention. It was tucked into a belt under Guin's long brown coat. He clenched his jaw and reached for his sword hilt ready to drill the man for answers only to remember the guard had his blade. He took a deep breath and relaxed. This was not the time nor place for it anyway. The old sot must have seen the spontaneous movement of the swordsman, as he gave indication with a quick warning glare from the corner of his eye.

Kallias felt he must inquire of Guin's weapon. He hopped from his stool to the one next to the old man. He leaned close. "The weapon you have, they are common here?" He gave Guin an accusing look.

Guin half turned his head in Kallias' direction. "Ya always greet people this way?"

"Forgive my manners. I am but looking for answers, my friend," he replied to him.

The older man took a swallow from his drink, poured anew and looked past Kallias to the little one at the end of the bar. "Men's talk, Sipsie. Take yar cup with ya." Obediently the little one left the inn. Then Guin turned his attention to Kallias as did the men at the table, ceasing their idle murmurings. "Odd manners at that. Information before greeting and suddenly I'm yar friend." He looked over his shoulder at the other two who suddenly pretended not to be paying any attention. "I'm Guin. Who are ya?"

"Kallias," he said with a nod.

"Well, Kallias. ya're the stranger here and it's a volatile question ya ask." He sized Kallias up and then straightened himself. Kallias could see he was not as the others were in stature, but like himself, Guin was taller and larger. "It's a port. There're all sorts here. Men as well as weapons." He looked again to the two trying to hide their pretense. "What brings ya and from where?" Guin turn his body and attention toward Kallias, but moved his glass slightly to keep it in front of him. His trousers and shirt showed wear and a need for washing.

Kallias paused. How much should he say? To find Asadia required some openness. "I'm from afar, the Glimmerbarrens of Baresi. I come to seek a man." At that he made a swiping motion across his own face with his fingers. "He has scars that run his face. He is bald and carries a weapon such as yours."

Guin's sandy colored, shoulder-length hair fell from a receding hairline to shroud his weathered face with streaks of white and gray. His graying, scraggly beard dripped off his chin a palm's length before petrifying into place. It wagged up and down as he spoke. "He's dead. What'd ya want with him?"

"He is... dead?" The fear was evident in his tone as he repeated. Kallias persisted, afraid he may never find his sister. "And his men he travels with? The ones in burgundy hide armor?"

Guin leaned forward putting his face close to Kallias', the spirits on his breath heavy. He whispered in a husky voice. "It isn't wise to speak of the Bloodfish men aloud. They've friends who'd as soon gut ya as look at ya and—" He glanced at the table. "Cowards who'd hand ya to them to gain favor." He took a drink and poured. The bottle was nearly empty. Then the old fellow spoke aloud, "I don't know what ya're talking about. Here, drink with me." He took a glass from the other end of the counter and poured the last of the spirits into it and shoved it in front of the swordsman.

Kallias took a sip of the spirits and hissed as its liquid fire ran down his throat. He gave a sigh of hopelessness. These longship men were feared here. This was evident. He contemplated quietly as he held the glass in his hand.

Chapter 5

The door opened with a bang as an official looking man entered the inn. Behind him walked the first guard from the gate. "This the one?" the official asked.

"Yus that's him," replied the guard.

"Ya was told ya couldn't have a weapon in town." The official waved a finger at Kallias.

He faced the official with a contorted, confused look. "The guard has my weapon."

"Yus he did. Ya stole it back."

"Now Jolben, this man's been right here all afternoon." Guin spoke up.

"Keep out of this, gaffer. I thought ya'd left on a ship from here long ago."

"I did, Jolben. Left on several ships. Always seem to come back. I like Murie's gold," he said and raise his glass to the official then took a sip. He held his liquor without slurring a word.

Jolben looked to Kallias. "I'll have to search ya."

Guin turned his face away slightly.

"He be sittin' over yonder, Jolben," reported the other fellow at the table with Beullus. It had not been apparent until now how much this one resembled a pointy nosed mouse. He motioned Jolben to the corner table.

Jolben waved a hand at the first guard who went and examined the area then shook his head. "Right then. Stand up," the official ordered Kallias.

He was hesitant at first but stood as commanded, arms out, cloak pushed back.

Jolben pointed at the sheathed poniard upon Kallias' thigh. "What's that? Be ya holding out? Hand it over."

"It is but a field blade." Kallias growled but unstrapped it, handing it over to the official.

Guin clamped a hand over Kallias' arm drawing it back from Jolben before the officer could take the knife. Then he drew himself up off the stool and stepped around to Jolben's side. His movements were slow and deliberate, as he stood head and shoulders over the smaller Jolben. "There's no such law here. Why this man?"

Jolben shook perceptibly then looked at the first guard, who was but a few inches taller than himself. He raised a weak hand. "He... uh... he claims he come over the mountain—alone. On foot he came."

All eyes turned to Kallias and the respect shone in Guin's eyes. "Did ya indeed?"

Kallias nodded to Guin's inquiry. "I have."

"He's lying!" squeaked the mousy man.

"Ain't no one survive that," agreed the other.

"Clap yar traps!" shouted Guin at them. "Ya believe a man can't live a night in the forest. Cowards and fools all of ya."

Jolben showed offense. "Here now, no need to shout. Go on back to yar drinking. No harm done." He waved the back of his hand to Kallias to keep his knife. "No sword here. It's fine."

"I demand to know the whereabouts of my sword! The guard said I could trust him to keep it safe!" Kallias barked as Jolben waved him off and turned to the door. The two men at the table gawked, wide-eyed as Kallias took a step forward and stood defiantly.

Guin stood behind Kallias, a sneer across his face. Jolben turned to the first guard. The guard hemmed and hawed a moment. "I... I'm... it be stolen. But I'm sure it'll turn up. We'll investigate." He turned hopeful eyes to Jolben.

"Yus, that's it. We'll investigate." Jolben pushed the guard in front of him and hurried out the door.

Kallias growled his anger through clenched teeth, then spoke. "That sword was my father's and his father's."

"Don't worry," said Guin, "it'll show up. When it does, ya can sliver the thief with it." He sneered again and staggered a step before returning to his stool and hunkered over his glass as he was when Kallias first came in the door.

"So, how'd ya do it?" asked Beullus. "How'd ya get from the mountain to here? Kill lots of kervplik and wixxon did ya?"

"Brigands too no doubt," remarked the other.

Guin hovered. "More terrifying things in the woods than hunters and claw beasts." He took a drink which he could not refill.

Kallias watched the door a moment in disgust, the men's questions far from his mind. He returned to Guin's side and sat with a grunt. "More terrifying?"

"Rekinnder."

"Fantasy!" cried Beullus. "Those don't exist."

Kallias swiveled in his stool to listen.

The mousy fellow chuckled.

"A horrifying creature that can become anything? Ya happen to see ya self, mister. Ya kill ya self immediately. That's the safe thing they say." Beullus laughed aloud. "Not likely."

Guin looked over at Kallias. "I believe they exist. I may've even seen one once. Hard to tell. But if they do, they're feared and hunted. Ya ever see one, kill it quick. Ya won't but have one chance."

"How'd he know? Huh? Tell us that gaffer. How'd anyone know till it be too late and they lay bleeding inta the dirt?" Beullus asked.

"Easier to kill a kervplik hunter. Can't miss them, noisy, ugly, big brutes. Ya can smell them coming." The mousy man tapped his mug on the table. "I need another ale."

Kallias faced the bar. This place became a storehouse of information indeed. Was Spiritdancer a rekinnder, the shape shifter they spoke of? He feared for her safety and withheld any mention of her during their talk of the creature.

The town outside seemed quieter, the rays beaming through the cracks of the inn door slowly faded as the sun edged towards the horizon. Guin finished his drink. He picked up the bread and put a silver coin on the counter top. "That'll cover ya," he said to Kallias. Then he put a knotted piece of cloth upon the counter at Kallias' elbow and walked with careful step out the door.

"Thank you," the Blade Dancer responded. The dark-haired man mused for awhile. Then it occurred to him that he was not being dismissed but was expected to go after Guin to learn more. He took the cloth in his hand and followed out the door only to find Guin was gone. Kallias walked around to the back of the inn and unfurled the cloth. Inside were three small Glimmerstones. A vague memory teased at the corner of his mind and was lost. He looked around and discreetly pocketed the gems. Kallias had questions to ask and a sister to find. Where could Guin have gone? He returned to the front of the inn with eyes searching in all directions. He finally looked to the bay and caught sight of Guin sitting at the edge of a pier. Kallias walked across the sun bleached wooden planks and seated himself alongside Guin.

"Didn't think I was so fast or that ya'd follow so slowly."

Kallias grinned at the remark and raised his eyes to the sea. "You hold your liquor well."

"It's all illusion," replied the older man. "Ya're far from home."

"I am." He appraised the older man again. *Full of surprises this one,* he thought, then said, "So you know my land."

"I've seen your kind. Pale faced, dark haired people."

"You've been to Baresi? Rockscrest? You picked up these stones yourself?"

"I've been lots of places."

"But these," said Kallias as he pulled the wrapped stones from his pouch. "They're only found in the desert near my home."

Guin stared out over the bay watching the fishing boats come in past the promontories that separated it from the open sea. "Not only, but these did."

"Do I know you? I seem to recall..."

"I doubt it. Let me tell ya what ya need to know. Men come from the north, longship men. They gather whoever they will and whoever they can't kill. Some people have saved themselves if they have something to offer. Like the akinn of this town." Guin ripped bits of bread from the loaf and threw them into the water.

"Akinn?" Kallias asked.

"The race of these people. Ya never see akinn before? Light hair, sometimes a bit o' red in it. Short and shorter. Certainly ya noticed how tall ya are here." Guin chuckled.

Kallias showed no amusement. He knew what it meant that the akinn feared longship men. This town was in the pocket of his enemies. Fish splashed and snapped at the crumbs below. Guin raised a hand and swept it wide in front of him to the left and right. "The land there and there that almost meet at the sun, hug this harbor and surround it with kinnir-like beasts. The wixxon to the north, the kervplik to the south and east. Nearbeasts and beings of strange powers." He regarded Kallias. "Ya've seen some of them no doubt. Difficult not to have run into them coming through the forest over the mountain. I don't know how ya survived. But that's why yar sword was taken. Ya pose a threat."

"What? They hold my sword for fear of me?"

"They tried to hold yar sword." Guin chuckled. "I can't imagine who'd steal a sword. Far too many cowards here for that. That's very odd. Not odd that it could be stolen. The law here's a mockery." He shook his head and broke up the rest of the bread loaf. "Ya're strong enough, clever enough, something enough to've come from the land into this bay town. That means the delicate balance they hold with yar enemies is at risk. The akinn're cowards but clever ones. They keep themselves alive by guile. And they allow the Bloodfish Navy to run over the town whenever they come to shore here. Clever deceitful fools. They don't know what to think of ya. They don't know what to think of me either. They don't dare touch me or anger me because they fear the Bloodfish more than kervplik and wixxon alike. And I... was a Bloodfish man."

Kallias' heart beat fast. *He's a longship man? Then he, if anyone, can help me find my sister.* Kallias asked, "Are you not one any more?" Guin shook his head. "They raided my people and took my sister." Kallias continued with sad hopefulness. "Will you help me?"

Guin chuckled. "I wonder at yar mind plainsman. Perhaps the winds of yar grassy slopes or the heat of yar sandy dunes effects yar thinkin'. What makes ya ask me for help?"

"You know more of them than I. You were one of them. I must find my sister." Kallias turned his gaze back toward the market place to hide the tears if they should come. The streets began to empty, leaving but one or two persons walking about, while the inn began to fill with patrons ready for an evening meal.

Guin took a deep breath and held it a moment before speaking. "Bloodfish are ruthless raiders. Ya join them or die." He waved a hand in the air. "Unless they're not interested in new crew. But they're also a suspicious lot. They keep a mystic aboard their ships to control the weather, keep sea monsters away and to advise them of what to do to ensure success, long life, riches, anything and everything. One of these mystics got to be a bit too influential. He had all the others killed as pakao by their own boatmen. That was no long time ago.

"There was a story about a day when the nearbeasts would come to the call of a mystic and they'd drive kinnir to the Point of the Gald. But it'd be a woman of dark hair and dark eyes that'd bring the mystic to ruin or something like that. She'd save her people. We're all of fair hair, those of us has any at all, and light in eye color. They probably raided yar village and took yar sister because she's dark of eye and hair, isn't she?"

"She is, of course. We all are," he replied as the image of his sister returned to his minds-eye. Asadia was as he was, pale skin with obsidian hair and dark eyes, his were blue, hers near black, ardent, with an inner fire.

"Well where else were they apt to find a dark-haired people? And what're the chances that if they found dark hair they'd find such eyes as well? They want to make themselves yar sister's people. They're trying to avoid the terrible powers of a high mystic that way, to avoid their fate. Yar sister won't likely be harmed. The one man who'd've touched her is now dead. His idea for making a Baresian woman one of them died with him." He took the flintlock from his belt and handed it to Kallias. "This was his. It's called a flintlock. Comes in many sizes. Careful, it's loaded." As Kallias took the gun, Guin reached under his long coat and pulled two long barrel flints from behind him. "These're mine." He laughed menacingly.

Kallias carefully examined the gun turning it over in his hands. It was clumsy and heavy. He thought deeply about all Guin had told him. "These navy men took my sister and killed my best friend just to avoid the wrath of a mystic?" He peered down the barrel.

Guin smartly brushed the weapon away from the man's face. "Well I'm sure Pluth had another reason. They raided yar village to find such a girl. I'm sorry ya lost a friend. How many ships were there?"

"It was all so quick. I'm certain some of our women escaped. But a few, my sister—I confronted one man. Then pursued the scarred one. Then I heard a whistle and all went black." He gingerly touched the wound on his head at that.

Guin nodded. "They'd take as many young untouched ones they could find. At least one for each ship and more to sell to other longships, if there were so many to be found in yar village. If not, they'd gone on to other Baresian villages close enough to the sea for a raid."

"That means Olkem at least."

"There's a place in Kanratu where the men of the ships who claimed yar village make their home. The bald captain, Pluth, was from there. The other ship 'n' their clans were to bring their offerings there as well. Now his manly part 're nailed to the door post of yar women's prison, shriveling in the heat and warning others what'll happen to them if they should sully the sacrifice before the prophecy's fulfilled."

"Sacrifice! No!" Kallias nearly jumped to his feet, but Guin grabbed his arm, holding him in place.

"Not to kill, sacrifice. The women are too important to them for that. Don't get yar ire up... yet. They been waiting for the mystic to make his choice first. Then they'll portion the women out to navy captains maybe. That fishing boat with the orange flag hanging from the yardarm goes south to Kanratu in the morning. I'll be on it."

"Then I shall come!" Kallias exclaimed and belted the pistol.

"Ye mean ye'll go. No one's going to let ya out of this village alive. Except perhaps me."

"I must get my sword!"

Guin sighed. "Calm ya self, Baresian. I'll look for a sword for ya. Meanwhile, ye've but one bullet in that pistol. Ya know how to fire it?"

He pulled it from his belt and stared down the barrel again. "I've never held one before."

"Ya could blow yar face off now and save Jolben the favor." Guin took the gun from Kallias. He demonstrated. "Ya pull back on the hammer like this until ya hear it click. Ya don't pull back far enough before letting go ye'll set it off and waste yar bullet... or kill ya self. Once it clicks and sets, ya point and try to keep yar hand steady. Then pull the trigger. That's this here." Guin showed him. "It has a kick, so try to keep it pointed at whatever or whoever ya're shooting." He released the hammer and handed the pistol back to Kallias. As he spoke, he gazed out across the darkening bay. A light blue fog could be seen in the distance as the last of the sun disappeared leaving its fire reflected upon some smattering of clouds over the fog line. "Now, ya can't stay at the inn. Ye'll be dead by morning." Kallias belted the pistol at his back. "By now everyone knows that a dark-haired kinnir of stature has come into Saungtau Shore. They know the story, and know about the raids. They suspect yar purpose and yar prowess. Ye'll not be able to board that boat in the morning either. Ya must get some rest. I'll show ya a place to hide. Then ya must get up before the dawn hours and get out through the gate and take the road south."

"You have my thanks," said the swordsman as he stood and glanced about.

Guin tossed all but one of the drier corners of the crumbled bread loaf out onto the water and stood. "Come," he said and led Kallias through side streets until they reached a rough, wooden booth against the wall of the town. "Ya won't be bothered here. Cover up. I'll attempt to find yar sword. But if I can't, I'll bring ya one." He handed the crust of bread, about half the size of his fist, to Kallias. "This isn't much but ya won't starve. How will I recognize yar sword?"

"It's a curved long blade with an ornate black scabbard. It shouldn't be hard to find," he said as he crouched low against the wall and pulled his ragged cloak around himself.

Guin nodded then pulled a wooden plank door down in front of Kallias to further hide his presence. "I'll awaken ya when it's time. Ye'll need whatever prowess that brought ya over that mountain if ya're going to recover yar sister from the Bloodfish. So sleep well."

Prowess? My prowess is a cat, maybe the dreaded rekinnder. What good was all my training except to make a fancy dance? Kallias sat gazing through the planks, mulling over everything he had experienced thus far and letting the tears fall silently. Eventually he nibbled on the fishy-smelling crust and waited for the longest night of his life to put him to sleep.

Chapter 6

Kallias slept fitfully in the cold, damp air. Near dawn a decisive footfall approached the shelter and stopped a moment before Guin rapped lightly on the door. "Awaken, Baresi, it's time." He then lifted the panel. Pre-dawn light touch the hazy morning air with promise.

The man stood tall over Kallias as if he had gained in stature from the day before. Guin had a fresh newness when he cleaned up. His hair tied back, his beard neatly trimmed, he wore a robe with mid-length sleeves and the burgundy cuirass of the Bloodfish navy over it. The robe split at both sides, revealing dark canvas trousers and pale deer hide boot-like leg coverings tied with straps of brown leather that crisscrossed up his calves ending just below his knees. "I brought ya some provisions." He offered a hand up to Kallias. "No one in this town has yar sword. Whoever the thief, he's long gone." Then he handed a longsword in a tooled leather scabbard to Kallias. "Here, take this. Ye'll need it. One bullet won't keep ya alive the three days' journey ahead of ye." He also handed him a package wrapped in oiled cloth. "There's enough to last ya most of yar trip. Dried fish, meat and bread. There's some fruits, too." He tucked a second, smaller package under his arm. "Murie's bread."

Kallias belted the longsword about his waist. It felt cumbersome and heavy at his hip, but it would have to do. He tucked the food away in his pack as he listened. "Am I to head south? How will I make it out the gate?" he asked as he slung the pack over his shoulder.

"I'll distract the guard. Once ya're outside go 'round the east corner and along inside the woods until the trees meet the road. Best to keep to the road unless a caravan comes. More protection that way. I'll take the boat and meet ya in Kanratu."

Kallias took Guin's forearm in his hand with appreciation in his eyes. "Let us make haste then, my friend."

Guin clasped his forearm briefly and nodded, then headed east along the wall to the south gate. When he came to the roadway, he motioned for Kallias to stay back while he stepped out onto the street and opened the gates pushing them unnecessarily wide to gain the attention of both guards. He strutted out boldly and turned westward to draw their attention. "Ya two! Asleep at yar posts are ya?" He accused, engaging them in their own defense as he watched for Kallias' egress.

Kallias darted to the gate wall. The guards had their backs turned to him as they approached Guin, enabling the swordsman to slink quietly out and around the corner. Kallias made his way to the forest edge east of town. Keeping behind trees and boulders until he was well away, he arrived safely at the road below the cliff where he had first seen the town. Guin and the guards were barely visible at this distance.

Ocean waves could be heard in the distance as the forest started to awaken with the hum of insects and birds. Occasionally small creatures scurried through the fallen leaves as he headed towards his destination. It was mid-morning before the Baresian found a soft sandy patch off the road behind a large boulder where he could sit for a repast. Sunshine broke through the trees spreading fingers of light over and around the brush and between the trunks of conifers. He removed an apple from the bundle Guin had given him, buffing and polishing it before sinking his teeth in, snapping off a bite. On top of the package Guin had placed a soft leather-covered water bladder complete with shoulder strap. Evidently, he meant for Kallias to have one in addition to his own. On it was dyed the image he had seen tooled on Guin's cuirass, the same as he now noticed on the scabbard. It appeared to be the pakao fish with a kinnir form riding upon its head. The form had its hands raised high, and there was some sort of star between its palms. Having finished his morning meal, Kallias pushed the fruit's core into the ground. Uncapping the water bladder, he took a deep swig before running a forearm across his beard. *Why did Guin leave the longship men?* He would ask when they met up again, if it was not too personal a question.

Just then the snap-crack of twigs breaking off to the northwest caught his attention. It was followed by a sort of soft crunch, but then nothing, neither more sounds in the distance nor an approach. He listened intently for a few moments. All he heard were the cicadas singing, the tree frogs chirping and the occasional buzz of a fly or mosquito in his ear. Ready to travel again, he crept out from behind the boulder onto the road again. The sun warmed the dew from the forest floor. It's light danced through the branches of the trees and fell upon the road forming odd patterns of shadows, which swayed occasionally with the ocean breeze. Thoughts ran freely through Kallias' mind in the peacefulness of the day. Three days and he would free his sister, if he was not already too late. There was some assurance in what Guin had said. At the least he was no longer afraid of her eminent death.

Something down the road caught his attention. An animal, dark in the shadows, crept out of the brush. It appeared to struggle as it dragged some cumbersome dead thing along between its legs before letting it drop. Kallias sprinted hastily into the trees and hunkered down behind one. The serlcat dragged the thing along again for a few paces, then dropped it again when Kallias disappeared off the road. She crouched and let her ears pan for trouble and sound of him. That is when Kallias got a good glimpse; it was Spiritdancer, or at least he hoped. Mistaking an identity could prove troublesome. He stepped cautiously back out onto the road, holding his arms out with his palms facing her. "Spiritdancer?" he called out. If it was her, he would know from body language. *That and from not being mauled.* He chuckled at the thought. Spiritdancer's ears perked up and she took an attentive pose. Suddenly she crouched again and her ears flattened back as she emitted the warning cry of the predator cat. At the same instant Kallias could hear the crush

of sand and the report of a pistol behind him. A whistling
projectile passed him, and the serlcat disappeared.

"I got it!" A man shouted victoriously.

Kallias spun to face the voice, half drawing his sword.
"You fool!" he growled.

"Whadda ya mean? I just saved yar life!" Guin waved his
smoking pistol in the direction of the cat's escape. "That's a
serlcat, a most dangerous and cunning creature. And we'd
better finish the job before it comes up behind us. Besides, its
coat'll fetch a very handsome price. Ya've no idea how rare
these animals are."

"No!" Kallias exclaimed, shoving the longsword back in
place. "That cat is my friend, Guin. Leave her alone. She is
how I made it over the mountain."

Guin looked nervously into the forest and around him.
"That's impossible. A serlcat won't get close to kinnir.
They're elusive and dangerous —very dangerous, especially
wounded ones. I'd rather thought there were none of them
left. But I see I was wrong. Come, we must find it, before it
comes back around for us."

Kallias' face reddened. "We'll go, but you're not to kill it.
I'll show you."

"If it was yar friend, it isn't now. Trust me. It's wounded
and will rip us apart if we don't get it first." Guin continued
to peer into the trees.

"Why are you not on the boat?" Kallias' visage became
even more confused and sullen.

Keeping his eyes upon the trees, Guin put his un-fired
pistol in his belt and then took a powder horn from the same
belt and began to reload the other gun. "It seems someone
recognized my mystic's garb. Maybe they figured my talking
to ya last night was a sign of betrayal to the Bloodfish men.
There was a party waiting for me as soon as we got away
from shore. I persuaded them to run aground instead.
Unfortunately, it ripped a hole in the hull." He finished
loading his weapon, then had a pistol in each hand once
again.

Kallias rested a hand on Guin's pistol and shook his head. "Trust me," he said before making his way deftly through the trees, seeking signs of the cat.

Guin followed him, not relinquishing his hold on the guns and keeping one eye over his shoulder. "I'll watch yar back. But ye'd better get that pistol out or at least the sword, though I doubt it'll do much good. They're cunning creatures and will ambush."

"She is not just a serlcat, Guin," he replied as he jumped a log and stopped short a moment.

"Whadda ya mean?" Guin eyed Kallias suspiciously and halted before the log.

"She's a spirit of the forest. My guardian." Kallias raised a hand over his brow and scanned the area.

"A spirit?" Guin turned slowly on the balls of his feet, cautiously peering into the woods behind them. "Ya don't mean what I think ya mean, do ya? A rekinnder is a far more dangerous and unpredictable hater of kinnir."

"Don't know the term," Kallias retorted, "But whatever she is, she helped me." Again he made his way, zigzagging between trees. Kallias could see a few drops of blood along the jagged path he took.

Guin followed. "Alright, she helped ya. Why? She'd have kept far from ya or if she felt threatened, would've leapt upon yar back and killed ya with a single crush of serlcat jaw." The path wound around and eventually came back to a point just a few steps away from the log in the brush behind where Guin had stood watching for her. "Ya see? Circled b'hind us," he said.

Kallias followed the blood trail relentlessly as it continued back toward the road, never slowing pace for Guin. "Nonsense. Keep your pistols down." He feared for her safety yet knew at the same time she could take care of herself. He climbed up a gully made by water erosion and back onto the road with a slight pant of breath. His trail led him to where Spiritdancer dropped the thing she had been dragging. It was long and black and somewhat flat. Kallias peered both ways then ahead. He looked in awe at his sword. Then he swung his cloak to one side and knelt, his boots creaking as he bent low grabbing the scabbard blade. He watched down the gully as Guin made his way up and held his sword high. "You see?! We must find her!"

"That's yar weapon? She's the thief?"

He nodded vigorously and smiled. "Yes!"

Guin stepped up onto the road and un-cocked his pistols. He turned toward the woods. Holding his arms up and his pistols upon his open palms in a surrendering attitude, he shouted, "Hear me rekinnder! I didn't know who ya were nor of yar nature! I mean ya no harm! I am Guin, mys..." He was cut short as the cat sprang from the shadows and hit him hard in the chest. One pistol skidded across the road as he landed upon his back with a solid thud and escape of his breath. The serlcat pressed her weight upon his chest with her snarling teeth inches from his face.

She growled.

"No! Spiritdancer! Please, you must understand. He has helped me as much as you." Dropping his sword, Kallias stepped forward. "Spiritdancer, please." Carefully, he ventured forward and rested his palm on her shoulders.

She hesitated before jumping off Guin's chest and shaking a back leg. Then she stepped, limping on the hind leg, around behind Kallias, away from the longship kinnir who gasped for air. Guin coughed and remained upon his back for another moment.

Kallias picked up Guin's pistol and offered him a helping arm up. On his feet again, Guin accepted his pistol from Kallias and returned both to their places at his back. Then he observed the serlcat as she sat licking the wound on her hind leg. She appeared calm enough, so he ventured a step toward her. She growled. He halted. "It'd be wise to let me see the wound."

Kallias bent low to examine the wound. He nodded to her, then motioned his head to Guin. Guin tried another step and was given another warning growl. "She won't have it."

Kallias crept much closer to the cat. "It looks like just the skin was grazed but with a fairly deep cut."

Guin bounded down into the gully and was gone a short while. Oddly he made no sound as he came and went other than the occasional soft shush against the sand of the road when he was quite close to Kallias. Guin returned holding a few leaves and a small vine that oozed a milky sap. "Put this on it. Then bind the leaves over the wound." He handed them to Kallias without receiving a growl from the serlcat.

Kallias held the cat's eyes with his as he took her hind leg in his hand. She permitted his touch as she turned a hard gaze upon Guin, who raised his hands and stepped back. A sneeze and tail twitch let Kallias know he could go ahead. He wrapped her wound as instructed, binding the leaves over it. He scratched her chin before standing to face Guin. Spiritdancer inspected the job and then, satisfied, took her place beside Kallias as if to claim him and warn Guin a final time.

Guin looked from the serlcat to Kallias. "I'd not have believed it possible. And yet, I may be dreaming or too drunk to know the difference. Though I've not had anything at all to drink this day. Perhaps it isn't today yet. It must be I'm still sitting at Murie's bar looking into the amber and having the most fascinating dream." With that, he plucked a hair from his beard. "Ouch! Nope. Not drunk or dreaming."

Kallias chuckled. "Guin, here, offered his help to save my sister, Spiritdancer. She's being held near Kanratu," he said. She licked the back of his hand with an accepting expression and then glanced between him and his sword as if acknowledging his receipt of it.

Guin checked his rucksack and pointed to the scabbard upon Kallias' belt. "Might I now have the return of m'father's sword?"

Unlooping the scabbard, he handed it back to Guin. "My thanks for allowing me the use of your blade. And my thanks to you, Spiritdancer, for giving me back mine," he said, retrieving his sword. With his free hand, he stroked her head. She purred her appreciation.

Sword in place, Guin readied himself, stepping beside Kallias opposite the cat. She had other ideas though and neatly slipped behind Kallias and put herself between him and Guin. "So ya think he needs protection from me? Suit ya self, pakao. Ye'll get no arguments from me." Then he leaned forward toward her. "But so ye'll think on it, I shot you." He pointed. "Not him." She sneezed indignantly at him, then faced forward. "Fine." He spoke then to Kallias. "Let's hope for an uneventful three day's travel."

Kallias smiled at the conversation. He secured his once lost blade back to its rightful spot. He had felt naked without it. Once he was ready he started ahead. "Yes, let us hope."

Chapter 7

They walked silently for hours, the two men with the cat between. The air was light with a gentle breeze. The shaded places were as cool as the sunny places were warm while the morning pressed on toward midday. As the shadows of the trees stepped to the edges of the road and the sun shone more directly upon them, Guin move away to the eastern edge for some shade. "Let's look for a place to rest for the midday."

Kallias nodded, wiping the soft sheen of sweat from his brow. "I can see a small clearing that way, through the trees." He pointed east, past Guin. Guin headed for it picking his way through the overgrowth. Kallias followed behind as Spiritdancer pushed her way past them and up ahead. "Guin?" He braced an arm out in front of his face as a branch came flying back. "Why did you leave?" He continued, "Leave the Bloodfish men, I mean. You did say you were one as if it were past, though you're wearing the cuirass."

Spiritdancer sniffed and examined the entire clearing before lying next to the single log near its center. From the far end of it, in a crescent moon shape, was a small berm of rounded gray rocks with dense grass and leafy plants growing all over it. Guin entered the clearing and plopped down across from the log, facing the serlcat. "Didn't exactly quit the Bloodfish. 'Twas two years ago," he began then stopped and rummaged through his rucksack taking out some dried fish and a biscuit. He looked at the cat. "I assume ye'll fend for ya self in that form, pakao. I've given Kallias provision already. Ya needn't concern ya self for him." Spiritdancer casually turned her head toward Kallias as if ignoring Guin. Kallias sat cross-legged in the crescent of the clearing, facing the two as he searched his pack. He pulled out a biscuit and smoked meat.

"Recall the story I told ya on the docks? That a mystic would make himself all powerful and would rule the nearbeasts of the forests and marshes and bring them down on the rest of kinnir?"

Kallias nodded as he bit off a chunk of meat and chewed purposefully. He swallowed. "Yes, the mystic."

"What do ya know of mystics, their nature, and what they do?"

"My people have shamans and sages. Is this the same?"

"They're like shamans. Yar sages are learned of scrolls and books?"

"Scrolls and books, yes. But most knowledge is handed down by the sages. They are also teachers."

Guin nodded and broke off another small bite of fish and put it on his tongue. Spiritdancer got up and leapt into the forest with a casual air. He looked after her and listened a moment. Then satisfied that she was not inspecting some possible trouble returned to his tale. "Shamans and mystics come by certain powers naturally, but must study and work hard to develop them. This pakao, the rekinnder, isn't the same. No mystic or shaman can become another creature. Though some can make themselves appear so by illusion. Ya can't pet an illusion." He opened his water bladder and took a healthy drink before resealing it. "Two years ago, a mystic of the Bloodfish navy began to absorb the abilities of other mystics serving the longships. His name is Yungir..." He paused as if to say something outside of the story but thought better of it. "Yungir used an incantation in a tongue none had heard before. Therefore 'twas impossible to refute or protect against. Those it didn't kill recovered their abilities. Together they proved a threat to Yungir. He started a rumor that one by one labeled each of the others as the one prophesied about. The Bloodfish captains and their crews conspired against their own mystics to prevent the prophecy from occurring. Those mystics wanted nothing to do with it. But that didn't matter. Fear was the master. The mystics began to run and hide. Each one that was found was burned to death or gutted and fed to the sea monsters." He finished his biscuit and fish and took another drink from the skin canteen. "So after I was killed and my body burned, I kept hidden. Then came to Saungtau Shore with my cuirass but kept m'robe tucked away for this day. I heard about the raids and returned to Kanratu briefly to see the women they'd brought there. And to protect them. After nailing Pluth's future to the doorpost, I left again. I didn't want to draw undue attention."

"You were killed and burned? Yet you sit here?" Kallias eyed Guin.

"Fortunately, I wasn't gutted. That would've been harder to pull off."

"You continue to surprise me. Then you're a mystic, too. And my sister, she was well when you saw her?"

"If 'twas indeed yar sister, she's safe—was safe, when I left. There're other women there as well. But this one, one of the younger women, her eyes were as ya say, black fire. She defied the captain and the others took strength from her. So, he attempted to violate her. His men turned their heads to feign ignorance. But I was waiting for him. Ignorance and stupidity're brothers." Guin looked skyward a moment. It was clear and blue and beautiful. "The only thing violated was him. The women were ensconced in a hutch in the center of town after his body was discovered. My last act was to nail his parts to that doorpost. Yar sister, at the time, was put in there with the other women."

"Then we must save all those women we can. How is it that this woman, perhaps my sister, is prophesied as being a savior? How will she ruin the mystic's plans?" he inquired as he unclasped his cloak and packed it away. The air was gaining in heat and humidity. He watched Guin with a hint of respect in his eyes.

"I've no idea. What I've learned is that the native people of this land have a different tale. Perhaps it's the same tale but told differently."

Kallias tilted his head curiously and listened. "We need a plan." He stood and paced about the soft clearing, rubbing his goatee.

"Just so." Guin let his eyes follow Kallias. "These people, the akinn, believe a dark warrior will come and bring an evil time upon them."

Kallias paused and turned to Guin. "Dark warrior?"

Guin nodded. "Despite yar pale complexion. I think they believe ya're the one. Because the first part of their tale talks about the kinnir of the sea pakao bringing raven haired women to their shores and about the rising of the nearbeasts. Still one tale's as vague as the other."

The warrior chuckled. "They believe me to bring evil? That's absurd."

"In their minds, all magic is evil. The dark one'll stir up magic. So, are ya a shaman as well?"

"I'm a swordsman, as was my father. Nothing more."

Guin smiled and a wizened twinkle glistened in his eyes. "Aye, that's true. Just as predicted." He rose to his feet. "Where's yar pakao? We should press onward."

Kallias scanned the woods surrounding the clearing. "Spiritdancer!" he called out.

Guin climbed up on the berm of stone to look into the forest. As he did, it broke suddenly, crumbling beneath him. Guin tumbled to the grass behind it.

Wide-eyed, Kallias ran to one side of the mound to look after Guin. The shine of something buried within the rubble met their eyes. Guin rose gingerly and checked to see that he was unharmed. "Are you all right?" asked the Blade Dancer. Then he noticed the rubble was not stone and dirt but a mound of many skulls and men's bones in which was buried bits of whatever may have been their clothing. "I've never seen so many bones!"

"I'm fine," Guin replied. "This is from long ago." Then he reached into the rubble and drew out a bright red stone. "I've never seen so many gems. Somewhere in this heap must be a courier's pouch or something." He held the ruby up to the sunlight. "No kinnir did this. Must have been a place for kervplik hunters at one time."

Other stones and personal belongings were inside the heap. Kallias poked around the rubble of skulls and bones. "We can't spend much time digging about." Kallias examined several broken items. "Some of these skulls are crushed, as well as blades. Do you think they'll come back?"

"No, it's old. We'll mark it to find later." Guin pocketed the ruby. After this he picked up a few more stones of various colors and a necklace and dropped them into his bag.

Just then Spiritdancer leapt into the clearing. She climbed atop what remained of the berm and rumbled a warning at Guin from over Kallias' shoulder. The warrior put a hand up to squelch her fears. "We have much ground to cover before nightfall," Kallias said, anxious to leave.

"Let's go. I'll not forget this place." Guin responded and smiled warmly at Kallias. "We just became rich, Warrior. I'll put my mark on a tree by the road." Kallias nodded once and began to march towards the road.

They continued quietly along the way for some time until the sun stretched the shadows and cast an orange hue upon their steps. Spiritdancer had ceased mistrusting Guin with Kallias and walked at his right side as Guin walked to his left. "So, do yar people have any stories or prophecies, Kallias?" Guin's mellow voice cut through the long near silence of the late afternoon.

Kallias closed his eyes briefly as stories ran through his head. One in particular grabbed his attention. He cleared his throat. "There are many stories, Guin. Our people's history is mostly an oral one. We would gather around the elder sage as children and listen. Some stories were repeated by mothers to get their children to behave. And just as many were told to youths, as a moral guide. But there is one story that is quite a riddle, which comes to mind. I don't even know why it's told."

"Ya know it clearly enough to tell it?"

"Of course. It speaks of a man, a gardener, who planted a seed. A vine grew from the seed. It wasn't what was expected to grow. But it grew into a twisted aberration, overtaking the man's home with its creeping branches. The gardener hacked it away, but the more he cut it away the more it grew. So, the man set out on a quest, to where giant fire pakao lived to make a plea for a blade that would stop the plant. The pakao showed him another garden, a dead one, and gave him the task of reviving it. It was not the man's fault, but the garden couldn't grow in such heat. So he was cast out of the mountains until he could set things right. He found a little flower that grew around a precious stone. The gardener brought the stone back and buried it in the pakao's garden. From that stone grew a blade of fire. The grateful pakao gave him the blade to cut down the vine. He was poised before the wicked plant, and ready to charge and sever the vine. At the same time, the great plant prepared to snarl him in its roots and pummel the man with boulders and dirt." The warrior stopped with the tale.

Guin nodded and listened. "Then what?"

"That's the oddest part. Most stories would have the man kill the vine, maybe find treasure or, at least, live a long happy life. In this one a small flower, with petals of shimmering white, fell from the sword to the ground between the two and brought peace to the gardener and the vine. The vine pulled away from the house and produced as it was meant to."

"Strange story."

"Mhm." Kallias nodded.

"What's it mean?"

"I have no idea." He took a swig from his water skin, then laughed.

"And there's nothing in yar tales about the men of the longships or of some of yar people being taken or traveling away across the seas?"

"No. Lots of them about sea monsters though. One elder spoke of dreams he had in which a great fish swallowed the wives working on their husbands' nets. A swordsman jumped into the water and killed it, then split its belly open. They all walked up out of the sea again."

"Ya sound as if ya don't believe it pictures what's happening to ya now." Guin held amusement in his voice but was not taunting. "Ya shall have to show me this fine sword of yars when we stop again."

"That was a fish, not men. The dream had nothing to do with the killing of my people by vicious kidnappers."

"Prophetic dreams and stories're like that. They leave out what makes 'em seem real, especially to those they're most about," the older man said, then fell silent.

Kallias stared unbelieving at Guin. After a long moment the Baresian said, "I would be honored to show you my blade."

The serlcat paced onward, ears moving.

Later they camped without fire and ate cold, dried food. Towards the end of the first day, Kallias noticed that Guin did not eat at all and drank little water. When he asked, Guin told him that he had taken no real provisions. After all, he was expecting to be on a boat and in Kanratu much sooner. So Kallias split his provisions and the cat tended to herself.

As the shadows grew long on the second day the thunderous roar of water could be heard and Guin turned to Kallias with a smile. "Finally. Loshith Falls. We've got water." He led them downhill into the woods to the west. Spiritdancer had already disappeared in that direction. Kallias stepped out of the westward woods into a clearing. To his surprise all the noise of a great falls came from one not more than half again his height. He gazed up to where a spring shot from the earth along a rise then cascaded down the rocks in its white hailing mist storm upon the water below. He sauntered downward to the stream bank. Bending near to the ground beside the drinking cat, he ran his palm over her head and neckline, giving her a tender pat. "Definitely fresh water." So saying, he filled both skin canteens and slung one crosswise over his shoulder so that it rested on his back as he stood. Kallias filled his lungs with a contented sigh as he peered around his environment with admiration. Golden hummingbirds darted back and forth over the stream to the flowering bushes on either side. The conifers grew very tall here, past the top of the spring, higher even than the road above.

Guin came upstream with a large handful of berries and seeds, with some juice resting on his beard. "This place kept me alive for three days once." He put the berries in Kallias' hands. "Tonight we'll have a small fire as long as the pakao looks about first." He inclined his head toward Spiritdancer, who ignored him and went about cleaning off the bandage and leaves from her leg. "What's the matter with ya?" He put his hands upon his hips and gestured as if scolding a child. "I've as much as apologized. I'm not a danger. Ya know that now. So what is it?" He then turned to Kallias. "It's yar pakao serlcat. Ya reason with her."

"Scorn many females before, have we?" Kallias smirked with his remark to Guin. "Perhaps it's because you call her a pakao." He looked towards her. "Spiritdancer, will you, please?" He asked and made a gesture. Spiritdancer purred a quick answer and bound into the woods.

Guin scowled a moment, murmured something under his breath, then took a small pouch from his rucksack. He found a large flat rock to sit on at the bank. From the pouch Guin produced a small thick stick slightly longer than the width of his palm. He unwound a sinewy string with a pumice stone tied to it. The pumice was riddled with holes and from it, along the string, which was about the length of the man's forearm, dangled a hook. Guin dug his hand into the mud at the side of the rock he sat upon and in quick order produced a fat grub which he impaled upon the hook. Then he tossed the line into the water just above an eddy and watched as the rock floated into the gently whirling water.

Kallias walked along the tree line gathering small dried sticks. Returning to a level spot in the clearing, he dropped armfuls into a pile.

Guin watched the stone disappear and the string snap taut and pull upstream. "Ha! Ha! Got it!" He jerked his hand up. He reeled the sinew in by looping the string around the stick, pulling and yielding until he hauled the fish out of the stream. "Two more and we've evening meal." He removed the hook and threw the fish into the clearing where Kallias stood.

Kallias bounced on his toes as the fish flapped about. He unsheathed his blade and struck a blow, severing the fish's head. "You are a man of many talents, Guin." He threw the fish's body and head on top of a nearby rock. Next, he dug a slight depression in the level ground and neatly spaced the sticks up into a pyramid shape. In the middle, he stuffed it with moss and dried leaves. Taking a small pinch of the moss, he struck two stones over it. It absorbed the spark quickly and set ablaze. This he threw into the middle of the pit.

Later the fire lit their faces as they finished their meal of fish and berries. They talked. Kallias showed off his sword. Spiritdancer lay next to Kallias, leaning upon his leg with eyes half closed purring occasionally in response to a light touch. Guin's countenance had changed remarkably since they reached this wee haven in the woods. He smiled into the fire. "I'll tell ya another story. A short one as I don't know that this one's so much a story as it's what little history is known about the rekinnder." He drank a healthy swallow of water to begin his tale and capped his water skin. "Once there was a being. No one even knows what sort of being but not a nearbeast. 'Twas more between kinnir and akinn. This natural creature came from..." He paused to think, then continued, "No one knows where. It showed up one day in a small town much the same way ya showed up in Saungtau Shore." Guin picked some fish and seeds from his beard and brushed through it quickly. "This being was first a beggar. 'Twas gladly fed by the akinn as back then they were less suspicious of strangers. Then one day the kervplik attacked a little farm outside the town. When the alarm went up, this being transformed into a giant hideous monster and plowed through the streets towards the farm. Now as the story goes, it ran the kervplik away from the farm and chased them into the wood. But when the being came back, it was treated with fear and suspicion. Now I'm certain ya can understand why. But the creature didn't. It began to terrorize the citizens. It raced into their dreams at night and into their homes. It took away children, they say, right from their beds and would transform itself into the likeness of the children to be fed and cared for by the parents. Except when they would attempt to discipline the child, there'd suddenly be some animal pakao in the child's place. Finally it was caught and killed. But before it died they say it sired or birthed others like itself. No one knows who or what or where. But every rekinnder that's discovered is hunted, and so what few remain have taken to some forest or other and become legend. Most don't believe in them any longer. But I saw the change in a creature once and know..." He looked upon Spiritdancer who had stopped purring. "There's at least one."

Kallias enclosed himself in his cloak as the night breeze crept into the area only to be met by the defending heat of the fire. Cold and heat battled and danced as he listened to the story and placed his hand gently upon the cat. "Fear tells bad tales. Shall we take turns at night watch?" he asked with sleepy eyes.

Guin's eyes met the blue light of the eyes of the serlcat. "That's up to her if we need to. I'll call ya pakao no longer if that's what'll suit ya. I don't know if ya need sleep. There're many stories, some which say the rekinnder doesn't sleep." Spiritdancer gave a wide sweep of her tail from behind Kallias to the other side of her and then curled herself up next to him and closed her eyes. Guin shrugged. "I'll take first watch then."

Chapter 8

Kanratu sprawled out upon a wide coastal valley and surrounding rolling hills. From a vantage point in the trees where the three stood, the road dropped like the handle of a gravy ladle into the urban bustle. The docks were clearly visible, and amongst the fishing and merchant vessels in the bay were three longships. They out-sized the other ships by half again the length of the largest merchant ship and as much high. Their carved and painted bows resembled the pakao fish. All were securely anchored now, two beside the docks. Of the three, none had hoisted sails.

Guin pointed to the center of town and turned to Kallias. "It'll be tricky getting ya into the middle of town without being seen."

Kallias nodded once. "Shall we wait for the cover of night?"

Guin agreed. "Let's find a good place to wait out the day. There's a bluff through the trees there to the east. It comes out where that large rock is. We can make our plans."

Kallias rubbed his beard a moment, then smiled. Finding a tall stick, he picked it up and wrapped his cloak tightly around himself. His cowl pulled far down covering his face as he hunched over and leaned on the makeshift cane. In his best crotchety voice, he said, "Spare a coin for an old man?"

Guin chuckled. "That'll certainly do it. Let's go up and see the layout of the city. Then the old man'll have to go in."

Guin led the way through the trees where the terrain began to climb. Then he continued southward where it leveled out. Soon they found themselves standing on a wide flat rock. He immediately got down on his hands and knees and crawled to the edge and looked down into the city. The serlcat disappeared somewhere as soon as the town was visible. Kallias crawled down alongside Guin. He shielded his eyes from the sun with his hands as he surveyed the city. "Where is our destination?"

"Right in the middle of town." Guin pointed to the spot where they had stood beside the road. "We'll approach from there and follow the road. From here ya can see the fence 'round the forger's yard. If ya stay to this side, ye'll come to a street." He shifted his weight to his right elbow and looked further over the edge. "It's the same road as this one heading up into those hills there. But on the ground ye'll have to look for a street lamp. Ye'll go in after the lamplighter has visited this part of the town. Otherwise he serves as town crier. Ya don't need ya self announced coming in." He looked back over his shoulder and around. "Where'd yar serlcat go?"

"She does that." Kallias smiled.

"She'd be more helpful if she stayed to hear what 'tis ye'll be doing. And if she's a rekinnder, to take a form that can speak."

"I imagine she is listening and planning ahead." Kallias grinned and looked over his shoulder for the cat.

Guin gave Kallias a thoughtful gaze before peering again over the town. "I hope she's protective of ya so much as she seems. So ya walk the road in, go behind the smith's and forward to the first lamp. Then head towards the docks for two lampposts. The house ya seek will be southward on the west side of the street amongst three other houses. From here ya can't see its roof. The house on this side's that tall one there with the double chimney to one end and single on the other side. The house ya want's one of the two small ones that face it. If they haven't taken it down, ya might recognize something nailed to the doorpost. Be watchful of the Bloodfish men who may be in the house, but otherwise it isn't guarded."

Kallias nodded as he overlooked the town. He scooted backwards till he was far from the edge and anyone's view, lest they should happen to look up, then stood and dusted himself off. "You will be staying here?"

Guin rolled over on his back. "No, I must go down now. I've some business to attend if we're going to be successful. Getting in's the easy part of this. Getting yar sister and the women out, that'll be hard. Unless ya happen to have a place for them all somewhere nearby?"

Kallias' lips curled inward with a frown. "I have no clue where to lead them."

"As much we need as needs us I'm afraid." Guin rolled back and scooted off the rock, standing and brushing himself off. "I only hope my friends're both alive and willing to help. I didn't leave here on the best of terms." He turned his head seaward briefly. "When ya get to the house, go into the darkest shadow ya can find and wait for me. And if yar friend shows up, perhaps she can help us with the locks or some way to get inside."

Kallias nodded and peered at the surrounding denseness of the trees a moment. "I will wait for you, my friend." He turned back to Guin.

"If anyone sees ya, old man, keep bent and look small as the akinn. Nod a lot and whine. Ya might get kicked, but that'd be good. If ya must move away from the house, go where ya can keep yar eye on it. No matter how long I'm delayed, I'll be there." Guin nodded to Kallias. "Until we meet again." He grasped Kallias' forearm for a moment then disappeared into the trees. Some few minutes more and Kallias could see Guin on the road walking into town with a sure step, whistling.

Kallias waited till the sun started to tiptoe on the horizon. He crawled to the rock's edge and watched for the lamplighter. The city's streets soon became deserted.

As candles and lanterns and stove fires were lit, the eyes of houses opened, glowing of a yellow-orange. The only noise that rose into the night was the distant din of a tavern. As the twilight royal blue became navy and moved into the blackness of night, two small lights bobbed their way through town winking and blinking between houses. Soon a small halo of light went on far to the south of the rock. Then another on this side of town lit up. Then another south, then one to the west glowed. The lamps were lit in a zigzag order back and forth. Two lamplighters moved from the southeast area of the city toward the northwest of it and then down toward the tavern.

The Baresian stood, taking his stick with him as he made his way down to the road and paused about a hundred yards from the city. He donned his old man guise once again and took a deep huff of cool air. It was now or never. His stick poked into the soft soil of the road as he hobbled closer and closer until it clunked on the cobblestone. He peeked up a bit to see the smith's anvil on the sign. It swung and creaked in the breeze. He made his way behind the shop, coming to the first streetlamp. A giggling akinn couple, embraced in each other's arms, walked past paying no mind to the surroundings. Kallias crouched more in his hunched posture to better emulate akinn size. From under his hood, he peered towards the sounds of the docks. "Two lampposts down, one house of three," he murmured to himself as he made his way to the landmarks Guin said would be there.

Bent over near the last lamppost, he turned to the southwest. There loomed the large house and behind it, the shadow of the cliff overlooking it from afar. He slunk to the dark side of the first house to the west, and moved his hand along the wall to take a peek around the corner. Much to his surprise, it was unguarded as Guin said it would be. As he began to come around, he heard the voices of two men nearby. The warrior froze.

The voices softly broke off and the sounds of footfall on the cobblestone could be heard retreating into the distance. Kallias quickly made his way to the second house. There nailed to the door, the shriveled remains of a man's genitals hung on by threads of sun-dried flesh. He grimaced. His stomach turned as he tried to push the door open only to find it locked.

"Hey, gaffer! Get away from there!"

Kallias grunted and remained hunched at the shout.

"What're ya lookin' for old man?" A tall, husky man stepped down from the porch of the large house. Had he always been there? The great, heavy door closed behind him.

He lumbered down the walkway towards the street and Kallias.

"Respect your elders young man, I'm trying to get into my house," Kallias responded quickly in a hoarse voice without facing the sailor. His heart pounded.

"That isn't yar house ya stupid drunk! That's Captain Pluth's home. Can't ya see its windows're boarded up? He's dead." The man was easily upon Kallias in a few strides and dragged him away from the door with a rough hand. "Yar kind don't live this far up the grade. Get back down the docks, ya fool." With that he shoved the old akinn man between the houses roughly so that he bumped against some crates. Kallias gave a disgruntled humph.

"I'm goin' for a drink and when I get back ya better had found yar house. Stupid akinn drunk." The man lumbered off along the lit street then around the corner towards the docks.

The Baresian stood in the dark, his heart pounding. At the feet of the old akinn disguise, several rats were disturbed and squeaked amongst each other rudely. A side window of the house had been boarded up. Peering between the planks he saw the utter blackness of the interior, and the only sounds he heard coming from within were the squeaks and chatter of rodents. Where is Guin? He wondered, as he concealed himself in the shadows of the crates.

The rats continued to gather about his feet. Then one by one they slipped into a hole in the stone beneath the wall. Soon the squeaks were numerous and some movement could be heard inside the house. Suddenly a light from another room shined through the cracks between the boards as a door was opened inside. Kallias took a peek. "Better get som'pin' to thin out these rats, Bask. Them wimin'll be screamin' thar heads off." The ruffian left the door ajar and disappeared into the other room. Around the other corner of the house a dim light emanated from between the boards of another window. In a moment two men entered the dark room and began chasing rats out and beating at them. The swordsman ducked away to the other window.

Kallias rubbed the rim of his sleeve against the window's glass, removing the dust from the pane. Torch light danced and bobbed about, causing the shadows of the women to wave in rhythm on the wall. There appeared to be six. Most huddled together except for one hooded figure, who remained in the corner. His heart thudded as he waited for the right moment to try to slip inside unnoticed.

"Has yar cat joined ya yet?" Guin was suddenly behind him.

Kallias jerked at the voice. "You shouldn't sneak up on people like that," he whispered. He put his index finger over his lips and gestured to the window.

Guin peered in through the boards. "Looks like there're five women. Do ya know how many men're inside?" Just then a scurry of rats ran in various directions from the back of the house. A small white figure bounced up to Kallias. It was an ermine with a black nose and tail tip. In its little mouth, it carried a ring of keys.

"Look at what the rat dragged in." Kallias chuckled quietly and scooped the critter up, taking the keys.

"Looks as if ya were right. She was listening and making plans." Guin's tone was almost reproving. "So now we can go in easily. They'll not expect anyone other than their shipmates. Did ya see how many men, Kallias?"

"Two went inside, though another may return. He left towards the docks. He said this was Pluth's home."

"Really? How ironic. His jewels made it home without him then." Guin sneered as if he relished the memory of his kill. "Well then, prepare yar sword. When we leave here we'll go up the road east keeping to the shadows. There's a cave not far out of town. It'll afford us some temporary safety." Guin paused. "Kallias."

Kallias let Spiritdancer crawl into his pack, then unsheathed his blade beneath his cloak. "Guin?"

"We mustn't let a cry go up from the men. Ye'll have one chance to strike."

The warrior replied with a firm nod. "Ready when you are."

"Then I'll go ahead. They'll mistake me at first and hesitate at the sight of my robes. Ya make yar move then."

Guin held his hand out for the keys. "Once we're inside, close the door until we're prepared to move the women."

Kallias placed the keys in Guin's hand and stood behind him, his knuckles white as he gripped his sword. "Right."

They crept to the street side and peered around the corner of the house. Seeing the area deserted, they continued to the door. Guin found the house key, slightly larger than the other two on the ring, and put it inside the lock and turned. The latch gave and the handle moved easily as he opened the door. Guin stepped in sharply, giving Kallias plenty of room to maneuver. Kallias took a moment to ensure the streets were clear, then entered behind Guin.

The two sailors stood abruptly at attention then one of them spoke. "Why yer not an admiral yer..." The words caught in his throat as Guin's sword was out of its sheath and the tip of it hit the man's vocal chords. The brute staggered and grabbed a great ax. He put his hand over his throat and lunged at Guin. The other man was caught off guard as he fumbled to remove an awkward bell-shaped pistol from his belt. Guin's blade found its second mark to the charging man's heart, as the guard's momentum drove the thrust in. The man's cutlass, held high over his head, slipped from his hands, hitting the floor with a thud and pang.

Kallias took time to shut the door behind them. When he turned into the room. The man had leveled his blunderbuss at Guin's head. Kallias quickly struck the man at the base of his skull with the pommel of his sword, knocking him to the floor instantly.

"Is he dead?"

Kallias shook his head. Guin gave Kallias a meaningful look the Blade Dancer could not deny. Kallias swallowed hard but failed to act.

"If he's alive we're dead," said the Bloodfish mystic. Guin opened the door to the darkened room and dragged the other man's body inside.

Kallias gave a sigh as he stood over the smaller sailor's limp body. He hesitated with pity as he hovered the tip of his sword over the man's heart. "Forgive me," he whispered. Just then the man's eyes opened and widened with fear to see his death coming. As he raised his gun, Kallias drove the steel through the man's chest. Bile rose into the swordsman's mouth as he watched the light of life leave the fallen sailor. He pulled the curtains back on the nearest window, threw open the pane and thrust his head out, retching into the alley.

Suddenly he was jerked back into the room by the collar of his cuirass. Guin spun him around and grimaced. "Whadda ya think ya're doing? Ya wanna draw attention to us?" He pulled the window closed and then the curtains. With a corner of one curtain he wiped at Kallias' mouth. "Clean yar self up then get the women out. I'll take care of him." He handed the keys to Kallias and lifted the body.

Kallias finished the job of cleaning his mouth and goatee, took the keys and approached the frightened women. "We're here to free you. Quickly. Are you all here?"

From the other room Kallias could hear the strike of a sword upon something, then some moving about. Soon Guin returned to the front room and began chanting. "Osaracor lafthias metel ne. Osaracor lafthias metel asim."

"Kallias!" The voice called out from the cluster of women. The woman pulled down her cowl letting her shimmering raven locks fall.

"Roselana, you're safe," he called back to her as she reached out. "Is my sister here?" he asked.

Roselana shook her head violently. "No."

"Come, come!" Kallias ushered the women out of the room one by one.

As they entered the front room they saw their jailers seated at the table as if carrying on a game and drinking. Startled, the girls backed into each other, but the men ignored them and mumbled unintelligible speech. Guin stood sweeping his hand above the floor as the last of the blood disappeared. "Go 'round by the wall. The blood's still there and we don't want to make tracks," he said, indicating the path they should take. The group, with their jaws dropped, hugged the far wall, their eyes never leaving the scene.

Guin stepped gingerly to the door checking the floor to see if he had picked up any blood on his boots. Satisfied, he cracked open the door and checked the street. He closed the door again but kept hold of the handle. "Deserted. Follow me and stay close to the walls and in the shadows. Kallias ya must seal the lock behind us." Guin opened the door and slipped out, guiding the women first into the dark alley.

Kallias closed up the house. In one quick movement, he shoved the key in and jerked his arm downwards snapping it off in the lock, then slunk along a wall after the women.

Guin led them at a quick pace, stopping only to look around corners. Keeping to alleys and shadows, they made their way up the east road and beneath the overhanging rock. He continued along the dark side of the road until the town lights were behind them. "Cross here and up that incline." He pointed. "I'll be right behind you."

The shadow variance along the starlit road was surprisingly easy to discern. However, the moon had not come up yet, causing greater darkness through the trees. Kallias took the lead and helped the women up the slope. Suddenly a bright blue light lit in front of his nose, blinding him. Instinctively with a swift half-step back, he drew his sword only to have it wrenched from him and tossed aside by unseen hands.

Chapter 9

"Stop!" barked an unseen speaker. "Where's Guin?"

Kallias leaned his head back as the light charged his face. "Who asks?" he replied, shielding his eyes.

"Never ya mind if ya want my help." The voice, as raspy as Kallias had made his own while disguised, emanated from an old akinn with a beard that hung to his chest. The light shone from a stone at the top of his staff.

"I'm here, ya old badger." Guin stepped up from behind the group. "I was making sure we weren't followed."

The old akinn held a hand out to his side. In an instant, Kallias' sword was in it. He handed the weapon to the swordsman, then spun on his heels without a word and walked away, touching his staff to the ground. With every step the light white-blue glow of the stone reflected off his long gray hair. "Follow him," Guin said.

Kallias nodded and followed the old man and his bobbing light as Roselana caught up to his side. "Where are we headed?" she asked. Kallias shrugged.

The old man continued through the trees then down where the road could barely be seen. At last, he turned sharply across the road and into the trees on the other side and directly into a cave. "Keep coming," he rasped. Soon the long dark tunnel wound about and there appeared a warm yellow glow. The cave opened out onto a large cavern. In the center was a fire and a large pot with something cooking. Around the fire at some small distance were three sets of three bedrolls laid out. Beside the fire on a flat rock were bowls, spoons, cups, and a large water jug. "Make yar selves at ease." He growled and stepped to one side, keeping his head down.

Kallias planted himself on a bedroll as the women gathered around the large pot with bowls in hand, scooping its steaming contents. Roselana prepared and brought him a bowl, seating herself next to him. The other four women each chose a bedroll and began to quietly converse amongst themselves. Kallias turned his eyes to the old man as he studied him.

The elder akinn stared at the ground, his long dull hair falling around his face. He rocked upon his feet, leaning on his staff. "Where's the other woman?"

Kallias' had been sure he counted six from the window, but when they entered the house, there were only five. Kallias had no answer and was himself puzzled about the old man's question. "Other woman? I was sure there were six, but we are all." He could see that the question was directed to him alone. Guin stood with his back to them and chanted with his palms facing the tunnel entrance. Soon the cavern appeared to surround them completely, leaving no way in or out.

"Where's the sixth woman? Never am I wrong." The old one pounded his staff into the soft dirt floor.

"My..." Kallias paused, then continued. "My sister, Asadia?"

"No, not the one ya seek, Warrior. To Durgrinstar they'll take her." He began to walk around the fire and stopped in front of each woman, pounded his staff at his feet and called out, "Pia! Pia!" for each one. "Pia! Pia! Pia!" When he came to Kallias he stopped. "Ye're man of prophecy, Warrior. Ya bring danger! Where's the sixth woman? Ya see I've prepared for all. This is the place of six women and three men." He indicated the bedrolls.

"If you know more than I, then why are you asking me?" Kallias responded with the frustration of the wrongly accused. Guin merely finished his spell casting and sat upon a rock, remaining outside of the conversation.

Then the old man brought his head up and faced Kallias. He had no eyes, not sockets as if they had been cut out, but no eyes, as if he had never had them. He placed the top of his staff with the light stone upon Kallias' shoulder. "Pia! Pia! Tsia!" From Kallias' pack the little ermine ran up over his shoulder across the staff and up the elder's arm.

"No!" shouted Guin and leaped up. He snatched Dealla off the akinn's shoulder and dropped her quickly into Kallias' arms then physically rotated the old fellow away.

"That's the woman. And the danger. It be rekinnder pakao!"

"She's his protector. Ye'll not harm her! She's under my illusions."

"Ya lie poorly, Guin. What have ya brought me into? I warn ya. Kill it or it'll bring death."

Kallias defensively huddled his arms around the ferret, Spiritdancer.

"How is that in yar vision, old man?" challenged Guin.

"I've not yet seen how."

"Nor to whom I'll warrant. Let it be for—"

"And what danger do we possess in this prophecy?" Kallias asked defiantly. Roselana eyed the weasel and shifted a bit away. The other women whispered even more at the talk of a pakao, their spoons stopped clacking against the bowls as they all glanced nervously between the eyeless one and Kallias.

The akinn wheeled back to Kallias. "Ya bring a pakao inta a place of hiding and want to know what danger? Do ya not know what it is?"

Guin looked at Kallias and shrugged. "Tell him the prophecy, old man. And by all means what ya've seen."

The old fellow pointed his staff at Kallias. "Everyone knows prophecy who should. It's of akinn people that one will come, a dark-haired warrior to rise up trouble. He'll stir up pain and torment and plunder. He'll break the peace of the akinn people. Behold the kinnir, Pom da Guin." He lowered his staff to point it at the ermine in Kallias' arms. "I know ya, warrior. The sign of yar trouble making in yar arms now. Defender of the abominable. Ha! It protects ya? Ya're the protector!" Then he turned on Guin. "Friends ya said. Helpless in need, runnin' from the Bloodfish, ya told me. Never said rekinnder. Never said the dark warrior."

"There is no mention of rekinnder in yar akinn prophecy, Pom Talek," Guin argued.

"Nevertheless, it's here and..."

"Enough! I need to save my sister, and I need to get these women home." Kallias' face flushed red and the veins stood out on his neck with the pressure of his anger. "We didn't start anything or bring any trouble! Blame that on the longship men, your Bloodfish men. They brought it to us!" Kallias took a quick, deep breath, vainly attempting to calm himself. "And this one is Spiritdancer. She is a forest spirit like those of ancient times in my land. A savior."

Roselana shifted again comfortably close to Kallias. In a soft shy voice she said, "Kallias is a good man. Can't you see that he's here to rescue us?" The Blade Dancer took another breath at Roselana's words. This time it worked.

The old akinn stood silently for a long moment, then said quietly, "I'm indebted." Then he pulled a bedroll a distance away from the others and sat upon it cross legged with his staff resting against a shoulder.

Kallias addressed Guin. "What's in Durgrinstar?"

"It's the mystic's capitol." Guin picked up a bowl and scooped a generous amount of the stew into it. He sat across from Kallias with the covey of women to his left. "It's far north. But we can't go there on foot." He ate solemnly.

"He knows something that he isn't saying," Kallias whispered to Guin, leaning in. "He is indebted?"

Guin nodded and pointed to himself with his spoon as he chewed. Then after swallowing he spoke. "To me. I saved his life when it was forfeit. So until he saves mine, he's indebted to me. I don't think he'd have hesitated otherwise." He nodded at the ermine nibbling from Kallias' bowl. "But he's a seer. We'll need him."

Kallias nodded at that, as hand over hand, he absentmindedly stroked the ermine's silky coat. "Then we can trust him to help get us to my sister?"

Guin spoke as if Talek were not sitting right there. "He can tell us what to do and what to expect. He may volunteer to come so far with us. In which case, we'll be fortunate indeed. He can't see everything. But maybe what he does see can help us avert dangers."

"Easy to volunteer another's skill, is it? And just how will ya take so many women? And where will ya find a ship? Ya're impertinent, Pom da Guin," the akinn said.

Guin inclined his head behind him, listening to Talek. He set his own bowl down and prepared one for the seer and took it to him saying, "That I am, Pom Talek." Then he returned, picked up his bowl and resumed eating.

Roselana gently placed her arm upon Kallias' shoulder. "I wish to help, Kallias."

He nodded and smiled at her. "But he's right. How will we find a boat? And how will I take all of you back home?" He sighed at the thought.

Guin also considered the women, though his eyes lingered upon Roselana a bit longer. "Perhaps the women can help retrieve yar sister," he said. "Are they able and willing?"

"Are you mad?" cried Kallias. "What sort of man are you? I'll not put these women in harm's way!"

Guin raised a palm upward in mock surrender. "Fine but... do ya intend to go after yar sister or not?"

"Of course," Kallias retorted, "but I'll go by myself if I have to —if you're not coming."

"No," Roselana objected. "I'll help you. You know I can if I have a sword. Not as good as you or Omarion, but you know I can be."

The women quietly talked amongst themselves. Heads bobbed up and down before the tallest of them stood. "I am Jamila. We have no families now. No home, no husbands; all killed. We are alone so far as we know. You have our willing help, such as it is, brother Kallias."

Kallias did not know their names, but recognized some faces. "You —all of you? Willing to help me find my sister?" He placed his bowl down and put a hand on Roselana's arm. "She's all I have left of my family as far as I know. She and you." He spoke first to her and then to the rest. "And now we all become family."

"And so it unfolds," the seer said with his mouth full. "Behold yar crew and yar army, Warrior." Kallias' eyes darted to each of them as the seer spoke.

Guin raised an eyebrow. "I'm impressed." When Roselana turned her eyes toward Guin, he busied himself scraping his bowl and filling a cup with water. He raised his eyes again to the group. "What do ya ladies know of fighting and sailing?"

"You're all serious about this!" Kallias exclaimed. They each nodded eagerly as he looked at them.

"In Olkem the women of our village fish, so we sail. But fighting we know not." Jamila responded to Guin. "Ours are hunters. Warriors are the Rockscrest guard."

Guin eyed Kallias and his ermine, then hailed Talek. "How long, old man, until we're too late?"

Talek responded, smacking his lips as he finished his meal. "Ye'll not be late."

The mystic rose to his feet. "Then we must discuss our plans. Ya must all be prepared for stealth and maybe to defend yarselves. Kallias, we'll have to find a place outside of Durgrinstar." Guin stepped over to him. "Yar sister'll not come to harm. I promise ya. Talek'll tell us when it's time to go. Can ya trust me?"

Kallias offered his free arm. "Of course, but—" Spiritdancer hissed.

"Then we begin now." Guin clasped the warrior's forearm and met his eyes, ignoring the ermine. "I'll outline our plan. I'm called Guin," he said to the women meeting the eyes of each in turn. "Please tell us yar names and whatever skills ya feel ya possess which we might use for aid in such a rescue, or in keeping us alive until it is accomplished or anything else ya can think of." He sat.

Jamila, still standing, spoke first. Her posture upright and her voice commanding and well spoken. "I am Jamila, wife of the late Ganim, a councilor and the commander of our people's hunters in Olkem. Our hunters are not swordsmen but spear carriers or wielding clubs and knives. We are the south seaward sweep from the coast to the crevasse where the Valandree fled. We also guard the wetlands of the plateaus. I know much of organizing as I have listened in and offered advice to my husband for the council. I know not how to wield a hand weapon and know little about throwing a spear, but I can learn."

A slight girl stepped up next to Jamila, who put an arm around her. "I might be able to. I'm Charlise. My father served under Ganim as a border guard to the wetlands as far as the crevasse. I played with my three —had three brothers." She faltered a bit. "Two were fishermen, harpooners, and one served with my father. They'd play with me at throwing a harpoon. I think I can remember something about boats, too. I know how to repair nets and sails. Otherwise I just stayed home with my mother and cooked." Some tears came to her eyes as she scowled at Guin's armor. "They —who wore that —burned my mother alive in our house."

Guin also scowled and nodded. "I'm sorry I wasn't there to stop them."

One of smaller stature than the rest stood up. Her hair was dark as the others' but a highlight of red shimmered over the top of it as she bowed her head to them. "My name is Pekoe. I am from Alamtel, southeast of Tiernon. I don't know any of you. I came with Sarad to visit his family in Rockscrest and announce our betrothal." Tears flowed suddenly and freely along the dirty tracks that had evidently carried them down her cheeks before. She sat again.

"I'm sorry," Kallias said. "I knew him and his family. I had no idea he had returned from the inland tribes—" His voice trailed as he looked with pity upon Pekoe. He swallowed back his own sorrow. "Pekoe, what skills have you?"

She turned pained, tearful eyes towards him, shook her head and shrugged. "Herbs, medical apothecary. I was being trained in healing."

"That is of great value, Shasha Pekoe," Guin said softly.

With an outcry that rent the heart of them all and brought tears to every eye Pekoe cried, "A hole as big as my thumb! Sarad's blood spat all over me! I —I cou-houldn't stop it! A-and then the... the man grabbed me-he an—"

Charlise quickly pulled the young woman to her bosom and held her as they cried.

Dealla moved uneasily in Kallias' arms as she heard these women speak. By their tones and demeanor, she gathered that they spoke of such bravery and such horror as her own kind had known. *Do they speak of being hunted? Do kinnir hunt their own? If so, why are they with the longship mystic?* Her nose twitched as she pointed it toward Guin, whose eyes were turned away.

Another whose hair was a dark brown, stepped forward, wiping tears from her face. "My name is Zetrine, also of Olkem. My father and brother were smiths and tinkers."

Kallias nodded. "I knew them well."

Zetrine continued. "But I wasn't. I don't know if I have any useful skills other than what is common, but my brother and I used to play at sword fighting when we were children and were taken to Rockscrest to see the Dance of the Blades. I would like to learn to use one. He died defending me with a garden hoe." Swallowing hard, she held her head up with an attitude of resolve. Then she sat next to Pekoe and rubbed the weeping girl's back.

Kallias offered her a sympathetic nod. Then the young Roselana rose off her knees and dusted her festival robe. "I'm Roselana. I'm quick and agile. I will do what I can to help. Though I haven't many skills, except as Zetrine said, what's common. But, as Kallias knows, I would often play at swords with my brother, Omarion. He taught me much of what our fathers were teaching the boys. I kept up practice."

Kallias squeezed her shoulder as she sat again. "You do him great honor."

"Ask the warrior what the pakao said to him." Talek spoke up as soon as the women had finished. "It doesn't show itself and join with ya. Why is that? I can't see the woman inside but to know she's there. And many a great beast in that one I see as well."

Guin faced Kallias and the ermine. "Rekinnder, show yarself. —Kallias?"

Kallias shrugged as the ermine lay upon his forearm. "I don't even know if she has a kinnir form. I haven't seen one yet. But she has a voice." Remembering the guttural language of the huge nearbeast, he looked down at the oddly dark-blue, beady eyes and snagged-toothed grin of the critter. "Don't you?"

Spiritdancer remained comfortably on Kallias' arm. Now here was more reason than she had had in a long time not to take the vulnerable form. *Does he understand? Probably not. Perhaps he will understand that I yet needed him and he needs me.* She said, "Chit chit," to let him know she was with him and the women. She knew they spoke of horrible things that happened by the hands of longship men. Their voices sounded of revenge. *My enemies, too,* she thought, though not in words. *They should start with this one, the mystic, if that is what they want.* Dealla would fight all right, and she knew quite enough about it too.

Kallias rose and carried the weasel away some few feet from the group as they converged and talked. "I need your help, Spiritdancer." He confessed quietly to the ermine. Spiritdancer's bright eyes sparkled up at him attentively. "I— we cannot do this without you. I wouldn't be here without you." She blinked, knowing enough of his words; need and help, you and I. With that he set her down and gestured with both hands that she should rise up. "Can you not become kinnir?" He patted both hands upon his chest. "Do you have hands?" He turned his hands over, back and forth, while reaching out toward her. "Two feet?" He raised one foot then the other.

She understood, but her fear was too strong. In this enclosed space two of her enemies sat, who only saw her as a pakao because of the lies they had heard. She was certain of what Kallias was asking her to do, and she feared it. So many of the kinnir race around her at once. She cowered slightly and swished her tail but did not take her eyes off him. *No. He did not understand.*

"I need your help. These women are not warriors but sisters, daughters and wives." He gestured towards them. "Anything, Spiritdancer, I would be grateful for. You're not a pakao, and I will stand up for your honor." Having finished his request, he left her there and returned to his bedroll.

She wanted to help him, maybe even to help the women. But to show herself? Spiritdancer sat a moment looking at the group as they murmured about what they may be able to contribute. *Run!* her body shouted at her, but she was drawn to stay. *I will show them I can be formidable.* She scampered to the side of the cave where the firelight made her ermine shadow dance against the wall. *Leave now,* her heart told her. But it was torn. For whatever reason that eluded her now, she wanted more to be with him. *Do not make me regret this, Kallias,* said her wisdom. She sat up on hind legs and put her small ermine nose in the air. A sound of wind rose around her. The dust turned at her feet and a spire of yellow-white light rose around her. Kallias stopped unlacing his boots. He watched in awe with the others.

The shadow on the wall disappeared then reappeared as unformed. From the ground uncurled a figure, lean, and strong in appearance, a woman, just as Talek had said. As the spire subsided and the dust settled she appeared, attentive, one foot forward. Her elbow length platinum hair floated outward as if a strong breeze blew through the cave, though it touched no one else. Her skin was a warm olive complexion, her eyes like blue flame. She had strange ears that fanned out at the top with three points connected by a thin membrane of skin. Her gown, at first like a powder blue chiffon, clung to her. Then it reformed itself over her torso and legs into an armor of colorful pearlescent scales. She held out a hand, palm down, toward the fire and a line of it jumped to her as if in a stream. It formed a longbow, fiery and fancy in appearance. She held her other hand out and again the fire jumped to it creating an arrow. This she nocked and in one motion swung about and released it to land at the base of Talek's staff, causing him to jump to his feet. The staff caught fire. Immediately she reached out her right hand again, and the water from Guin's cup flew to the staff and covered the fire, freezing it in ice. After which Talek kicked it, breaking up the ice so it would melt away. With her right index finger she touched her chin. "Dealla." She said simply, then turned fearful but defiant eyes to Kallias. She steadied herself. She nocked another arrow, pulled directly from the fiery bow, ready for the retaliation that did not come.

Kallias snapped out of his speechless gawk and offered a kind smile to her. "Spirit... Dealla. Come, sit, please." He indicated an empty bedroll beside Roselana, who had returned to her own.

"She scorched it," Talek complained, running his finger over the damaged staff.

Guin stood, mouth agape, hands in the air, cup on the ground. Dealla hesitated. Her eyes shifted from Guin to Talek to the women then back to Kallias. The fire weapon blew out. Suddenly and without quite so much fanfare, she slipped into the serlcat form. Her feeling of protection back, she approached the group. "So that's it," Guin said as he watched her graceful step. His tone of gentle understanding belied the stern glint in his eyes. He lowered his hands. "Ya're afraid. Indeed Kallias, I don't know how ya managed to gain her trust, being kinnir as ya are." Dealla stopped short of the group and waited.

"Tomorrow then we'll head out for the Point of the Gald. That's the tip of the peninsula. There we'll find a small encampment of the Bloodfish. The four of us'll do what we can to secure a boat. Then we'll go on to some place near Durgrinstar where we can stay and prepare our approach. For now, we get some sleep." Guin made markings in the dirt to indicate where they were and where they had to go. He looked again at Spiritdancer and Kallias. "She'll likely want yar protection tonight, Warrior." Spiritdancer looked at Kallias as Guin added, "From whatever fear 'tis that haunts her. Though I've a pretty good idea."

Kallias gave a nod of agreement and took his bedroll to the far corner where he settled down to rest for the next day's journey. The serlcat, went to Kallias and laid down between him and the wall of the cave. She shivered slightly before laying her head on her paws.

Chapter 10

The cave had cooled only a little as the fire died without any tending. Talek awakened Kallias with a nudge of the scorched end of his staff. He held a finger to his mouth then motioned Kallias to leave his things and follow, alone. Kallias covered the cat with his cloak. He laced his boots and tied them tightly around his calves then, out of habit, strapped on his sword.

Talek led Kallias faultlessly through Guin's illusion. Neither the pale orange glow of the embers nor the seemingly endless stone enclosure made it difficult for the seer. Kallias followed in his tracks, clasping his arms about his shoulders in the chilly night air. *Where is he taking me?* Kallias thought but did not bother to ask. He stared at the back of the seer's robes, as Talek's staff poked in the soft ground with each precisely placed step. They continued a short way from the cave entrance where Talek stopped and turned to Kallias. "Yar Asadia hasn't yet left Kanratu."

Kallias looked hopeful. "There's time. We should wake Guin and go back to get her."

Talek nodded. "No, but ya can save her. It's why I tell ya now." He looked back toward the cave. "One alone may be able to go in and find her and bring her out unseen. More won't make it. She is on one of the ships. I can't tell which it is. Ya mustn't get caught. There's much danger in that. Now look." Talek pointed his staff westward. "We walked in a great loop to hide where we were going to come here. But the road is just there where we crossed and to the west ya go. It's but a short distance. Make haste."

"You have my thanks, Talek." Kallias said and set off for the road. He looked back once, feeling the seer's blind gaze upon him.

"She'll sail at the rising of the sun!" Talek called out after him. Kallias turned westward setting a quick, deliberate pace. He had no idea how long he slept before Talek awakened him. A full moon, now high in the night sky, lit the way with its soft, silver light. Kallias looked skyward. Clouds gathered. A stiff breeze blew. He realized these as possible helps or hindrances to his need for stealth. On the breeze, quiet night sounds filled the background to the crunch of his boots as Kallias trotted toward Kanratu.

Kallias slowed as he approached the empty streets. Evidently Guin's illusion had kept the alarm from being sounded. No one walked the streets and only an occasional light could be seen from any window. He stuck to the shadows, zigzagging through winding alleys as he made way to the seaport. From the safety of a fisher's shed, he scanned the docks left to right for any longship getting loaded and ready to leave at dawn. Two ships were tied to the pier and one sat out in the bay. A Bloodfish sailor appeared on the deck of the closest to him. In the absence of other signs of life, Kallias reasoned, *That must be the boat.*

He watched the longship man for a time. Scenes raced through his mind of all the possible outcomes of his approach. It was necessary to take the man down quietly in order to search that ship. Then he heard a voice and the longship man turned as another approached him also on deck. "Fie!" Kallias exclaimed, causing the sailor to glance his way. The Blade Dancer backed further into the shadow against the structure.

"Gimme a light fer m'pipe," said the newcomer. The other obliged.

"Y'hear the mystic chose his wench?" The first asked him. "Ye seen her? Which is she?"

"One of Pluth's." The second drew upon his pipe and blew a smoke ring then looked around.

"Pluth's dead. Which ship they taken then?"

"Pluth's of course."

"He's dead. Task should go to another cap'n."

"Maltax is another cap'n."

"Maltax is first mate. Don't knows I'd wanna foller his orders."

"Well ye don't have to now, do ye? It ain't the ship ye serves on, is it?" The second one shook his pipe. "Cripes, m'pipe's gone out. Gimme 'nuther light."

"Get yer own next time." The first gave him a light from a small flint stick. "Maltax'll be made Fleet General. See if he don't."

Kallias focused his awareness on the other ships. Which one was Pluth's? He could not afford to make any mistakes. The other docked ship appeared deserted. Then he noticed the lights on the anchored one. They were not only the ship's lanterns but there were lights in what appeared to be windows at the stern of the longship.

"I need a distraction," Kallias spoke softly to himself and slid opened the small bait door near his foot. He rummaged inside for something to throw. Suddenly, a strong gust of wind blew through. The nearest lamp post, and the longship man's pipe blew out, for which the watchman exclaimed curses. "That will do," Kallias muttered and darted quickly and quietly to the pier. Traversing the distance under the cover of a now clouded sky, his silhouette vanished, as black as the night sea. The longship men found the night winds distracting as they failed to find another match. Too busy to notice a mere streak of silent shadow, they retreated to another section of the ship. The wind gave up its fierceness. At the end of the pier was a small fishing vessel. It tugged at the rope binding it to the post. Kallias jumped in and untied the bond. He unfurled its sail. The gentler breeze pushed into the sail with a soft poof. Soon the coble cut quietly across the seawater. He laid low in the belly, a single hand upon the rudder to steer around the larger longship's bow.

From the anchored ship, he heard a low growl as a watchman stood at the port side, clearing his throat and spitting into the sea. The guard squinted hard towards the incoming craft but did not discern the approaching swordsman. Just then an opening in the clouds threatened to expose him in the moon's full light. "Bah! Damn fish," growled the sailor and turned away. It was close. The glowing lanterns became larger and brighter as Kallias neared. Another look would reveal the little boat for what it was. But the man was gone.

The wind died, and the clouds parted. Kallias jerked the rudder as the little coble came to a slow sideways halt. With a quiet thump, it's hull rested alongside the larger one. Kallias held his breath, waiting for discovery. When no alarm sounded, he fastened the binding rope to the anchor's chain. He climbed the chain to the top, then raised his head for a peek. Hooking an arm over the railing's edge, he swung a leg up and pulled himself across the rail, belly down, rolling onto the deck noiselessly. Besides the splashing sounds of the night sea upon the side of the ship, Kallias heard the clink of a heavy key ring marking time with the watchman's approaching boot steps. He made himself small in the shadow behind the anchor wench. He waited for the man to turn and move towards the stern. There were two cabin compartments on this huge vessel, one fore and one aft. He crept to the nearest small door at the bow and raised the latch. It was easily done, allowing him to slip inside the vestibule of a cabin.

Kallias shut the door behind him. The pale kiss of the moon's beaming gaze through large portholes cast an eerie light throughout the cramped room, creating deep shadows from everything. *An odd place,* thought he. A set of steps rose to his left from the entry to a loft which he could barely discern. Around the room, the tops of bookcases were covered with strange collections and artifacts. Among them were bottles and alchemy utensils he had only seen in a shaman's gallipot. Kallias took interest in the desk that marked the center of the room. He noticed a familiar object. When he reached for his sister's decorative comb, his sleeve knocked over a small pedestal holding a crystal orb. The round ball landed hard on the wooden desk with a bouncing thud. A cough responded from an alcove bed behind the steps. Kallias held his breath, releasing it when the only reply was a grumble as the covered bulk of a man rolled over to settle back to sleep. The sway of the ship rocked the sphere left to right in a game of teeter-totter. Kallias grasped at it and missed. The glass ball shot across the desk. He caught it with a quick hand. Again, Kallias held his breath to hear if the man had awakened. Assured of his safety, he held the festival dress comb up to what light there was and felt its carvings with his thumb. It belonged to Asadia for certain. Now if he could only find where she was being kept.

The sleeper's grumbling snore snapped Kallias from his examination. He slipped back into the shadows of the vestibule near the door. Obviously Asadia was not in this room, but where? He had not returned the orb but placed both objects in the same hand. Almost as if in response to his thought, the small orb shone a soft white light. Taking form inside of it was an image, another room which held an occupant. Behind her a lantern lit the room and the various accouterments of a captain's cabin. The occupant was indeed Asadia. Kallias surmised that she must be in the rear of the ship where he had seen the windows from shore. Just then he realized that the moonlight seemed very bright now. He had lost the cover of darkness outside. This was going to be tricky.

Kallias noticed a robe hanging from a peg by the stairwell. He packed away the crystal ball and comb in his cuirass, then nodded to himself firmly. *I got away with it once.* After donning the robe and with the cowl draped over his face, he opened the door. The brightness came as much from the approaching dawn as the moon. He had little time left to find Asadia and escape. The watchman paused from picking his teeth and cleared his throat as if to begin saying something. Kallias raised a dismissive hand, shooing him away. The watchman shrugged and returned to his lookout.

Kallias strode confidently towards the doorway at the stern. He did not bother to look back but pulled open the door and entered. *Ha! I did it yet again!* he mused. This door led to a small, enclosed companionway with a narrow stairwell down to his left and another door in front of him. Light lined the perceptible cracks around the door. He stepped up to it, resting an ear against it. He heard the soft cry of a woman, the sound of hopelessness. "Asadia," he said her name once inaudibly and pensively to himself. "Sister! Asadia! I come to save you!" His heart skipped at the sound of his own voice. After such stealth, a whisper seemed unusually loud.

He heard movement from inside as she rushed to the door. "Kallias?"

Kallias put a palm on the door. "I'm here, Sister."

"I thought I'd never see you again. The door is locked." Asadia spoke in hushed tones with her mouth close to the door jamb. Kallias tested it, despite her declaration. He grumbled. "The guard has the keys."

"What shall we do?" Asadia moved about on the other side as if searching for something. "I can't find anything to pry it open with, Kallias. I tried earlier."

"Stand back, Asadia." He took out his curved blade and wedged its point into a crack. Then, levered his weight on the hilt as he pushed into it. The wood creaked. With a loud click and a crack something broke free within the door jamb and the door came ajar. Kallias swung it open and hurried inside, closing it behind him. "I thought I'd not see you again either. We must escape," he told her as they hugged each other tightly.

The front of Asadia's dance skirt was covered in dry, dark blood. "Not too soon either," she responded quietly. "They were going to take me somewhere. I think they meant to sell me."

Are you hurt?" Kallias appraised her a moment with a worried expression. "Yours or someone else's?"

"The blood? It was from the man who took me on this boat. He... he tried to force himself on me. He almost did, then the most horrible thing. I saw him above me and a sword came right through the middle of him. The man—"

"We haven't the time. You can explain later when we're far away." Kallias took her hand in his. "There is a guard outside. Perhaps many more sleeping. My boat is tied to the anchor chain. That's where we need to be."

She nodded and followed quietly. Kallias paused a moment in the companionway to listen. Then he opened the outer door just enough to check on the guard. Outside, the morning sun's rays stretched like golden fingers above the distant mountain range. A few paces from the door stood not one but three men, including the watchman. He closed the door quietly, turning to Asadia. Before he could utter a word, they heard the talk and movements of the men below. Kallias pushed her back into the room and closed the door. Its broken lock prevented it from latching, so they braced a chair against it. "This will not keep anyone out," he whispered, "but perhaps it will buy us some time." He examined the small windows.

"Too small, Kallias," said Asadia, "I thought to escape that way but couldn't fit." She showed him an open window with its latch broken.

Something hit the side of the ship and a great hubbub ensued. A loud crack and then a splash followed. Kallias cringed. "Damn, we've lost the skiff. I had it tied to the anch..." Suddenly the door banged open sending the chair flying to one side. Kallias drew his sword and stood in front of his sister. Three men stepped in, each armed with a flintlock longer than Guin's, all aimed at the swordsman. A large burly man with a ruddy complexion and wild reddish brown hair, which stuck out in all directions, stepped to the center of the group and sneered. "Ye wanna return m'robe?"

Kallias remained in defensive posture. He could feel the uplift of the ship as the wind caught its sail and it began to move. His heart dropped. "I'm sorry I've failed you, Sister," he said to Asadia without taking his eyes off the men.

The burly man raised his hairy brows. "Sister is it? Drop yer sword."

This must be Maltax, the captain those sailors argued about, Kallias concluded. "Let us go!" He barked the command as if his confidence had not waned, but was sure the blood had left his face.

Maltax nodded to the man at his left. The sailor responded by moving to one side and aiming his weapon at Asadia. "Now, ye'll give up quiet or both be dead." He tilted his head to the right, speaking to the man at his elbow. "Let's take him far as the reef and throw 'im overboard. We'll let the sharks decide his fate."

"Aye Cap'n." The other approached Kallias and easily took his sword as Maltax laughed. He gave the sword over to his captain and then returned to bind Kallias.

"M'robe first." Kallias pulled off the robe and slung it across a table. Maltax gestured to the man to his left and the two men grabbed Kallias, bound him and dragged him onto the deck. Another man came into the cabin and did the same with Asadia.

Once outside, Kallias could see they had come a long way from shore very quickly and were making good time going further away. "You won't get away with this." Kallias tried to hold certainty in his voice, though he doubted if Guin or any of the others would be motivated to save Asadia without him. He had failed Spiritdancer, too. He only hoped she could protect herself against Talek. Besides which he had only Talek to trust to tell the others where he was.

The ship bucked over a set of waves that rolled over an unseen shore. Kallias could hear breakers in the distance though the shoreline behind them was barely discernible. "So perhaps ye'll be able to survive. Can't kill ye outright ye bein' a relative 'n' all. Ye might even swim as far as that island." Maltax pointed Kallias' sword to a large rock to the south. "Of course, ye'd hafta be rid o' yer bindin's." He signaled to a man, who then tied up Kallias' feet with the long end of the same rope, as others picked him up. When Asadia cried out, a sailor roughly clapped a hand over her mouth.

"And ye'd hafta be able to ketch yer breath." With that the man who bound him stuffed a rag in Kallias' mouth. "An' ye'd hafta avoid gettin' et by sharks and sea beasts. Then the islands full o' sea beasts. They might not take to ye." Maltax pushed his face to Kallias'. "Yer clever to make it this far. I respects that. I'll help ye out a bit." With that he threw Kallias' sword overboard. "There! Fetch!"

The men swung Kallias over the side.

Chapter 11

Spiritdancer awoke with the sun as always, despite its inability to shine into the cave. She did not feel Kallias next to her and so turned her head toward the fire pit, expecting him there. Then she jumped to her serlcat paws in a panic, as his cloak dropped to the ground. The others slept soundly yet. Where would he go? How could he find the tunnel through the illusion when she could not feel past it even? The illusion held its place as Guin slept with one eye open. Spiritdancer could not trust Guin nor the seer, Talek. If given the chance they would likely kill her. Only the one called Roselana seemed close enough to Kallias. Spiritdancer nudged her.

"Mmm, what?" Roselana moaned and opened her eyes. She started at sight of the serlcat before recalling the situation. "Oh, Dealla. What is it?" She looked around. "Where is Kallias?" Spiritdancer paced along one side of the rock wall where she was sure they had come in. "You don't know?"

The serlcat went to stand in front of Guin. She looked at Roselana and when certain of her attention, bat Guin sharply on the top of the head with a soft paw. Then she leapt to one side as the awakening Guin swung a fist at her.

"Guin!" Roselana said, "Kallias is gone."

"What?" Guin yawned and sat up sleepy-eyed.

"Kallias is not here." Roselana repeated as Spiritdancer returned to pacing across that section of wall.

"Where'd he go?" Guin looked about curiously.

"Guin, the illusion. Dealla can't see past it."

Guin waved a hand and mumbled a few words. As soon as the tunnel entry was visible, the serlcat bolted through it.

Spiritdancer picked up Kallias' scent and raced along the path he took back to Kanratu. Where the road crested above the east end of town she halted. There was a great deal of activity in town. The longship men were alerted to the missing women and were beginning to search the town for them. Spiritdancer took the form of an osprey and flew to find Kallias.

Spiritdancer spent time flying over one rooftop after another looking and listening for some sign of Kallias or Asadia. She searched in a zigzag pattern over the city from east to west until she reached the docks. Then she heard a man on one of the longships. "Naw, 'tis the other wimins they's lookin' fer." With some thought she connected the talk of women to Kallias' purpose. There had been three ships yesterday. She scanned the horizon and far out westward she could see the vanishing dot of a ship. Spiritdancer took wing after it.

Kallias heard Asadia scream and call his name as the cold sea swallowed him. He had filled his lungs before hitting the water but the rag in his mouth soaked up water quickly. Pressing his tongue against it, he attempted to minimize the threat of drowning. He watched the dark shadow of the ship's hull as it moved swiftly away. *It's their mistake to keep my hands in front.* He yanked the rag from his mouth. On a rock of corals his blade glinted in the diffused sunlight. If he could reach it he could free himself. He was near to passing out though. The Baresian dolphin-kicked his way to the surface and gulped air until his lungs were full. Then he dove down kicking hard to get to his sword. The small crystal orb and his sister's comb fell from his cuirass into the depths.

Something large swam past him. Kallias halted and pulled himself upright. Sharks. There were at least three of them wandering around him just where the water became dark. All he knew about sharks was that they tasted good. He had no intention of giving them the opportunity to find out if he tasted good too. He prepared himself to strike at the next one that came close. His binding would not make it easy.

Tucking his legs up to make himself small, Kallias gave himself room to kick. A shark twice his size approached. He struck out at it barely touching somewhere next to its dorsal fin. It swam away. He prepared himself again. This time a smaller one came near him. He struck again. A miss. Again and again they came at him. Each time he faced them kicking hard and often striking them. Suddenly, they all retreated. Fearful, Kallias looked around for something even larger and more terrifying. Nothing. He had won.

Again, he went up for air and again dove deep for his sword. This time he got it. Immediately he cut loose his feet and kicked himself to the surface. With some manipulating he managed to wedge the point of his sword into his boot, brace the hilt against his chest, and cut his hands free. Then he sheathed the blade and swam for the rock.

Spiritdancer swept through the air quickly, leaving it behind her wings. The ship sailed with the wind, and she had to do better to catch it. When she did, she perched upon the yardarm. Her keen eyes examined the deck for Kallias. There were longship men only. Then a large one stepped out of a doorway at the bow followed by another. "We'll leave her there only 'til we git the latch fixed to m'quarters," the first man was saying. "If any more come lookin' fer her, I'll slice 'em open and drop 'em in by pieces. I'll be glad to git to Durgrinstar 'n' be rid o' this business." The two continued across the deck to another door at the stern and disappeared.

The bird flew around the two ends of the ship, stopping where she found purchase upon a rope or sill to peer into the rooms. Something was wrong. A woman was there, but Kallias was not. Then she realized Kallias had been thrown overboard! But where? Spiritdancer flew high back toward shore circling every little way to see if she could see any signs in the water.

Kallias swam. His arms ached, but he kept up his pace against the tide. Thunderous barking filled the air as he came nearer to the rock. He could distinguish the shapes of seals. They laid basking and socializing for a mid-morning's break. He panted and halted, clinging to a mass of barnacle-covered rock as he finally made it to the islet. He rested a moment taking a deep, swallowing gulp of air. He coughed violently until he heaved the salt water in his guts back to its origin. His head began to pound as if a band of Baresian drummers played a war dance there. A "kree" sounded from a bird of prey circling high overhead. He squinted as he gave the winged figure a swift glance then pulled himself out of the water. Volcanic rock and barnacles scrapped and cut into his hands as he climbed up. The smaller seals slipped into the deep blue depths once aware of his presence. The larger bulls ignored him. Others barked while some stood their ground with chins held high. They almost seemed to smirk as they reserved an indignant warning pose with their chests pushed out and backs arched. Kallias buckled. His muscles finally gave way to exhaustion. He laid faintly on his back, watching the ship with his sister, a tiny dot in the distance, as it vanished. His heart sank. A tear rolled along his cheek, its unforgiving bitterness even saltier than the cold waters that slapped the rocks. The bird rotated high above. Ignoring it, he stared into the powder blue, morning sky.

The osprey spiraled down, first slowly, then made a dive for Kallias. He flinched. She threw her wings wide just as she reached him and settled gently on the rock above his head. Then Dealla assumed the rekinnder form he had seen in the cave, only dressed in what appeared to be a light blue ethereal gown. The barking of the seals ceased. She stepped around to Kallias' side and knelt beside him.

"I failed, Dealla. She was in my arms. Now she's gone. Beyond my reach." Kallias sat upright and groaned, his eyes fixed on the vanishing point. He shook a fist. "They'll pay. I'll find them and free my sister. But not before I feed that captain to the sharks." Kallias coughed, choked back the tears and wiped his nose with a salty, wet sleeve. He then turned his attention to the rekinnder. "I'm glad you found me, Spiritdancer." Bringing himself up on his left knee, he spat out into the water and swiped the other sleeve across his now pale face. "So, how do we get off of this rock?"

She glanced out to the sea where the ship had gone and then around toward Kanratu. She pointed to the shore then put her fingertips to her chest and spoke slowly. "Mele Spiritdancer d'gaffini ekuine." Then she put her fingertips upon Kallias' chest. "Kallias..." She searched for a word. "Kallias sail."

Kallias rose to his feet with a frustrated sigh. "Sail? Sail what?"

Dealla smiled, stepped to the edge of the rock and dove into the water. In a moment, a bottle nosed dolphin stuck its head up out of the water and chattered at him. Kallias stood soaked, shivering and angry. But Dealla's form brought a smile to his face. He dove into the water coming up beside the dolphin. She nudged him, bringing her dorsal fin up under his arm, waited until he had a firm grip, then set off towards the peninsula. She started slowly, gradually increasing speed over the surface of the water, making it easy for him to keep beside her. It took very little time for them to reach the shoreline. The city still resounded with the near frantic activity to find the missing women. Spiritdancer paused south of Kanratu just out of sight from the port. Kallias stood in the shallow tide. The dolphin pushed herself out toward the sea again and disappeared momentarily. Then as he watched, she launched herself out of the water high into the air arching towards the shore. A worry flashed across his mind but for a blink when she landed upon the padded paws of the serlcat. He walked out of the water to her, his mouth agape. She was completely dry!

Kallias' teeth chattered as he limped along behind Dealla in sopping boots. When he attempted to wring his long hair free of the salty water, his arms ached like never before. His wrists, red with rope burns, evinced the stark reminder of his defeat. He groaned.

Spiritdancer stopped inside the trees. Her ears had been doing their work. Thus far, there was nothing in the woods around Kanratu nor on the east road ahead. They would make it back to the others without a doubt. She turned to Kallias with a reassuring gaze, when she noticed his discomfort. How could she have been so thoughtless? Effortlessly she shifted into her rekinnder form where she could more easily manipulate the elements. With a gentle hand on his chest she stopped him. "Alaf olent d'Kallias." She spoke softly as if to comfort something within him. A cloud of vapor lifted off his head and body and in the breath of a butterfly he was dry. She could do nothing about his aching arms nor the rope burns, but his body ceased quaking immediately.

"Thank you, Dealla." Being dry helped him muster up the spirit to continue. Asadia was gone from Kanratu. But before Talek had told him otherwise, he had expected her to be in Durgrinstar. *Not beaten yet,* he told himself. Kallias put his hand over Dealla's as it lay on his chest drying him. "We have to regroup." Dealla yanked her hand away nervously, then slipped into the serlcat form. After selecting their path, she checked over her shoulder frequently to be sure he followed.

Later they entered the cave through the tunnel. The illusion was again in place but because of the living beings inside, Spiritdancer could detect the pathway and led Kallias through the apparent wall of rock.

"Kallias!" Roselana squealed with relief. At sight of the returning duo, the others stood. "Where were you?!" she continued.

"I almost saved her, Roselana." Kallias accepted a hug from his friend, though he hardly felt worthy of it. "But they captured me, I was helpless. Thrown overboard as fish bait."

Talek stood aloof from the group, his head inclined towards Spiritdancer. Guin's eyes narrowed as he cast a scornful look at the errant warrior. Then Jamila spoke their thoughts. "What were we to have done had you not returned? It's good that you live, though. Yes, very good you're still with us."

"I had to chance it. It's why I came."

"And you'd have sacrificed the rest of us?" accused Zetrine.

"Yes... no!" he stammered, "Not... I mean... It wasn't as if I planned to fail. If I had succeeded, we'd all be heading home now with no more talk of you all having to defend yourselves or sneak into a city. Look, I lost this time, but it isn't over. We're back and no worse off than if Asadia had already been gone."

Guin shook his head. "Maybe, maybe not."

Talek's head jerked up. "We must leave. The alert's gone up and a search is made for the women. We mustn't leave trace of our being here."

"Yes, we heard the alarm go up when we reached the shore."

"Ya weren't seen were ya?" Guin moved instantly upon the old akinn's words. Kallias shook his head. The older man doused the fire with water and threw sand on it besides. Then he gathered up all he could into his pack and Kallias'. He handed Kallias his satchel and cloak. "I'd thought ya might not return. I'm glad I was wrong."

The women rolled up their bedrolls, tucking cups, bowls and utensils into the folds, then tied them with rope and slung them over their shoulders.

Chapter 12

Pekoe tread softly, her sandals creating footprints inside of those left by Guin and the others on his heels. She glanced back now and then, warily, but curiously studying Kallias and the serlcat following in the back. The misty morning air cleared gradually as bits of sun shone along the dusty path. Spiritdancer walked silently at Kallias' side. Pekoe could not refrain from casting continuous glances over her shoulder, because behind them with every swish of the cat's tail, the dirt and dead leaves swirled as if a breeze followed them in the otherwise still morning air. As the forest stirred to life with the sun's warmth, an eerie silence fell among them. Kallias, aware of the young girl's questioning gaze, caught her eye and smiled. Alarmed, she snapped her head forward, then jogged up to Roselana's side. The serlcat paid no notice as her ears worked at screening the sounds of the forest and road around them.

"Is he a pakao, too?" Pekoe asked Roselana quietly.

The older girl glanced back at Kallias with a giggle and a shake of her head. "No, I've known him since we were children. He's my brother's friend." She spoke softly as she put her arm around Pekoe's shoulder reassuringly. "I'm not sure what to call the strange one, but he wouldn't be happy with me if I called her a pakao, too. I think it would be a good idea to get to know her."

Spiritdancer glanced up at Kallias, putting her ears forward as if to ask something. Catching the glance, he shrugged. "Guin, how far to go?"

"Most of the day. It isn't really so far as it feels. We cross into the woods soon and leave the road," he called back.

Kallias sighed. He noticed the serlcat's ears as she scanned about, alert. For now, they were all safe. He wondered if he would read her as well if she took her kinnir form. He wanted to speak to the woman, Dealla, now he had seen her and knew her name. *I want to know more about my hero and companion,* he thought, but his lips would not move. She was exotic and beautiful despite the rekinnder stigma.

The group carried on as the morning sun swept down through the trees ever brighter. The road crested the gentle incline they had been walking. It dipped and turned eastward. Dealla wondered if perhaps Kallias would suspect her now that she had shown herself. He had not touched her, had not pet the cat as he had before. Questions and self-chastisements ran through her rekinnder mind, not in words but in feelings and images. *Have I lost something? It was probably a mistake showing myself like that. They all mistrust me now, don't they? I should not be with them. Better to follow from a distance inside the trees.* The faux-breeze behind them with which she cleared their footprints suddenly stopped.

Kallias fell back a bit from the group as Spiritdancer leaped through the brush and vanished into the forest without so much as a sound. "Dealla? Spirit..." He called out her name quietly. He peered into the trees, then nervously towards the group, now more than ten yards ahead. Guin paused as the seer tapped him with his staff. He looked back to see Kallias alone catching up to them. Without a word he tread onward.

Soon Guin stopped and waited while they bunched up together. Guin searched through the brush. "There's a large stone like a duck around here somewhere. It may be over grown with berry vines this time of year. Help me find it. It's been some long time since I've used this path."

"Stone in the shape of a duck?" Jamila asked. As everyone else dug around in the bushes, she rested a hand up against a mound of vines only to have her arm fall slightly inwards. "Here!" she called out as she ripped the vines away from a boulder. The top was rounded with a flat extrusion like a duck's bill. "A duck," she announced, "or at least half of one."

Guin chuckled. "Good work. We go along the back side of it just here." He pointed the way and the seer stepped into the wood as if he saw every plant, every leaf and vine. The women followed him, then Kallias. "She around here somewhere, like before?" Guin asked Kallias as the warrior stepped past him into the woods.

"Spiritdancer? Most likely."

Guin nodded. "I don't know if we can trust her, Kallias. She has a fear inside and a hatred. I saw it in her in the cave. And Talek is no friend of rekinnder or the stories about them."

Kallias nodded his understanding but quickly defended her. "She saved my life, you know. I wouldn't be here without her. I don't know anything about your stories. In my land there is no word rekinnder. Creatures that change shape are legends, spirits of the wilderness, helpful to travelers, like her, helpful to me."

Guin said no more about her but again took the lead, following a narrow, worn animal trail. "There's a spring up ahead. We'll stop for midday and rest there."

Charlise sighed. "Finally, a rest." Her sandal clad feet had become scratched and bruised from pebbles and twigs kicked up along the way. As they trekked down the narrow path they could hear water rippling over stone. Here flowed a quick-moving stream, quite narrow this close to its source. As soon as they happened upon the clearing, the women lifted their skirts and sat to wash their feet.

Talek found a broad rock to sit upon and took a satchel from under his robes. He pulled out some dried fish wrapped in parchment. "Pass this about and share. There should be berries in abundance here to supplement."

"There weren't any berries on the duck rock vines," objected Jamila.

"Lots of different kinds. Some in bloom, some fruit. Surely ya can smell them?"

Guin took the fish after Talek had helped himself to a generous serving. He carried it to Roselana first and held it out to her. "Ya look..." He smiled as she turned to him. "Ya... all look very hungry. Go ahead and have yar fill. I've provisions of my own." Roselana picked from the fish before passing it down the line. Guin addressed the group. "Refresh yar selves well. The place we're headed is not meant to be reached by foot. It's close enough, but rough going. We'll be picking our way through brush by animal trails," he explained. "Stay close. Pay attention so ya don't get separated."

Zetrine waved a hand. "I don't like dried fish. I'll go pick berries." Using the hem of her dress, she dried her feet and tied her sandals back on, then headed upstream into the nearby brush. Soon after she had disappeared, the peaceful atmosphere was split by her scream. Everyone leaped to their feet. With weapons drawn, the men ran to her defense. Kallias found her first, not far from the clearing with her hands over her face. She pointed to a large rock where a skeleton sat interwoven and locked in place by various plants, its death grin peeking through the growth. The women circled around Zetrine, calming her and each other.

Sheathing their swords, the two men investigated the find. "It's been there for a while." Kallias bent low and moved the vines around. "Though these probably grew faster than our desert vines with so much more water."

"Wasn't kervplik. The bones're still together." Guin noted. "Attitude says whoever it was wasn't going to the spring here. He was facing something or someone."

Kallias sifted through the remnants and picked up what he first thought to be a stick. As he drew it up from under the layer of vines it turned out to be a longbow shaft barely worn from the elements and still in usable condition, though only half of the bow string remained.

"Rekinnder," Guin said looking at the bow. "I've not known another race or creature in these lands to use a longbow except them, not since powder and gun anyway. Any sign of what killed it?"

Kallias handed the bow to Roselana and cleared the leafy overgrowth from the rest of the remains. "No clothing," he remarked.

"Well there wouldn't be, would there?" Guin stated the question. It was true. Nothing remained stuck to the skeleton that indicated it had worn anything other than at its waist, where there hung a tattered leather belt with a dagger sheathed in it. He picked around the bones and looked to Guin with a shrug. Guin shook his head sadly. "This one had kinnir form, held a weapon. Fear can do horrible things."

Kallias slipped the belt and knife from the bones and handed them to Charlise. Roselana ran her finger along the bow's shaft clearing encrusted dirt from it. "Look, inscriptions."

Guin turned. "Can ya read them?" She shook her head in response. "Let's give a burial to the bones," Guin suggested.

"No. 'Tis best leave the pakao as is." Talek stood behind them now, pounding his staff as before. "'Tis evil. Don't touch it."

Charlise dropped the dagger at the old seer's words. Kallias picked it up as he rose to his feet and motioned his hand back towards the clearing. "Let's gather again at the stream." He touched Zetrine's elbow. "Don't stray far."

Guin again surveyed the bones as the others stepped away. As if to ensure he was not observed, the mystic peered into the trees around him. He reached into the remains and took something small out, putting it into a pocket of his robe. He then checked over the skull and the ground. After a few moments, he gazed around the area again and finally joined the others by the spring.

Talek returned to his seat upon the rock, firmly planting the end of his staff in the ground in front of him. "The image mine, of an empty place of death. There a ship is also dead. When the sun has gone below the waters a pyre will burn."

"A dead boat?" Roselana inquired. "Like a ghost boat?"

"He's being dramatic. He means unusable. Has a hole in its hull or something." Guin responded.

"'Tis dead and was a box of death to those last upon it." The old akinn spoke with a mysterious tone, thrusting his eyeless face toward the girl. Roselana wrinkled her nose and backed off. She made her way to the gathered women, past

Kallias, who was busy examining the dagger. All but Zetrine were there as the sun rose to the center of the sky.

"Have ya anything of real value to say, old man?" Guin inquired.

"That's all I see." Talek rested the staff against his shoulder and let the tension out of his body.

"Well the encampment isn't far. That way." Guin pointed due south. "The women should keep in the trees while the three of us make our way into the camp and find a small boat to use." He looked again at the old man then back to Kallias. "If yar pak... yar... if Dealla will join ya, we'll be the stronger ones should fighting be necessary. If there're too many men, we'll wait for the cover of darkness."

Once the group left the road, Spiritdancer went in search of her own repast. It took her to the opposite side of the roadway. There was little to hunt on the west side. She had gone quite a distance through rocky terrain in search of pika when she heard the scream. She bound across rocks and through the crags back down into the trees to the road. She sniffed out their trail quickly. When she arrived at the stream they were all returning from wherever they had been. No one appeared upset. The one called Zetrine headed away from the group.

Spiritdancer crept through the trees and underbrush silently. She found an elevated fault line above the area Zetrine explored and padded noiselessly along it. As the others grouped back at the stream, she followed Zetrine watching over her, one ear on the girl and the other alert to forest sounds. The hilly wooded area afforded an overhead view of the young woman but an easy jump if some protection was needed. Zetrine stopped to pick some small red berries. Hungry as Dealla was, it made no sense to leave them now. Another hunt would take too long. She contented herself with rest. The serlcat made herself visible on a grassy overhang near Zetrine, if the girl were to look around. Spiritdancer turned her ears in several directions. When she was satisfied that all was safe, she lay upon her belly, feet forward.

Kallias turned the elegant dagger over in his hands as he examined it. The pommel, a tarnished silver, held a red gem set in its socket. Its weathered scabbard felt softer than he expected as he examined the grip, made from a black onyx stone securely held with the same soft deer hide, and the guard, a slightly weathered steel with a larger matching gem set in the middle. Its blade was longer than the poniard he kept strapped to his thigh. Grasping the hilt in one hand and the sheath in his other, he pulled. The scabbard was oddly better preserved than the belt and released its hold easily. Well protected from the elements, the blade shone brightly in the midday sun. From handle to point, it sported intricate gold designs similar to those of the bow. "Guin, here's another with markings. Can you read these?" He laid the blade across his palm, the hilt towards Guin.

Guin looked at the blade and shook his head. "They're not mystic writings nor akinn symbols and the Bloodfish rarely write anything. This must be rekinnder, Kallias. I can think of nothing else. Ask her when she returns to ya." He walked up the small stream to the egress of the spring itself close to the rocks and brush where the skeleton still rested exposed. There Guin silently filled his leather covered water bladder.

As Kallias started to run his fingertips over the inscriptions along the blade, a blue light like an electrical charge, began to swirl about the blade and his fingers. He quickly pulled his hand away. When he tried again, nothing happened. *Perhaps I imagined it,* he thought.

"Where's the other girl?" Guin asked Kallias upon his return. "It's time to go."

Kallias separated the sheath from the stiff decaying leather of the belt, returned the dirk to its place and tucked it into his own belt. He stood and gazed about. "She's still picking berries close by. I'll look for her."

Guin nodded. "Everyone with a water bladder should refresh and refill them at the spring itself. Then we'll continue. It isn't far now."

Kallias found Zetrine tying up a small handkerchief filled with berries. "We're ready to leave, Zetrine, Spiritdancer." He smiled to the serlcat sitting protectively over the girl. Zetrine glanced over her shoulder. Startled, she jumped as she realized the cat had been so close. "Come, come, I have some things I must show you." He motioned for the serlcat to join them as he turned and followed Zetrine back to the spring. Spiritdancer leaped off the overhang gracefully, landing noiselessly upon her serlcat toes. "You know something of the meaning of these designs?" He spoke as they walked and produced the blue tinted steel with the gold etched line work. "We found a longbow with similar designs."

Spiritdancer stopped. Her ears came forward in recognition. Then her eyes asked the question of its finding.

"They were discovered on some remains obscured in vines just near the springs. Guin believes..." He cut his words off short as the cat sped off in the direction of the spring.

Spiritdancer sniffed around the skeleton. Finally, she lie down in front of the remains. She flattened her ears. Her chest rumbled with a disturbing growl.

When Kallias and Zetrine reached the gathering, Kallias stepped around the brush far enough to see Spiritdancer. He then returned to the group quietly.

Guin hooked a thumb upstream. "Taking up a vigil, is she?"

Kallias nodded. "Let's go." He gazed back over his shoulder and sighed.

They crossed the stream and began moving along another animal trail. It continued meandering through the forest for some ways, passing through a small meadow and around some large boulders, continuing downhill and to the south. Their path ended abruptly at a small dirt clearing from where the ocean could be seen and heard distinctly. Guin held a hand up to halt the group. Across the clearing a few trees stood leaning away from a drop off. Their windswept branches with close-growing clusters of leaves, stretched toward the bare spot of land as if bowing to their greater cousins on the other side. Even the greater trees where the group waited in the shadows, sported the gnarled, semi-stripped branches polished by the force of wind storms.

The mystic stepped into the clearing and waved Kallias to his side. Speaking quietly, he pointed through the trees at what appeared to be two small thatched rooftops. "The encampment. It's a place of..." he searched for a word. "meeting for the longship men."

"How do we get down there? It drops off here." Kallias likewise spoke quietly.

"We'll go to the right. It slopes down through the trees, bit of a trail, bit of cover, too."

"Shall I prepare and hide the women nearby?"

"Last time I was here I was going that way." Guin hooked a thumb over his shoulder. "Aye. Let's prepa—" He stopped as the old seer walked right past them and headed toward the encampment. "Wait, old man!" Guin growled. Ignoring him, Talek disappeared into the trees.

Kallias sighed as he rested his palm on the hilt of his blade. "Talek had better be good at foretelling the future, Guin."

Once Talek had set off, the women joined the men. Guin scanned their faces. "Wait here. I'll follow him." Guin went after Talek as silently as possible. Kallias crawled on his belly to see over the cliff edge. An eternal minute later from his vantage point, Kallias could see the two exit the trees, one after the other. The old akinn was soon standing between the two huts.

He turned and called back. "Behold the empty place o' death!" Guin halted in his tracks.

(Selected Translations on page 295)

Chapter 13

Meanwhile, Dealla waited for the noisy footfall of the kinnir to fade from her hearing range. Standing upright, she pulled into rekinnder form only, leaving herself cloaked in the black-spotted silver fur of the serlcat. She knelt before the skeleton and placed a gentle hand on the skull. "Ak Mehanna! Atlo falke juet awa omwa da?"[01]

Until this day, she had not known what happened to Mehanna. She investigated now. The kinnir had taken the knife and the bow. With the exception of one arrow, Dealla found Mehanna's quiver behind and beneath the bones. It was enough for Dealla to make assumptions. Mehanna's bow out meant she intended to defend herself. However, she did not flee. She must have tried to talk; she knew her assailant. Immediately the image of a kinnir wearing the removable furs like those of Guin's came to mind. Anger welled up inside her, the same jealousy which had separated her from her beloved Mehanna an eternity ago. How could her own sister take up with one of those who had instigated the ages long war against the rekinnder and who were responsible for their mother's disappearance? "Palae mile awa von kinnir, shiive Rekinnder et awis?"[02]

Mehanna had chosen a kinnir mate. Dealla saw them once, pressing their mouths together. Then the male bound Mehanna's waist with a belt and a shiny, sharp weapon that shimmered in blue like water reflecting the morning sky. Perhaps the belt kept her from transforming to fly away. Quivers and bows were made by rekinnder to drop instantly so they could change form and flee. Their weapons were tooth and claw or quickly created of materials naturally found everywhere. But this dagger, which her sister called "hanna" or gift, from the kinnir was treacherous. It bound her body. Dealla knew it was a mistake for Mehanna to accept. She recalled her furious words at the time. Unfortunately, the more Dealla tried to coax Mehanna away from this kinnir, the greater the gulf grew between sisters.

Finally, Dealla ran away. She meant to worry Mehanna. It worked. It was cruel. Dealla could feel her sister's anxiety in the land when she transformed into the serlcat. She knew Mehanna followed her southward. But when regret seeped into Dealla's heart, she knew that Mehanna had given up searching for her. The roles reversed themselves. She headed north to their last nest only to find it long abandoned. She could track Mehanna in the goz, with sense and scent. Just when she thought she was close, Mehanna disappeared completely. Dealla lost direction. Her search meandered. The only explanation was death, but Dealla denied it. How could she apologize otherwise? So instead she chose to believe that Mehanna had left this land with the kinnir. That somewhere she was alive.

"Sege ala d'shrivez? Uene shrivez awo ala hol da!"[03] Dealla berated the skeleton with many "how-could-yous" followed immediately with as many abject apologies for having left her unprotected from the traitorous kinnir. "Zet jakala ka sega leot awa d'ala, von zet mahij pez leot ele awo awa. Atlo rivesh eot ele? Zon uez bosae ele."[04]

No tears came to Dealla's eyes. She would save them for the funeral. One suspicion repeated itself in her mind. In fact, for her it was a certainty. HE had betrayed her sister, killed her. Dealla swore revenge. "Alle, alle d'awa, Mehanna! Tiiti juzaum kinnir! Shiive von gradin mis dö mis juzaum!"[05] She tried to remember his face, but she had never seen it completely. Mehanna kept her away whenever he came around. Never mind. She remembered his scent.

As Dealla pulled the plants away from the rock and ground to weave a funeral basket for the bones, she discovered a second skeleton. A full set of tiny bones curled, half buried in a mound of dirt beneath Mehanna. "Uene uratol döj, waling kinnit."[06] Dealla gently dusted the soil away and lifted the bones. They all fit in just her palm! What little creature had been killed by Mehanna's fall? Head, hands, feet, short tail, perhaps a little marmoset? This collateral loss of an innocent, unwitting, little creature gave evidence of the abhorrent nature of the kinnir. She vowed also to this little once-living thing, she would find the guilty man and kill him.

Fourteen seasons of lonely denial, of attributing the worst motives of abandonment to her beloved Mehanna, vanished the day Dealla watched the solitary kinnir jump and spin and swing his sword, defeating some invisible enemy. A strange attachment and inexplicable fears accompanied her when she walked with him. Dealla thought she understood Mehanna then. But this evidence of certain betrayal, the discovery of these bones, caused her deep concern about Kallias the strange, dark-haired kinnir. He would not kill her as the other had killed her sister! Betrayal did not seem to be in his nature, but for the reason of his friendship with the longship man, she remained wary.

Chapter 14

No one moved. Six pairs of ears strained to capture the sounds of Bloodfish sailors. Nothing happened. The old akinn continued into the body of the village. Guin crept down to the huts and peered around the corner of one of them. Then he turned back and called out. "It's as the seer says, empty!" Guin continued into the village and was soon lost to Kallias' sight.

"Come ladies." He marched alongside the women as they paraded down the path towards the village. They soon stood in the midst of a ruins with their backs to three hovels, each held above the sand on wooden legs. Their first impression of the small encampment was of desolation. A single gull screeched overhead.

"A little boat!" squealed Pekoe. The next moment she frowned. "Aww, the stern is crushed. Must be the dead one."

Kallias turned to Guin. "I thought you said there would be boats here. There isn't even a pier."

"There never was. Ships just anchored. It's as if half the encampment has been wiped away." Guin took the scene in slowly. "This wasn't ever a regular camp for the navy, but there was always someone here. Always."

"What could have done this?" the warrior asked.

Talek stepped around him and muttered a single word. "Maogra."

"Not the sea monster," corrected Guin. "There would be signs. Looks like hurricane on the beach. There's nothing left of the posts. These three huts here still stand but there were two more, there and there." Guin pointed at empty sand beside two of the bungalows. "But, we've weathered hurricanes before," he continued. "This is a clean sweep. There should be cabin debris. The base posts should be sticking up out of the sand or something."

"What are you saying, Guin? They've just disappeared into thin air?"

"I'm saying I don't know. There probably was a hurricane. But that isn't what cleared the encampment out. I'm sure of it. It hasn't been a long time either. It may be why the women were taken into Kanratu. Place of death, bah." He clawed a piece of driftwood out of the sand then tossed it away.

"Could be our death he speaks of," Kallias said flatly.

Guin snapped his head around to the swordsman. "No, they carried out executions here."

"Yours?" Kallias raised a brow.

"Mine and worse. It wasn't a prophecy, that part."

"Let's hope not. So what are we to do now?" he grumbled. "I have to find my sister."

"I don't know," Guin replied. "If they've taken her to Yungir in Durgrinstar, they'll be there in a few days."

"Then we do the same. Maybe we can steal a boat in Kanratu."

"What? All of us? With every boatman and akinn searching for us? We can't sneak in; we just got out." Guin scowled at the absurdity of the idea.

"Then we go without the women."

"Wait. You can't just abandon us here!" objected Zetrine.

"Who's abandoning us?" asked Jamila, drawing the attention of all the ladies and gathering them to the conversation.

"No one. We can more easily steal a boat at night and come back to pick you up," Kallias explained.

"That'll never work. It's suicide." Guin folded his arms.

"You have a better idea?"

"Look, we're all tired." Guin sighed. "Let's look around and see what we can find. At least we can get some sleep and maybe come up with a plan once our heads are clear."

"Fine. Spread out. See what you can find. Anything we can make use of." Kallias waved a hand toward the others.

Kallias and the women began to search around in the huts. Each hut was a single room with a suet-burning heater-lamp hanging in one corner, three beds, a hewn wooden table attached to one wall with a single leg holding it up and two or three stools. There were one or two windows in each, though the intermittent sunbeams gave little light. Under some of the beds they found boxes with rope, candles and other items.

The beach wrapped about the Point in a horse-shoe shape. Its eastern side curved north along an unrestrained beach while the west, more rugged and troublesome to travel, meandered northwest, as most of its beach was tapered and rock-strewn where the forest and cliff side met the sea. Guin walked the beach to the east. Meanwhile the old akinn sat upon the overturned hull of the small, broken rowboat, making obvious his determination to be of the least possible assistance.

Roselana happened upon Kallias in one of the huts as he sat on a bed, blowing the dust from a small wooden carving of a boat. It was incomplete, most likely a gift from an away-from-home father to his son. "How does it fit?" She twirled about in a leather cuirass dyed of a deep red wine, much too large for her, but a belt held it fast to her torso. Leather bracers and shin guards protected her limbs.

"Good find. Make sure the others know to gather what they've found and meet me outside." As he set the small toy aside, he thought, *We may never know why you were left here unfinished, little boat.* Reaching under the bed, Kallias pulled out a crate and held it in both hands. He left the dimness of the hut, moving to the center of the village where he dumped out the crate's contents. Small drops of misty rain touched his face.

"Kallias!" Charlise came around the east bend along the shore. "There's a boat!"

"Head for the trees!" He stood ready for anything.

"No! No, it's not coming this way. It's beached!"

"Where?"

"There! Come see. This way. We're saved! We just have to get it back in the water." Kallias began to follow her when Guin appeared from the same direction.

"Except that it has a hole in it." Guin approached ladened with another crate; a loop of rope hung over his shoulder. "Won't sail, but there's salvage aboard. Looks like yar army has found some gear," he said to Kallias, indicating the women as they exited huts. Roselana, in her new found cuirass, and the others grouped around the men. Guin put the rope on the crate and set them next to the one Kallias had dumped out on the sand.

The sun dipped into the water just then, shrouding the world in the deep royal blue of twilight. "Look there!" Guin pointed at a distinctively orange glow and silvery smoke up the hill behind the huts.

"Is the forest on fire?" cried a worried Charlise.

"The rain will put it out, won't it?" asked Pekoe.

"Rain might be too light depends on how—" Guin was interrupted as just then an eerie, howling cry that sent chills down the spine, filled the air.

Kallias drew his blade. "Is it one of those kervpliks? Get behind me, girls."

"What is it? It's frightening!" the women wailed, as they gathered close behind him.

"Pakao's cry." The old akinn pounded his staff. "I told ya. Warned ya I did. It's that pakao. Certain I am o' that."

"What does it mean? Is she hurt?" Kallias rejoined. His eyes never left the hillside. The howling continued, but nothing came out of the woods at them. He returned his blades to their black, ornate scabbards and started for the trail. Guin caught him by the arm. "Let me go! She might be hurt!" Kallias jerked his arm out of Guin's grasp.

"Of course she's hurt," answered the mystic. "She's mourning the loss of her family."

Pekoe stared wild-eyed at the others, petrified. Charlise covered her ears. Zetrine slumped to the ground and also covered her ears. Jamila's eyes began to run with tears. "Please, make it stop," she cried to Kallias. The sound disoriented them as it cut deeply to the emotions of their own losses.

"It must take its course." Guin turned sharply to the old akinn. "That's the funeral pyre ya talked about, isn't it? Ya wretched old being."

The cries took on the mournful sound of a dirge traveling through the trees, howling like the wind.

"There's a fire? I couldn't tell." The seer with his eyeless face and hence tearless feelings just leaned against the broken skiff.

Kallias gave a glance of bitter distaste toward the old man. "I have to help her."

Guin stopped him again. "There's nothing you can do but interrupt a funeral. It's her way. Let her get through it. Help me with the women. Best to try to concentrate on other things," Guin called over the wailing as he took Zetrine by the elbows and made her stand up. He pulled her hands away from her ears and spoke to her with a steady voice. "Don't listen to it. Check the packs. See what there might be left for a repast." However, as soon as he released her hands she clasped them over her ears again and collapsed, crying, to the sand.

Then he turned to Charlise and took her up in his arms. "Ye've got to busy ya self. Try not to think about the cries. Jamila," he said, turning to the eldest, "the evening meal. Maybe there's fish left?" Guin took one look at Pekoe who had curled up in a ball with her head tucked into her arms and decided he could do nothing about her. "Kallias, please. The women!" he pleaded.

Kallias turned a painful glare toward Guin, then scanned the distraught women. "They've all lost someone. I've lost..." He swallowed his words and trembled.

Charlise cried. "How—how can you—think—of—food at a time like this?"

Kallias lunged in Talek's direction. At first, the akinn prepared to defend himself. But Kallias moved past him to the broken stern of the little skiff. He began ripping at the hull. His movements were fierce with fear, despair and anger. What violent emotions the mourning howl had stirred in him!

He did not like the thought that such a powerful spirit creature could elicit such pain in all of them. He stopped only after he had scraped his palms and gotten slivers beneath his fingernails.

Only Roselana stood, quietly staring up at the fire. Guin approached her slowly. When he stood in front of her, she faced him. Her face, wet with tears and the soaking rain, which by then had dampened everything, held the most peaceful expression. He felt puzzled by it, but also hopeful. "Why doesn't the rain put the fire out?" She put the question to him innocently like a curious child.

Guin put his lips next to her ear. "I imagine it's because fire is one of the elements she controls. Like she did in the cave, remember?" He dared not speak much above a murmur as if he might break whatever spell she was under that kept her so serene.

"Of course." She paused and raised her eyes to the fire again before continuing. "I saw my brother fall. I don't know what happened to my parents." She brought her dark eyes to meet his. Her voice quavered. "Are we going to get Asadia back?"

Guin nodded. "First we need to help your sisters here to get hold of themselves. Perhaps we can get everyone into the cabins to sleep?"

"I have a better idea." Roselana turned to the other women. "Come on. We should go into that hut there." She touched each one of them on a shoulder and pointed to the center hut, closest to the source of their anguish. "Let us give in to the mourning cries. We can do our own life songs, honor our brothers, husbands, beloved fathers." She lifted one woman at a time to their feet. None of them fell again, not even to their knees. "You have a life song in Olkem, don't you, Jamila?"

"Y-yes. It would do us good to... would do us..."

"Good to sing together in one of the huts. Out of the rain and the dark, yes?" She finished Jamila's thought and silently ushered them towards the little hovel.

Guin cleared the treasures to a spot beneath the nearest hut out of the weather. They could inventory what things they had found tomorrow. Kallias stood with an armload of wood, pieces of the skiff. Guin approached him and put an arm around Kallias' shoulder. "Let's get some rest." Kallias dropped the firewood, allowing Guin to lead him to the east hut. Talek followed silently.

As the women's voices were raised in a sweetly sorrowful tune, the sound of rekinnder cries began to die out in the distance.

Kallias sat on a straw bed leaning against the wall with legs straight, crossed at the ankles. He picked the slivers from his fingernails and palms. In his lap lay the little unfinished toy. His throat burned as he strained to keep from crying out as Dealla had done. Clenching his teeth helped some. Finally, he spoke. "What are we to do?"

Guin sat at his feet. "The more we can salvage from the ship, the more we have to work with."

"It'll take too long. We have to go now," Kallias rasped.

"You heard what Talek said. These women are your army. They're going to have to learn to fight."

"Unarmed?"

"Maybe we can arm them. Let's see what we can do. We don't even know everything the ship has to offer yet."

"Too long! What's to become of Asadia while we're here playing at fighting? We need to be traveling!" Kallias raised his voice with his frustration.

"Look." Guin leaned in, keeping his voice quiet but firm. "Took ya three days from Sungtau to Kanratu. Over night there and another day to here, all by road and footpath. With kinnir out searching we can't go north by road. Can't go up the beach to Kanratu either. That leaves up the east and over the mountains."

"We could do that. I did it."

"Ya came across, one person, with the help of yar pakao, yar Spritdancer. But is she going to hold off a full tribe of kervplik on her own? Because with a group this size we'll draw attention. Kinnir, akinn or kervplik, none of 'em will leave us alive. And if by some miracle we survive all the way to Durgrinstar on foot, it'll take us maybe two months or three. These women'll be tired, hungry and ignorant of how to save their own skins. Ya want to try to take a tower full of men like that? We do that, yar sister's still lost. The best we could hope for is some of the women might survive and be taken by the Bloodfish as wives."

"We could still steal a boat."

"Maybe we could." Guin sat back. "Maybe we sneak in at night like ya did. Then someone misses their boat come morning. We might be up as far as Sungtau when they fire the guns. Every town has 'em. Big ones facing out to sea. It's why I brought us here for one. No guns. They go off and every longship hits the sea full sail to the wind. Again we get caught."

"Then what're we to do?" The warrior's eyes reddened with angry, unshed tears. He swallowed hard.

"We listen to Talek. He'll tell us how much time we get. As long as we have, we teach these women to defend themselves, and we build a boat."

Kallias sniffed and wiped at his eyes and face.

"We can salvage enough wood from the longship to make a little caravel, sea worthy, big enough for us. The three of us can put it together in a few weeks, maybe a month. No matter how ya cut the jib, Kallias, it'll take time or lives. I'd rather take the time."

The howling had died down to intermittent cries which kept the atmosphere solemn. Guin continued. "We've training to do. And I think we might as well do it here."

"What if Talek tells us it's time and we're still not ready?"

"If we don't make it in time to save her—" Guin paused. "We avenge her."

Kallias nodded, relenting to the reasoning. "What happens if they come searching here?"

"They're a superstitious lot. I've a feeling whatever chased them from here will keep them away. It'll be the last place they'll want to come. But, for now we'll keep a watch."

"I hope you're right. I also hope we aren't in danger from whatever it was."

"Yar rekinnder's cries 've died down now. She's not meaning harm. If she were—" He cut himself off. "Let's get some sleep." Then Guin turned to the old seer, who was settling down to rest. "Talek! You're first watch tonight and no guff." The old akinn grumbled and got back up.

(Selected Translations on page 295)

Chapter 15

Work on the funeral pyre for the lost rekinnder began as soon as Dealla reached an overlook from where she could see the ocean off of the Point of the Gald. First she collected and built up enough wood to rest the bone basket as high as she stood. Then as the sun sank, she used stone to spark a fire. Her control of the element did not extend to causing it to spring from the very air. Once the blaze engulfed the catafalque, she knelt before it.

Dealla began to cry. Like the smoke, her cries filled her surroundings. Bereft of all hope of forgiveness from Mehanna, Dealla gave herself over to wailing into the zenu of Iasegald, that which connects all things in the world. She sat on her heels as the fire grew around the pyre. As she leaned with her hands upon her knees, the points of her ears slumped listlessly forward, her long platinum hair draped around her, partially shielding her naked form. Only when an explosion of sap threatened to collapse the catafalque she raised a trembling hand to manipulate the rate of burn.

The words of an ancient prayer-song filled her mind and heart. Though she could not recall learning this song, it came forth howling, rolling, flooding from her soul, tingling every cell with emotion as she sang.

Amahal Mehanna. Essio d'ele.
Amahal ka vamase d'elwa lalipre.
Padekoi pez azenu d'Mahanna.
Rawnhaj Iasegald von rabnio d'ira.
Mahij ka lapret von lipret, wele zet gaio.
Iabriz owila olive d'awa.
Padekoi haiekala oliv enade.

Fri sel isa urume zon zonda.
Amahal ka azenua, ka selendo gald.
Amahal Mehanna. Mile owi urume.
Net fri iaowi ele d'olive awa gaio.
Rawnhaj Iasegald von rabnio d'ira.
Ele Dealla da, de-alle.[07]

Mehanna had cared for her from Dealla's infancy, from
the time their mother had drawn the kinnir hunters away
from her babies. There were many things Dealla could do
that Mehanna could not. Dealla excelled in the number of
forms she could take and of elements she could control.
Because they lost their mother before Dealla had been fully
weened, she was still closer to her birth knowledge, called
womb memory, which allowed her to retain more ancestral
knowledge than Mehanna. She could describe creatures
neither she nor her sister had ever personally seen.

But Dealla feared they were the last, she and Mehanna.
Dealla remembered everything about her mother. She
remembered fleeing one new nest after another. Their life
together had no village in it, no safe home. When she had
grown, when she was alone more, Dealla slipped into the
akinn villages. She made outer skins, fur that was not fur,
scales that were not scales, all in an attempt to fit in, to
cohabit with the akinn and kinnir races, only to be rejected
and hunted whenever she was found out.

The details of this history of their mother, herself and
Mehanna, Dealla cried out after the song. "Tolukuez azenu
d'awa. Mahij rekin gald. Awo ma ka zonda."[08] Thus she
ensured that Mehanna's memory followed her sister's energy,
filling the void left by her death. It would not be missing
amongst their ancestors.

She remembered the little creature and named it Zefebn,
meaning little monkey or marmoset. Finally, all her family she
mourned and all rekinnder who died at the hands of the
kinnir longship men. "Zet zon due d'elwa? Net d'elwa—zet...
ele da."[09] She hoped more of her kind still lived some place in
the vast gald. "Zet due. Tiiti awis."[10] She pleaded for guidance
to find them.

As the flames and memories dimmed, sweet voices of melancholy rose from the encampment. With her anguished cries subdued by song, a new sensation washed over her. The fullness of a tribe, of belonging, germinated in the core of her being, as did her determination not to die the last rekinnder in Marisko.

Chapter 16

When his eyes opened, it took a few moments for Kallias to recall where he was and why. He was alone in the little dark room. A tightness clung to his chest. In his right hand he still held the toy boat. He pushed open a shutter of the window above the bed. The weather was disappointingly gray, a sign that the rain had continued through the night and would probably go on all day. But that was not what held him. He was still mourning his fallen friends and family. "We don't have time for this," he told the toy as he dropped it to the bed. He had slept in his clothes again despite their more civilized environment.

Outside, everyone else sat around a campfire. Surprisingly, there was no rain. Not surprising was the lack of talk. Charlise rose and brought him a little tin cup with some sort of tea. Then she whispered to him, "We've saved a bit of fish, berries and hardtack for you. It's all there is."

"Thank you," he mumbled and sat on a board which was laid out next to several other boards. Each of them had one to sit on to keep relatively dry, though none of the boards were big enough to save their clothes from the wet sand entirely.

As Kallias ate, Guin broke the silence, first by clearing his throat. "Kallias, here, and I agree..." He paused for a wordless approval from the Blade Dancer. "We agree that most of our options are too risky. Heading north without a ship is the greatest risk. Stealing one from Kanratu would set up a new alarm. So that's out. Now it'll be up to Talek to say if we have time to train this army before the woman, Asadia, comes to a bad end. Talek?"

The seer rocked where he sat before replying. "The sail is yet full towards Durgrinstar."

"How much time? What will happen when they arrive?" Kallias dropped his hands to his lap.

"I have no details. I will know more after she arrives." Talek's insensitive tone fed the swordsman's sense of futility and anger.

Kallias began to speak but Guin continued before an altercation could ensue. "It gives us time then. Thank ya old Pom." Talek took the appreciation as dismissal and left the group. Guin continued, "There's the broken ship up the east coastline with things we can use. Two decks worth of space to explore below with a lastage in the aft. Two upper decks including the bridge. If she's the lost Tidal Gull, we're in luck. She was carrying a cargo for Kanratu."

A misty rain began to fall, soaking things as it had the day before. Kallias returned to his morning repast.

"Can we fix it?" asked Pekoe.

"I don't know. Let's take a look." Offered Guin.

"Indeed. Good," Kallias said with finality. "If we're all ready, let's see this ship." Finished with the meager meal, he brushed his hands together, then glanced about for the old seer. "Where's Talek?"

"Here." The old akinn lifted his staff from behind the wreckage of the rowboat. "I lay myself down as I became tired." He did not venture to rise but stayed as he was.

"You're going to get soaked and sandy under there," warned Kallias.

Talek gave no response.

Guin explained their situation. "We're on the point of a peninsula here. Where the beach disappears to east and west, it turns north. On the west, if ya travel far enough ye'll come to Kanratu. It's narrow and stony, but a fresh water stream is that way. On the east, there's no sea town until reaching the mainland. The ship's that way."

"The dead ship I've seen," said the seer, raising his staff once again.

"Yes, Pom Talek, we know." Then to the little band of Baresians he said, "Come this way." Guin took the lead as always, but soon allowed the ladies to pass.

He raised a hand to slow Kallias. "There's also plenty of sailcloth we can use for more than just our boat. The hole in the bulkhead goes inward like it hit rock, but there's nothing close enough here to've hit it. It's strange. Not only because it ought to've sank rather than beach itself, but because it's pointing seaward, like it backed up onto the shore." He spoke quietly to Kallias alone as they walked side by side.

"You think a hurricane did it?" Kallias inquired.

Guin shook his head. "Too little damage to 've been dropped and the salvage is in too good a condition." Then Guin changed the subject. Looking back over his shoulder, he asked, "Do ya think she's gone?"

"I don't know, Guin. Maybe she still mourns. Maybe she's done with us. Whatever her story, she's a... not a pakao. Please, speak no more ill of her."

Guin held something out to Kallias. "I found this." He put a lump of molten lead into the warrior's hand. "It was lodged in the backbone." He indicated a particularly distorted part. It had been molded into a ball at some time. "A bullet."

"A gun?"

"Aye a blunderbuss by the size of it. Flintlocks 're somewhat smaller in the barrel. I don't know how old the corpse was, perhaps two years or three. But, it can't have been longer than that."

"Yours?" Kallias asked bluntly.

Guin eyed him and contemplated. Then he took out one of his own flintlocks and handed it to Kallias. "They don't fit. I promise ya, these're the only guns I've ever owned. I'm not saying I've never killed a rekinnder. Only that I've never knowingly killed one. And I did not kill that one."

"I wouldn't know how to tell if you did." Kallias handed the flintlock back.

Guin took the distorted bullet and held it to the barrel opening of his gun. "If it won't go in, it didn't come out. Too big, see?" Guin handed the bullet back to Kallias. Then returned his gun to its place at his back.

"Didn't mean to sound like I mistrusted you after all you've done, Guin. I..." Kallias hesitated.

"It was fair to ask. I take no offense."

The light rain stopped as the sun winked between dull gray clouds. "Looks like we might get some sunshine after all," noted Kallias. That was at least something to feel glad about.

They reached the ship in a short time. Up close it was enormous. Planks lay inside, where a large gaping hole allowed entrance. It was half as tall as Jamila, the first to enter, and twice wide as high. "Watch yar step as ya go in! Doesn't look like a very big hole when compared to the entire ship, does it?" Guin marveled. "We'll not be able to take everything from here in one trip. Not even with as many as we are."

Charlise entered second, behind Jamila. The cold sea water rose to her ankles as she stepped past the mound of sand at its entrance. "Ah! My skirt is wet now!"

"Tie it up," said the older woman, who had already done so with her own skirt.

Kallias bent in half and slid a foot in after nodding to Guin. He stepped to one side then held a hand out to help the other women pull themselves through. As the last one disappeared into the darkened hull, Guin took a quick look around. Finally, he entered as well, bending deeply at the waist to get inside.

It was dark but Zetrine could see a crusted salt line about knee-high along the walls of the hull with water sloshing beneath it. "Looks like the tide comes in and doesn't have time to go out before the next," she said, pointing. The breech afforded dim lighting, though breaks in the clouds occasionally added a bit more light through the boards above them.

Jamila showed the others how to tie their long skirts up above their knees. "We will have to change these later. They will not serve us in this situation."

There was little even in the way of debris floating about down below. "I didn't check the hold." Guin told Kallias. "Perhaps we can do that, while some of the women go above? There's a companionway up front with steps from the orlop deck to the galley. And another to the main deck." Zetrine, Charlise and Jamila headed through the deeper water then upward. Roselana and Pekoe stuck with Guin and Kallias.

To the stern and barely visible, the wooden door to the cargo bay hung on but a single hinge. Guin held the door with a hand at either side and gave it a rough shake. The hinge broke loose from the door jamb, and Guin set it aside. "Good piece of wood that." He entered the bay which was much darker, affording little more than shadows to discern its contents. The sounds of a thud and the clatter of metal rang out as Pekoe bumped into something.

"Oof!" She growled with frustration as she rubbed her forehead. "It's too dark in here!" She reached out blindly.

"Careful there, Miss," Guin said, reaching a hand out in her direction. She took hold of his arm at the sound of his voice and positioned herself behind him. "What was 'at ya ran into?" Guin kept his hand out as he stepped that way. "Sounded like a... aha!" The sound of the metal against the post was unmistakable as Guin took a lantern down. "Now to light it. Here hold this." He handed the offending lantern to Pekoe and rummaged around in his pockets. Then he produced something no one could see.

"What is it?" Roselana asked, coming up behind Pekoe.

"A lantern. Smithy made and... everyone cover yar ears." With that brief warning Guin shot off his flintlock and ignited a bit of cloth on a stick. Then he took the lantern from Pekoe, opened the shutter and lit the candle within. Soon there was a halo of light around them. "And glass encased. A very clever use for sand, the making of glass."

"It's the Tidal Gull all right. That looks to be an anvil there," Guin continued, stretching his arm forward to shine the light on it. "And if I'm right a..."

There came the thunder of three pairs of feet overhead. "What happened? What was that?" The ladies cried out from the front of the ship down through the stairwell.

"Just a bit of powder. No trouble," Guin responded.

"We're fine!" Roselana called up to them. "I found a hammer."

"I found a pot!" called down Charlise. "A big ol' pot to make soup in! It's heavy. There's lots of things in the kitchen. Come see." The full compliment of them followed her not only to the galley but out onto the top deck, where the sun, high in the sky, had chased off the threat of rain.

They pulled down the sail and unwound rope, folding and looping to make them cart-able. Later they all explored the few compartments and the two rooms of the ship. "If you ladies will start bringing these things down to the hold, we'll go down and get ready to move it all out." Guin and Kallias headed downward followed by Pekoe.

"It'll be good to find something to go in that pot if we can. Though I doubt they found anything stored in the galley." Guin held the lantern aloft as they walked about the various crates and packages in the hold.

"We forgot about hunting or fishing. That's going to take a lot of time. Feeding ourselves to keep up strength. We're going to be too late, Guin." Kallias regretted his words as soon as Pekoe let out a small helpless whine.

"Then we'd best waste no time." Guin gestured to the boxes and other items around them. "Let's get busy hauling this out of here. Grab what ya can."

Kallias slogged toward the exit with a large crate in his arms. Quickly, he dodged to one side as the large iron pot tumbled down the steps. Kallias dropped the crate and cursed under his breath when it broke open.

"Sorry!" Charlise winced.

"It's all right," he said and rolled the pot out onto the shore. Afterward, the women filled it full of items from Kallias' broken crate and more.

The sun lay upon the horizon to the west as they exited the ship with the various treasures they found. It had taken them the whole day to explore the ship and move much of its contents to the opening. Charlise carried the pot by one handle as Kallias carried by the other. Trudging along behind them, Guin and Roselana carried a long roll of sail with more items wrapped in it. They were followed by Jamila, Zetrine and Pekoe, each with their arms full and with more things strapped to their backs.

Thus, the group returned to camp where the akinn sat beside a fire. "Ah just in time." He made a grand, sweeping gesture towards the fire and beyond. "There is warmth and meat." Opposite him lay three rather large, odd-looking creatures, dead beside the fire. Other than the rabbits, they were the same rodents as Kallias remembered Spiritdancer bringing to him. Talek continued. "There is a cook among you, at least one, yes?"

"Yes!" Charlise piped up immediately. "But, I've not had to skin... or uhm... clean a kill before. The menfolk always brought them to the kitchen cleaned"

"That's all right, I can," announced Roselana.

"Me too. And me," chimed in Jamila and Pekoe.

"Where did you get them?" asked Kallias, not attempting to hide his suspicion.

"They inhabit all these woods. Can't throw a rock without hitting one." Talek laughed and Guin joined him. Kallias gave the seer a sideways look.

While they waited for their repast, the menfolk sat huddled together out of the way. Talek offered nothing to the conversation except a few disapproving grunts. With a repetition of his admonishments about the dangers of any other option, Guin again convinced Kallias that stealing a boat would be a fatal choice.

When Charlise finally called them to eat, Kallias remained aloof. Guin brought a bowl of the meat to him. "Don't be sulking. Ya'll worry the women."

Kallias answered as soon as the mystic squatted down beside him. "Those women are not warriors, Guin. You're all here because of me. I can't ask them...I can't ask any of you to...to maybe have to kill someone." He hesitated as pained eyes revealed the horror he felt at the memory of the forced kill in Kanratu.

"If we kill, it will be only because we must. What ya did was necessary. Ya have to know that."

"I suppose I do, or would not have done it."

"What is it ya call yar Baresian warriors?"

"Blade dancers."

"Pretty sounding name for soldiers. Being a warrior means understanding that ya deal in death. ya're trained not to hesitate."

"Maybe I'm not meant to be one. We haven't had a war in a hundred years. I don't think there is a single person alive in our village who has ever had to kill someone." He almost voiced the exception of himself but then recalled the raid. "Until the raid. I don't know if any of us killed any of the Bloodfish even then, except perhaps Omerion. I certainly didn't. Only one down on his back—" Kallias cut his words off and poked at the rat meat.

"Ya're talking crazy. We're all here because ya're brave enough to go after yar sister. These women were taken also. Ya see anyone else coming for them?" Guin sat, keeping a knee bent. "I'd not've known anything more about these women. I wouldn't 've bothered myself with anything about their lives beyond Pluth's stupidity if ya hadn't come along. Everyone of us has chosen to stay with ya and get yar Asadia back."

For a long while, they sat in silence, neither touching his food. Shadows grew long. "Eat up, warrior. Ya have an army t' train."

Kallias nodded and both turned their attentions to eating. There had been few seasonings with which to dress up the rodent soup, but it didn't seem to matter. It was a substantial meal, with large hunks of meat.

Kallias attempted a smile. "Rat is growing on me."

Guin chuckled. "It's called a cavy. It's larger than a rat."

The seer finished his meal, set his dish to one side and stood. This would be the first of his nightly forecasts about Asadia. Talek rarely said or did anything other than what Guin required of him, except to tell his visions. They would all become accustomed to this standing and waiting for attention soon enough. When the chatter around the campfire ceased, he pounded his staff into the ground three times. He spoke slowly. "Have no fear. Asadia is unharmed. The loss of her brother is her only pain of heart. She mourns. She's arrived in Durgrinstar. That's all I've to say now."

"She thinks I'm dead," said Kallias to Guin.

"More importantly," Guin replied with a smirk, "Yungir will think yar dead."

It seemed an odd quirk of fate that there were three huts and in each three beds. Jamila and Zetrine took the central hut, the other three women the southwest hut and the men the one toward the east. Dealla was not among them, though there was room for her. The beds were generous for singles and though the straw-filled mattresses were lumpy, the ropes which held them in place were firm. All in all, silence now brought comfort here. No more pyres burned. No more mournful rekinnder cries rang out. They all drifted off to sleep in a short while.

Then Kallias was awakened by the mystic, who nudged the old akinn awake. "Come on. We're going outside."

The old man grumbled. "What's this about?"

"Hush. Just come with me." Guin ushered him to the door and pulled the blankets from his own bed. Then he turned to look at Kallias. There was barely enough light to make out his face. Guin motioned with his head toward the hanging lamp which glowed softly as the suet burned away. A figure stood next to the wall beside the shuttered window. Guin closed the door behind them.

The long white hair was unmistakable. She had returned and in her most kinnir-like form. Dealla pressed herself against the wall, fearfully. Every move she made created a soft wisp of flower scented air around her. Kallias lifted himself upright in the cot. His eyes, accustomed to the dark, let him see the faint details of her silhouette, the surreal glow of her hair, her face beautiful in shape but a blur for any detail except the twinkle of her large, strange, blue on blue eyes. "Dealla?" he called out to her softly. He shook his head to clear the feeling of being between the realm of awake and asleep. "Is that you?" He knew it was of course, but what else was there to say?

She quickly crouched down at the edge of his bed the wisp of air wafting over him, first cool and then warm and scented. Her face could be seen now and her eyes appeared swollen and red from crying. "You're still in mourning," he said barely above a whisper.

The blue of her eyes glowed as when she walked the night forest as the serlcat. The tops of her strange ears had folded down like one closes their fingers against their palm. Her voice was soft and trembling. "Zet iajue ele da."

The strange words reached his ears. Though he did not understand them, they elicited a feeling of utter hopelessness that wrenched at his heart. Kallias did not know how to respond at first. Her presence and fragrance filled his senses, making her visit seem dreamlike. Without hesitation, he reached out and palmed her cheek. Her flesh was cool against his warm hand. She looked hopeful at him. He cleared his throat. "I have so many questions of you. I won't let anything happen to you. You're safe here," he said, his voice soft as hers.

She slipped her arms up around his neck and brought her face close to his. Once more, her intoxicating scent overwhelmed him. His arms, reluctant at first, locked around her. His eyes closed and opened as he inhaled the fragrance of flowers that clung to her hair and skin. His lips felt the heat and softness as hers brushed against them. Their breaths mingled. *Am I awake? Is she really here in my arms?* It all faded in a moment of eternity.

"Mele d'ele gaio kuita," she said as the air about them swirled. Then she pressed her lips to his and the room spun. Her body became warm beside him, and as if in a dream, her bare skin touched his.

Chapter 17

Many leagues to the north in Durgrinstar, Maltax and two of his men entered a large council room. Asadia, with hands tied and a sack cloth over her head, fought against her bindings.

"Bring her forward," said a figure sitting on a high-backed chair on a platform with three such chairs upon it. The walls were lined with two sets of benches against them all around on three sides of the room except where the doors opened into it.

Maltax motioned to his men. The two pulled the struggling girl to the foot of the platform beside Maltax and left her there.

The figure wore a cloak and hood. He rose slowly from his chair and stepped down the three steps to the floor. "What is your name, sailor?"

"I'm Captain Maltax, sir."

"Well, *Captain*, why is she bound?" He stood before her with his cowl concealing his face.

"She tried to escape, High One."

"Well, of course, she did; she's frightened. Take the sack off her head ya barbarous mackerel."

Maltax did as instructed. The girl blinked hard and squinted against the sunlight streaming through an open window above the thrones. Asadia's hair fell across her shoulders and down her back in long, silken, raven curls. Her onyx eyes shone in fiery defiance.

"Ah, that's better, isn't it?" Yungir's grin could be seen.

Maltax held her by an arm as Asadia fought to free her hands. "What do you want with me?" she shouted. He shook her.

"That isn't a good way to begin a friendly conversation. Let me show ya how." Yungir pulled back his cowl. "My name is Yungir. What's yars?" Long ashen blond hair cascaded to his shoulders; his skin was a rich tan; his light-gray eyes were large and long lashed, his lips full and his smile generous. Yungir was, to the surprise of the two, young and beautiful. He glanced between them. "What?" he asked bemused. "Oh, ya thought I'd be older. A wizened mystic? Well at least old as most experienced mystics should be, eh Maltax?" Yungir walked around them. "No, we mystics start young. I merely discovered a way to advance faster than any other. That makes me the best." He returned to where he stood before. "Now, dear, what's yar name?"

Asadia clenched her teeth and returned only a glare.

Yungir raised a hand as if to strike her and went red in the face. She flinched. Then he calmed. "Alright, more generosity. More bees with honey 's the wise saying. I'll have him release ya and untie yar hands if ya promise not to run."

When Asadia stopped glaring, Yungir nodded to Maltax. Maltax cut her free. Immediately, Asadia snatched the knife from his hand and slashed toward his throat. The rough sea dog was too quick for that however, and took the gash on his arm. Seeing she missed, Asadia dropped it and bolted for the door.

"Stop her!" As soon as Yungir had called out, a gurgling sound was heard. Something shiny lashed out from somewhere near the platform and Asadia froze in her steps. Yungir walked over to her. Asadia's eyes widened in fear and followed him as he crossed in front of her. Around her throat gleamed a silver thread. She made a choking sound. "By the hairs of a dagginshee, ya're turning blue already. Release her!" At his command the thread dissolved and Asadia fell in a heap at his feet. Maltax picked her up roughly. "Stop," Yungir said quietly and held a finger up to Maltax. He let her go and again Asadia crumpled.

"Good. Now we can talk a bit," said Yungir. Asadia whimpered through angry tears. "My father always told me, 'if ya truly want a thing, go at it patiently and persist.' So ya can see how truly—patient—I am." He whispered for emphasis, then paused in expectation of a comment that was not forthcoming from his captive audience. Then he threatened. "And persistent." He bent at the waist over Asadia, switching to a saccharine sweetness. "Now little nameless one, why did ya try to kill the captain here? I was standing right there. The hesitation cost ya yar escape." Still bent over, Yungir swung his body toward the door and back, visually measuring the distance. "Or perhaps not. But ya do hate him so, more than me. Why? Go ahead yar voice is free. The pain'll go away gradually."

"He..." she rasped, "killed my brother."

Yungir stood. "Ah, the raid. I understand it was horrible. I, of course, had nothing to do with that neither directly nor by order." As he spoke he observed Maltax, who was shaking his head. "No?" asked Yungir. "No what?"

"Her brother come after her."

Yungir paled slightly. "A dark-haired warrior?"

"Yes, but he's drowned now. I had 'im tied and throwed overboard to the sharks."

Yungir bent again and this time lifted Asadia gently to her feet. "I'll give ya a show of good faith." He led her a few steps away from Maltax, then turned and abruptly motioned with his hands as if pulling something from the air, tying it and pushing it at Maltax. "Arun fet shaun d'oleigoz shishakeen." With an explosive flash of light, Maltax was cast in stone. "There. Bad man all gone. I'll have him taken to the sea. How's that?" The terrified girl shrank from him. His face reddened as his ire rose. "Stop it! I've done everything nice to ya till now!" He hissed, "Speak to me! Tell me yar name!"

"Asadia," she said in a small, nearly inaudible voice.

"Huh?" He leaned towards her and grabbed her by the jaw. "Say again."

"A-Asadia," she whimpered.

Yungir brought his face to hers, holding fast to her chin. Then he relaxed gradually. He let his eyes travel down her form then back to her eyes. Suddenly he released her and snapped his fingers. Two small creatures shuffled forward from somewhere behind the platform. They were bipedal with little round, bald heads, hairless cat-like ears, large dark eyes, without irises or whites, and a natural lip-less grin.

"These're wixxon. Don't be fooled by their appearance. The thread that stopped ya is one of theirs. They can be most unpleasant when riled." He turned and snarled at one of them who responded with a show of a mouth filled with pointed, jagged teeth and held up large, clawed paw-like hands. Then he said to the wixxon, "Bathe her. Put her in some appropriate clothing to mourn her brother. Ask Kaig. Ya're not to harm her nor let her escape. She'll acquiesce soon enough." Her eyes widened as they approached. The wixxon each took one of Asadia's hands and led her away.

When the girl was out of the room, Yungir turned to Maltax and again chanted and cast him back to his normal self. The captain coughed and doubled over. "Take whatever men ya need. Search all of Marisko, even the forests. Make sure there're no more brothers lurking about. Find the other women. Then kill them all. I want heads! Any man trying to keep one of them gets the same as Pluth. And pick up yar knife."

"Yes, High One," he replied and coughed again. Sweeping up his dagger from the floor, Maltax hurriedly left the room.

Yungir wiped his clammy hands off on his robe. "A dark-haired brother…"

Once left to herself, Asadia tested every exit. Failing to find an escape, she paced through the tower rooms of her prison. Two fancy rooms, a bedroom and a sitting room, were well-furnished, warm, spacious and brightly lit by tall, slender, locked windows. The only door, also locked securely, exited into the stairwell.

Following the sound of the latch, three wixxon entered without knocking, bringing food, black clothing and a bathtub. They manipulated her, taking her by the hands, a wixxon to each side. First, they sat her at a small table in the sitting room and place a fine meal before her. One remained at her side. The others placed the tub beside a desk in the inglenook, a sort of closed-in balcony off the bedroom. While the two took turns traveling in and out of the room to fill the tub, the third kept its shiny black eyes on her. When she leaned across the table to look through the doorway at the others, this one slid into her view.

"I'm not going to try running." She rubbed her neck. "I know what you can do," she told it. With some exceptions in their neutral beige coloring and height, they appeared to be without personality, without gender, without any identifiable individuality. She sat back in her chair again, but the wixxon stayed where it was. "You can't make me eat, you know." It blinked but said nothing. "If you force me, I'll just puke on you." Again nothing. "Are you the one with the key to these rooms?" Nothing, not even a blink.

When her bath was ready, the two returned and took her hands again. When she resisted, they dug their sharp claws in but just enough to cause scratches when she jerked her hands away. They stood a moment, buzzing and chirping at one another. Coming to a decision, they moved as a unit. Two took her each by arm and hand, digging their claws in slowly. The third waited behind her ready to pull the chair away. Until she stood, the pin-point pressure of many little nails increased.

At the tub, each began the task of undressing her by pulling at the fine satin material of her festival gown. "I can undress myself!" she snapped, "Stop it! Let go!" None of this worked. They only nodded with their natural grins unchanged. Finally she shouted, "You're going to rip it!" and slapped at their hands. This stopped them for another buzzing conference, giving her time to begin removing the dress herself. This act of cooperation saved it from a possible shredding, though the blood stain had likely ruined it anyway.

"You could give a lady some privacy to bathe." Her tormentors stood watching. Asadia dropped her dress to the floor, leaving her undergarments on and crossed an arm over her chest. She raised her free hand to make a spinning gesture. "Or you might at least turn around?" When again there was no response, she untied her half-slip and stepped out of it.

Still in her chemise and undershorts she stepped into the tub. This caused some confused clicking and humming as the three looked to one another. Finally, they did their best to bathe her and her underwear. Once she had been thoroughly rubbed with lye soap, she was made to stand while rinsed with water from two buckets they had set aside for the purpose. To accomplish this, one stood on the desk chair to do the pouring. Then in unison the three pointed to a large towel on the desk and to three black gowns on the bed. At last they all left Asadia to finish up by herself.

Some time later, three others, distinctive only by their robes, entered the room. These bailed the dirty water out of the tub through the window. "Will you leave the window unlocked?" As usual there was no response. When all evidence of her bath and uneaten meal were removed and the other dresses hung in the chifforobe, they relocked the window. Asadia sighed.

Then the first group returned. Seating her at the vanity, they began working on her hair. When her long, black hair was braided and wound into a knot on top of her head, they pinned a black, beaded headdress to it and draped a black, shoulder length veil over her head and face. Tears welled up in Asadia's eyes as she was shrouded for mourning.

Asadia remained seated and crying before the vanity mirror long into the night.

Chapter 18

The sun rose through the window facing the east. It shone upon Kallias' pillow and nearly into his eyes. He was alone in his bed. There was a grumble behind him as the old akinn began to stir. Guin rolled over and coughed himself awake. Kallias awoke slowly at the sound of grumbling and coughing. He lay there a moment gathering his thoughts. The memories were there, but difficult to grasp, as they seemed to slip from his mind's reach like a dream.

Guin sat up at the edge of his bed and put both hands on his head. "What a headache! Must have been the cavy soup."

"No ya fool." The old man awoke, immediately alert. "Ya should have a headache. Why'd ya take me outside to sleep on the cold ground? Huh? Wake me from my sleep with the gibbous moon behind cloud cover and not for a night hunt? Ya say nothing, just 'come with me,' and outside we sit until nearly dawn! Ya deserve a headache and a backache, where my staff strikes ya!" The akinn shook his fist.

"What're ya talking about old man? I slept all night right here." Guin moaned and rose from his bed. A light dusting of sand fell from his blanket, unnoticed except by Kallias. Guin's hair hung down around his shoulders. He looked more the drunken old man than the mystic longship man he was. He stood and gave Kallias a nod and then stepped outside in just his trousers. At that moment Kallias knew his experience was no dream. He arose silently and swiveled in his bed with the blanket covering his lower half.

The akinn got up and put his robe on over his under garment and loin cloth. He tied it in place tightly and then stretched out his hand into which his staff jumped. As soon as he was in possession of the staff he looked with his eyeless face at Kallias. "That pakao came to ya, didn't she? I can feel it in ya. From yar spirit it vibrates. Pakao she is. And she has ya." Without another word, Talek shuffled out the door, closing it roughly behind him. Its gate-like construction caused it to bounce back open. The akinn cursed and pulled it shut.

Kallias shook his head at the akinn's failed attempt to slam the door. He blushed inwardly as he realized he was naked beneath the blanket. He searched for his black leather pants, put them on, then laced up his boots and stepped out of the hut.

Outside, there was a heated discussion in progress. Four of the women were voicing complaints to Guin. With one hand on his forehead, he responded. "What do ya mean? Which things? Which she? Charlise? Where is she?"

"Not Charlise," the others replied, "the pakao girl."

Roselana saw Kallias and took the matter to him. "She has taken my bow. I had it under my bed. She came in the night and stole it from under my bed."

Kallias ran his palm over his beard before responding to Roselana. "I'm sure it was taken for a reason, Roselana. After all, it wasn't our bow to begin with." He offered her a comforting smile.

Roselana bobbed her head. "I'm sorry. Of course, of course."

Talek said, "A pakao and a thief now. I warned ya. We're not safe in our own beds."

Kallias folded his arms cross-ways over his exposed chest, letting his scowl rest on Talek. Despite the akinn's lack of eyes, Kallias felt Talek project a murderous stare his way. "You can keep that to yourself, old man."

Jamila repeated herself to gain Guin's attention. "She finished up the soup we had left over and cleaned out the pot entirely! She's an animal. You'd think she'd hunt for herself. Anyone know where to get eggs or anything? We're going to have to spend most of our time hunting and gathering to feed ourselves now."

"Jamila! How inhospitable. Is that how the Olkem tribe behaves? " Kallias spoke sharply, which startled them all. "Dealla did hunt. And she brought her catch to us. Tell us, Talek. You didn't hunt the cavies at all, did you?"

"Never said I did, only that it was easy." All eyes turned to him, shocked. "Still, her thieving wasn't limited to a shared meal."

Jamila shook her head and turned away, ashamed. "I'm so sorry, Kallias. I didn't realize."

"Of course, Jamila. None of us were expected to." Kallias turned his attention to Guin who sat by the fire rocking slightly, his head in both hands.

Pekoe and Zetrine added that Dealla had taken quite a bit of rope, all of the rodent hides, some mending awls, and other tools they were not familiar with but which they knew to have been in one of the crates. "Who knows what else she took," exclaimed Zetrine. "We hadn't counted everything yet. Suppose it was something we really needed?"

"I'm sure there was no malicious intent. Let us calm ourselves a moment," Kallias replied with a sigh.

Charlise approached the group with something wrapped in a cloth. "Here. I knew there was far too much meat for the soup last night so I boiled the lard to make this oil cloth to wrap the rest of the meat in. We will have this for first meal plus some more berries Zetrine found this morning. It should be a delightful repast." With a cheerful countenance, she looked around at the disgruntled group. When she saw the sober faces, she added, "What's the matter? Something happen?"

Roselana began to speak about the matter, but Kallias put a hand firmly on her shoulder, hushing her. "I will find *Dealla* and speak to her." The emphasis on her name ended the discussion with a commanding tone. He returned to the hut to finish dressing.

"My head's killing me," moaned Guin.

"There's some tea here. Let me get you a cup." Charlise picked up a cup and went to the fire where a small pot was boiling. The herbs were fragrant and tied in a small white cloth for steeping. She ladled out a portion into the cup and handed it to Guin.

Kallias approached Roselana as they were all about to sit down. "Here take this. I have my own, and I know you know how to use it." He handed her the dirk found by the skeleton.

She took it with thanks, though chagrined. "I didn't mean to make a fuss."

"It's all right." Kallias gave her shoulder a squeeze.

During the morning meal, their plans were made. "Alright, ladies and gentlemen, if I may have yar attention, please." Guin stood and then thought better of it and pulled a crate over to sit upon. "Here's what's needed. We must build our own training area. And build our own boat as well." He sipped tea. "The skills we've got are these; Kallias to train with swords, Talek to teach us to defend ourselves when unarmed or with a staff maybe."

"Now ya have me teaching them? Ya're pushing the debt, mystic," Talek grumbled without raising his head from his dish.

"Ya're the best at it, Pom Talek. I'll show what I know of seamanship and boat construction and whatever else. I hope to find enough iron and steel to make some weapons." He looked about as he said these words, then looked to Kallias. "There's a small anvil deep in the hold of the ship. Maybe there are also some forging tools." Guin continued. "I propose ya all learn each of the fightin' skills the best ya can. Then each of ya choose what suits her best. When the time comes, Kallias and I'll lay out strategy and tactics. Remember, if we can accomplish our goal without fighting we will. But if it should come to blows with the longship men, we'll give them an unexpected offense." Guin looked at himself in just his trousers. "I'll go get dressed. Then we'll start."

After the morning repast, Charlise cleaned up the dishes. Guin approached her. "Thank ya for the tea. Took the headache away immediately. What was in it?"

Charlise looked up from her pans. "I have no idea, ask Pekoe. She's the healer. It woke me up with its fragrance this morning. Must be some kind of flower."

"Pekoe?" Guin inquired.

She shook her head. "I didn't make tea."

Talek chuckled. "Know the pakao, I do. She expected ya to have pain in yar head. Left ya the cure. Ya know why don't ya?" His tone was accusing as he turned his face toward Kallias. "Why not tell him, eh, Dark One?"

"I'll go find Dealla and meet you all here," Kallias said, ignoring Talek. Guin disappeared into the hut.

Kallias held palm's edge to his brow as he peered up the wooded hillside. If he went to his left he could use the winding trail they had walked down. "Or..." he said aloud, "a shortcut." It would be a bit of a climb. Directly behind the huts, the ground sloped up to a cliff face eight or ten feet high. Thick tree roots jutted out from the dirt and rock, promising an easy climb. Gripping one and then another branching root while catching footholds on others, he scrambled upwards, as loose stones and dirt flew in his face, causing him to turn away. Once he pulled himself up over the side, he stood and took a couple of deep breaths. His eyes lit up at the spectacular view over the encampment.

"Right. Well done, Kallias." He dusted himself off head to waist. "But walk around next time." He imagined he would have to hike back towards the spring as somewhere between here and there was likely to be where Dealla had mourned for her dead during the night. No sooner had he stepped away from the scenic view than he saw to one side of the clearing something that could only be a nest. There were several smooth vines woven together in an ovate form and covered with a variety of grasses, leaves and other plants. There was no sign of the pyre. "Dealla?" he called out.

A soft coo came from behind the Baresian. The serlcat stood attentively, toe forward, one ear on Kallias, the other moving. "Spiritdancer. We're getting re—" He paused a moment. "The others are accusing you of stealing items from the camp." Spiritdancer listened. "What I mean is... do you have the bow?" Kallias pantomimed shooting a bow. Again she merely stood attentively. "There were other things too; rope, hide, mending tools." He enacted each of them as he listed them, though he doubted any were recognizable by his poor acting skills. "Have you seen them?"

The serlcat responded with another "coo" and headed across the clearing. She led him not far behind her nest to where a bush grew in front of a hollow place in the trunk of a broad oak. There she stopped, twitched her tail and looked back at him.

Kallias pulled the bush aside. Inside the hollow were all the items they mentioned and some bit more. She stood beside him as he surveyed her little trove. "And here they are." He attempted to pet her, but she backed away. "I'm sorry. They think of you as a pakao, perhaps understandably for them. You're unknown. But I know better." She moved between him and the tree, shouldering the bush back into place over the hollow. "Well, I don't understand," he said, "but I trust you." She nudged him away with her head. Her body brushed against his leg as she stepped back towards the path to the shore. He dropped his hand gently across her back as she passed him and felt her shutter beneath his touch. "I really don't understand. Come down to the camp. We all need to work together. And they can get to know you, all right?"

Dealla made no attempt to change form but led him back past the clearing to the forested pathway. Just before stepping out of the trees behind the huts, she stopped. When he caught up to her, she bounded back up the hillside into the forest and disappeared.

Talek had the ladies lined up in two rows on the broad sandy beach to the west. They each held their arms wide and touched fingertips to give themselves a measured amount of room. Talek walked between them, stopping front and center of them, then called for their attention.

Guin, watching the ladies from beside the campfire, turned to see Kallias heading towards him. "Did ya find her?" he asked.

"I did. She might be around shortly," Kallias responded.

"What did she say about the missing things?"

"Nothing. But she has them." Kallias left it at that. "This a warm up?"

"Talek's taking the first part of training. That frees us up to pull the forging equipment from the ship."

"First, warm up body!" Talek commanded firmly and loudly. "Then defense stand exercise."

Kallias glanced back over his shoulder at the group as he and Guin headed for the ship. "Defense stand makes it sound like how to become a target."

Guin continued on the former subject. "I thought we'd all make practice swords from some of the wood pieces. That way they can feel the weight. Ya think it wise to have them make shields? Longship men don't use them, but that may be a blessing."

"Small, light shields. An excellent idea. But it might take too much time to fashion practice swords. We'll fetch branches."

"But they need to feel some weight."

"I know, Guin. When they have some skill, we'll let them use our swords."

"All right. We can keep the forge close to the wreckage. That is if we have the makings of a forge."

"If not, then what'll we do?"

"Hope Talek knows what he's doing, I guess. "

"A stick wielder's moves? I don't even know if we should allow the women to take swords against guns, let alone sticks or nothing."

"Won't ya be wielding sticks at first anyway?" Guin chuckled.

Kallias grinned but shook his head. "It isn't the same."

"Aren't Talek's moves like your dance of the blade?" Guin asked. "I saw ya with yar sword last night. I thought ya were mad and going to take yar frustrations out stabbing at the air."

"No. I mean, it's different with the sword. The blade dance movements are supposed to be the most advanced. Sometimes I think that part is only for meditation. We didn't do much dancing when our village was raided. Mostly it was running and striking. Maybe I can teach them enough to keep them from getting themselves killed, maybe place some strikes to disable. That would be success enough, provided we live."

"Longship men don't dance. I should try it sometime."
Guin chuckled.

Kallias laugh. "We should spar sometime. Then I'll know
which I am, warrior or dancer."

Many crates in the hold required both men to carry them
out one at a time. After emptying the aft chamber, the two set
to opening the crates, taking inventory of the goods and
separating usable wood from scrap. The yield of a slack tub,
hand bellows, various tools and nine crucibles caused Guin to
shout in triumph. "Now we've but to build a hearth and find
every bit of iron and steel not in use."

When the simple body movement lessons were
concluded, Guin called the girls together to go to the ship.
"We're going to salvage wood from the ship for shields and
boat parts. Kallias and I will be using hammer and chisel as
wedges to pry the boards loose. Then yar arms are needed to
pull the planks off. There are also a bow saw and two axes in
the crates we found. These are for the damaged boards, to
clear them out of the way. Please don't chop at anything
without instruction first. We need to preserve as much as
possible. Any questions?" He looked from the girls to Kallias.
"Ya have anything ya want to add or for them to do
especially?"

"Not at the moment," Kallias replied.

Guin nodded and the group set out for the ship, tools in
hand. This time even the old akinn went along. He was silent
in his work, strong in his hands. His only comments were an
occasional harrumph uttered when Kallias passed close by
him. After the third time Guin poked the seer with a stick of
wood. "That's enough. If ya can't say a kind word to him, old
man, say nothing." Then he added before the elder one could
object, "And no sounds either."

When they had worked to exhaustion, they returned to
camp and were greeted by another gift of meat. This one was
a small deer, hung from cross poles. It had been skinned and
cleaned and was without head or horns. Three crows sat
upon it picking at the thighs. Kallias scattered the scavengers
with a wave of his arms. They squawked defiantly but

eventually flew off. "We have our next meal and then some," he exclaimed.

Guin dropped a load of scrap wood he carried and motioned for the girls to drop the planks. "Roselana and Zetrine take these and split them lengthwise to get several long thin sticks of them." He handed each of them some of the smaller wood pieces. "Jamila ya remember the broken oars ya found in the hull? The ones we thought to make swords from?" Jamila nodded. "Go get them. I've an idea." The three women trotted off to get the items they needed. Guin seemed quite excited. "Let's build a smoke box. We'll have jerked meat to keep us up through our work days." He smiled at Kallias.

Charlise busied herself making a quick dish from large hunks of brisket Guin sliced from the carcass. The late midday meal consisted of some of the roasted meat and more berries found by Zetrine, who still preferred fruits to fish.

Afterward they pitched in with building a small cabinet with a frame and leg posts made from the oar handles. The drying racks were made by laying the thin-cut sticks across the frame. Several planks were cut to form the walls of the box and the entire thing was held up off the ground by the posts extending down into the sand. Beneath this another fire pit was made. Wood chips were soaked in a pan and a small fire was started under the box. Inside the box, which had a cover that opened at the top, strips of the venison were hung, filling it. The entire unit stood about three-and-a-half feet tall. Once the fire made a sufficient amount of coals the soaked wood chips were added and smoke filled the box. All day the group took turns making sure the smoke and heat did not go out. Though it required traipsing back and forth from the ship, it provided each of them with short breaks from their other work.

That evening there was another repast of the meat, a sampling from the smoker, only this time Charlise surprised them with a meal like they had not had in a long time. There was something like potato but with a sweeter taste and a gravy with mushrooms and onions which was poured over the meat as well as the white potato-like pieces. "Zetrine found these vegetables when she went to fill the water bucket," she explained to the surprised faces.

"There's a meadow just this side of the stream if you go upstream east a bit," reported Zetrine. "And while we were climbing about the ship, I saw the rolling hills to the northeast side are covered in vegetation of all kinds. Perhaps I can go see what we can use of that?"

"Of course, ya can." Guin held his bowl up in salute. "To the keen eye of our herbalist! We should have you fetch water more often." This was followed by the others, raising their bowls and calling a salute of their own.

"Preserving myself," explained Zetrine. "I'd rather not eat meat, you know. And now, I don't have to." She beamed and held up her bowl of vegetable stew. "I know the gravy is from the meat, but I'm not complaining."

"Be careful not to go wandering too far alone. And let us know when you do go," Kallias requested.

"Of course," she replied.

After that, some time was spent in making baskets and gathering a supply of vegetables in the mornings before the first meal.

Chapter 19

And so it went day after day into the second week with little difference. Mornings filled with hours of exercise, and combat training. Afternoons filled with collecting materials for the forge and disassembling the old, broken longship. The rest of their time was spent in fishing, preserving meats left for them by Dealla, finding vegetables, cooking, cleaning, sewing skirts into pants, eating, personal hygiene, and often honing new sticks for practice swords. Before bed, Pekoe made poultices and salves from the many herbs gathered by Zetrine, and applied them to everyone's aching muscles and open cuts and scratches.

At the end of evening meals it became a habit, before any separated from the fire, that Talek stood to speak. The group fell silent immediately. The teacher of hand combat pounded his staff and repeated words they all had nearly memorized. "Asadia is unharmed. She's of good health—" It was at this point that the day's message would occasionally differ. One time it was to say she had arrived in Durgrinstar, another to say she was not jailed. Most often the message was benign. "She's taken food and water. Her will is strong." Such meager details often produced an audible sigh amongst the women.

Kallias awoke several evenings to the door closing behind Guin and Talek. The figure of Dealla stood in the dim glow of the lamp each time. Kallias arose in his bed and watched her quietly. Dealla stepped closer to him. The intoxicating fragrance lifted from her in a gentle movement of cool air. "Mele d'ele gaio kuita," she whispered.

Each time she said the same words. Kallias had no idea what they meant but was able to repeat it back to her. More often Kallias said nothing but embraced her body against his. As they lay together, he felt the synchronous thudding of their hearts.

Time melted the nights together after the first three or so repetitions of this wonderful dream. It would barely begin to collect itself in his memory when two nights passed without her coming. Then once again she came and whispered the words and brought his lips to hers with her hand at the back of his head. Many evenings had come and gone as had many dreams. The world spun away, and Kallias knew nothing more for a certainty until he awakened in the morning with the moaning of his companions.

The mornings held no surprises, no arguments, no accusations any longer. These mornings, Talek also sipped the tea meant for headaches. Charlise and the ladies prepared the morning repast from the meat and odd vegetables. Everyone ate in relative silence. Talek made no more comments to Kallias. 'It has become routine,' Kallias thought. 'And they all know.'

Then one day, Guin broke the silence. "Up until now Talek has done morning training, Kallias after midday. All of the swords are finished, meaning only two short swords. The rest of the metals are brackets and nails for the boat. Forge work is done. The old ship's a skeleton, as will soon be the new, but the work has been too slow. From now on, Kallias and the women can get on with training in the mornings, but we all must work on the boat after midday." He sipped some tea.

Shirtless under the rising sun, Kallias sat on bleached driftwood at the fire. He looked over the brim of his bowl as he drank down the broth of the morning meal. "Fair enough," he said and took a swipe at his beard with a forearm. "Then we'll use swords starting today. If we may borrow yours, Guin?"

"Certainly," he responded with a gesture, "by my bed." Guin continued. "Our huntress benefactor has not managed another deer in a long time and the cavies are few and far between as well."

"Maybe she's tired of hunting for ungrateful people," Pekoe suggested.

Objections were raised in a hubbub until Kallias raised a hand. "We're not ungrateful, no, as you all say. She probably has to venture further away for game or she has other things to do."

"I saw her here the other day and told her we were thankful. I think she understood me," added Roselana.

Guin said, "All right, so more fish is needed. Talek, if ya'd not mind fishing and gathering of the mornings, I'll accompany ya when I can."

"About time," grumbled the old seer. He appeared to want to say more, but a tilt of Guin's head kept him still.

Pekoe pointed seaward to sinister, dark clouds that blazed with bright blue pulses of light. "Guess we better make haste."

Guin followed her gaze. "Perhaps a half-day away. It doesn't look to be coming this way. Season is changing." He knit his brow, concerned with the passing of time. Then he smiled to hide it. "No worries."

"Summer comes as does the time." The old akinn announced.

Kallias stood and slapped the sand from his trousers. "On that note, let's get to lessons." It took great effort for him to keep his anxieties about Asadia in check all this time. He clenched his teeth as this pronouncement of Talek's brought his fears back up into his chest. After quickly retrieving Guin's sword and his own gear, Kallias tugged his boot laces tight and strapped on his black leather bracers, then cinched up his cuirass.

The lessons took place to the west of the huts past the rough, narrow shoreline, so they would be close to the stream. After they had the basic moves down, he paired each up. Charlise and Jamila with the short swords, Pekoe and Zetrine with their honed branches, and he with Roselana, who used Guin's sword. They each followed Kallias' movements of the offensive while Roselana on her own took what Kallias had taught about defense and parried his strikes. Then he switched roles with Roselana so they could learn to parry as well. "Try the spar now. Jamila and Zetrine on first offensive, Charlise and Pekoe defend."

Kallias listened to every clink of steel and smack of wood and shuffle of foot, watching their moves. "Bucket's empty. I'll fetch more water." He headed for the stream.

Charlise howled, "Aaiiee!" She dropped her sword.

"Sorry! You're bleeding!" Jamila cried out. The girls all rushed around their wounded friend.

Kallias turned sharply. He dropped the bucket and ran back to Charlise. "What's the damage? Let me see." Two knuckles of her right hand bled only a few drops from the broken skin. "Open and close your fist." She did so. "Wiggle your fingers." She did this with ease. "Nothing broken. But listen to me now. You can't all stop and rush when one of you cries out in pain or sees a little or a lot of blood. And never, ever drop your sword!" he scolded. "It's life or death. You're likely to get more than cracked knuckles. But unless you absolutely can't stand, you fight with every last drop of blood!" He checked one face after the other to see that each one of them understood the importance of his harsh words. Then he softened. "But don't bleed. You let them do the bleeding, right?"

"Right, right," they said one after the other. Pekoe pulled a strip of cloth from a pocket and wrapped it around Charlise's knuckles.

"Now switch up ladies!" Kallias commanded. Satisfied no one was seriously hurt, he continued to the stream.

Later that morning, Guin sashayed into the lesson. He had covered his bare chest with his cuirass and was carrying two wooden swords he had made. The women stopped when seeing his approach, causing Kallias to turn. "I don't recall making any wooden swords at the forge." He laughed and handed his sword to Roselana.

"Wouldn't want to kill each other." With a sly grin, Guin gave Kallias one of the well proportioned practice swords, and the two faced off.

"Hmm. Well-made in the likeness of your own. I did not think you needed a lesson, Guin, or I would have invited you." Kallias smirked. Roselana backed away and the others, including Talek, gathered at a distance with her.

"Oh, but ya did. The first day here ya said we should spar." The swords met with a, "Clack! Clack!" as Guin struck and Kallias parried. Guin chuckled. "What is lesson one, Sword Master? Taunt the opponent?"

Clack, clack, clack! Again, as Kallias struck and Guin parried. "But will you learn the lesson, Mystic?"

Guin advanced in earnest and the sparring began. "Ya see, ladies, my own sword is larger and thicker than Kallias' fine curved blade. So I'm accustomed to more weight than this little wooden piece gives me." He swung the formed stick about easily, switching from right hand to left and often using both hands. Meanwhile, Kallias moved to meet Guin's tricks and match him, though never placing both hands upon his wooden sword. His footwork was flawless, keeping Guin's strikes just short of contacting their targets. "Be aware ladies, a Bloodfish man'll press on ya looking for any opening." Forward and back they went, strike, thrust and parry, neither making any apparent headway. "Ya know, Sword Master, yar dance is rather pretty."

"Thank you, Mystic. Your brow is rather sweaty." Kallias spoke the truth, for where they seemed an even match, Guin was working hard to maintain it. Kallias spun about giving Guin an opening to his advance. Their bodies collided as Guin lunged forward. Kallias parried, turning their swords inward between their bodies and then pushing outward, throwing Guin backward.

Guin recovered quickly, lunging at Kallias. The Blade Dancer leaped and turned away.

"Aaahhh!" Guin shouted out as his cuirass twisted aside and a large red scrape appeared along his ribs. "How did ya manage that?" He touched the wound gingerly. "That's going to bruise."

"You threw your body too far forward. You let me use your weight against you." Kallias continued his attack as he spoke, forcefully backing Guin towards the tide. With a jump, a spin and a kick, he knocked Guin on his back into the water. "I hope I didn't break your rib," said Kallias as he lent Guin a hand up.

"No, I don't believe so. But had ya that sword of yar's, I'd hate to think." Guin turned to the others and smiled broadly. "Well, ladies, ye've got a fine master teacher here! I'm going back to boat building." He gave Kallias a nod of respect and walked away, shaking water from his pant legs and holding his side.

Kallias retrieved Guin's wooden sword and held it out to him. "Are you giving up?" Guin walked onward to his work and simply held up his free hand as a mild refusal.

This set a merry tone for the rest of the lesson.

After some hours of lessons and practice, they realized it was about time they returned to the campfire for a midday meal. The scent of a fire and meat roasting reached them almost all at once. Guin was the first to put down his work and head for the promised food. A spit had been rigged over the fire and something like a small boar sizzled and dripped fat into the fire, popping and splattering. No one was around as Guin peered into the woods and in every direction looking for Dealla. There were more tubers roasting on the rocks around the fire as well. He took up a position at one end of the spit and began to turn it. Kallias was next to follow his nose with the women at his heels. They marched quickly to the campfire.

"I have never smelled anything so delicious in my life!" little Pekoe exclaimed.

"Isn't quite done yet, ladies," replied Guin, turning the pork consistently. "Ya can go back to yar practice for some little while yet." He waved them off. "Kallias, a word please?"

Pekoe frowned, and her stomach agreed. With an "aww" and a whimper, the girls returned to their swordplay, though this time staying on the camp side of the rocky portion of the beach.

"Very well. That is if Roselana can keep her eyes unlocked from you," Kallias said. It did not escape his attention when Roselana quickly turned away, pretending to be interested in the practice whenever she caught Guin watching her.

Guin gazed appreciatively at the woman in the distance as she moved her sword through the air with exactitude. "She's pretty good with that," he said smiling, then brought his attention back to the roasting pig. "Speaking of women... I must ask something of a personal matter to ya, Kallias." He looked up at the swordsman to see his reaction as well as hear it.

"It's about Dealla, isn't it?" Kallias returned the gaze.

Guin nodded. "I'm sorry. But I must ask. Ya see, Talek tells me she comes to ya at night. That she awakens us and puts a spell on me, and now on him as well, to cause us to leave the hut. That's why we have headaches in the mornings. And she always leaves the tea that takes the headache away."

"What would you have me say?" Kallias returned. "Sometimes, I don't even know if I am dreaming it up. But by what you're telling me, it's real enough."

"It isn't right, Kallias. Ya're being bewitched by this pakao. What'll she ask of ya once ya have yar army trained? It isn't trustworthy. She feeds us, I know. I'm grateful. But I'm fearful as well. I'm mystic. And Talek isn't without some powers besides the seeing. Yet she can come in our sleep without our knowing and put spells on both of us and enchant ya? She's dangerous and doesn't even join us here. If she would just—" He shook his head in frustration. "Ya've got to stop her or... or something, Kallias."

Kallias nodded as Guin spoke but felt in his heart that he was not enchanted. There was something about her which drew his spirit to her. "It isn't magic that draws me to her," he replied. "But I will talk to her."

"Is it done yet?!" Pekoe called out.

Guin poked the pig with a knife. The meat broke easily but did not fall. "Looks like it. Get the others." Guin added a quick comment to Kallias. "Make her stop, Kallias. If she doesn't, I'll have to consider her a threat. Ya understand?" He stared hard a moment into Kallias' eyes.

"Understood." Kallias turned his gazed to the fire with less interest in the roasting pig. "I'll speak with her tonight."

"Perhaps—" Guin began.

"I said, 'tonight'... when she comes," he retorted, then fetched the women to the meal.

Kallias sat some distance from the group, leaning against a hut facing the camp. As hungry as he had been, the thoughts of what he would say spoiled his appetite. He barely picked from the thick slabs of pork in his bowl. He stared upwards at the plateau where Dealla's nest was. As much as he cared for her, getting the boat built was more important than curbing her nightly calls. Kallias did not feel bewitched, though he did feel something—for her. However, it had to wait. He must keep his mind on his sister's safety for now.

Guin gave instructions as they ate. "The work on the new boat'll be slow at first. I've a lot to show ya, and ya must be patient while I do. There'll come a moment when ya know all ya need to work on yar own, but today isn't it." Guin promised that the setting of the keel and frame would be the hard part requiring all of them. "Talek and I set some logs down as runners. We'll build her atop those so once she's done we'll be able to launch her. We've also selected out the portions of the old keel, the kelson and the frame and ribs to the size for the boat. As before, when we pulled the planks from the ship, don't go hacking away until ya got the go ahead. So finish up. We'd best get moving."

Kallias was first to set his dish on the food preparation table. "Fine with me. The sooner we leave this place the better." He marched toward the lumber pile, shouting over his shoulder. "Don't take all day!"

"What's the matter with him?"

"He's a lot to think about, Pekoe. He'll be fine once the boat takes shape. You girls take whatever time you need to eat, but not more than necessary." Guin scraped the remaining morsels from his bowl into his mouth and followed after Kallias while still chewing. Talek did likewise.

One by one the women finished up and headed for the work to be done. Finally only Charlise and Pekoe were left. "Will you stay and help clean up?" Charlise asked when Pekoe stood to go.

"Of course. There's a lot of meat left. Kallias barely touched his. What should I do with it?"

"We don't want to waste anything. I usually put it all in the cauldron and cover it with the linen, then salt it. The gravy will go to the bottom. The salt will stick on top with the cloth." Charlise took another mouthful. "We need to start sharing the cooking and serving more. I'm always last to finish."

"Don't worry, Charlise. Guin said take your..."

"Pekoe! We need you here!" It was Kallias shouting. "Come. Let Charlise clean up!"

"Oh, bother! I'm sorry, Charlise. I didn't take the meat from the bones. Is that all right?"

"It's fine. Just put the cloth..."

"Pekoe! Let's go!" He shouted again waving her over with a broad arm stroke.

Pekoe hastily covered the meat in the iron vessel and wiped her hands on a rag. "At least that's done."

Charlise watched her go then turned her attention to eating. By the time she too had completed her meal, Kallias was again calling for her to hurry. "What IS your problem?" she shouted back. Kallias turned away. There were only a few dishes left when he called her a second time. She put them all into the wash bucket to soak and headed for the boat building.

Barely noticed by any of them during training, the distant storm moved off as Guin had said it would, leaving the sun to march across the sky with but a few clouds to cross it. Indeed the afternoon's work under a hot sun took its toll on their patience as well as their backs. They stopped frequently for water. By the time the frame of the boat was ready for nailing, the horizon glowed a deep orange. "Post some torches," commanded Guin. "We can't leave her like this."

We've got to get the ground futtocks secured and a couple of uppers before we quit for the night."

Before they stopped, the night sky had filled with stars. The torchlight grew dim by the time Guin announced the end of the evening's work. Tired and aching all over, the women slumped into heaps around the campfire to eat. Not having eaten much at midday, Kallias ate ravenously of wild carrot and the reheated remnants of boar. Despite their fatigue, the group sat for a long time after Talek's usual announcement of Asadia's current condition of mourning. Pekoe and Zetrine poured liniment into the palms of each of their friends to be rubbed into sore muscles. There was no conversation.

Kallias felt as if the heat of the day did not leave after the sun sank. "I think I'll turn in early, if you don't mind." Without listening for objections he entered his hut and collapsed into his bed without undressing. If Dealla came tonight he would not have the strength for her. His talk would have to wait.

Chapter 20

After cleaning the dishes up, Roselana and Guin stood by the campfire, talking. She fingered a black pearl gripped in a gold talon setting that dangled from Guin's neck. "When did you start wearing this?" she asked.

"Yest'day. The clasp was broken; I fixed it. I found it a midday's walk out of Saungtau Shore with some gems, too." He removed the necklace, placing it in her hand. "I'll make ya a map where I found 'em. There's more."

"What is it? I've never seen such an orb." Roselana raised a brow with piqued curiosity.

"It's a black pearl. Rare ya know." Guin took it from her and put it around her neck. "It's said the wearer will have good weather and good fortune on the seas."

"I can't take this, Guin. It's—"

"Ya will," he commanded. "It's my expression of yar value to me. And when this is all over, I hope ye'll allow me to ask something of ya."

"Ask what?"

"When it's over." He chuckled. "Seems yar other Baresians have lost their stamina. Besides Talek and myself ya're the only one not to bed early."

"I probably should be in bed. I think I'm quite sunburned," she confessed. "Feels hot."

"Perhaps some cool night air first?" Guin asked.

They strolled arm in arm along the beach, up the broad east shoreline, until the last hut hid the camp's fire from view. Further up the coastline, debris from the old ship's bow nodded slightly at the shush and crash of waves. "If that doesn't get washed away, we'll have to salvage it for firewood."

Roselana asked Guin, "How did you become a mystic?"

Guin spoke quietly, letting the mellow tremor of his voice wash seductively over her. "It's a secret, not kept by conspiracy nor agreement but by the gald." They faced the sea and Guin stood behind Roselana and put his arms around her waist.

"Ya mean ya don't know how ya got yar magic skills?" she asked, as she placed her hands on his and leaned back upon his chest.

"Do ya know there's one energy that moves through all creation in Iasegald?"

"Everyone knows that, don't they? We're brought up with this knowledge. Our people call it the Force Of Life."

"That's a good description. And how do yar people tap into it?"

"Tap into it?" Roselana faced him without much disturbing his hold on her.

"Ya know. Use it."

"The shamans move life force to heal or protect, but otherwise, it's just there. It just exists." Her dark eyes searched his face.

"Did yar shamans never tell ya how they invoke such power?" The inquisitive gaze he gave her also held an obvious longing and adoration for her. "Did they never tell ya to do the same?"

Roselana shook her head. "The only thing I know is when a shaman has been called to aid the sick. He or she might ask us to make poultices or teas that we all use, but they have a way of... I don't know. Making it work better."

"They get yar help but don't tell ya the truth." Guin tilted his head. "So ya believe the power exists but that ya're separated from it?"

"I guess I've never given it much thought at all. Our healers and guides are born with some ability and taught the rest by other shamans. I suppose no one ever asks about the rest of us."

"Many would likely not believe it anyway. That's the way of it. Every kinnir has this energy, some are born with ready access. If it's recognized in a child, then the wee Pom will be taught to develop it. I believe it's a matter of work and education, but possible for all."

Roselana eyed him curiously. "Are you saying I could be a mystic or a shaman?"

Guin shrugged. "Not all the mystics realize the power of the average person to do or be anything they wish."

"Yungir does though, doesn't he?"

Guin's face hardened at the mention of Yungir's name. "All the abilities any man wishes to possess should be earned, not extracted through the living energies of another man. Not that way. Yungir found a shortcut like washing rice through a sieve. He didn't keep with his teaching."

Roselana touched his face. Her voice was soothing. "It'll be all right. We'll stop him."

"If I could but find out..." Guin stopped short. Then he placed his hand over hers upon his cheek. "Ya want to learn to do illusion?" Roselana smiled her response. "Then turn around." He moved her by the shoulders until he was again at her back. "Now, pick a spot on the ground in front of ya." Roselana did so and kept her eyes on it. "We use concentration words to help focus the energy we'll call. Ya know what a campfire looks like."

She giggled. "Of course."

"Keep picturing a campfire in that spot. Choose yar words."

"How do I know what words to choose?"

"Well ... hmm. Experience." Guin chuckled.

"That isn't funny." She scowled at him over her shoulder.

"I'm sorry," he said without sounding like it. "At first ye'll need to use some sounds like ya might be trying to clear yar head. I'll teach ya some chants another time if ya like. But for this just use open sounds like, aaaahhh. Or vibrating sounds like, mmmmm. Because ya want to use the energies which exist outside of ya and bring it through yar being. I'd say use ha ma rah nee."

"What does that mean?" Roselana asked.

"Nothing. But saying a real word isn't what ya're doing yet. Ya're vibrating ya self to keep yar focus on the energy but using sounds that resonate in yar being. Ya want to keep yar head open. Mah does that. When ya get to Rah, ya best growl the R for yar chest. Understand?"

"I understand."

"Focus on seeing a campfire on the ground. Slowly say, 'Ha Mah Rah Nee.' Then bring yar hands up and around in front of ya, imagining that ya're taking the energy and pulling it in through yar body, and then ya're throwing it to the ground. When ya throw yar hands toward the ground shout the word pyro."

"Pyro?"

"It means fire."

"Why don't I just say fire?"

"Because it adds to yar focus to choose a word ya'd not use in ordinary conversation. And it sounds more mysterious, too." He smiled roguishly.

Again, Roselana glanced over her shoulder at him, this time with a laugh.

"Ya have the most beautiful laugh, Roselana." He gazed lovingly into her eyes. "Well, now. Let's try it."

Roselana stared at the spot, then slowly spoke the syllables, drawing each one out until it was almost sung. She repeated this three times, then motioned with her hands as instructed. After bringing them to her chest she pushed outward and said, "Pyro."

The two waited. Nothing.

"What did I do wrong?" she asked.

"Ya don't think ya can." Guin spoke softly in her ear while smelling the scent of her hair. "Try again. This time, know that ya have everything ya need to make it appear. And call yar word out loud like ya mean it."

Roselana tried again, this time closing her eyes as she imagined pulling strong cords of energy into herself and then through her hands.

Behind her, Guin followed her hand movements. Roselana cast toward the ground. "Pyro!" she shouted. A campfire appeared right where she expected it to be. She squealed with delight but then spun toward Guin and sobered. "You did that, didn't ya?"

"No, ya did it ya self," Guin denied.

"But I felt a tingle through me, and it came from you."

Guin shook his head then shrugged. "Might have gone through me as well. But it didn't come from me, Roselana. I swear to ya." She pouted. "When ya're ready to believe it, ye'll see the truth," he continued. "It isn't the limit of yar personal energy. If it were, it would drain ya more. Later I'll teach ya some real magic words for access, control, manipulation... all that. Perhaps yar leaning isn't illusion. But if ya keep trying with the illusion, whatever is yar's will show itself."

Roselana checked back, but the campfire was gone. "What happened?"

"Was illusion, Roselana, never real."

"Can you teach me more?"

He held a finger under her chin. "If ya're willing to work at it."

Roselana beamed and nodded. He gathered her up in his arms and kissed her.

***

Afar off in Durgrinstar, a black headdress and veil lay across a small settee at the foot of Asadia's bed, ready to put on at a moment's notice. After countless days of leaving her alone with only the wixxon to serve her, Yungir had called for her to be brought to the audience room. The wixxon took her, shrouded head to foot in black. He requested her presence for a meal but did not specify when that would take place. She refused his invitation at first. However, she bartered with him to have the seaward window left open and unlocked. Since then, Asadia sat alone in her rooms looking out to the sea with nothing to do but wait to be fetched for a meal. But the meals continued to be brought in by the creatures.

A particularly short wixxon entered her room and traipsed to the desk in the inglenook beside her chair. "Is it time for evening meal with your master now?" she asked and began to rise.

The little one shook his head and motioned for her to sit back down. When she did so, it set a book and plume centered on the desk and opened a squat black ink bottle, which it set into the inkwell cradle. This one did not attempt to take her hand or move her, but stood quietly staring with his white-less eyes and natural grin and patted the book with a small clawed hand.

"What do you want me to do?" she asked.

The little creature nodded then whistled through flaps of skin on either side of its oddly flat nose. When she did not respond, the little one began a soliloquy of clicks, gurgles and flute-like tones as if telling her a full story. He opened the book, picked up the plume and waved it over a blank page. Then he held the writing feather out to her.

Asadia took the plume, put it down and closed the book. "You can tell your master I don't want his gifts. I want nothing from him. I only agreed to a meal. He may not have killed my brother personally, but he was certainly the cause." The unwavering little wixxon reopened the journal and pushed both book and pen toward her. Asaida shoved them back to the creature. "No!"

He returned them more insistently. She engaged him in a pushing match where pages folded and tore and the plume began to split. Finally the little nearbeast stepped forcefully forward as he slid the items to her, opened his maw and hissed through his pointed teeth. Asadia jumped up, grabbed the ink bottle and dumped it on the journal with the clawed hand still covering it. Ink splashed over the plume, book and desk as well as the wixxon's paw-like hand and robe.

Through his odd gills he screamed an ear-splitting pitch. Asadia dropped the bottle to cover her ears. With his menacing jagged teeth still showing, he spat what appeared to be two strands of light which immediately spread net-like over Asadia's nose and mouth and wrapped around her hands and head. Unable to breathe, Asadia collapsed to the floor. Suddenly a guard and two wixxon burst into the room. "What's the commotion here?" yelled the guard. At sight of the answer, he grabbed a water pitcher from the vanity and poured it out over Asadia's wrapped head. The net instantly dissolved. The two larger wixxon quickly ushered the little fellow out of the room.

"Are ya all right?" the guard inquired.

"Yes, I think so," she responded.

"I'll see it's dealt with," said the guard, leaving Asadia to dry herself off.

Hours passed without another visit from the wixxon and without a meal. Then the familiar click of the lock sounded and in they came. Four wixxon, their ears drooped and heads down, carried a stretcher on their shoulders with a cocoon, body-shaped and heavily wrapped in their webbing. Behind them the guard stepped in and replaced the water pitcher. "Hang it from the sitting room window," he ordered the creatures.

Asadia's eyes grew wide. She jumped from her seat at the seaward window. "STOP!" she shouted. "What are you doing to him?" Overtaking them at the adjoining room, she snatched up the water pitcher and flung its contents onto the face of the little wrapped wixxon. The bearers dropped it to the floor. Asadia began wiping away at the melting web around its face. "No, no! What did you do to him?" The little creature lay lifeless, eyes and mouth sealed with more of the sticky web. Deprived of air, its skin had turned from its naked beige to a dark blueish-black.

"It could have killed you, Miss," explained the guard defensively.

Asadia turned toward the guard. Behind him in the doorway, holding a bouquet of flowers, stood Yungir. "How could you!?!" she screamed at him through her tears.

Yungir dropped the flowers. "Throw it into the sea," he said quietly, then turned and left. He did not call her to evening meal that night.

Chapter 21

Spiritdancer laid at the edge of the precipice overlooking the encampment. From this vantage point she heard every word exchanged beside the campfire. With the exception of Talek's prophetic announcements, the men's talk was all about fighting and boat building. The women's talk centered around caring for one another. With enough experience listening to the people in the villages, Dealla had a broad grasp of the common kinnir and akinn languages. She had never cared to speak to them, and so found it difficult to formulate responses when she wanted to converse with Roselana.

She had kept watch over the kinnir since the day after Mehanna's release to the azenua. Her connection to Kallias developed a feeling of strained desperation. She missed the ease of their wordless communication. But, it was Roselana she felt close to since then.

Dealla recalled her fist broken conversation with Roselana. Hunting meat for two had been difficult enough. Finding prey to feed nine was impossible.

One day in the camp not long after their arrival, disturbed from her work of skinning two meager rabbits, Dealla heard footfall. She looked up to see Roselana entering the campsite from the east carrying a bucket. Dealla prepared to run, but Roselana stopped her.

"Wait! Please!" she called. Dealla turned back. "Please don't go. I—we want to thank you." Dealla stood listening. Roselana gestured to the rabbits then to herself. "We're so grateful for your help. Thank you." The dark-haired woman explained the last words with a bow of her head.

Dealla quickly explained why and how she cheated the gald of its innocent creatures. She apologized for not hunting fairly; that their meat was robbed of the vitality of a flight for life. Mid-explanation, she stopped. The expression on the Baresian woman's face told her Roselana had not understood. Of course. She alone spoke Rekinnder. For the first time, this caused some frustration for Dealla.

How could she convey that to use the power of her luring scents and colors to entrap these creatures caused a fear at their sudden demise rather than the strength of the will to live? How could she say that all of those who ate would be stronger too, if she had given chase instead? It was the way life energy passed on in the meat, the way life was served even at death. But with so many to feed, she could not spend the time to chase nor take the chance of a miss. Dealla sighed. Facial expression and gestures did not make up for the difference of languages. *If only she understood Rekinnder*, wished Dealla.

"It's all right," Roselana said and set the bucket down. "We don't expect you to be able to feed us all, though you've done a pretty good job of it." She put a hand on her chest. "I'm Roselana. We met in the cave, remember?"

She understood? Amazed and a little confused, Dealla nodded, stretched a hand out to the woman and then brought it back to her own chest. "Ro-zay-lah-nah. Day-ahl-lah."

Roselana smiled. "Yes, I know." Then she pointed to the rabbits. "Rabbits," she said.

"Pakeke," Dealla responded.

Roselana repeated the word, "Pah-kay-kay." Next she pointed at the ash and coals. "Campfire. Only it's dead now."

She's willing to learn. Dealla felt delighted. "Hilio. Mele ia io." Which was not a translation of Roselana's words but expressed the use of a campfire instead.

Roselana repeated the words with an elated smile. She pronounced them effortlessly, which was great encouragement to Dealla. She picked up the bucket. "I have to go." She gestured, then held the wooden pail aloft. "Bucket, water."

Dealla nodded, but instead of giving Roselana two more Rekinnder words, she repeated, "Bucket, water. Go." That was the beginning.

Roselana had caught up with Dealla twice more within a week. After that Dealla looked for opportunities to catch Roselana alone. They exchanged a few words each time, though Dealla hesitated to repeat most of the Kinnir words and felt grateful that Roselana did not push her to do so.

When she saw *them* together, everyone had retired early and left them unchaperoned. Roselana walked with the longship mystic, Guin, let him put his arms around her and pressed his mouth on hers. Never mind that she, Dealla, had done the same to Kallias. That was different. He was under control. Kinnir did not ordinarily control nature in the gald. This was the mystic's doing. This was the fate of Mehanna all over again. She watched them leave the beach. As they headed back toward their separate bungalows, Dealla left the precipice for her own nest. She would eliminate him after they retrieve Kallias' sister.

Something was wrong. Dealla awoke in the darkest part of evening when the voices of the forests were most silent. There was a sound though, carried inland on the warm ocean breeze, not a singular but a composite sound of voices. Hums, not words, reached her thrice-fluted ears, and yet, not hums either. Then a scent reached her, horrible, threatening. Dealla leapt from her nest. She had built this one in the trees, so the leap required a brief transformation mid-air, allowing her to hit the ground upon her toes. Immediately she moved in serlcat form for speed and rushed to the encampment. At the center of their quarters she recognized the bile. *Belly fire.* She listened. A choking cough, moans. She sniffed the camp. Things had been cleaned up, but to her keen animal senses the remnant scent of pork hung around stacked dishes.

She raced into the brush, zigzagging through the undergrowth until she found the small clearing where ginger and basil grew. After collecting root and leaf enough for eight, she tied them up in a broad leaf wrap. Another transformation allowed her to take to the sky with her makeshift medicine bag, returning to the camp more quickly than in the cat form.

Once again into the more human-like rekinnder form, Dealla entered the hut where Roselana, Jamila and Zetrine slept. She touched their burning foreheads, then immediately woke Jamila, pulling her from her bed outside to the corner of the bungalow just in time as the woman vomited the poisoned contents of her belly into the sand. Dealla left her there to awaken Roselana and draw her out to relieve herself in the bushes.

Zetrine alone showed no signs of illness, no fever, no moaning, but deep in sleep. *This one does not like meat,* Dealla remembered. At a nudge, Zetrine shooed her with a sweep of her arm. Dealla tried again. "What? It's still dark," Zetrine complained.

"Zaytray," Dealla called her, "Zaytray, come."

Zetrine awoke and pulled back at sight of Dealla so close. "What are you doing?"

Dealla stood and motioned her to come. "Jimio iakin jez io," she explained with a sense of urgency, patting her stomach and backing towards the door.

"I don't understa... What is that smell?" Zetrine covered her nose and mouth. Her eyes widened with realization. "Someone's ill!" She sprung from the bed and followed Dealla outside.

Jamila sat upon her knees clutching her stomach. She moaned as she rocked to and fro. Dealla entered the other women's hut and brought out Pekoe and Charlise, neither of whom wanted anything more than to crumple to the ground. Roselana came staggering out of the brush and leaned against the hut.

"They need to be in their beds, Dealla!" Zetrine called to her. But, Dealla went instead to the wrapped herbs and began to open them. Zetrine approached and immediately recognized the roots and leaves. "I understand. Get the fire ready I'll prepare them."

Dealla turned the ember log and stoked the fire with kindling. As it lit, she left Zetrine to tend to it and entered the men's hut. The scene was much the same, though the floor was filthy with regurgitation beside both Talek and Guin. She felt their fevers, but all three men slept soundly. She took Talek's staff. Holding it at its narrow end she rapped each of them soundly on a hip to awaken them. When Guin rose she tapped him again to get him to look at her. Then she pointed to the open door. "Go out!" she ordered. Guin nodded and picked up Talek as the old man began to sit up. Once both were on their feet and heading out to the fire, Dealla dropped the staff and turned her attention to Kallias.

There was nothing on the floor nor in his bed. His head and body was hottest of all of them, but he lay silent. She shook him. "Kallias," she spoke close to his ear. "Juet, Kallias, come. Zet iaowi jez io." She shook him again. "Kallias. Kallias, sae ira!" A fear took hold of her when he did not respond.

Dealla hurried out the door to Zetrine, who had gathered the others and was busy wrapping blankets around the girls. "Zaytray! Kallias, zet saira!"

"What's wrong? What do you mean?" She followed Dealla inside to see Kallias unmoved. Zetrine also shook him. "He's out. I don't understand how it could effect him this badly." She turned to the worried rekinnder. "We have to get some of the tea into him." Dealla nodded, understanding only that Zetrine would help with the steeped herbs. As she watched Zetrine pull the blankets from the beds and head back out to the others, she returned to Kallias's side.

It seemed like an eternity, though it was but a few moments before Zetrine returned with a cup of the hot liquid. "Hold him up." Dealla understood her words and gesture. The two of them held him and took turns blowing on the tea and spooning it into Kallias's mouth. At first, he responded to this nurturing with jerks of his head, spilling most of the tea down the front of him. Eventually, the two managed to get about half of the tea into him and laid him back down. "I hope that does it. We'll give him more after awhile." She patted Dealla's hand and returned outside where the rest sat around the fire quietly sipping from their own cups. Dealla gazed after her for awhile, watching the woman go to each of her friends and the two men, making sure of their comfort. Were all the women accepting of her? *Perhaps,* she thought in her Rekinnder, *it is the dark hair that aligns them with Iasegald.*

***

Yungir sat at one end of a long banquet table, gazing ahead at a vase of fresh flowers in the center. Suddenly he snatched up his silver plate and threw it spinning into the vase. Roses and baby's breath leaped upward as the vase shattered, tossing shards of glass in a wide spread and causing the woman at the other end of the table to jump and flinch. Water flew with the glass, then cascaded down upon the table and floor. The plate skittered onward, bumping to a halt against a bowl of fruit, while the roses dropped into the ruins of the vase and bounced to stillness.

"There. Now I can see ya," he said. Asadia stared at the dishes of food before her. Like a shadow, she sat garbed in a black satin dress, buttoned up her neck, with close fitting sleeves that terminated in lace around her wrists. Her hair was tied up in a tight knot at the base of her neck, barely visible under a semi transparent shroud. "Ya haven't touched yar breakfast. Look there. Ya have fruit and meats, three kinds, eggs. Did ya want some wine?"

She sat silently.

He picked up a goblet of red wine with his left hand. "Ya don't mind if I drink wine at breakfast, do ya?"

Glaring at him from beneath the black veil, she trembled with gritted teeth and did not answer him.

"Good. I don't care anyway. Ya probably won't like a lot of what I do." He took a swallow, leaning back in his chair with his right arm on the armrest. "We'll wed in the summer. I always wanted a summer bride. That'll give that stupid sea captain a chance to look for any more brothers ya might have come to Marisko."

At the mention of the sea captain, Asadia raised her head sharply and growled at Yungir. "You turned him to stone."

"Aah... about that," he said with a wry smile. "Ya don't think I meant to be rid of him do ya? He's good fodder in case someone comes to threaten me."

Asadia spoke through clenched teeth. "I have hundreds of brothers. They'll come for me. And when they do, they'll spill your guts out on the floor."

Yungir laughed and raised his cup. "Well said! I like a girl with spirit." He lowered his arm, his head and his voice. "I hear the lie in yar words and the fear in yar trembling tone. No one's coming. Ya'll draw closer to me. Every day a bit closer. Ya'll stay in yar tower room and stare at the sea and wish ya could see yar home. But ya'll never leave here again. I'm patient, like I told ya. I'll see ya break. Ya'll beg to marry me...in time." He paused then added, "Not too much time."

Suddenly he leapt from his chair, drew a dagger and slammed its point deep into the wood of the table in front of him as far forward as he could reach. Asadia flinched again.

"Kaig!" he shouted. Instantly a manservant appeared at his side. "I want this table cut off just there." He pointed to the knife. "Have the craftsman move the legs and refinish it." He gave a brief savage look to the woman, then stomped out, shouting his final words as he left. "Next time we sit down, I want to see her face!"

Chapter 22

All was stillness engulfed by a shadowy emptiness for what seemed an eternity. Time had no importance, no concept. Kallias sat upright in his bed. A soft indigo aura colored the world, as if the radiance of a full moon emanated from everything.

Guin and Talek shuffled mindlessly out of the hut door. "Guin! Talek!" he called after the two, though they did not react. Incensed, he hurried after them grabbing Talek's shoulder, pulling the old soothsayer around. "Talek!" he growled as the old man's body twisted toward him. Yet Talek's head uncompromisingly stayed facing away from him. Astonished, Kallias stood with his mouth agape while the men marched out of the cabin. The warrior cried out and dropped to his knees, clutching tufts of his black curly hair. "Aaahhh!"

The hut shook without a sound, then suddenly ripped away from the floor and disappeared into the air. Before him stood a small, grotesque creature with cat-like ears and sharp, menacing teeth. Kallias stood with sword in hand. He became twelve years old again. His father, unseen somewhere behind him, commanded him. "Center yourself for battle." The cat-being lunged at him.

Young Kallias struck swords with—Maltax? —amidst a furious battle in a strange place, somewhere like his home but not his village at all. Kallias searched for the cat-like nearbeast while chaos encircled him. The heat of burning wood licked his back. Huts were aflame. His muscles strained as his sword grew large and heavy. Kallias grunted through clenched teeth, grasping his sword with two hands, a thing he never did. Maltax's eyes glowed red when Kallias struck him down.

Suddenly someone stood at the top of a mountain, which appeared like a huge rock. This one raised his hands high causing a great fiery cloud to circle over his head. From it, molten rock rained down upon people, who had appeared with him all around the foot of the rock.

The weird little creature returned. It ran on two feet, leading a pack of kervplik hunters towards Asadia, Roselana, and the other women. Kallias shouted and charged towards it. Meanwhile kervplik stumbled head over heels in all directions. With each momentous roll, they became solid rock, boulders of tremendous size. Shouts and screams filled the air. All attempts to jump out of the way were futile, and people were soon trampled by rolling stones.

Kallias froze. Before him, the little thing grew into a fearsome, fiery giant towering over his head, though the young blade was once again the man. His father was nowhere to help him. But there stood Guin, fighting the giant creature.

Kallias waited as Guin battled toe to toe with the brutish fire monster. A fell swoop of the giant's fist flung Guin's hapless body through the air. In a thought Kallias appeared under the belly of the beast. As it raised its boulder sized fist in the air to smash Guin, Kallias leapt forward, piercing the only soft spot of the creature, its armpit. It burst into flame and diminished. Suddenly in its place stood Dealla, her eyes wide and frightened. "Kallias?" She called out weakly to him and fell to ash.

Kallias cried out, "No! Dealla!"

"Kallias? Kallias, wake up. It's alright. Everything is fine now. Your fever has broken." Dealla's soft voice came to him out of nowhere.

She lives? She speaks Kinnir?

Then it became another voice. "Kallias—I think he's waking up!" Jamila got up from his bedside and called out through the open door of the hut.

Kallias opened and closed his eyes a few times. He took in all the blurred faces as each of them, dead in his dream, filed in through the door and stood around his bedside quite alive.

"Don't get up too fast," said Jamila putting out a protective hand to stop his attempt to sit up. The others made various exclamations that ran together in his ears.

The garbled sounds became clearer and the faces more detailed. "Dealla, Guin!" Kallias exclaimed. "I thought you were dead. I thought you were all dead."

Guin shrugged. "Same here."

"What happened?"

"Ya got a fever, belly fire. We all got it. Jamila was down two days. Ya been down for nearly five," explained Guin. "Good to have ya back. We were worried."

Talek grumbled. "At least we've not had to deal with morning headaches."

"Quiet, Talek," ordered Guin.

"You feel like getting up?" asked Roselana, handing Kallias a cup of cool water. "Here. Go easy." Kallias sat up, and drank slowly from the cup she handed him.

"We should let him rest still," suggested Jamila.

"Yes, rest a bit Kallias. Then we'll talk." Guin ushered the others outside leaving Roselana behind.

"Guin and I took turns with sword training. I'm not sure I have the dance steps right, but we've been doing some offense, too. Guin said he doesn't know your style but—It's alright though, we haven't forgotten it." Roselana watched Kallias drink his water as if he were doing an amazing thing. "I'm so glad you're alive."

He handed the empty cup to her. "We must get back to training. Time is valuable." Kallias twisted to place his feet on the floor.

"Wait!" Roselana held a palm against his chest. "Ya haven't a thing on."

Blushing, he coughed, cleared his throat and clung to his covers. "And what of Dealla?"

"Dealla saved us from the illness. But, I'm worried, because she hasn't been around since that evening." She gave Kallias an earnest gaze. then looked into the cup and smiled. "Would you like more water? You don't have to get up right now. It's late in the day. We did lessons already. We've been working on the boat."

"I'm fine. But I must relieve myself," he said.

"Oh dear, of course. Your clothes were soaked with sweat, so we washed them. They're there." She pointed at the small wall table, then stepped out the door, closing it behind her.

Kallias donned the leather trousers and laced his boots. He slipped over his torso the now crisp white linen tunic. He mused. *They actually stopped to do laundry after two months or more? I hope they're all clean, too, or I'll smell out of place.* Then, as was his custom, he tied his poniard to his right thigh. It was then he noticed Pluth's flintlock was missing. He looked about for it to no avail. His sword hung on a bedpost. "Well as long as I have my sword. If someone needs that stupid gun, I'll not deny them," he told himself.

Kallias shuffled out of the hut past the camp into the woods. In a short time, he returned, beaming happily in the sunlight, fully recovered.

Kallias returned to the hut, because he realized he had paid little attention to his grooming since chasing after Asadia. He vowed to change that. His hair had gotten very long. He examined a fish-bone comb, one of two in the camp. Each one in the group kept tabs on shared personal items. This ensured an immediate and violent eradication of any parasitic insects showing up. Assured of a clean comb, he took pains to get the knots out of his hair. Then braiding a long thick strand, he used it to tie the rest into a tail behind his head.

On the east side of the camp, a short way from the high tide line, rose the sizable hull of a boat, about one quarter the size of the great longship, which had been dismantled to make her. A ladder leaned against the west side and Zetrine stood at the top bringing up a long plank being handed to her by Pekoe and Jamila. Guin walked along the top edge of the boat as if balancing on a wire. Pekoe turned to see Kallias and waved, quickly returning her hand to the heavy plank.

Charlise leaned over the stew pot stirring. "Good to see you're up, Kallias."

He turned to Charlise and smiled before gazing hungrily into the pot. "The boat is coming along. Then again I've been gone for several days, haven't I?"

Charlise smiled weakly. "It'll be ready in a little while. We've been eating mostly vegetation since we became ill. She...Dealla, left us a couple of pheasants the morning after most of us recovered, but nothing since, and none of us have seen her. We don't save over meat or fish anymore, unless it's smoked. We burn the leftovers, because I—" Her words caught in her throat and tears welled up in her eyes. "I'm so sorry, Kallias. It was my fault. I poisoned us with the boar meat."

"Stop, Charlise. It isn't anyone's fault. You can't say for a certainty that it could've been prevented." He stepped over to her and put a comforting arm around her shoulder. "We're all alive. Punishing yourself will help no one and will only hinder you. Let's act upon what we've learned and grow. It'll make you a formidable warrior. Consider that I, that we all, have survived the threat of a death. In fact, I'm glad it happened. There is less to fear now."

"Thank you, Kallias." Charlise sniffled and wiped away the tears.

"Tell me about the pheasants. Tasty, were they?"

The smile returned. "Oh yes and such beautiful feathers. I kept some, though she already plucked all the most colorful and long ones." Charlise shrugged then continued to stir the stew. "Today we have crayfish with basil, rosemary, spinach, onions and little potatoes. Zetrine's meadows produce a cornucopia."

"Smells delicious." Kallias gave her shoulder a reassuring squeeze before venturing toward the boat. He picked up a light plank of wood and handed it up to Pekoe. "Guin, how long till it's finished?"

Guin looked down from his perch. "Greetings stranger." He laughed. "We've about another eight days' work on the hull and decks. Then the sail, lines and trimmings to do, another few days."

"Your cross beam seems heavy to one side." Kallias gestured to the slant of the yardarm. "A bit long, too, isn't it?"

Guin laughed. "It's set for lateen riggin's. Triangle sail. She'll cut quicker athwart the wind."

"I see. Well it's a good thing I'm not designing her then!"

Guin added, "These women are fantastic carpenters! They mastered the use of the tools very quickly, though it was necessary to take turns." Something was said by someone inside the hull and Guin turned his attention to her. In a moment, he took a couple steps back as Pekoe passed a light plank up to Zetrine, and Zetrine turned it over to Guin. "They're like ants upon a hill!" he crowed. Another comment was made from the feminine voice below and Guin laughed and handed the plank down.

After a moment, Charlise called out for them to come to the evening meal. Guin called to those unseen inside the boat and moved again upon the edge of the hull. A hand appeared and he reached for it. The old akinn stepped upon the hull catwalk and made his way to the ladder. The girls cleared the way and held the ladder for him as he descended. Then Guin leaned over and brought Roselana up out of the hull. When she emerged, he put his hand upon her waist, smiled into her eyes then guided her to the ladder. Soon they were all seated around the fire with bowls of crayfish stew in their hands and cups of water at their sides.

Four days without eating was evident in the way Kallias devoured his food. Once his initial hunger was sated, he peered around at the others gathered. "I know you haven't seen Dealla, but do you know where is she? Has anyone gone up to see if her nest is still there?"

"Ya're the only one who's seen her nest, Kallias. She's never joined us here." Guin answered. "She brings meat, then disappears. We never see her. All we know Kallias, is that—" Guin stopped and looked at the faces around the camp. They all knew, they had all been there.

Jamila gave voice to their experience. "We might not any of us be here if it wasn't for Dealla. Well, and Zetrine."

Kallias gave the woman a quizzical look. "Zetrine?"

"I didn't get sick, because I only eat vegetables. We think it was the pork."

Kallias thought for a long moment, then quietly said, "Poor Dealla. She must feel guilty." He exchanged a knowing glance with Charlise.

The sun cast long shadows from every rock, plant or item on the Point of the Gald. It still provided enough light to continue work for a short while as it perched just above the horizon. Kallias sat his bowl down and strolled away from the camp to the boat and examined it quietly.

"Think he's alright Guin?" asked Roselana.

Guin followed Kallias with his eyes. "I can't say Roselana. But he'll have to satisfy himself that Dealla may be gone, if she feels guilty enough."

After Talek's usual announcement, Charlise and Zetrine took the pot and bowls to wash in the stream. Jamila picked up the corner of a sail and began sewing the hem. The others talked quietly around the fire as Guin walked over to Kallias. "It'll be a fine vessel."

"Fine vessel," Kallias repeated, patting Guin on the shoulder. "I can tell she isn't your first." Kallias ran his fingers along the hull, feeling the smoothness of the wood.

"No, every longship man learns first to make a ship, then to fight, after that..." Guin dropped his head slightly, for just a moment, staring thoughtfully into the sand. His eyes became gentle as he continued. "My son and I built a boat many, many seasons past, when even I was young and invulnerable. 'Twas half this size. I'd been a longship mystic as was my father and I passed it on along with all my skills."

Kallias raised his brows with interest. "You have a son? He is a mystic, like you?"

Guin nodded. "I do. He's a mystic, not like me. He's...much better at it, stronger force, quick to learn. When his mother died, I spoiled him. I couldn't say 'no'. He...he was so small and willful and beautiful, like his mother. A good protector of his longship until this damned..." Guin stopped on the upwards tone of his tale leaving something unsaid.

"I think I would enjoy having a son," Kallias said wistfully. "Where is he now?"

Guin stared at the hull of their boat, tracing a finger along the wood grain.

"Oh, the mystics were—" Kallias broke off. "I am sorry, Guin, I didn't mean to..."

Suddenly the air was filled with the screams of the two women down the beach toward the stream. Guin spun around. Zetrine and Charlise raced toward the camp. But nature made quayside of uneven rock and constricted beachfront. In the high tide, skimming the shallow waters and working its sail-like dorsal fin, was a saber crispin. It lunged and snapped at the women whenever the terrain forced them near the water's edge.

Kallias looked around and grabbed an ax. He ran at the monster. Guin followed, pulling his pistols from his belt.

Charlise fell. Zetrine stopped and ran back to help her up. The crispin came at them. Talek was there in an instant to ward the fish off with a blow from his staff. Guin fired off one shot then the other. The creature jerked slightly as each bullet hit but did little to stop it. Then Kallias reached it. He leaped over the monster as the thing thrashed its open maw in his direction. At the same time, he swung downward with the ax., bringing his full weight to bear upon it. It hit its mark squarely in the creature's head, splitting it open as Kallias landed upon the sand and rolled against a rock.

He took the blow to his ribs but quickly regained his feet. Kallias took in a deep breath of sea spray and coughed, checking that no bones had broken. The monstrous fish flayed about until it expired. He quickly checked to see that the women were safe from the would-be devouring pakao of the tide. "First battle won. So much for the fearsome maogra!" he crowed.

"Not a maogra, Kallias. This is a saber crispin. And now it's food." Guin crossed over to the southwest hut and retrieved a couple of carving knives from the tool crate.

Kallias rested beside the carcass. He had only just recovered from one malady; he did not need another.

"Ya all right?" the mystic asked.

"It's going to bruise, but nothing's broken."

"This'll make fine salted steaks and smoked meat. No more thin, crayfish soup," Guin said, returning to Kallias.

Zetrine and Charlise were met at the fire by the other women who comforted them and hugged them. Roselana called out, with a worried tone, "Is it dead?"

"It is!" Kallias replied.

Jamila patted the girls on their arms as she spoke to each one. "There'll be more danger and attacks than that in Durgrinstar, girls. Let us take to heart Talek's lessons on being aware now."

"Always practical, Jamila," said Pekoe. "Are we to expect fish to attack us when we find Asadia?"

"I'm just saying we mustn't be complacent. If a fish can attack, how much more so will a man?" Jamila picked up some material she had been working with and headed for her hut.

Roselana looked after her then to the others. "She's right. I know you had a scare. We're glad you weren't fish food. But we're to be warriors now, right?" They each nodded and attempted a brave countenance.

Charlise turned to see the men coming towards them with large chunks of the fish in their arms. She grimaced but spoke softly. "Thank you, Kallias and Guin, Talek... and Zetrine, for saving my life." Zetrine nodded and added her thanks to the men.

Kallias merely smiled to the thanks and traipsed behind Guin back to the carcass. "You said eight days until we set out?" he asked as he cut several larger slabs and stacked them in Guin's outstretched arms.

"Eight for the body, I'd say a ten day and the boat 'll be seaworthy, ready to stock. Then we'll take a few days to gather our needs; preserved foods, bedding, cooking and cleaning items and the like. About a two-and-then-some days' sail to Durgrinstar." Guin adjusted a slab of the fish before it slid off the stack in his arms.

Kallias scowled. "It's taking so long. I don't want to lose her, Guin. She's all the family I have left."

"From the start, I didn't keep from telling ya it would take months. The difference is we'll be prepared. And that is the difference between life and death to us all." Guin adjusted his footing as Kallias added another cut of fish to his armful. "Hold Kallias. I think we've all we can preserve of the fish. We'll cut the rest up and bury it in pieces tomorrow. We'll pack most of this in salt."

"Are we going to have enough salt?"

Guin harrumphed. "While you were yet sleeping in your illness, we set up means to keep our food better preserved. We've a system to collect salt. Gathered a sackful and then some."

"We can smoke some of it." Kallias lifted a few slabs into his own arms. "With the sun going down we'll have to lay the salted pieces by the fire."

"We'll cook some up and oil it, too."

Kallias returned to a previous conversation. "I must seek Dealla out before we leave."

"I understand. I suggest at sunrise. Take someone with ya. We'll bury the fish in the morning." Guin tossed fuel on the fire and prepared the smoking cabinet as three of the women helped to cut the meaty fish into thin strips, steaks and planks. "Rub the salt in a bit, ladies."

Pekoe came out from one of the huts with a slightly large, aged bottle. "Look what I have! I tripped on a loose floor board some time ago and found someone's stash. I'm glad I didn't throw it out." She giggled. Guin lifted his head with a smile.

"Hand that here," ordered Kallias in a good natured tone. She put the bottle in his hands. He tilted it and dusted off the label then tossed it to Guin.

Guin caught it with a quick hand and turned it around. Nearly every available iron platter and pan was filled with fish. One pan sat directly on the fire. What was not in the pans was in the smoke cabinet. Guin popped the cork from the bottle with his teeth and smelled the contents. He chuckled with the cork still between his teeth and generously sprinkled some of its contents on the frying fish. A splash in the fire caused it to flare. Then he removed the cork from his mouth. "Get out the cups. We need some of this!"

Pekoe pranced to the request and returned with cups. Half-way back she dropped a cup. When she bent slightly to pick it up, another fell in its place. She did this several times and gave a frustrated sigh. "Let me help you with that." Charlise giggled and grabbed a few of the cups. Both returned to Guin with smiles.

"Now this is pretty strong spirits, and one bottle isn't going to go far—" He paused while pouring a little in each cup. "But a little extra for the scare to the brave girls." He tipped it a second time for a few added drops into two cups. Then he took two empty cups from Pekoe and held one out to Kallias. "And extra for the hero as well." He poured a generous amount into Kallias' cup then some into his own. "This'll help pass the time as we wait for the fish. Say, Charlise did ya happen to find a pipe in that captain's sea chest?" Pekoe took the bottle and poured some for herself and Roselana. Then she poured a bit in another cup. Roselana took it to the hut where Jamila was.

"Mmm... how did you know?" Charlise pulled a pipe from a small crate of odds and ends and handed it to him.

"Ah perfect!" Guin got up and stepped over to where Charlise often kept vegetables and took from there bits of kelp they had collected on the beach some time ago. "The dry kelp burns harshly but it gives a fine restful odor." He stuffed the pipe with this and lit it from the campfire with a twig. He took a few puffs then handed it to Kallias. "Try it."

"Restful odor my staff," countered Talek. "Stinks worse than a kervplik."

Kallias looked at the pipe doubtfully before trying it. He gave a loud hacking cough and blew the smoke from his lungs. "Ugh!" He grunted and cursed colorfully though quietly. He washed it down quickly with the spirits. "Ack! Great stuff." He coughed again.

Guin laughed wholeheartedly. "Well it isn't for everyone."

Talek then stood and handed his untouched cup to Kallias. "Spirits block such energies as is needed. I'm now to retire." He picked up his staff and headed into the hut.

Pekoe coughed and grimaced at the spirits. "This burns, too." She smiled good naturedly and tried another sip, which sent her into a coughing fit as she handed her cup to Zetrine and grabbed a water bladder.

Jamila came out of her hut with her cup in hand, followed by Roselana. "Thank you." She handed her cup to Guin. "If you do not need me to watch the fires, I will also retire."

Guin took the cup and shook his head. Jamila returned to her hut. "Did she really drink it that fast?"

Roselana laughed. "Downed it in one swallow. Such is the wife of a counselor and commander of hunters."

"I'm impressed," he returned, then took another swallow. "We're losing company fast, Kallias."

"Looks that way. More for us!" Kallias raised both his and Talek's cups with a grin. But, he thought better of the idea and poured Talek's back into the bottle.

Soon Pekoe, Zetrine and Charlise also took to their huts for the night. The pan-fried fish was cooled, covered in oil cloth and salt, then given to Charlise to put in the keeper chest in the south hut. Finally, only the three sat at the fire, Kallias, Guin and Roselana. Kallias gazed blankly at drying crispin and the smoking cabinet.

Roselana held her cup in both hands and stared into the fire turning her eyes slightly from time to time to look at Guin. Guin refilled the pipe and sat with his cup in one hand and the pipe in the other, also feigning a stare until he glanced at Roselana. This exchange of glances went on for some time. Finally, he cleared his throat and spoke. "The smoked fish might be alright to cover now. I'm sure it'll be finished by the time the fire dies out," he said.

"I suppose you're right," Roselana replied. She did not move from her place nor did Guin.

Kallias emptied his cup. He caught sight of the exchange when he put it down. "I see. Guess I'll retire, if you don't need my eyes, too." He winked at Roselana. Not waiting for an answer, he stood and walked towards his hut. "Sleep well you two."

The tease gave her cheeks a flush. "Sleep well Kallias," she replied.

Guin sat up. "Good rest Kallias."

"Are ya warm enough?" Guin asked as he moved closer to Roselana. "I've something for ya." Guin handed her a small bag of stones. "Take these. Some day they'll come in handy maybe. There's a map where I found them in there, too."

Inside the hut, Roselana's replies barely reached Kallias' ears. With the light, fuzzy-headed feeling, he heard a soft feminine murmur, some movement and the low rumble of Guin's voice as the couple spoke quietly. Kallias drifted off to sleep, thinking of the couple and their developing relationship.

After that evening, Kallias frequently saw Guin and Roselana together in the twilight, talking, walking and laughing. They also appeared to be playing some sort of magic game, chanting and moving their hands. Sometimes lights of various colors flashed; sometimes oddly shaped items he could barely make out appeared; sometimes dark shadows or even things that, by what he overheard, only they could see, resulted from these castings.

Kallias considered what an avid student Roselana had always been. She learned from everyone; her brother, Guin and Dealla. In doing so, she uplifted those who taught her. She was now more than his best friend's sister, she had become his friend, too. And, she was shaping up to be a powerful warrior in her own right, capable of wielding sword, dagger and longbow, able to speak and translate Rekinnder, and now, likely becoming a mystic, mastering the art of magical illusion. *Omerion would be so proud if he were alive to see this.*

Chapter 23

"Kallias! Kallias!"

"Asadia?" Kallias saw the longship man throw her over his massive shoulder and climb aboard his ship. The next instant a monstrous saber crispin was carrying them away. It was the longship at sail and Kallias hurried to create a sail on the fishing boat to pursue. He wedged the flat of a paddle between the seat at the stern and the storage box. Then he cut up the net and used its roping to tie his cloak in place with its corners out to the oarlocks. "Kallias!" The longship disappeared and left him and his tiny fabricated sailboat bobbing in a vast sea.

"Kallias!" Kallias awakened. The moonless night, lit only by the stars, darkened the room considerably. "Kallias!" The sound of Dealla's voice was distant and yet as if right outside his window. Inside, the room buzzed with the heavy snore of the old akinn. Guin moved slightly on his cot. Kallias sat upright, listening. Was he dreaming? He crawled from the bed silently and approached the window. He opened the shutters. The chilly night sea-breeze caressed his face softly.

"Kaaalliaas!" Her melodic call came from the forest up the hill, like someone searching for a lost child. "Kaaa-llii-aaas," came the eerie call, carried by the breeze and sung.

The warrior peered over his shoulder to be sure his fellow hut mates were still fast asleep. Satisfied, he grabbed his boots and snatched up his cloak. The click and creak of the door suddenly seemed so much louder than he had ever noticed before. Once outside with the door shut behind him,

Kallias slipped on his boots and cloak and headed up the pathway to the ridge.

The sea heaved behind him. He stopped. Something like a huge dark shadow rose up out of the water. The dim reflection of starlight, which danced upon the waves, blacken out beyond the horizon and up into a portion of the bespeckled sky. His heart raced as the edges of this darkness writhed back and forth, suggested a tremendous form, then sank. An odd sucking sound, like something being dragged, brought his attention to the beach. The whole incident took barely more than a breath of time. And suddenly, the dark against the darkness was gone. Something had dragged away the saber crispin, something much, much larger. After straining his eyes futilely against the night, trying to see more, Kallias gave up and returned his attention to the hill and Dealla's call.

He perceived not only the call of her sweet soft voice, but also her fragrance, wafting invisibly towards him. It dissipated quickly. Had he imagined it? Without her luminous eyes to guide him the going was slow, despite how familiar the path to the clearing was to him. Her nest was gone. Parts of it were scattered about. There was no sign of Dealla nor her serlcat form. The strong sweetness of a night jasmine filled his nostrils from a plant close by. An irresistible emotion of disappointment, then fear for her safety flooded his chest. Where was she? Was her voice but an illusion? Was he still dreaming?

A soft whisper came from the trees. "Kallias."

"Dealla?" he called back just as gently, darting his eyes blindly into the trees. Through the rustling leaves high above came a soft halo of light from branches deep within the woods. It flickered for a moment. Then he lost it. With hands out, he searched his way through the tree trunks towards the glow. He quietly called out Dealla's name repeatedly.

Suddenly something dropped in front of him. "Kallias." Dealla's quiet voice came from above him. He could make out her white hair, her blue-on-blue eyes and the form of the knotted rope she had dropped down to him.

He gripped the rope and pulled himself up hand over hand until her eyes met his. He repeated her name softly, "Dealla."

She ducked away as he placed his feet on the platform. Behind her on a low table several sticks shimmered a fiery red. As the embers died out, a subtle florescence emanated from Dealla's bow, which leaned against the massive trunk of the tree. It filled the small space with a pale white light. She made a sweeping gesture, smiling to him. "Juet awa. Piira ka kuite jaia."

There seemed to be little enough room for both of them. Dealla motioned with a slender hand to each corner as she spoke in her native tongue. "Jaia d'selendo." In one corner was a new nest, more elegant than the last and covered with furs. "Doisha d'vezj." Beside that lay a stack of longbows and leather bracers and quivers. Extending across the other side were two planks side by side creating a table. "Farnio ka vezam."

Kallias hunched slightly as he stood next to her. His eyes followed the small tour she offered. "This is quite the home you've made for yourself." He smiled.

"Home?" she asked.

"Hmm," Kallias brought a hand up, rubbing at his dark beard in thought. "Home, yes. Where you live. This." The last he said with a wave of his hand.

"Mele home," she said with a smile, her eyes soft upon him. "Ach! Jalita et." She looked skyward to show the leafy ceiling which was dense and reflected back the soft glow of her bow. She pointed upward with one hand. "Piira evia. Wain, Kallias?"

Kallias took in her enchanting beauty. The exotic shape of her ears fascinated him. His eyes followed her long slender arm upwards to the foliage. "Peerah ayveeah?"

Dealla nodded continuing her radiant smile. She touched the trunk gently, then tapped it with her fingers as if trying to get its attention. The branches and twigs of the natural ceiling unraveled in the center to form a skylight, showing off the speckled night sky. "Haiaive," she said melodically.

His sucked in a quick breath. This was like her manipulation of the fire and water in the cave, but so much closer. It startled him to have nature around him obey her.

Kallias recovered quickly and stood upright in the tree house. "High – ivy?" He repeated the word as best he could. It came out awkwardly.

"Hah-ee-ah-ee-vay." She instructed. "Haiaive."

Kallias gazed upwards. "What is it?" He pointed at the twinkling stars amidst the backdrop of the dark black space. "The stars? Or do you mean the opening?" he asked, moving his hand in a circular motion. "Or how the tree moved? It's fantastic."

Dealla looked into his eyes and laughed. She hoped someday he would speak her language with her.

"You called me here to show me your tree house," Kallias said. His tone was not ungrateful though he chuckled involuntarily. "What can I say? It's marvelous. But I had hoped you would join us down in the camp. This looks very—permanent." Kallias managed a weak smile in an effort to hide his disappointment.

"Eo faleke jaia kuite. Tolu d'elwa rekin kuita. Piira haiaive d'haiaive piira." She rattled off the Rekinnder in an excited tone, proud and happy with her accomplishment. "Bosae Kallias sel?"

Kallias shrugged. "I may not understand, but you are delightful when you're happy." Taking her hand gently in his, he brought her to him. As he raised her chin to kiss her, she quickly, shyly pulled away. He smiled, but it was evident he was confused. "For all those nightly visits, you certainly can't be shy. Is this coyness?"

Dealla did not have the Kinnir words to express her meaning. She attempted to explain how it was her own fault to mislead him so. He came to her call and now wanted something from her. But she was stronger than Mehanna. And he, Kallias, was no mystic. He was not in control. "Faleke wopik d'ele d'awa. Uez zet hol awa," she explained. "Ushen elwa d'Asadia. Fet mahij awa."

He attempted again to kiss her. She pulled back. "I don't understand," he objected. Hurt and confusion filled his eyes. "You come to me at night, over and over. But in the daytime I can't even pet the cat any more without feeling a shudder, and now you shrink from me? What's going on?" He pulled her back to him and held her tightly. "I won't hurt you. Please don't hurt me."

Dealla's eyes searched his. She waited, neither resisting nor relenting.

Kallias breathed heavily and swallowed hard. The pain filling his eyes was almost unbearable. She could not deny feeling something for him. It twisted inside her now. She had been so happy just a moment ago, showing him the nest and the work she was doing to help them all. There was a fullness to that joyful feeling unlike any experience she had before. This feeling though, here in his arms so tightly held, did not feel good. It hurt inside like the shame she wanted to impose on Mehanna to break her from the kinnir. This guilt mirrored the guilt and fear when the connection to Mehanna had been broken. It crushed her heart like the loss of all her people at once.

Kallias slowly released her, placing his hands gently upon her cheeks. He wiped tears from her eyes with his thumbs. Only then did she realize she had been crying. Was it for herself or Mehanna?

"I'm sorry," his voice cracked with unshed tears. "It hurts me to feel rejected by you, but I don't want to hurt you. I love you, Dealla. I have from the moment you showed your beautiful self to us in the cave. I only wish I could explain or... or at least understand why—"

She could not bring herself to cast him away. She stopped his words with a kiss.

Kallias lifted her and took a few steps forward. Gently carrying her until they reached her nest. Still embraced in each other's arms, he lowered them together down upon the furs. Her body lay cradled in his arms.

Dealla swept a hand gently down his chest over his shirt. As if by some command the air lifted it from his skin. She removed it over his head.

Kallias brought his lips to the soft flesh on her exposed neck and shoulder. She wore the silvery-blue ethereal gown he had seen her in on the seal rock. His hand clutched her knee and swept up her thigh until it rested on her hip.

Dealla felt the twisting again inside. Her own confusion and fear of losing control. Perhaps this was the kinnir's magic, befuddlement. She altered the intoxicating scent her body released as her hands moved over his chest and ribs. She would have to keep control of him until she could figure out these feelings. She would not die the last rekinnder of Marisko. If he was true, she would find out.

Kallias closed his eyes, unaware of the changing air. She cleverly undressed him, then turned him, letting him slip to her side to continue with a dream all his own.

She had work to do.

Just before dawn the chilly night air woke Kallias. He did not realize when it was he had fallen asleep in Dealla's arms. But, she was not in the nest. Something yellow, like lamplight, caught his attention. Kallias raised himself upon an elbow. Dealla sat naked with her back to him. He admired her graceful curves as he considered, *This is the first time I've actually seen her.*

Dealla made a sweeping gesture he could not make out. Something on the table emitted a bright glow briefly. Then just as quickly dimmed. Kallias covered himself with a fur and moved in the nest to get a better view.

She began to play with her hair as he watched. It appeared to be a pantomiming of her washing the long strands of crystal white until she moved more furiously like scrubbing laundry against itself to remove a stain. He chuckled quietly at this odd game.

Dealla turned and smiled at him over her shoulder just as her hair stood high with its static charge like wings raised up. With her back to him again, she stretched her hands out. A group of sticks crackled into light like a bright electric dance as if of fingers of lightning. In its brilliance, Kallias could see the sticks were arrows, two sets of them; one upon the small table-like board and another set below the table. Dealla held a hand over each set as the arrows filled with the strange statically charged bolts, which ran down her arms from her hair. "Electric," Kallias said quietly.

"Electric," Dealla repeated. "Liojin." He smiled and nodded. Excitedly she picked up a fist-sized gray rock and held it up. "Gozib," she said frankly.

"Stone or rock," he responded. The electricity died down and her hair fell back into place.

"Stone. Gozib." Then she showed him two small indentations at one side of the table. Kallias had to crawl out of the nest to see them. He shivered, naked in the cold. It was then he noticed she had covered herself in a silvery, velvet gown. *When did that happen?* This morning was filled with wonder already.

What Kallias had thought was candlelight was a small open fire burning in one of two little bowl-shaped dents of wood. Dealla evidently controlled it. A circle of water filled the depression next to the fire. From this one, a snakelike line of water rose up and froze. Then as she drew her hands over another set of arrows the ice shattered to fine bits and was absorbed by them.

With a birdlike quickness, she turned her expectant grin to him. "Ice," he said.

For each element, she exacted the Kinnir word from him with great eagerness. Her inquiries did not stop with elements but continued with parts of the body and certain of their functions; shoulder, burden, arms, strong and such. As the world began to brighten with morning mist, he felt overjoyed in her presence and to have taught her so many words. *We're truly connected now,* he thought. And communicating, understanding each other.

Around her tiny little home in the tree, Kallias could see how everything was within an arm's stretch from where she sat. Beside Dealla's bow were two quivers, filled with arrows, one set with white feathers another with black. The arrows upon the table were also fletched with colored feathers. There were sets of blue, red, yellow, green, and gray spotted, three each on top of the table. Many more below each solid-colored set had two brown feathers and one of the color matching the set above it.

As sunlight filtered through the trees, Dealla took two quivers from the pile of bows and leather-made goods. One she handed to Kallias. She showed him the tooled inscriptions running lengthwise down the outer curve. Then she brought his index finger to the top carving. It glowed green beneath his finger. She touched one upon the quiver in her hand, and showed him it shone a silvery gray. Dealla picked up the arrows with gray spotted feathers and put them in the quiver, indicating he should do the same with the green fletched ones. He did so. They filled the rest of the quivers in the same way.

Her silvery gown deepened in color to a dark gray-blue. Its texture transformed into a hard, scaled cuirass and leggings. An involuntary shiver rose up his spine when he witnessed her shift of clothing. This time he had to believe it. *It crawls like a living thing over her,* he thought. He shuddered as he dressed himself. "It's just the cold air." Kallias said aloud, though she busied herself clearing the table and likely had not seen him. *I remember everything. That was skin against my skin and no dream.* He tried to recall the evening. *She used air to undress me,* he remembered. *It was such a dreamlike motion. No wonder it was so difficult to believe or remember before.* The thoughts of what occurred after that, he struggled to recapture. Her own clothes vanished at his touch but then what? He glanced sideways at her as he pulled on a boot. *Why not? She has fur she can grow and manipulate as she changes from one creature to another. It makes sense she can create clothes. She is perfect as she is.* A satisfied grin pulled the corners of his mouth up. He did not need to recall everything. This was love.

Once her little home was tidied, Dealla took a fur from the nest and wrapped the bows up in it making sure the bowstrings were not tangled. This bundle she tied up with a leather strap and handed to Kallias. Kallias took the bundle and cradled it under an armpit. "Dealla, you have my many thanks. You're amazing."

Dealla stood with a satisfied sigh, beaming, happy and childlike. She strapped together the shoulder harnesses of

four of the quivers. These she slid over Kallias' arm and
shoulder. Then she handed the end of the strap to him,
looping it around the bundle of bows, leaving him a free arm.
She did the same with the last three quivers, hefting them to
her own shoulder and picked up her bow. Once again she
smiled. Her eyes held affection for him as she indicated he
should descend the rope.

Chapter 24

Asadia stared, mouth agape as the vicious wixxon shredded her veil. "Fine! I don't need it! I don't care what you do!" The creature tossed the ragged bits into the sea-breeze outside her window. With a whir and a click, it marched to the door. The other two took hold of Asadia's arms and the three led her to the dining hall.

A short while passed as she sat at what had become her end of the table. Every few mornings, she was brought down to take breakfast with Yungir. Since that dreaded first meal when neither of them ate, they sat and ate in silence. But at each new visit, the table had gotten shorter. Now it was half its original length.

"Thank ya for not wearing the veil," Yungir stated flatly, not looking up from his plate.

"I didn't have much choice. Your little monsters ripped it to pieces."

"Ya really should cooperate more when I send them to do a task for ya. They're there to serve ya." He set his fork down and lifted his head. "I can't punish them every time they lose patience."

"I don't need them to bathe me, and dress me, and do everything. I'm quite capable of caring for myself." Defiance filled every word.

"Then ya'll come down for evening meal tonight." He rose from his seat, approaching her slowly. Asadia watched him, moving only her eyes until he stood by her right shoulder. She cringed as his hand touched her hair. He pulled the comb from the woven bun the wixxon had fashioned, and let it fall. Then he brushed his fingers through her long, curly locks. "It's very silky." She shuddered. He pulled his hand away.

With speed and unexpected strength, Yungir spun her chair around to face him, knocking her knee against the table leg. She flinched, scowled and grit her teeth against the pain. He lifted her face gently by her chin. "It is not my purpose to harm ya. I will send the wixxon with a dress for the evening. Mourning time is over. Courtship can be courteous or torturous. That's up to ya. I suggest ya cooperate, because it'll be the dress or ya'll come down naked." To emphasize his words, he grabbed the collar of the black gown and ripped the bodice open down the front, causing black buttons to fly everywhere. Asadia clasped the top together to cover her breasts. Yungir stood, dropping his arms to his sides. He made a dramatic show of not looking at her. "Thank ya for allowing me to see yar face and for the pleasure of yar company. Ya have lovely eyes."

Asadia sat silently scowling, eyes focused away to her left. Yungir grabbed her face and brought his own down to it. He was half a finger length from her. "Yar polite response is, 'ya're welcome, Yungir.'"

She trembled. "Y-your wel-come," she managed to rasp out. He released her and gently brushed her cheek.

When he left, Kaig came to clear the table. No wixxon or guards came to take her back up to the tower rooms. "Am I supposed to wait here?" she asked.

"I dunno Shasha," he replied.

After Kaig had gone, Asadia sat a long time. Then, without letting go of her gown, she returned to her rooms and shut herself in.

   ***

They entered camp, Dealla behind Kallias. Everyone was up. Some stood around the morning fire. When Kallias appeared, the women came almost as a unit at him with their accusations. "Where were you?" "We were so worried." "You should have awakened one of us. We would have gone with you." As this barage of comments assailed the couple, Guin, Talek and Pekoe walked up from somewhere along the shore.

"All is fine," Kallias reassured them and set the bundles of quivers and bows down. "We are both fine," he added with a turn of his head and a smile to Dealla, who stood behind him to one side.

Dealla looked at them nervously. This was her most vulnerable form. *Run away!* Her body told her, but she trusted Kallias, and they needed her.

"Dealla has provided us with arrows and bows, which we will learn to use," Kallias said as he motioned to the bundles. He added, mostly to the women present, "Please make her feel welcome in our company."

Roselana stepped forward. Dealla responded in kind. The clandestine language lessons had given Dealla confidence. But when the others rushed towards her, Dealla flinched and retreated to Kallias.

"Back up! Back up!" With arms spread, Roselana urged them away.

"Let her be if she doesn't want to come any closer." Talek was relentless. Despite his omission of the word, his tone said "pakao" nevertheless.

"Let's not overwhelm her," continued Roselana, giving Talek a sideways look. Then she turned again to Dealla. "We want to welcome you, Dealla," she said confidently. "We are very happy to have you join us here. Please come and meet everyone, personally." She gestured with her palm up to each woman. "This is Jamila, and Pekoe..."

Dealla began to laugh and say, "Jah-meela, Pee-koh, Zaytray, Shahlees, Rosaylana, Kah-lee-ahs, Tay-lohk, Koon."

Roselana interrupted her, "Goo-in, Guin" she corrected.

Dealla shook her head and tried again. "Kuin," she said which sounded more like queen.

"Well I guess it's better than coon," Guin remarked with a hearty laugh.

"She didn't say any of them correctly," grumbled Talek. The women objected in a cacophony of repeated names with various odd syllables and laughter.

Kallias laughed, then broke up the joviality with a command. "All right, all right. Let's take these to the training area." He picked up the bundle. All but Talek followed him.

Guin spoke quietly as they moved away from the campfire. "Something has dragged away the crispin carcass."

"I heard something last night. Another crispin?" guessed Kallias.

"I don't think so," replied Guin and stopped Kallias so that the dark-haired man faced him. "Something bigger. It left a trench in the sand as if coming down atop of it, adding weight and dragging." Guin's sober expression gave Kallias the feeling that he was expected to know the significance of this. The warrior shook his head. "Maogra, the sea monster ya mistook the crispin to be."

"There are always tales among fishermen, Guin. None have been prov..." he hesitated as he recalled his first encounter with the saber crispin. "None by name. Talek mentioned this creature when we first arrived here. You told him no. What are we in for, Guin? Tell me this time."

"We must keep our eyes open," cautioned the older man, "and bury anything that might attract it. We'll be fine." With that Guin let the matter rest, but leaving Kallias in an agitated state for some time.

The women huddled around Dealla and Kallias as he put the quivers down and untied the bundle of bows. Dealla began laying the quivers and bracers out in a row by sets.

Their eyes eager, Jamila, reached out and claimed a bow. "These are so lovely. Thank you Dealla. Can we have whatever we want?"

Kallias looked to Dealla, who had either not heard or not understood. With a bob of his head, he said, "Pick what suits you. There is much more to learn."

Jamila picked up a bow and the quiver with the red fletched arrows. Dealla stopped her and took the items. "Brikar d'awa."

"What did she say?" Jamila turned to Kallias. "She is taking it all away... Kallias." Jamila began to be indignant.

"Oh, uh... brick-ar. That means... uhm... It's a body part I think. She told me but, I can't remember them all." Dealla touched Kallias' arm. "Be patient with her. I'm sure she has a reason." Kallias asked of Jamila, then responded to Dealla's touch with a questioning look. Dealla handed the bow to Charlise and the quiver to Roselana. Then she touched a carving upon Charlise's bow and it shone blue. "I understand now," Kallias said. "She 's made a specific bow and quiver for each of you. Probably the bracers as well. Match up the insignia on them and the colors. I'm sorry I misled you."

"Colors? You mean the fletching? What does it match with?" Roselana asked.

"The top inscription on the bow. Just touch it like she did and see." Kallias demonstrated as he held up a bow and touched the designating mark. It shimmered with a fluid green light. He handed the bow to Dealla and she turned it over to Jamila with a nod.

Jamila looked over the finely crafted weapon and touched the symbol as Kallias had done. With an expression of disappointment, she picked up the quiver with green fletched arrows in it. The carvings were a match. "Well, I guess she didn't know red is my favorite color. She made each set for one of us only. Does that mean no one else can use them?"

"I don't know, Jamila. She will tell you in time." As he picked up each of the bows, he handed them to Dealla. She in turn gave each their own, allowing them to discover the colors for themselves, the silvery-gray to Pekoe and the yellow to Zetrine.

Roselana found her bow, the last one, which was the one found with the rekinnder skeleton. The writing on this bow was more extensive than those carved on the quiver or bracers. Only one sign was the same, the second from the top, that shined red when she touched it.

When they had all received their sets and put their bracers on, Dealla began her lessons. To Jamila, Dealla smiled softly and touched the three symbols on her bow, lighting each up as she spoke the word for it in her native tongue. Jamila's disappointment became a scowl of confusion. Dealla touched the center mark and translated. "Gozibri awis. Gragoz awis." Of the top inscription, which became green at her touch, she said in a well-rehearsed cadence, "Gozib. Stone, strong." Then she touched the larger carving at the base of the others, which was framed in a square, separating it from the others in style. "Arm, brikar, power d'Jah-mee-lah."

"You mean it says I'm powerful? And this will crush my enemies?" Jamila asked, obviously impressed now. "Exclusive to the user. Amazing." She smiled as Dealla nodded. It was the first smile any of them had seen from Jamila. The others were now anxious to know what their signs meant and gathered around the rekinnder, only Roselana held back.

Dealla tapped Pekoe, who had pulled an arrow from her quiver to examine the gray spotted fletching. Dealla touched her own head, pointed to her own eyes and then to Pekoe. "Rarid von frusent awis. Hilma. Smoke, think. Head, eyes, think, see d'Pee-koh."

Pekoe smiled shyly and shook her head. "I am not sure what you mean by that, but thank you, Dealla."

To Charlise, with the blue inscribed bow, she spoke as with the others. "Shaiz awis. Niolo. Ice ..." Dealla fought for the right word. "Burden, carry, carry, carry." She turned to Kallias for help. He shrugged.

"Endurance?" asked Roselana.

Dealla smiled and shrugged. "Niolo. Ice, burden. Shoulders, en-du-rance d'Sha-lees." Then she turned to Zetrine in the same manner. "Mrez awis." Dealla traced a zigzag pattern from the sky to the ground. "Liojin. Electric. Feet, fly d'Zaytray."

"I guess that means I am fast like lightning." Zetrine grinned at Kallias.

Kallias smiled in return. "I saw her touch these arrows with the elements she's talking about. You're quick on your feet, Zetrine. And your arrows I think were made electric for that reason."

When she came to Roselana, Dealla ran her fingers lovingly over the bow. A single tear glistened at the outside corner of one powder blue eye. An azure liquid light swirled over the bow similar to the white radiance Kallias had witnessed coming from Dealla's bow. The symbols filled the length of the upper half of the outer face and were mirrored on the lower half.

Dealla spoke slowly as she read the group of carvings. "Juet sel azenua d'zenu. Sel hil; sel nio; sel io; sel goz." As she touched each inscription, it would spring into a color for a moment; white for air, blue for water, red for fire and green for earth. "Fobridis Mehanna d'hil von d'nio. Fobridis Roselana d'io."

Next, Dealla showed Roselana the name square on her quiver differed from the one on the bow. Then she touched the square on the bow which shone a pearlescent white. "Rekin d'Mehanna." With her palms facing the ground, Dealla made a motion as if patting two children on their heads, one a bit taller than the other. "Mehanna," she said of the taller and of the shorter, "Dealla." Roselana nodded her understanding.

Dealla moved a finger over the left side of Roselana's cuirass as if writing upon it just above her heart. "Essa io d'Roselana." At the mention of Roselana's name the writing Dealla drew shined a fire red and seared into the cuirass. "Shiive awis. Io. Fire. Heart fire d'Roselana."

"You mean passion," she replied. "I 'will' take good care of Mehanna's bow."

All this time Guin stood behind Kallias with rapt attention on Dealla.

Days passed as the new training was added to the routine and slowed their work on the boat.

Chapter 25

Some days later, Guin sat fishing at the deepest point in the stream before it opened out to the beach. Here the area was slightly concealed and generously shaded, though it afforded a panoramic view of the sea and the long empty beach to the north. His line yanked in his hand again. Guin brought the fish up from the water and unhooked it. Then he un-looped another line from around a stub of the tree root and ran it through the fish's mouth and gill. When he set it back into the water, the fish struggled to swim free but was brought up next to a half-dozen others on the line. "I don't expect ya to come along, only to keep mum a few days."

Talek sat behind Guin, leaning against a tree and facing the ocean, his staff lying at his feet. "And in the meantime what am I to say that won't stir him up to race off before all is prepared?"

"That's obvious now, isn't it?" Guin fed out his line again. "But what's it mean? Ya say her courtship has begun. Are we out of time?"

"Naught but that her mourning time has ended. He intends to win her." Talek huffed, arms crossed. "Yar swordsman won't be liking that news."

"If ya're saying she's consented to permit Yungir to court her, ya're right. Kallias isn't going to like that." Guin snuggled the handle end of his fishing pole into a pile of stones. "So don't say it like that. Ya know how to make things vague."

Talek spat. "'Tis all the more evil upon us that his sister is the chosen one. Already begun has the suffering, as the search for these women spreads through Marisko. How long,

Pom da Guin? I don't like that ya cause me to assist him against my people."

"I'd have ya assist me, old man."

"And the other, too? Ya know 'twas her—"

"Ya've no need to remind me!" Guin spat out. "That rekinnder pakao seduced..." Guin's voice trailed off as he stared into the swirling eddy of the creek, ignoring the tug on his line. He whispered, "Everything would be different if it weren't for rekinnder."

"'Tis all the same now, no changing it. Give me leave to my people, Pom da Guin. Ya've already let us delay another eight days for training."

"He's done nothing to yar people. Ye'll stay awhile longer. Yar words are to keep him calm, that his sister is in no danger, while the rekinnder teaches the women her weapon." Guin pulled out an empty hook, baited it again, and returned it to the stream.

"None would dare harm the Baresian woman. Not to their purpose, as ya know." Talek said with certainty. He lifted his staff from the ground and leaned it against his shoulder. "Told ya all that occurs with the woman. What ya knew and what ya knew not, know ya now."

"Ha! All but the most important. All but when. Keep him calm, Talek, and he'll keep the pakao calm."

The seer stepped around the mystic and squatted so they were eye to missing socket, and snarled as he spoke. "What are ya thinking, Guin? She's a great danger especially to the two of us. She mistrusts us and our magic."

"There in the cave, did ya not see her? She spoke no word nor made motions with hands nor body except to reach out for what she wanted." Guin's eyes glinted as he spoke.

"I noticed. 'Tis her nature. Set fire and ice upon my staff as well. 'Tis permanently scarred. That's why she's dangerous and needs be destroyed."

"No. She's a right to life same as us. She teaches more than archery to the women. She teaches them words."

"Curses."

"Power. I know now how he learned to do it. I've an idea, a way to diminish Yungir."

"Or perhaps ya intend to rival him?"

"Yungir's gotten too much power too quickly. He's forgotten his lessons of discipline. It's all gone to his head. I need only learn to do the same. Then he'll—"

"Absorb yar energy like the others. He'll test ya and ye'll let him. Ya care too much for yar—"

"Enough!" Guin snapped. He pulled in his line and packed it away, then rose to his feet. "Remember to whom ya speak if ya're wanting to keep speaking."

Talek clenched his teeth and got to his feet quietly. "But one last viewing I've to tell the warrior. Includes the time for ya to leave here. After that, I'll go. 'Tis the last I do for ya, Pom da Guin."

"And ya'll keep mum."

"So long as I can." He walked back towards camp, stabbing the ground angrily with the end of his staff punctuating each step.

As the days continued and Talek's messages remained unchanged, a concentrated series of archery training sessions took up most of their daylight hours. Dealla first showed the other women how to use bow and arrow effectively as their range weapon. Then she taught them with a few words of her language how to call upon the enchantments with which she had imbued them.

Dealla instructed by example, by signs, by touch and infrequently by word. When she spoke in her tongue, it was received by confused looks and sometimes scowls. Only Roselana took an interest in learning the language. She would repeat phrases and words until Dealla could find an explanation she would understand. Dealla delighted in teaching the women to use their bows and more so in teaching her language to Roselana. She soon lost her mistrust of them though never of Guin nor Talek. Guin did not let his interest in Rekinnder be known outright, but he paid more than the usual attention to the training lessons, especially those given by Dealla. Roselana and Kallias observed his acute attention to the lessons.

Kallias had become comfortable with the time the
archery lessons added to their boat building and preparations
for departure. Ten days passed then twelve. Finally the day
came when Talek stood and pounded his staff after the
midday meal. How strange it was for him to speak his
message before the end of the day! Kallias and the women
were certain something had happened to Asadia. And they
were not yet prepared.

"Kept in the high place of Durgrinstar is Asadia.
Bereavement ceases for her. At that time, her garments burn
and she'll be dressed in fine raiment. Thereafter toward the
service of the longships her strength of mind is to bend, for
which reason she was taken."

Kallias cursed under his breath, then spoke aloud.
"Service of those pakao bastards. I'll kill any who lay a hand
on her."

"Six ten day and some ya worked here. Another ten day
and ya must requite yar kinnir, Warrior. Taught ya all I can.
Told ya all I have to say. Now, I go." And with that, Talek
walked out of the camp heading northwards up the coast to
Kanratu.

"Hold a moment!" Kallias shouted and rose up to go
after him. Guin leaped forward and caught Kallias by the
arm. "What isn't he saying, Guin? He never tells me
everything! I need to know!"

"Ya know what ya need to know, Kallias. Ya sister is well
and we have time to finish everything and load up."

"You're just going to let him leave like that?"

"He's served his purpose. Let it go."

Chapter 26

It had been four nights since Talek's last message. Kallias strolled away from the evening campfire as Dealla spoke and laughed with the other women. Perhaps Roselana was helping her with the Kinnir tongue. It was good Dealla had become comfortable with them all. He could not help but think that the absence of Talek was helpful. The old akinn never told him all he needed to know about Asadia; of that Kallias was certain. But at least now he had a timeline.

As he began his quiet meditations in preparation for his dance, Kallias heard Guin's voice and wondered who he might be talking to. He stepped around the bow of their new boat and looked toward the wreckage. Guin stood over a pile of rubble by the remains of the old ship mumbling his mystic's language and moving his hands. Kallias stopped to watch from a distance.

Guin's movements were brief as he made the rubble appear to catch fire. With a wave of his hand he removed the illusion. Then he repeated the spell, only he spoke the word Dealla had been teaching Roselana, the one for fire. The illusion repeated as before. However, this time when Guin waved the illusion away, the rubble had become charred and small embers faded in the cool night air. A line of blue-white smoke rose away from it.

Kallias watched as Guin repeated the experiment again and again substituting the rekinnder's words for ice, electricity and stone. Each time the illusion without the new words left no trace but with the words became more than just illusion. Only Pekoe's word for smoke, had no effect at all.

***

About half way through the meal, Yungir put his utensils down, sat back in his chair and spoke kindly to Asadia, "Ya can move about the tower and grounds. But ya keep to yar rooms. Why not enjoy yar freedom?"

"You call it freedom when I'm followed wherever I go? I can't go past the archway without your guards stopping me."

"It's for yar own protection." Yungir continued, "There's often dissension in the streets among the wixxon and akinn. So it's dangerous. For yar own safety ya'll remain up here. Why not see what it is ya have? Everything is visible from the butte... well, not much of a butte, more like a big rock. But ya can see the port, the city, and much of the surrounding countryside, some rolling hills and valleys, horses and equinoi." He paused. "The mountains in the distance sometimes have snow on them. They're... majestic."

"Mm. I've seen all that from the tower rooms," she responded quietly.

"Suit yar self, but I'll be taking the chance to show ya how pleasant yar life here can be." Yungir returned to his evening meal as he talked. "Ya'll have fresh flowers every morning to cheer ya. Ya may take yar midday in yar room if ya like, but come down for ya morning and evening meals."

"So, nothing new," she responded flatly.

Yungir ignored her comment. Again he put his utensils down, looking up from his plate. "Anything ya want or need, ya've only to ask." He leaned forward as if to tell her a confidence. "When ya've done with yar meal, I'd like ya to join me in the garden. Kaig will show ya the way." Without waiting for her to reply, Yungir rose from his place and left the room.

Later, Asadia stood in the center of a small paradise. All around her an aesthetic arrangement of trees, bushes and ground cover grew, some colorfully in bloom, others in a rich variety of greens. Yungir stepped out from the midst of this with a salmon-colored rose in hand. Asadia searched her surroundings with a quick eye. Stone pathways wound about groups of foliage in every direction with no indication of where they led.

"It isn't a labyrinth, if that's what ya're thinking. The exit is behind ya and to the left if ya're thinking to run. Of course ya're still on the butte."

Asadia took a visibly deep breath and remained where she stood.

"Good. This is for ya." He held the rose out to her and waited. His facial expression remained passively insistent. Finally, she took it without a word.

"I thought I should tell ya a little about myself. Walk with me." He held out an arm and again, waited.

She sighed. After a moment of staring at the flower, twirling as she rolled the stem between thumb and forefinger, Asadia slipped her free hand onto the proffered arm.

They turned down a path that wove around a cloverleaf-shaped set of flower pods. Each pod had been designed in rings, like a target, with pansies, then marigolds, then snapdragons of many colors, and bulls-eyed with roses of a single but different color for each pod.

"Why?" she asked.

"Why... what?" He took her hand and looped her arm in his, then put his hand gently atop hers. "Why would I tell ya about myself? Because we're to marry. Or perhaps, ya really want to know why I have a garden." He gave her a saccharine smile.

"No," she replied, "why me? And why kill my brother and why—"

"Stop, stop, stop," he said with a surprisingly humorous tone. "Yar marriage to me saves the gald. At least, that's what I'm told."

"That doesn't make any sense. Besides, I'm already betrothed to Omerion. I want to go home."

Yungir took an audible breath and slowly shook his head. "Then where is he? Did he come with yar brother?"

"Maybe."

He faced her. "I can tell by yar unshed tears ya believe as I do. He isn't coming for ya. Either he doesn't love ya or more likely, he's dead."

"No!" Angry tears poured down her cheeks. "He loves me and will come for me!"

"Ya've been gone all New Season long! Only yar brother came for ya and he's dead. Ya have no one but me." Asadia shook her head violently with every word he said. "It's the Bloodfish Navy that's responsible. It's their superstition and akinn prophecy to blame. But they offered me the choice of a bride to end the killing of mystics. And when I saw ya, I knew where they'd taken ya from. I recognized ya right off."

"You know me?" Tearful surprise filled her eyes and disbelief followed anger in her countenance.

"I met ya when I was a boy. Remember this?" Yungir opened his mouth and stuck out a tongue of fire. When her mouth dropped he closed his with a smirk. "Ya remember me now, don't ya."

"Please, let me go home."

"I can't do that. If I let ya go, the Bloodfish might do dreadful things to ya. They've likely made whores of the rest yar dark-haired friends already. Ya're alone and helpless. But ya don't have to be." Yungir stepped close to her and put an arm around her shoulders. "I can give ya everything, power and respect. Agree to marry me and everyone will do anything ya say."

"I don't want them to," she muttered.

"They will anyway because I'm the most powerful mystic anywhere in Iasegald. They fear me, so they will fear ya too." Asadia set her jaw, shook her head and swiped away the tears. "Let me show ya something. Ya can see the garden in all its splendor. Focus on that group there." After murmuring a few words, his hand burst into flame causing Asadia to jump. "Now look." He stretched his fiery hand and with another incantation, it left his hand and the pod burned to blackened ash."

Asadia cried out, "Stop! Please!"

Yungir laughed aloud. "It's illusion. See?" He brushed a palm across her eyes and everything was restored. "But it doesn't have to be illusion." With that statement and a short command, he flicked a finger at the rose in her hand. It caught fire, but unlike the flames of the now restored pod, heat from this one caused Asadia to drop the flower. It lay at her feet and burned until Yungir stomped it out. A mess of scorched petals, leaves and stem was all that remained. "I can do much more. I have every power any mystic of the Bloodfish Navy has ever mastered." He circled his hands around each other. Then stretched out his left hand towards the nearest rose bush and pantomimed picking one from the bush. A red rose snapped at the base of its stem and floated towards them. "I have telekinesis and levitation." The rose halted mid-air in front of Asadia. "Go ahead, take it." She hesitated. Without touching it, he pushed the rose toward her face. "TAKE IT!"

She quickly snatched the rose from the air and held it away from her.

"There isn't another mystic with all the abilities I have." As if pulling something invisible towards him, Yungir clenched his fist and drew it to his chest, emphasizing his words. "From every mystic I've reaped the essence of their talent so I could learn every kind of magic there is."

"Reaped? Like harvested?" She wrinkled her brow, perplexed.

"Let's just say, I found a way to learn by soaking it all in. Ya see, the rekinnder race here are fully connected to Iasegald. It is as if the gald breathes through them. I met a lovely pakao who taught me how to speak her language."

"The rekinnder are pakao, evil?"

"Evil? No, not evil exactly. But they are vile creatures. This one kept me in a spell. But when she taught me her language, I learned more than just words. Ya see they manipulate the elements, the zenu. And there is one element that exists in, around and through everything. That is the spirit element, the azenu. The power of the azenua, the spiritual being, is expected to be born into the race. But I discovered that my illusions took on the reality of the zenu when I added the rekinnder's words for them. I just applied it to the azenu as well."

Her puzzled expression did not change.

"I didn't hurt anyone. They recover in time. But ya understand what happened, don't ya? I became the azenua. I,

though not a rekinnder, became The Great Power. Only—"
he stopped short.

"Only something went wrong."

"I didn't say that."

"Your face did."

"She would not yield her spirit to me. The ability to
change form, the ancestral memory connection, whatever it is
that makes the real magic. I only wanted to learn. But she
kept it from me. Even tried to kill me. She was the last or I'd
have found another to give it to me."

"What—happened to her?"

"Oh... we parted ways." With a wave of his hand, which
caused Asadia to draw back, he dismissed the conversation.
"Listen. I don't want to frighten ya or be angry with ya
anymore. It isn't my fault ya're alone and helpless in the gald.
But ya can make yar life easier if ya cooperate. Ya don't even
have to like me... yet."

She sighed.

"I'll leave ya to find yar way back. It'll be a good way to
see the grounds." He took a few steps then turned. "And ya
can't follow me. Because I know transmigration as well."
Another word and a snap of his fingers caused him to
disappear in a puff of smoke.

Chapter 27

Shadows stretched like long fingers reaching across the camp. The sun had shone between passing clouds in their quiet parade all day long. Now as it began its sleepy decent, it promised to bring a masterfully painted sunset. The light golden hue skipped across the water's surface, noticed only occasionally by the craftsmen on the beach. It had been a long, still day for the little rescue army as they worked at some final preparations.

With a tired sigh, Pekoe rose from the circle of those who were mending a sail for use with their new boat. She trudged a few steps to the water bucket and picked up the ladle. There was little water left. Pekoe drank what was there. She took the bucket and marched past the center of camp where Kallias was putting the finishing touches on an arrow. Kallias and Roselana lifted smiling faces to her as she passed them. She walked between the outstretched shadows of the trees towards the well-worn path to the spring. In a day or two they would be leaving to find Asadia.

"This batch is finished, Roselana," Kallias said. "Take them to Dealla, please, while I clean up the filings." He loaded her arms with a great many arrows and sent her toward the group sewing the sails. The bits of feathers smoldered against the embers as Kallias tossed them in. The wood shavings he collected into a small kindling box. Just then he saw Pekoe racing back towards him in a panic. When she reached him, she could not speak but clasped his arm tightly, panted and pointed back towards the stream. "What is it Pekoe?" Kallias responded. He trotted away to investigate, with Pekoe at his heels. He found where she had dropped the bucket. It seemed fine and had not spilled much. He looked through the trees, up the beach northward. Pekoe slapped at his arm several times as he picked up the bucket. She stared out over the waves and pointed.

Moments later, Kallias burst in upon the others at their sewing and chatting. "We must hide from view, up in the hills. Cover our tracks and put away any evidence of our being here," He commanded urgently. "No time to explain. Just do it! They come."

Guin was first to his feet. "A longship." It was more a statement than a question.

At Kallias' nod they moved. "We weren't seen because of the trees," he reported and doused the fire. The others speedily packed away whatever small items were scattered around the camp. Guin headed for their boat and soon it disappeared into thin air. The women shoved the sail and mending materials beneath the boards of one of the huts. Then each woman gathered her weapons.

Kallias and the girls made their way towards the forested hills, they swept the sand roughly with branches attempting to cover their tracks. Guin took the men's weapons from the hut and followed after. Roselana went back to sweep away his tracks as the bow of a longship came into view from around the trees and rocks to the west.

They were too sluggish, Dealla noted and hurried them up the hill. She lifted her arms gracefully. A whirlwind of air moved around her and blew the sand swiftly. Foot trodden, half-swept sand became ripples, natural in its appearance, as if no one had stepped foot on the Point since the last typhoon. Then she slipped into her serlcat form and bounded into the forest behind the others.

They were well away from being out in the open. Through a hidden recess of boulders and vines they watched as the longship's hull came into full view.

Moments later, the Bloodfish sailors cast the anchor, and disembarked by dropping a small boatload of men over the side. The tide brought the small boat to a soft landing just where the crispin's body had been dragged back into the water. There was much unintelligible shouting and guffawing as men climbed out of the smaller boat and began to walk around the campsite with their guns drawn.

"Leg of a dog!" Guin exclaimed. "We left the meat smoker exposed! And the target dummies."

"There is no meat in the smoker. I put it all away," assured Charlise. Then with less confidence she added, "In the storage chest in my hut."

Kallias shook his head. "Perhaps they might not even inspect the huts." He winced as one ventured into the doorway of Charlise's hut.

After a long moment, the man came out without anything in hand or setting up an alarm. He merely shouted, "Looks deserted."

"This place hasn't been used since the maogra came." Kallias recognized the voice and the man, Maltax, as the captain turned to squint his eyes up into the trees.

"Aye Cap'n. Though I don't recall this bein' here," said another as he hit the smoker with the butt of his rifle.

Kallias balled a fist. "That's him. The captain and his crew that threw me over. I'll gut him! Asadia might still be on that ship!" Kallias grabbed the hilt of his sword and was about to leap out.

Roselana grabbed his shoulder. "Wait."

"What're ya thinking man?" Guin hissed through clenched teeth. "Ya weren't on that ship yesterday. It's been months."

The setting sun caught Kallias' sword as he pulled it momentarily from its scabbard and replaced it. Maltax moved as if he caught the glint. He started toward the open way between the huts, calling a couple of his men to him.

Pekoe urged them in a quiet voice. "I think he saw us."

"Ssh," Guin hushed them. "We aren't sure. Stay quiet but be ready. And don't let the light hit yar swords."

"But," Pekoe was hushed with Roselana's cupping hand.

Guin pulled his flintlocks from his belt and quietly cocked the hammers back. Zetrine held her sword down into the shade and pulled it from its sheath. Jamila had steel in hand as they all crouched quietly behind the trees and bushes watching Maltax come closer. Just as the sailors reached the lower trees, a shot rang out from the campsite. Maltax and his men spun about and raced back to the others. A cry went up as well as several more shots were fired from out of sight to the west.

"What in the blazes is it?" shouted Maltax.

"A serlcat! It's just there, out o' range!" Some of the men ran out of sight before Maltax could order them to stop.

"Hold yar fire! Get back here ya sea slugs!" Maltax called after them.

He turned once again to look into the trees. Satisfied there was nothing amiss, he ordered a fire to be made and his men to settle in.

"They camp. The captain is down there. I can avenge my honor and my sister." Kallias growled.

"Yar sister 's in Durgrinstar. Talek's been tellin' ya. Ya get ya self killed now, she's gone permanently and the rest 'll never get home. Now keep to ya self, Kallias, or ye'll get us all killed." Guin held a pistol up.

Kallias backed off with a nod.

"They're settling. That means we've got a wait ahead of us." Guin looked around to each of the girls. Pekoe rubbed her eyes with a sleepy smile as Guin looked her way. "We need to keep a watch." Guin motioned to the girls. "Let's get further up. Try to get some rest." As they climbed up toward the clearing, a sudden rustle of bushes nearly caused Guin to fire his gun. He halted just in time as Spiritdancer leaped out of the brush into the group. "If I'd fired this, we'd be given away and ya'd be dead," he snarled and his face reddened with anger.

Kallias brushed a hand over Spiritdancer's head. It had been a long while since she had taken this form. There was no shudder this time. "We can't make a fire either. Hope everyone brought blankets," he said with a wry grin, knowing full well not even he had thought to bring anything except weapons. Fortunately, they had plenty of those. The women each looked from one to another and shook their heads. Kallias nodded. "I know. We'll have to make do with what we have until they leave. Take turns keeping watch."

Dealla appeared. "Jaia." She pointed upward and in the direction of her tree house. Dealla took Pekoe by the hand and Charlise as well. She made decisive steps away from the clearing and towards her home.

Kallias saw the wary expression on Guin's face. "What's she doing?" growled the mystic.

"She has a safe place for us to stay."

Zetrine looked between the men as they stared at each other, then followed Dealla. Jamila followed while Roselana stood beside Guin, her eyes pleading. "Fine," he relented. "But we can't see what they're up to from here."

"And they can't see us, either. Come," she said.

Kallias added, "You'll like it. She made a nice tree house." With that he gave Guin a hearty pat on the shoulder and followed behind Jamila.

Roselana put an arm through Guin's and smiled. His countenance softened.

At the tree house, Dealla made herself into a tufted squirrel and scampered up the tree. Then as rekinnder she lowered the climbing rope.

"I'll remain down here." Guin turned to Roselana. "Ya go up if ya can."

Roselana nodded and was the first to climb the rope and see the unusual home Dealla had fashioned for herself. It was small with a nest and what appeared to be a table and nothing else. Dealla busied herself spreading furs out across the flooring and motioning for Roselana and the other ladies to lay down as they came up. As soon as the five were snugly resting upon the tiny floor, Dealla diminished into the squirrel and descended the tree. She became the serlcat and found a place next to Kallias as they prepared for nightfall.

"I'll take first watch," Kallias announced. He pet the serlcat then rose to his feet, heading back the way they had come. Spiritdancer followed. Kallias positioned himself on the rim where he might be able to hear as well as see his enemy.

Maltax and his men made a campfire on top of the sand-filled pit. He cast his gaze toward the hillside repeatedly. A

sailor approached him. "Cap'n I'd like to take a walk about."
Maltax nodded absently and searched for something to sit on.

The hum of crickets stirred the air. Kallias noted the
sailor on foot wander away from the fire. Kallias' eyes locked
back onto the captain who had left him for drowned. "He
won't do anything," Kallias whispered to the cat, "It's getting
too dark."

Maltax walked around the front of a hut and to the three
short steps leading to the doorway and stopped. Something
beneath the hut seemed to have caught his eye. Kallias
watched him pull a canvas bag from under the step. Maltax
bent to examine it, parting the cloth with a drawn stiletto.
Inside was a steel tankard. As he hooked the handle and
brought it up, it swiveled on the blade and the remaining
contents of a liquid poured out. He sniffed. "Tea?" Maltax
dropped the cup into the sand. His eyes were aimed at the
dark trees of the hillside.

Suddenly a shout went up from the sailor. "Cap'n! Cap'n
Maltax!"

Maltax raced to meet the sailor, who ran toward him.
"What is it?"

"There's something there." The sailor pointed. "It's big.
I ran into it. But I can't see it."

Maltax's eyes went wide. "Invisible?" He looked briefly
up the hillside then back to the sailor. "Show me where."

The man took them all to the side of the boat which
Guin had hidden with the illusion. "It's here Cap'n. I swear it.
Ya can walk into it."

He demonstrated by walking a few steps gingerly with
his hands outstretched until he hit upon the side of the small
sloop. "There!"

Maltax pulled a flintlock revolver from his belt.
"Concentrate on it!" Maltax ordered. With effort most of
them began to see the boat. "Search the huts again. This time
turn everything over! Tear 'em apart if ya have to! Search the
boat, too!"

Kallias pulled back further into the shadows.

The men hurried to do as ordered. Soon the one who
had seen nothing in the hut Charlise lived in, came out of it

with a cloth-wrapped object in his hand. "Captain! I found a locker with meat in it!"

Maltax stood beside the covered fire pit scanning the ridge with narrowed eyes. "They're here. To the hill men! Take the women alive if ya can. But kill the mystic." Maltax took an arm sized piece of burning wood to use as a torch. Some of the others followed suit.

"Mystic?" asked one of the men with trepidation in his voice.

"Takes a mystic to hide something big as a boat in plain sight. And they're not on it. So they're up there. I thought I seen something shine earlier. Be ready with yar arms!"

Kallias backed away slowly from his hidden spot. Glad the sun had not fully set, he ran relentlessly, dodging trees and jumping fallen branches. Spiritdancer had already disappeared. The royal blue tint of twilight upon everything gave Kallias a surrealistic feeling as if it were a dream. Guin slept with one eye half open. "Guin! They found the boat!"

Guin fairly flew to his feet from his position against the tree. "Shite! Get the women up."

Spiritdancer shifted from serlcat into the squirrel and scurried up the tree, changed form again and woke the women. From the treetop, the women could see small bobbing dots of firelight as the sailors began their ascent. "Get your bows girls," Roselana said in a hushed tone.

"I want the captain," Kallias said to Guin.

"We need some strategy and quick," responded Guin.

"We have the trees for cover."

"I can shoot twice from a tree. After that, unless I've plenty of time for reloading, it's the sword. If we can get the women to spread out in the trees maybe."

"Yes. They'll be focused on where the arrows are coming from. We could circle them."

Roselana climbed down the rope behind the men. "It'll take too long to climb down and back up another tree."

Kallias peered up to Dealla. Her head appeared over the side, waiting for Roselana to step away from the rope so another of the women could descend. Kallias caught her eye. "We need to get the women high into the surrounding trees for an advantage, Dealla." He observed her large exotic eyes hoping she understood.

Dealla held his gaze as if absorbing the meaning of his words. Then the shine of her eyes flashed and she disappeared into her house. Suddenly a squeal went up from the women as the largest branches moved and stretched outward from beneath their feet, carrying them towards the neighboring trees.

"Stop it! You are frightening me!" cried Zetrine.

A shout went up from the sailors below. They had heard the women.

The branches continued to spread out. Dealla ran and jumped from one tree to another until a half circle of them had intertwined their branches.

"I'm climbing back up." Roselana did just so and then pulled the rope up after her.

Kallias checked to see all the women ready in their spots. Most were barely visible in the darkness beneath the canopy. They nocked their arrows. He gave Guin a confident nod before finding the thickest of tree trunks to use for cover while making his way flank of the approaching men.

Dealla ran along the limbs making sure the small branches and leaves shielded the women and they could shoot through them. "No word," she said to each of them. Then she found a place for herself and prepared to shoot. The noisy footfall of the longship men approached. Weaving through the brush and trees, each held his torch aloft to light up the forest around them. It was obvious from the branches when the searchers paused in the clearing and when they moved again. Not so obvious was Kallias' stealthy movement between the trees. Only Dealla's night vision could make him out, slipping from tree to bush to tree to rock.

Something moved and a shot rang out. "Do ya see them Barlash?" called Maltax. Dealla held her breath as Kallias crouched behind a boulder. Barlash's random shot was a near miss.

"No something moved there," the man called back. "We can't see a thing Cap'n!"

Maltax held his pistol high as well as his torch. "Then fire at anything that moves."

Someone moved near Maltax and he fired his pistol. The cry of one of his own men rang out. "Shite!" He put the pistol into its holster and drew his sword. When the man was shot, the others ceased moving forward and listened and watched for each other. When they stopped Maltax stopped. "They're close now mates. Arms to the ready." Maltax held his torch out in the direction of the man he had shot. He was not dead but lay moaning and clutching a leg. "They'll come at us from the trees if they're smart." He yelled out. "Let's burn it!" With that he threw his torch forward and right to the foot of the tree that held Dealla's house. The other men threw their torches as well. Some landed clear of anything and burned alone but a few ignited the underbrush below the trees. It did not work. Dealla manipulated the flames and choked them out. The fires appeared to extinguish themselves for no apparent reason.

In response to the failed attempt, a volley of arrows flew from the darkness high above the men. Two of them hit their marks. Men cried out. "Shite!" Maltax grumbled and took refuge from the raining death. He took advantage of the time to unholster his pistol and reload it.

"Maltax!" Kallias jumped out from his hiding spot.

"Ya're supposed to be dead!" Maltax fired a shot. At sight of the gun, Kallias ducked behind a tree. The bullet whistled past his head. It hit a tree and sent splinters airborne all around. The weapon's one shot round was spent as the barrel smoked. Maltax dropped it and drew his sword. "Come on ya bastard!" Maltax roared with an arm out, waving Kallias onward.

Kallias charged with a snarl. They met in the middle of the forest with a loud reverberation of steel. "You should have killed me when you had the chance!" He yelled.

Maltax shouted, "Perfect! Looks like this be my second chance, dog!"

Kallias and Maltax pushed their weight onto each other as they rivaled blades. The swordsman spun full circle to his right, giving way and causing Maltax to stagger forward.

Kallias' curved blade caught the man's underarm, cutting through the leather and flesh.

Maltax howled in pain as he gripped his side. The captain scanned around and saw his crew overtaken with volleys of arrows. He ran. Kallias chased, but slid to a halt as Maltax stopped short and put his sword in his left hand, pulling forth a second pistol. The captain pivoted. "I'll not miss this time!" He cocked back the pistol's hammer with his thumb. He faltered and it clicked futilely.

Around them, the men fired wildly into the trees. Guin fired at the places where the flash of powder could be seen. He hit his mark with both barrels then reloaded. Once a cry went up from one of the women, but none fell from their places. The arrows continued to rain down upon the longship men. One of the men shouted a retreat. It was not Maltax, but they all began to run down the hill. Guin left his place behind the tree and pursued the fleeing men. The women still sent arrows after them. One of these nicked Guin and he dove for cover into a bush.

Surprised to have another opportunity, Kallias tightened his grip on his sword. His eyes burning volcanic with sudden emotion, he charged with a battle cry. "For Asadia!" With little more than starlight to see by, he closed the distance between them fast. Maltax reset the hammer and fired his round hastily. The bullet grazed Kallias' shoulder but did not slow him down. Maltax dropped the pistol and deflected Kallias' overhead blow with an upward thrust of his broadsword. He grunted as their bodies crashed together. They pushed against each other neither giving way. Kallias dropped one hand to his thigh. An instant later, his little dagger sank deep into the captain's stomach.

Maltax looked into Kallias' eyes with disbelief. With his free hand he grabbed at the knife hilt and backed away from the warrior. He yanked the blade from his torso. Madly he charged with the dripping dagger in his bloody hand. Kallias deftly sidestepped, letting the wild haired captain careen past him into some bushes. Maltax wheeled about, paused and gasped for air. "Ya're quick but not quick enough!" He exchanged the poniard for his sword and charged again.

Kallias took a step, then leaped with a twist of his body. The flash of his blade cut through the air as it met Maltax's momentum. As he came full circle, Kallias closed his eyes, listening. The moment his feet touched the ground, Kallias froze, body leaned forward, one knee bent, blade poised at the completion of his swing. The gald fell silent except for the distinct thud of a large body and a smaller object hitting the leaf covered forest floor. Slowly he stood and sheathed his blade.

Guin came back through the brush from the direction of the camp, torch in hand, just in time to see the death blow to Maltax. He halted. The girls began to climb down out of their trees. "They're making a run for it," Guin said as he recovered himself. "They'll be setting sail for reinforcements. We've got to leave."

"We're not finished with the sail," objected Zetrine, the first to reach the scene. She shuddered when she caught sight of the disembodied head of the Bloodfish captain. Charlise joined the group with tears flowing down her cheeks. "Are you all right?" Zetrine asked her.

"It's just a scratch. I was more frightened than hurt."

"How much longer..." Kallias began.

"No time," interrupted Guin. "We must use it as is and repair what's left as we sail. It can be done."

"But we have no stores aboard," whimpered Charlise, trying to wipe the tears from her face.

"What is it?" asked Roselana when she approached the group with Jamila and Pekoe.

"We have to go," explained Guin. "Now." Dealla appeared behind the group and listened. Guin continued. "Charlise and Zetrine gather whatever food we have. Pekoe, Roselana and I will fill the water containers. Kallias, if ya, Jamila and Dealla will collect as many of these arrows as ya can find and bring aboard whatever other armor and tools we need. Oh, and get what guns and ammunition ya can find too," Guin added.

"You mean—" Jamila stopped short in her question.

"From the bodies, of course," Guin replied. "There are at least three of...four dead." He glanced at their expressions.

"Kallias will get the captain's weapons. Ya need not touch him."

Kallias' eyes met Jamila's then Dealla's. He observed the latter's expression for a long moment, then offered a small, subtle smile. "Let's go. We'll need torches."

Chapter 28

Kallias stood with a foot on the bow of the newly crafted vessel as it broke through the waves. His long, black, curly mane blew with the crosswind. Never before had he been on such a boat which moved so fast. His people built only small fishing dories. He felt exhilarated, almost as if he were flying. The journey to save his sister was that much closer to its end. He worried they may be too late. After all, if Talek thought taking her to this mad mystic was a good idea, he would not have admitted it.

Kallias surveyed his seaward bound companions. He left the bow watch, and Pekoe stepped up to it. Each of the women were armored in the rugged longship men's leather. *An odd humor of fate for them to wear the gear of the very people who caused such grief.* They no longer resembled the innocent young women he had once met in a cave. No longer pale and delicate, their ruddy complexions, muscular development and calloused hands attested to their training and strenuous work. Hardened warriors now, each of them came prepared for the journey and battle ahead of them.

They traveled a league west of the misty shoreline, topped with slopes and mountain peaks. Its lush green forest protruded from a white fog. As these became a mere jagged line on the horizon, Guin steered the boat northward. He cut a gallant figure at the wheel with his eyes locked forward, his wispy ponytail whipping and waving in the strong breeze.

Pekoe yelled from the bow. "Vessel ahead starboard side, Guin!" She pointed.

Guin steered the boat to port. "Did they see us?"

"I don't know. But, they're headed this way."

"I'll disguise us. But keep silent." Guin held his arms up and chanted a spell. When he threw his arms wide they were suddenly riding the back of a huge saber crispin. Zetrine screamed. "Quiet!" he barked. Zetrine covered her mouth. "Close yar eyes. Ya'll feel the boat beneath ya." Guin suggested. Charlise closed her eyes as did Zetrine. The rest remained still as Guin navigated them away from the path of the approaching ship. Someone on the longship shouted and pointed in their direction. Guin chanted other words and soon it appeared that the saber crispin with their sail disappeared beneath the surface and they floated upon nothing. The men on the longship lost interest and moved away. It had been close enough.

The longship turned heading further away from their starboard, eastward. Safety was assured them, but they all knew where the Bloodfish ship was going. Guin adjusted their heading north again. He watched until the longship was a thimble upon the sea. Then with a single word the boat took on its natural appearance.

Above them, they heard the screech of a falcon. The peregrine swooped down and landed on the Blade Dancer's outstretched arm, clutching hold of his bracer. He ran his finger the length of the bird's breast when the falcon's flapping came to a halt. Her darker feathers glimmered, reminiscent of the serlcat's silver-steel tinted coat, as she tucked her wings to her sides. Her bird-of-prey eyes darted keenly over her surroundings and scanned the water in the direction of the disappearing longship. She screeched and cocked her head to one side as if to question the longship's motive for the land it sailed toward. Then she rested her eyes on Kallias and blinked.

"When we come close to the port of Durgrinstar, I need you to fly ahead of us and report anything you find to be useful information," Kallias asked quietly of the bird as his knuckle ran the length of the creature's breast. Spiritdancer blinked again. Then she lifted wing, pushed off Kallias' arm and flew towards land to the east.

"Now where's she going?" asked Guin.

"To keep a bird's eye view of things for us," replied Kallias. He began pacing the deck.

"Durgrinstar is to the north. She's headed towards Saungtau Shores." Guin scowled and shook his head. "We're between the two about here."

"Where can we land in Durgrinstar without being seen?" Kallias' hair blew into his face as he came to Guin's side at the wheel. He swept it aside vainly trying to keep it from his view.

"We need to sneak in as close as we can away from port," he replied. "There's an inlet to the west of the city with a long beach front. We can bring her in on the high tide and beach her." Guin paused. His gray eyes met Kallias' gaze.

"Won't that make it hard to put her out to sea again? What if we have to flee?" He questioned Guin in earnest.

"Flee? Ya mean get away quick."

"Exactly. What if we get Asadia and then need to get away quick?"

"Hadn't considered that."

"What did you think we were going to do with only the eight of us? Take on the entire Bloodfish navy?" He was confounded.

"Well, I...uh," stammered Guin. "I figured we'd go in and fight like we trained. If we won we'd have our choice of ships, if not—" Guin hesitated.

Kallias waited. When nothing more was said, he searched the older man's visage curiously. Guin let his eyes drop slightly. "You're expecting we'll be dead!" Kallias threw a hand up. "Well that's perfect." He raised his voice with arguing so that the women turned full attention to the men. He glanced away past Guin to Jamila who had taken up the aft watch. Jamila Curled her lips in, then turned her face away. He lowered his voice and hissed through his teeth. "You might have said you didn't have any faith in our success. Do you even know how we'll find my sister...or if?"

Guin sighed, stared out over the bow and adjusted the helm. "Alright." He held silent a long moment before speaking reluctantly. "Talek saw exactly where she is and what's happening with her." He worked his jaw a moment.

"She's in the manse tower. The Mystics' Manse is on a tall rock overlooking the sea. The port is to one side and rough country to the other. Every child born gifted spends his or her first schooling years there, learning how to use the gift. I know it like I know my way around a ship. Yungir took it over when the mystics fled. And I can get us in without being seen—I hope."

Kallias peered ahead into the distance then spoke to Guin sternly. "So why the lack of faith?"

"She's definitely there. I don't know in which room. But, she's being prepared for her wedding," he added flatly. He turned his head to Kallias, eyes steady. "She may not want to go back with ya, Kallias." Kallias growled like the serlcat. Guin faced away again.

"She will not be wed. And who is to say she may not want to come with me when she finds I'm alive?" Kallias' tanned cheeks grew red.

"Each time Talek said, 'she has not been harmed this day,' he meant she'd been treated well that day. She was given gifts or was pampered or in some way assuaged and sought after. She's been courted all this time." Guin scowled and shook his head. "I swear to ya—"

"Well she won't. She's engaged to Omerion," he replied, interrupting Guin.

"Omerion." Guin's eyes held pity for Kallias. "Is that the best friend who was killed?"

Kallias' countenance dropped.

Guin explained. "This is what the navy meant to do, because of the prophecy. Make her one of their people to save them. This is how. She marries Yungir and he leaves the men unharmed."

"I'm here, to save her. No matter what." His expression became enlightened. "Ah! Is that why he said I would bring death and destruction?"

"Do ya still intend to take her from Yungir? Yar Asadia has been treated well. The wrong has been done to akinn and wixxon and the mystics of the longships." Guin looked at Kallias with some fire in his eyes. "He's very powerful, and he will retaliate. Death and destruction indeed."

The Baresian's mind had begun to swirl heavily with this newly realized dilemma. *To save my sister means to harm the people of these lands; to leave her be means to lose the last of my family. But it isn't any harm by my hand. What that mad mystic chooses to do is not on me or Asadia or any of us. Just as what he has done before, this is not.* He reasoned within. *No, there is no dilemma after all.*

"I intend to take her." Kallias spoke decisively but without animosity. Guin had been of great help thus far and probably intended to be helpful even now. He was not the enemy nor was the old seer, Talek. However, Guin's remarks caused a question to arise. "If you don't agree with me, why have you done all this? To help rescue someone who may not wish to be saved?"

Guin scanned the horizon and the sky around them as if searching for something. At last, his eyes settled on Kallias. "We won't know for certain until we see her. Besides, we began together, and I must also face Yungir, mystic to mystic."

Kallias tilted his head in response. "Aren't you concerned that he might do to you whatever it is he did to the others?"

"Because of Yungir many mystics lost their lives unnecessarily and others fled in fear." Guin worked his jaw and sighed heavily. "I could have... should have stopped him."

Kallias' gazed at Guin steadily. "No. You'd only have gotten yourself killed—really killed Better this way, unexpected attack."

Guin harrumphed. "True then, ya're right. But now, I know how to beat him."

"Let's hope you're right."

"But tell me, Kallias. Why has the rekinnder gone toward Sungtau Shores?"

"I know as much as the rest of you. I asked her to scout and she flew that way. I don't know if she understood me." Kallias turned about face into the wind with his arms folded to keep his cloak around him.

"I can't believe she misunderstood ya. We head north. I don't see her going nor coming from the north." Guin growled in his chest then continued. "She'll betray ya, Kallias. I've had a bad feeling about her from the start and didn't keep that from ya. If I had killed her when—"

Kallias gave a sideways glance to his left at Guin. "She could have killed us all any time. She had multiple chances. Who would she betray us to? Yungir? Your Bloodfish navy?" Kallias retorted quickly but with a calm demeanor.

"A rekinnder is dangerous and more powerful than ya can imagine. She has control over ya. Ya'll see, Kallias. If ya bring death and destruction, it's through her!"

Kallias lifted his eyes skyward. "I trust her. There's a reason she's gone that way and we'll know it soon enough."

"It's for yar sake I've accommodated her as well as I could. I continue to do so, but if she turns, I'll not hold back." Guin scanned the faces of the women as they exchanged glances.

Charlise spoke their thoughts. "Kallias, we stand with you. We don't believe she's a pakao." The others nodded. "Even though she is frighteningly strange," she added.

"She has fed us and taught us to fight with elemental arrows." Roselana spoke with determination and stared boldly at Guin. "How can you continue to doubt, Guin?"

"She's rekinnder. Ya just don't understand what that means." Resignation filled Guin's words as he looked upon her fondly.

The high chirping screech of the falcon could be heard overhead. Kallias shaded his brow. Spiritdancer swooped down among them and as her wings went upward to land, she changed in a swirl of blue light and stood upon the deck. "Kallias," she said, urgently.

"Dealla." He smiled and approached her. "There you are, already. What news?" Kallias glanced over his shoulder at Guin, giving him an I-told-you-so smirk.

At first, she rushed through her message in her native tongue. Then began again in Kinnir. "Swarm like ant upon hill!" she said excitedly. "Upon forest, upon akinn, upon Saungtau! Boats to port." She continued, gesturing to assist her speaking in the Kinnir tongue. In her excitement, she included the others, who stared with puzzled expressions.

"Kill, tie up, lock in places, break, destroy. With stick and fire and black powder!" These images they understood.

Kallias hurried to the starboard. In the distance, he could only make out billows of smoke. "Guin?"

"Kallias." Dealla's voice was low and foreboding.

"We're headed north. Nothing we can do about them, Kallias," answered Guin to his incomplete question.

Dealla touched him. Kallias regarded her as her hand rested on his arm. She rattled off a string of Rekinnder words. "No, Dealla. We can't save those people. We have to continue to Asadia." Kallias glanced to the women. They all shook their heads sympathetically.

She pursed her lips. "Eot d'maogra," she said frankly. Then in a single, smooth movement vaulted over the side and dove into the sea.

Many shouts went up, "No! Dealla! Come back!"

Kallias turned to Roselana. "What does it mean, eot d'maogra?"

Roselana stepped forward. "She said, 'the maogra can.'"

Guin called down from the helm, "Let her go. If we can't depend on her, we'll do without her. The very best we can do is stop all this as quickly as we can. If the wind keeps steady, we'll reach Durgrinstar in about two night's time. There's an inlet where we'll disembark. We must take everything we can with us." The women agreed and everyone returned to their stations, to their watches and their lines.

Kallias gazed out over the sea towards the coast. A strange long line like a path of smooth water cut through the ripples from the wake of their boat into the distance. Soon the rough current closed the path up and they sailed on.

Some time in the evening, though not long after nightfall, Dealla returned aboard the boat. She sat upon the anchor capstan, put her face in her hands and wept. No one asked questions. Kallias rubbed her back. No one said a thing.

Chapter 29

Kallias was the first to leap ashore as the boat landed. The women lined up in formation passing along and tossing the bundles of gear to Kallias. The last was tossed and he stretched out a helping hand as each of the girls jumped out onto the soft, wet sand. They quickly gathered packs and readied themselves. He and Guin carried as much of the supplies as they could without encumbering themselves, leaving lighter loads for the ladies.

"There's a small cave near the base of the rock. We can put our provisions there, then continue up the seaward face." Guin indicated the area with the sweep of a hand.

The city of Durgrinstar was visible to the east of their landing point. To this side of it loomed a great ragged rock upon which was a tall edifice. The southern side of this tower-like manse balanced upon a precipice overhanging the sea.

"That's the high point Talek spoke of. We'll find yar sister there." Guin shifted from Kallias to Dealla. "Could be we'll have to fight our way in. Best stay as ya are. We may need yar bow." He nodded towards Dealla. "If ya will."

They kept close to what trees and rocks ran along the beach until they reached the slope of land leading to the rock. There was no activity on this side of the town nor in the countryside, as this part of the world was just waking up. They scurried single file up the slope to a small indent in the rocks. This was the cave Guin spoke of. Here they stored their packs and checked their armor and weapons, gearing up for a fight none of them wanted.

Guin spoke in hushed tones. "There's another cave beneath the manse which leads out to the other side. It's used for traffic to the east inlet. We must be sure yar sister isn't whisked away through it. If we climb this side, we may get in with little resistance."

"How do we know where Asadia is?" asked Zetrine.

"I'll use my skill to search undetected. Once we're inside set yar selves up by twos to guard our way out and to watch for trouble." Guin nodded to the women and then to Kallias. "I'll go to search the higher rooms. There're three large chambers in the main body of the manse. One is a counsel chamber with long benches, one is a large open room for audiences, the third is Yungir's. I don't know what that one is like, but ya must go through the other two to reach it." He squinted at each of them as if trying to decide something.

"Perhaps Dealla should come with me. She's able to make herself undetectable in another way." Guin stared at her. She looked to Kallias.

Kallias shook his head at the thought. "She will come with me."

"Very well then." Guin shrugged.

Kallias returned with a nod. "Let's make haste."

"This way." Guin led them out of the small cave and around to the seaward side of the mountainous rock. Here large stones protruded from the precipice at odd intervals causing an uneven, zigzag pathway. Upward they climbed, clinging necessarily close to the steep face of the cliff where slick, sharp-edged rocks formed the only handholds along the way. Though it did not require scaling, footholds were slippery with the salty sea spray covering the rocks. Around westward then back to the seaward side the terrain led them. Kallias took a position behind the others to give the occasional boost or steady hand to the women.

The rising sun eased the morning chill as it pushed away the shade that had previously concealed the climbers. When they reached the top of the rocks, they lined up against an outside wall of the main tower. "We need to go around to the west side. There should be a way down into the courtyard from there. That's where we'll find trouble, so be ready," Guin spoke quietly when they had all assembled.

They hugged against the wall as their toe tips almost reached the falling edge of the flat rock. Each shimmied along behind Guin to the western side. A narrow path between the rough black rock and the tower wall led down into the courtyard as Guin had said. They began their descent here. As they reached the courtyard, the clamor of busy people echoed off the stone. Guin halted the group and signaled them to duck down behind the rocks. From the safety of the crevice they watched Guin and waited his command. "Bloodfish men," Guin whispered as three men walked across the courtyard from a doorway to the broad archway that led down into the city.

"Kallias," Guin motioned him to come forward. He slipped low and huddled near Guin. Guin held a finger to his lips, gestured with his head and slowly stood just enough to see clearly into the courtyard. Kallias peeked with him and followed his gaze into the area, taking in every detail with a keen eye. The building formed a backward L shape, where they hid beneath the tower wall being the short leg. At the corner was a shaded alcove with crates and bags piled against it. The long leg was covered with an awning. A door in the middle faced the open courtyard. Guin slid back down.

"I'll open the door for us. Swords and knives only if needed. We don't want to attract attention. Kallias, take the women to that corner there and then along the wall and inside once the door's open. If anyone sees ya, don't hesitate." He gave Kallias a knowing gaze and drew a finger across his throat. Kallias responded with a firm nod and regarded the women as they bobbed their heads and made ready.

Guin placed his fingertips upon his forehead and murmured something in his strange speech. He disappeared before them. Yet as they watched the place where he had been there seemed to be a ripple in the scenery around them. As soon as the ripple moved away from the wall it ceased and they could no longer tell where Guin was. They all stared long and hard at the door, bracing themselves for the quick sprint. The handle dropped and the latch released.

"Now!" Kallias said with an urgent hushed tone. They darted to the door as swiftly as it had unlatched and slipped along the wall awaiting Guin. The door opened fully. "In! In!" Kallias ushered them in and was immediately behind them latching the door softly.

They had entered a kitchen. Guin stood over a body, covering it with a large table cloth. He motioned for the others. "That way up those stairs. Then ya go to the left while I go right. Understand?" he whispered.

Kallias nodded. Ignoring the body, he made his way up the stairs with the women in tow, then quickly moved to the left as they separated from Guin. At the top of the stairs Guin went to the right and disappeared again.

The sun rose, beaming in through the high windows, casting but a few shadows to conceal them at the corners and door wells of the first room. Along both sides were rows of benches. Under the windows sat four high-backed chairs. There was but one door besides the one through which they entered. It was located behind and to the right of the raised platform on which the chairs sat. Kallias appraised the room from the darkened corner with the women bent low beside him. Finding the room void of life they slipped past the benches to the right of the platform quickly. "Wait!" he spoke in a hushed tone, stopping the girls in their tracks as he put his ear to the door to listen.

Silence.

He found the door locked but with a simple latch. He guided his small dagger down the jamb. With a small click, the door opened slightly, enough to peek in. "Alright, let's go." He quickly made his way inside with the others on his tail. The room was large without furnishings as Guin had said. A long, rectangular area surrounded on three sides with pillars afforded them some seclusion in the shadows. Curtains lined the walls all around top to bottom. Even the door they had entered through disappeared into the surroundings. The vestibule arched high above them but even more so did the ceiling of the central room. Through a sectioned glass skylight, sunlight cast a diamond shape to the marble floor. To the farthest end another platform rose along the width of the room and to its curtained wall, though without furnishings of any kind. There did not appear to be another door in the place at all. "Search the walls" Kallias said. They all felt along the walls, pulling the curtains away frantically.

Dealla reached out and grabbed Kallias by the arm. "Tiau d'pakin..." She did not get a chance to finish her words as suddenly a loud buzzing filled their ears and everything went black. The girls screamed. Kallias felt something like ropes winding themselves around him, tying his arms to his sides and his ankles together. Dealla spoke a Rekinnder warning. The buzzing began to emulate vocal inflections. The sound of quick and heavy footfall crossed the room. A man shouted, "Stop her!" Then the same voice cried out in pain followed by a thud. Kallias heard the door close just before the light returned to his eyes. Two longship men dragged Kallias to the center of the room and another man for each of the women pulled them from the curtains. Only Dealla had escaped.

Kallias struggled with the bindings. "Let me go!" He was shoved to the floor. Pekoe grunted. The others also struggled futilely muttering curses at the men. From the shadows near the platform, a small, wiry limbed creature shuffled towards them. It had large, dark eyes and a small lip-less mouth upturned in a natural grin and cat-like ears which stuck outward from its hairless head, rather than upward. It wore a plain, ivory-colored robe. All in all, the creature seemed appealing, though something about its gaze made Kallias feel uneasy as he slowly stopped fighting the ropy web. He curiously watched as the little nearbeast inspected him. Kallias had seen a number of new creatures in this part of Iasegald. This was his first wixxon.

The creature bobbed its head and two of Yungir's men stood the warrior upright and held him. Because his feet were wrapped so closely together, Kallias could not stand firmly upon them. The height of the wixxon diminished markedly. Even the akinn were taller by a palms width. It buzzed its language through its flattened nose, then opened its mouth to reveal two rows of jagged teeth.

"That's quite enough, Zizzix." The authoritative voice came from the shadows just where the wixxon had emerged. The creature bent low and shuffled back into the darkness. The speaker strutted forward to near the center of the room where he could behold the women as well as Kallias. He was a handsome young man, his silver eyes large and bright. "Well now, here are yar missing women." The mystic faced Kallias. "And this? The warrior the akinn were so worried about? Ya're supposed to be drowned." He laughed and approached Kallias. His robe resembled Guin's, but he did not wear the cuirass of the Bloodfish navy.

"Where is Asadia?!" Kallias barked as the mystic circled him. Unable to turn his gaze, he clenched his jaw.

"Asadia's fine. She's with me."

"You—are Yungir? She will never marry you!"

Yungir laughed derisively. "And who are ya to say she won't? She's prepared already."

Kallias grunted and struggled again but his feet buckled, his weight held up by the men. "She's my sister!"

"So she said. But yar yet alive though she mourned ya." His eyes held an unholy glee. He pointed at a longship man. "Ya. Bring her out here."

The guard let go of Zetrine. She slumped to one side, as another man grasped her arm with one hand, his other holding Pekoe. "You're hurting me!" Zetrine shouted at him. The man gave her a shake in response.

Asadia entered, dressed in a golden gown of fine, colorful, intricate embroidery, her head covered completely in a headdress and veil. "Behold my bride!" Yungir crowed. "Asadia, someone to see ya, dear."

"Asadia!" Kallias cried out with another futile struggle to escape his cocoon-like entanglement, his eyes wide. "Asadia!"

"Kallias?" Asadia sounded surprised.

"Tell him how 'tis that ya'll indeed marry me, Asadia." Yungir took her hand and led her right to Kallias. He could see her lovely features though the sheer veil.

"I'm to marry Yungir, Kallias."

A sullen darkness befell his eyes as he slumped to her confirmation. He shook his head. "No."

"Tell him. Tell him why." Yungir was adamant.

"He's so powerful. It will save lives, Kallias an—"

"No, no, not that reason why." Yungir pushed her away from Kallias so that she tripped forward a few steps before turning back towards him. "I'll tell him. It's because she loves me. And why does she love me?" He looked to Asadia. She did not reply, so he continued. "Because I'm kind. I'm not the evil one who brings destruction or... or... any of the... " He waved his hands about as if mad while he stumbled over his words. "The... prophecies babbled about by... mad akinn seers." He motioned to someone behind him and another man brought forward a battered and beaten Talek, who was dropped at Yungir's feet. "No, not me... I'm not the one to bring... death to the people... by kervplik hunters and wixxon mages. That's you. Ya're the... the warrior that brings death. Ya... Ya don't remember me, eh? I never forgot her." Yungir stepped away from the akinn and circled Asadia, brushing a finger down her veiled cheek. "Prophecies can be so handy for getting what ya want." He returned to Talek and Kallias. "Now we'll... be related and ya'll... ya'll become one of us. The great Kallias, Bloodfish warrior." He laughed lightly. "What a grand idea. Here to give away the bride."

Asadia said no more but lowered her head.

Kallias lifted his head with a brooding, disagreeable stare. "Never!"

Yungir's face reddened with rage. "Ya'll do as I say or ya... all of ya, will die!" He screamed.

"Yungir!" Guin's voice boomed out of the dark recess near the entry door.

As Yungir halted, the longship men armed themselves. Guin stepped out of the dark vestibule with both of his pistols drawn. "Tell them to put them away."

Yungir raised his hands. "Put them down ya fools!" he cried. "I knew it! I knew they wouldn't...couldn't kill ya!"

"Ya gave over too many for death, Yungir. It wasn't necessary."

Yungir held up a finger. "Do *not* scold me, Father. I've come a long way. It's the prophecy that made the men afraid. Not me. Tell them!" He commanded and kicked the fallen Talek sharply in the ribs.

Kallias growled. "You bastard!" Spittle ran down his lip. "We trusted you!"

"The warrior of dark hair will—" the seer began.

"Not that one. Shut up!" Yungir kicked the old man again.

Guin put his pistols away. "Ya let one get away, Yungir." As he spoke an armed guard brought in Dealla tied up as the others, though with ordinary rope. Guin motioned them to bring her into the light before Yungir.

"Mehanna!" Yungir looked as if he had seen a ghost. "But that's impossible!"

Roselana's eyes began to fill with a hopeless sadness as they laid on Guin. "Why?" she cried disappointedly. Kallias contemplated Dealla as he slumped again.

Guin gave no indication that he had heard Roselana. "Ya killed Mehanna. This is Dealla. I believe they were sisters."

"Sisters? I've yet to understand the breed." Yungir stepped up to Dealla closely. He sniffed her hair. Only then did she lift her face. She was gagged but scowled with cruel eyes at the mystic. "She doesn't have that intoxicating fragrance." He touched her cheek. "Have ya given away yar secrets, my lovely?"

Guin gestured to the women. "She's taught each of them one enchanted word to empower their arrows with elements. I've studied them and learned to weave them into my own magic."

"Very good, Father. It's how I did it. But she just wouldn't co-operate when she found out how I used that power of seduction to retrieve magic from the other mystics. It's a very, very strong power. But this one…Dealla is it? Ya'll give me the rest of yar abilities. The ones yar sister refused to let go."

The Baresian swordsman felt his heart torn. He had brought her here and her predicament now he thought was his fault. His hope sank and he swallowed hard. "I'll kill you if you touch her again!" Kallias barked at Yungir as the mystic's hand pet Dealla's hair against her will. The warrior's body jerked furiously in the grasp of Yungir's guards. They struggled to hold him.

Yungir moved slowly toward Kallias, the light of realization in his eyes. "She chose ya, did she?" He put his nose close to the man from the Glimmerbarrens and stared hard into his eyes. "Yes. I can see it. Come to ya at night, did she? Smell of flowers that went to yar head and filled yar senses?" He glanced back at Dealla whose eyes were filled with anger. "Tell me. Did ya remember anything?"

Kallias spit in Yungir's face. "You'll burn for this, but for real."

Yungir punched Kallias in the mouth, splitting his bottom lip. Then he wiped the spittle from his face with a sleeve. "Why didn't ya just kill him, Father?" Kallias grunted, then turned his unwavering angry visage in Guin's direction.

"I had no reason to kill him. He's got no power."

Kallias glowered up at him with a smirk and spit blood at him from his lip. "You'll pay for this betrayal, when I get out of this!" He spoke vehemently to Guin.

"Will ya?!" Yungir kept his distance from Kallias to avoid being spat upon again. "Do ya have destructive powers like the akinn believe, desert boy?"

"Yungir!" Guin attempted to silence his son again. "He's a swordsman. That's all. Once ya marry, he'll not be a threat to anyone. Ya have what ya need. Now end this."

"I can't, Father. I'm not the mystic of the prophecy. But this one *is* the warrior, aren't ya? Ya disappeared from Saungtau and frightened all the akinn. Ya stole the women from Kanratu. Then ya wouldn't even drown like a man!" The wicked mystic circled Kallias like a vulture.

"I'm sorry, warrior. 'Twas my word spread the prophecy," Talek again attempted his explanation.

"Shut up old man!" Yungir snapped. "What was I saying? Oh yus, the akinn became uncooperative. I had to send men into the city. I had to punish my dear friend, Jolben, and burn his precious buildings. That was YAR

FAULT!" Yungir screamed again. Guin stepped up to him and put a gentle hand on his shoulder.

"Lock them up," Guin said to the men.

They began to tote them all away when Yungir shouted out. "Not her! She's too dangerous. Leave her here." The men holding Dealla dropped her to the floor. Dealla hit her head smartly on the marble.

"Throw the seer into the sea!" Two guards stood the akinn on his feet. "No, wait!" At Yungir's command everyone halted. "Ya've precognition. I'll have a bit of that." The young mystic grasped the seer by a shoulder and mumbled. Immediately a radiant aura shined about Talek. Ethereal tendrils flowed up Yungir's arm and encircled his body then disappeared. Talek shuddered.

The gald held its breath an eternal moment as Yungir stood, eyes closed, one hand clutching the front of his robe over his heart, the other upon the akinn's shoulder. Then with the echo of his inhalation resounding hollowly in the great hall, Yungir released Talek. The seer collapsed silently in a lifeless heap.

"Now ya can throw him away." All was in motion again.

Kallias struggled hard to keep his eyes on his sister and Dealla, as his captors dragged him out. "Asadia! Asadia!" His call went unanswered as Asadia slunk quietly back into the shadows. "Dealla! I will free you. They'll pay for this!"

Chapter 30

The short, stone-walled corridor held several prison cells parallel, each enclosed with a wide, iron-barred door. Kallias heard the soft conversations of the women, the slight dripping of water and the scuffle and squeaks of the local vermin. Freed from Zizzix's imprisoning web only to be confined in a room of stone with a hand sized window high above, he viewed the dimly lit area which smelled humid with mildew. He paced relentlessly and glanced frequently out to the cell opposing his own. There Roselana sat on her cot with her head in her hands. Finally, she noticed Kallias and stepped forward to the bars. He ceased pacing.

Unspoken words were exchanged with sorrowful and worried glances at first. Kallias peeked left to right through the bars before speaking in a hoarse whisper. "We have to escape. They will only let us rot away in here."

Roselana shook her bars. "How?" Dirty streaks ran down her cheeks, the tracks of her tears. "Why did he do it, Kallias? He was so gentle."

"Isn't it obvious? He had this planned from the moment he met me."

"But... why?"

"What easier way of capturing your enemy than to have them befriend you unknowingly? Dealla is our chance. Maybe she's free already. Can you see her in another cell? Maybe a little animal with blue eyes? Spiritdancer."

Roselana peered left and right. "Charlise." She paused as the girl came to her cell door. "Do you see Dealla?"

After another moment Charlise responded. "No, she's not in here with us."

"No, Kallias, Dealla isn't within sight of any of us."

He sighed and gripped the bars hard. A rat scuttled by and he looked to it expectantly but it only left with some hay from the cot as quickly as it appeared. "Were you all stripped of belongings as well? Search for anything useful. I don't plan on staying here forever."

"Yes, we have nothing. But we'll look." The women retreated back into their cells.

Dealla lay upon the cold marble floor bound by ordinary rope and gagged with a filthy, oily cloth. Never would she let herself out to trust a longship man again. Running to Guin for aid when the others were captured was a mistake. It was a mistake to listen and not change from the vulnerable form. Her head ached where it had been hit and a large welt formed on her forehead. She squirmed about to see where Yungir might be. Had she been left alone in the big room? If only she could create a new form, but the bindings would not allow it. The mystic had done something with rope that the wixxon could not with its web. The footfall of a longship man came up behind her. "I'm sorry, rekinnder. Ya're too powerful. It's to our advantage that ya don't see that in ya self." It was Yungir. She felt the grief for Mehanna. Stronger still was anger, a feeling foreign to Dealla, but a feeling of power she had not understood. Was this what the mystic meant? She rolled onto her back and glared up at the murderer of her sweet Mehanna. The questions were in her eyes and he could read them. He had connected with her sister as she had with Kallias. Why would he kill her?

"Ya want to know about Mehanna and me?" He squatted down to peer into her face. Dealla could see Guin standing behind his son. "Mehanna... she was... wonderful. I loved her, truly I did. When she first came to me I was in the woods beset by a kervplik hunter. She rescued me. Yar kind are like that, saving the small from the large danger. So very... altruistic. I stayed in the woods with her. The seer had spread his prophecy then and I'd gone looking for that mystic. I found Mehanna. She could do the most marvelous things.

She didn't use words to do what she could do. It took me a long time to realize I needed the incantations. I had to use hand and voice. She needed only freedom." He pushed Dealla on her side roughly with a foot, then shook her bindings to be sure of their security. She kept her eyes on him. "Ya feel it like yar soul is bound, don't ya? Why'd ya separate from each other and live such solitary lives?" He smirked into her blue angry eyes. "And ya're angry. Have ya ever been angry before? Mehanna never, never was angry. She'd kill without emotion. Do ya know how evil that is? No, ya'd not realize that to be evil. There has to be... something... someone to control all the evil in this gald. When I learned the words, I was able to face any mystic and... suck out the very essence of their powers. Ya understand how important that is?" Dealla's eyes still held the question. He talked much but did not answer the why. She squirmed and asked again with heavy breath, angry and tearful.

"When she found out what I was doing, she quit speaking to me. I assured her I was not harming the mystics. Why'd she care? Longship men and akinn alike have hunted rekinnder. Ya know me now. I'm the Azenua. Me! A-ze-nu-ah." He tapped his chest with a finger. "But I couldn't feel it. Ya know, whatever it is that connects ya and lets ya change into anything. If I could do that. I could have the power of the wixxon too." He paused and stared at a spot on the floor.

Dealla growled her denial of his claim into the oily rag, bringing Yungir back to himself to continue his rant. "Nothing I tried would do it." His smile now became twisted and devilish. "Therefore, I did the same to her. I tried to get her abilities from her. It pained me to hear her scream out like that; truly it did." He drew the back of two fingers gently across Dealla's cheek. She jerked away and glared. "But I made the mistake of not binding her first. She'd not yield up her power. Instead she took her bow up. I had to shoot her. Self-defense, see? There now, ya have it all. Happy?" He sneered. Dealla struggled in vain against the bindings.

"Ya have the rekinnder now, Yungir. What are yar plans?" Guin asked his son.

"My plans are unchanged, Father. Only more peaceful. I don't have to exert myself so much. The men will clear the forests of kervplik and wixxon alike. The wixxon queens are locked away. Their young and drones are huddled in fearful little masses in their clod homes. That blasted buzzing language of theirs is impossible to speak. But I got a bit of telepathy from old Bashall. Remember him? They're evil too, the wixxon, but I control them. I'll have all the powers of every form of magic one way or another." Yungir strode about the room as he spoke and gestured as if taking in a vast scenery. "I'll rule everything from here. There will be... peace. My peace. I've thought of everything."

"Son, ya have that power and peace now, don't ya?" Guin attempted to reason with Madness.

"I don't have it all yet, Father. I must have it all. Even yars, but it won't hurt ya. A moment of euphoria and then yar back to the same as before." Yungir turned to Guin with a wild look.

"I understand, Yungir." Guin spoke evenly and convincingly. "Have ya also the words I've learned from the rekinnder's training? Will ya gain that from me as well?"

"I know more Rekinnder than ya do, Father. What I want is yar flair. Ya're the best."

"Ye have the power of illusion, Son. I taught ya all I know from yar youth up."

"But learning their spells at my fingertips! So easy!" Yungir held his hands palm up and wiggled his fingers. "Besides, I get essence. Every mystic has something different inside, something that grows. I have felt it each time. It's an energy. It carries a vitality that makes every spell better. And it's quite intoxicating." He laughed with gleeful menace. "Unfortunately, if I do it too many times to the same mystic..." Yungir lifted both hands with a shrug. "Oops! No more mystic."

"What abilities do ya hope to gain from her?" Guin nodded down to Dealla. "Wouldn't it be safer to destroy her instead?"

"No!" Yungir became incensed. "I'll have her abilities. Imagine being able to become anything ya ever laid eyes on or can dream. Imagine being able to cause any element to do yar bidding and all this without uttering a word."

"If it's part of their race it may not be magic as we know it. It's dangerous to toy with, Yungir. She should be killed." Guin pulled his sword.

"NO!" Yungir screamed at Guin. "She's mine to get what I can." He motioned to someone in the dark and two longship men came and lifted Dealla off the floor. "Take her to the courtyard."

"What of Asadia?" Guin asked as much to distract Yungir as to gain the information.

"We'll be wed. I'll take her as a sign of the men's obeisance. I'll become their leader. Prophecy all gone, no leading kervplik and wixxon against longship sailors. It'll be over." Yungir spun away from his father. "But I want that warrior to give the bride away. I think... Yes, I think that will stop him from whatever it is he's supposed to do."

"Nothing," came Roselana's frustrated reply. "I have a cot with nothing removable, some straw upon the floor and a dung bucket with rotting filth in it. What are we to do Kallias?"

Kallias stared at the licking flames of a torch in its bracket. They seemed to dance with his thoughts and emotions. He shook his head and snapped from the reverie. "We'll make it out Roselana. Did the others find anything?"

"Nothing here," came a reply from one of the other girls and "no," from another.

A door opened at one end of the long hall of cells and let in a stream of light at once blocked with the diminishing shadow of a man in a robe as Guin walked towards the cells. "I brought water," he said and held up a bucket with a dipper in it.

Guin handed a dipper full of water to the girls out of Kallias' sight first. As they drank and passed the dipper back and forth through the bars, Guin spoke flatly to Kallias. "Ya never recalled our visit to Baresi. I thought ya would. All this time. He's my son, Kallias. His beloved mother is dead. He's as much the only family I have as yar sister is yars."

"You think it excuses betrayal?" Kallias retorted.

"Perhaps not. But listen, please. I'm trying to save lives." Guin moved to another cell and delivered water to the two women there. "When he found the rekinnder, I told him it was dangerous to take up with her. He didn't listen. It's the pakao's fault. Before he took up with her there was no prophecy. Mystics were revered for their services. Then the akinn seers like Talek began to tell people about this mystic and some dark-haired woman and a war of some kind involving all the races of men and nearbeast. I didn't believe it. We didn't believe it. At first the navy tried to quell it by gutting the seers. I stopped them." He paused as the women returned the dipper. Then he stepped in front of Kallias' cell.

"That's why Talek was helping us," Kallias remarked. "And why he said so little."

"True. When the word went out that an all powerful mystic had stirred up trouble and couldn't be stopped, that even their mystics were dying, the seers—"

Kallias interrupted. "Why wouldn't they keep their own mystics safe? Ya make no sense."

"Because they didn't know who it was. They began executions trying to cull him from the league."

"Why didn't they kill him when they did find out? Why involve my sister?"

"By that time he was too powerful. He easily could kill dozens with the wave of a hand. That's when the part about the woman started. The fear that prophecy put into them made them desperate. Mystics began to flee. Someone suggested they find the woman who could stop him, and make a deal with her."

"That someone being you, wasn't it? Why didn't you just ask? Why raid?" He snarled his reply to Guin.

"I wasn't part of that. I didn't say where to—My intention was for them to go out hunting vainly while the other mystics ran away. I was, myself, kept for killing. Had I not the power of illusion I'd be dead. What I told ya is true. And ya can't tell me ya wouldn't save yar own life as I've done." Guin hung his head. "When they brought back the women—" He paused and brought his head up. "I didn't believe the prophecy at all until then. But, do ya not see how a simple marriage can end it all?"

Kallias shook the bars. "Set us free, Guin. The marriage will not change anything. And where is Dealla?! What have you done with her?!"

The mystic's eyes narrowed. "I've done ya a favor, bringing her to Yungir. Don't ya see that a rekinnder started it all? Once the last is gone, it's over. Rekinnder are dangerous, untrustworthy pakao."

"You dare speak of trust? You planned this."

"No. I—I didn't know what I'd do, but now I—-" Kallias lunged at Guin, grabbing for his throat through the bars, like a striking asp. It was futile. Guin did not even flinch as he knew he was far enough away from Kallias' reach.

This infuriated the Baresian even more. "I swear upon my father's sword. If she is harmed, Guin, you can count your manhood and his next to Pluth's!"

Guin stared into the bucket as if an answer was there. When he looked back to Kallias, his eyes shone with unshed tears. "I knew when I saw ya the first time, ya were the one to help me put an end to this madness. But ye can't kill him. He's my son, Kallias. He's gone mad, indeed... but, he's my son."

"I will save my sister. And Dealla will have her revenge." Kallias breathed heavily, his words adamant. "Son or not."

Guin pulled himself away from Kallias and towards Roselana. "Roselana, I'm sorry."

She gave him a hopeful glance but backed away from the bars. "We trusted you. And you betrayed us and locked us away like animals."

"Please, Roselana," Guin stepped closer to the bars. "It hasn't been since the death of Yungir's mother that I've opened my heart. It's... I had them bring ya here to save yar lives. Please believe me, Roselana. He'd have killed ya right then." Roselana held a speechless gaze with a shake of her head.

"You fear him, don't you." Kallias made a comment rather than a question to Guin's back.

Guin hesitated, peering over his shoulder at Kallias. Then he returned his attention to Roselana. She hid her grief-stricken tears by moving away from the ray of light that emanated from the small ventilation window high above Kallias' cell. "Roselana..." Dejected, Guin set the bucket down outside of Roselana's cell and walked out of the door, closing the light away.

Dealla braced herself against the post where she was bound. They had left her there for hours, until the sun began its afternoon descent. Finally, Yungir came out and studied her, pacing back and forth and glancing at her from time to time. Anyone who dared to stand blatantly in the courtyard to watch was shooed away, until Guin came into the area. "I haven't gotten an answer from him. He'll think about the reasoning I gave him."

"Reasoning?" Yungir gave attention to his father. "We could just make him do it. Perhaps the seduction can be used as persuasion on one without magic as well as on a mystic."

"Perhaps, but he may choose to give her of his own accord. After all, they could all make a new life for themselves here. Their desert has nothing to offer them since the raids. They have no families." Guin nodded with an expectant air.

"Fine, fine. We have time. I'll find out how to get from this one her abilities. So lovely, so... cruel. She torments me as her sister did." He planted himself, with feet shoulder width apart, in front of Dealla. She refused to lift her head to him. He began a soft chant. Dealla scowled and wrinkled her nose at the sickly-sweet scent that rose around the mystic. It was not the alluring scent of a rekinnder's passion but revolting to the senses. She grimaced and turned her face away. The magic of his mystic charms blended though and worked as if a siphon was drawing her life force from her. The vacuum against her cells caused Dealla to emit a muffled cry through the gag. Yungir seemed to be gaining something then stopped suddenly, eyes wide, and fell to the ground wiping at his body. "Get it off! Get it off!"

Guin ran to him. "What, Yungir? What is it? I don't see anything!" Guin was desperate and wheeled upon Dealla. "Stop what it is ya're doing!" he shouted and slapped her. It did no good as it was Yungir's own magic that stuck to him and burned.

Yungir ceased his writhing and stood once again scowling yet fearful of Dealla. "That never happened before."

"Are ya alright?" Guin asked anxiously.

"Go away, Father. I'll figure this out myself." Yungir stared at Dealla whose face stung with the print of Guin's hand.

"What can I do?" Guin began.

"Leave us!" shouted his mad son. "I have to have her power and I will get it." He spun wildly upon Guin. "Now go and I promise I'll not take yar power."

Guin nodded and slipped away into the manse.

Chapter 31

The door to the cell hall opened again. Someone entered quietly and closed it. Only the light streaming in across the floor and the shadow, before it disappeared, was in evidence. Then the light footfall of someone small and tiptoeing came through the silence. The women who had whispered amongst themselves at first had become quiet in their despair. Then the whispered voice of Asadia resonated through the stone hall. "Kallias? Roselana?"

Kallias hurried to his cell door. "Asadia," he whispered in joy. Roselana pressed her smiling face between the bars of her cell.

"Kallias!" Asadia rushed up to him as the other women also came to their barred doors. The light though dim was sufficient to see that her dress was tied up between her legs and her bodice covered with a Bloodfish sailor's cuirass. This one did not get the refit theirs had and was therefore a clumsy fit. "Dear Brother, I thought I would never see you again. You have no idea how overjoyed I was to see you and so... fearful at the same time." She attempted to hug him though the bars. Kallias held onto his sister for a long moment then examined her as he held her hands. She smiled though fear still reigned in her eyes.

"We must escape this place, Sister."

"Yes, that man, Yungir's father, told me where to look for the keys. I have to find them."

Kallias' eyes widened. "Guin told you?"

"He came to my rooms with tears in his eyes. He apologized. I haven't been guarded for days. But I was told to stay in my rooms this time. I was so afraid Kallias. But he gave me this cuirass and put your sword in a passageway. He's the one who saved me from that big man who took me. I didn't know who he was at the time. And it was for me to marry his son. But I don't understand why he's letting us go. Do you think it's a trick?" She seemed concerned yet determined.

"Perhaps he's changed his heart. Hurry, you must make haste, Sister." He squeezed her hands once. "Go."

Asadia nodded and then touched Roselana's hand as she passed her and went to some place at the other end of the hall. She was gone a long moment but then returned with a large ring of keys. She fumbled with them as she tried one after the other on Kallias' cell lock. She kept watching toward the door as if the keys could be heard outside. "I can't... I can't find the right one, Kallias."

He took them from her and tried each deftly in vain. "Last but not least," he said as the tension drew high in the room. With a turn, there was a click and exhaled sighs went up from cell to cell along the hall.

Suddenly voices and the scuffle of feet resounded outside the jail door. "Someone's coming!" Asadia whispered and ran for cover.

Kallias quickly locked his cell door and hid the keys within his belt.

First unintelligible speech then laughter emanated from somewhere close. After an eternal moment they moved on. Asadia crept out of her place at the end of the hall and returned to the cell. "We must hurry before I'm missed."

Kallias returned to his lock with key in hand. He freed himself and raced to unlock the remaining cell doors. Once freed, they all grouped together. "Where to now? How do we get out?" little Pekoe asked quickly.

"We must go out the way I came in," Asadia answered. "Then follow me. I know where to go. Be careful and quiet." She moved briskly to the door and listened as Kallias had at the door to the marbled room. She opened the door slowly and peeked out. Then she signaled to the others to follow and crept out the door and along the wall of another hallway. Some ways down she disappeared through another door.

Kallias ushered and guided the women in through the door, then followed last behind. Asadia closed the door as Kallias entered making him jump unexpectedly.

"I need my sword. Then you see the others to safety. I must find Dealla." He spoke quietly but urgently.

They stood in a storeroom about ten forearms length square. Asadia led him to a corner of it. "Help me push these crates aside. There's a door beneath." She began to lean her weight against a crate almost her size. "You can't save Dealla, Kallias. She's in the courtyard. Everyone will see."

"I can't leave without her," he said as he pushed.

"No, please, Brother. She's a pakao. She has you bewitched. Yungir told me how her sister bewitched him." She pressed a shoulder to it as did the others until the crate moved aside revealing a trap door.

"Don't believe it." He held her elbow gently. "I must."

Asadia pleaded fearfully, "No, please, I can't lose you again." She opened the trap door and allowed the other women to climb down first.

"You won't lose me." He held her hand as she began her descent, then climbed down after her, closing the wooden trap door behind them.

They all stood in the dark until Asadia struck a flint and lit a torch. She led them down a long tunnel. Just as a pale bit of daylight began to show through the other end, they found a mound of what appeared to be flour sacks and cloth. Jamila began uncovering this to find all their weapons; swords, daggers, bows and quivers of arrows. Even Pluth's pistol, which Guin had originally given Kallias, was in that heap. "I wondered where this had gone. Still only one shot in it." Kallias chuckled and pushed it into his waistband at his back.

"Oh, that came from the little old man without eyes," commented Asadia.

"Talek." Kallias knit his brow. "I wonder that he didn't use it."

"They're all here!" Charlise exclaimed.

"Not all," noted Kallias.

"Where's Dealla's bow?" Roselana asked Asadia, who replied with a shrug.

"At last," said Jamila as she strapped on her sword.

"We're close to the exit, Kallias. There's a boat out there we can take home. Please, let's go now," Asadia pleaded again.

Kallias contemplated Asadia and the opening end, then back towards the darkened side they had come from. "I will return to you."

"We," said Roselana.

"Yes, we all go," chimed in Pekoe and the others.

"Stand together or fall apart." Roselana nodded with resolve.

"You're all going?" Asadia asked incredulously. "For a pakao?"

"Not a pakao, Asadia," said Charlise. "Can you use a sword?" she asked and held her sword out to the young woman.

She nodded, taking the sword and scabbard. "Not as good as Kallias but well enough."

"Then protect yourself here until we get back," suggested Pekoe.

"We *will* be back." Jamila's voice held the conviction of her words.

"All of you? Why?" Asadia still could not understand.

"Yungir, is the pakao. I'm not bewitched but in love. Dealla is a being just as we are. And we have come too far together for me to allow him to kill her like he did her sister," he said as he picked up his blades and readied himself. "Please, understand." He embraced her once again. "We will return."

As they headed back into the darkness and to the door, the patter of Asadia's feet could be heard. She caught up to them quickly. "I'm coming too, then."

Kallias smiled and helped her up the ladder.

She reached the trap door and attempted to open it. "It won't budge!"

"Guin?" Roselana said.

"He must have waited for us to escape and then covered over the door for us," Asadia explained.

Kallias pulled Asadia from the ladder, then climbed it himself and pounded his shoulder into the hatch. It did not bounce the slightest. "There must be another way around."

"Only one other way out." Asadia pointed back to the exit. "But if we go out that way, it leads to the port and to the city. The only way back into the courtyard is through the city. We'll never make it."

"We try." Roselana turned and began the familiar march down the tunnel.

Kallias nodded and followed the footfall down the dark tunnel until it opened up to the brightness outside of the east face of the rock.

They halted at the opening to the cave and peered outside. A winding stairway of wood and stone zigzagged its way down the rock face some hundred feet. Just below them was the port where the stairs let out onto the docks. To the left of that, the city bustled with activity. longship men, akinn and a few wixxon went about their daily routines. Set apart from the other ships was a single merchant vessel, empty and waiting. Roselana tapped Kallias' arm. When he turned, she hooked a thumb over her shoulder to the right up along the thirty-foot rock face. "What do you think?"

"A lot steeper than the other side, but I think we can climb it!" he said and set about finding a grip and foot holds. "Follow precisely. Step where I do."

Jamila followed after Kallias, placing her hands and feet where he did. After her came Pekoe, then Roselana, then Asadia, followed by Zetrine and Charlise. They traversed in a diagonal climb. Each reach was an effort as they stretched their limbs to place themselves higher and higher. The merchant vessel seemed to shrink. "I... c-ca-cannot." The nervous whimper of Charlise reached the ears of the others. They looked back to find her only half way up and about ten feet behind, petrified with fear and clinging to the rocks.

Zetrine encouraged her. "You must!"

"I'll get her." Roselana began to climb down to avoid moving the others in their climbs. "Don't worry, Charlise. I'm coming." She chose each move carefully, deliberately. Reaching out a hand she grasped Charlise's bicep and helped her to find steady handholds. Kallias and the others waited. As soon as Charlise was moving again Roselana came up behind her. Suddenly Zetrine stifled a scream as Roselana slipped. She grabbed a sharp rock and dangled but a moment before she pulled herself close enough to the rock-face to regain a foothold. The blood oozed from her right hand as she tightly gripped rock after rock and tested each step with careful toes until she had reached the others.

"Almost there," Kallias gave out a heartening call as he began again the arduous climb to the rim still a few arm-span lengths away. "Don't give up."

"Don't look down, only up," Zetrine told Charlise.

Kallias' dirty-knuckled fingers came up over the rim, which on this side was but two feet wide along the foundation of the stone tower. Cautiously he crawled up onto his side. Bracing himself with a jutting rock to counter the weight, he offered a hand to Jamila. Each of the women gave him her hand in turn as they crested the apex and moved themselves flat against the wall. Finally, Roselana reached up with an awkward left hand. "It's difficult, Kallias. Grab my wrist. My right hand is too slippery." He held her left wrist and gave a tug as she helped to pulled her weight up. Then her right hand slipped and soon all her weight pulled against Kallias. She reached for him with her right hand and grabbed his boot top.

"Roselana!" Asadia started to lean forward over the ledge in an effort to help.

Kallias' hand gripped the rock where he anchored his weight. His knuckles and fingers whitened from the tight grasp. The dirt holding the rock began to upturn and loosen. He grunted and flexed his forearm as hard as he could, swinging Roselana towards Asadia. Zetrine grasped hold of Asadia and the others each took hold of one another to anchor them. Asadia stretched downward. Roselana let go of Kallias' boot and twisted in the swing. Asadia reached and clasped both hands about Roselana's wrist and pulled her to a seat upon the narrow ledge. Kallias let out a heavy sigh that kicked up the sand and dust his cheek rested on.

When they were all finally safe, Jamila led with creeping steps against the tower wall toward the west side. She reached the corner, stopped and peeked around. The wall shone a deep orange color of the setting sun and the shadows of the rock structure grew long across the courtyard where the mystic paced.

The others came to a halt beside Jamila. "Is it clear?" Roselana asked.

"Yungir is there. I can't see Dealla. The boulders must be in the way. Guin is speaking. Yungir is mad." Jamila regarded the others then turned to Kallias. "I think we can make it into the crevasse without detection."

He nodded his approval.

"We must go one at a time. Make sure no one is facing this way before you go around." She gave this last instruction before disappearing around the corner.

Chapter 32

Dealla glared at Guin's back as he retreated through the tower door. Then she focused her hatred upon Yungir.

There was good reason why he could not take her abilities. What she did was by virtue of her own soul energy. When she used words, it was to imbue things, to give power to what had no mind of its own. No magic would ever be imparted to him from what was not magic in her, though her life force could be drained from her. But his powerful magic which focused only against her, did not take into account the fact that she was not alone tied to that post. She carried a protector. What Yungir did not know would hinder him. In that moment Dealla realized that Mehanna had also not been alone.

Yungir paced before her, grumbling and cursing under his breath. Then he stopped. "Ya're less willing. Ya're detached from me. That must be it. Let's see... ah, the word for heart. I'll give ya heart towards me. A spell of charm with yar word for heart. How simple yar language is, once one learns some rudimentary concepts." He turned and paced a distance from her. "Let me see. Heart, that's essa, isn't it?" The mad mystic began to murmur. Then he raised his hands before him and moved them as if drawing a rope from one place and another to tie them together.

His incantation meant nothing to Dealla except "essa". Once the word was said he cast both hands forward at her. His magic did not turn on him. It felt instead to Dealla as if he might stop her heart. She concentrated on pulling life energy from the gald, she and her protector. Again the pain caused Dealla to cry into the rag in her mouth. For Yungir it was fruitless. "Ya torment me and refuse to yield! And ya're draining me." Yungir shouted at the obvious failure as the rekinnder's eyes continued to hold hate towards him. "So, to take yar power I must take yar life, is it?" Guin stepped back into the courtyard and gazed about. He remained quiet as he watched his son. As he wiped the sweat from his hairline, Yungir seemed to come to some realization. "I know what it is."

Dealla kept focused on Yungir and to what she would do when she was free of the binding.

"I have to use the word for complete." He chuckled. He walked about in circles with his head down thinking of the word he needed. "Faleke. That's finish, but does it also mean complete? Pressez, union but not whole. Nust? All?" He had gained a small audience of men. When Yungir saw the handful, who had stopped in their comings and goings to watch, he seethed and shouted, foaming at the mouth. "I told ya to go! I told ya all to leave me be!" Then his eyes landed on Guin. "Father! Don't defy me! They'll follow ya! No! No! Wait!" The last he said as Guin began once again to move away from his son. He made the mistake of turning back, for Yungir chanted with the seductive words he had learned to use of Rekinnder and cast it at Guin.

Guin cried out loudly, "Yungir!" Every muscle in his body strained. His face grew red and contorted. A ghostly image of Guin, himself, was wrenched from his body and floated in Yungir's direction, dissipating as he absorbed it.

Yungir's face twisted into a distorted smile like that of lustful ecstasy. "Sorry, Father. I lied." Then Guin fell face forward into the dirt.

Roselana had dared to peer over the rock as she heard Yungir call to his father. She slumped back down, tears running and hand over her mouth so as not to cry out with fear, pain and rage at what she had witnessed.

"Now go!" Yungir screamed at the others who quickly ran off. He spun about and bragged to Dealla. "Ya see that ghost? It's magic energy, renewable. I've no idea how." Yungir admitted with a mad snicker. "He isn't dead. I could do that to him again and again. Of course if I did, then he might die. There must be something like that in ya. Let it come to me."

Yungir called another spell up. In this one he repeated one portion of the phrase. "Arun fet shaun tolas ele d'rekin ali. Tolas ele d'rekin ali." Dealla struggled against her bindings and moaned and cried out. But when, even through the gag, her muffled cries grew loud to the sound of the serlcat's warning, the spell was broken.

Yungir screamed out in his rage.

Kallias nodded once to the group as he came back down from peeking over the rock wall. "It's now or never," he said in a hushed voice and touched Roselana's shoulder. She wiped her eyes and gave a slight nod. "I'll strike at Yungir and distract him. You all form a perimeter and unbind Dealla." He unsheathed his blade and leapt over the wall, hitting the ground with a deft roll forward. "You're mine, Yungir!" He charged the mystic quickly.

Yungir in his surprise threw up his hand and shouted the words that put an unseen barrier up. Kallias struck against the invisible wall as Yungir ran toward the front of the tower near the archway calling out, "Zizzix!" He touched his hand to his forehead and rattled off the incantation they had heard Guin use. Suddenly he vanished. The women did as Kallias had instructed and stood a half circle around Dealla, eyes alert and longbows drawn. Roselana went around behind Dealla with the rekinnder's dirk and began sawing at the knots that bound her.

"Coward! Hide behind your magic! Face me!" Kallias shouted out to his unseen foe. The barrier was gone as soon as Yungir was. Kallias' grip held steady around the hilt of his sword. He spun defensively as his eyes darted. "Face me!" He swung his blade blindly around him. His ears became keen on sound, and his eyes searched the ground for any disturbance. Kallias backed up towards the circle of women. "Unbind her quickly," he said as he kept a sharp eye on their surroundings, waiting for an attack. He knelt down and put his index and middle finger on Guin's neck. "He's alive."

Guin moaned.

Jamila pulled the rag from Dealla's mouth. "Kallias!" Dealla called out. Using Mehanna's dirk. Roselana cut through the bindings at Dealla's feet and began work on those around her arms and at her wrists. Kallias quickly came to Dealla's side and helped pull free the cut rope from her limbs. As soon as she was freed, Dealla placed a hand on each of Kallias' shoulders and blew lightly into his face. A soft sweet breeze swirled around him billowing his hair back as it had done for her the first time they had seen her rekinnder form. Dealla moved from one to another of the women blowing gently in their faces until each of them had their own breeze about them. Then she stood looking about her for a weapon or means to create one. "Tolu ka ele bow?" she asked of him.

"Roselana." Kallias spoke.

The woman unshouldered her bow and quickly handed it to Dealla. "Use it for Mahanna's sake, Dealla. I have a sword." Then she handed the long, encrypted dagger to Kallias saying, "You can make better use of this."

Kallias took the weapon in his left hand. He began to voice his thanks but, the expression was quickly lost as the sound of many running feet approached the courtyard. The report of a rifle shocked them all into awareness. There stood Guin on his feet, one hand pushing away the barrel of the shooter's gun. His other hand laid a deft blow upon the man's jaw throwing him back through the doorway. Guin pulled out his pistols and fired one into a wave of men coming in through the archway.

Kallias turned quickly as a man, charging sword-point first, came at him. Ducking and bringing himself up under the man, he used the momentum to toss the longship man over his shoulder to land hard on the ground. Kallias quickly dealt the man a fatal blow and in the same instant turned toward the remaining men. "Ladies, here's where all your lessons come in!"

Guin fired his other pistol at a man who aimed a gun toward the women. Then with the butt of it, hit another who came out of the door, knocking him over the body of the first man. Dropping his pistols, he took a rifle from the second and fired it into the crowd of longship men. They kept coming, barrels drawn and swords brandished. Some of them remained steady under the archway letting others charge past them.

Charlise pulled an arrow from her quiver and nocked it in a single movement as she had been taught. She pulled back and released once she chose her target. "Niolo!" she called loudly. The arrow struck one of the men beside the archway who had a pistol drawn. He instantly turned to ice. She stood dumbfounded at its success. Dealla stepped up next to her and fired off arrows after arrows into the crowd of men, hitting her targets, felling some, wounding others.

"Roselana with me. Jamila take Zetrine." Kallias pointed to the right wall of the archway as he and Roselana ran for the left wall. With their swords, they clipped and ambushed those foolish enough to charge into the courtyard.

"Kallias! Behind you!" Jamila called out across the courtyard. An attacker had found his way around the duo. Roselana was instantly upon him and drove her sword deeply into the man's chest. Gripping the blade by surprise, he let out his last breath, falling to his knees. The man gawked at her, bewildered, and finally collapsed to his side.

The mystic's wixxon stepped out of the door to cast his blinding spell upon Kallias. He missed but caught instead, mid-swing, those surrounding Kallias and Roselana. Pekoe shot off an arrow barely grazing Zizzix. Guin uttered a spell using a Rekinnder word. The wixxon screamed as he became caught in a blaze. When the spell died, so did the creature, charred black.

"Wait here." Kallias motioned with a hand to keep Roselana at bay. He charged around the wall under the archway. He found himself amid a fistful of attackers. There he began his dance. His blade moved like liquid steel drawing streams of white light in the early evening air. The gleaming edge found the unprotected parts of the men. Wielding both sword and dirk, Kallias' dance befuddled his attackers. They fell one by one as they swung to meet emptiness.

Dealla fired off a few more arrows before stopping to watch the magic of the dance she had first witnessed upon the beach so long ago. Fighters on both sides paused in their attacks as well, for there must have been some magic on the dirk as an azure glow spun a web of light around it. Oblivious to the show he was putting on, Kallias parried multiple attackers and delivered returning fatal blows. His body danced and weaved, dodging the lashing tongues of his enemy's longswords. The brutality his blades lay upon the men's flesh, the red of blood, the cerulean fire that the enchanted knife left crawling through gaping wounds, displayed a mesmerizing bouquet of death. The watchers returned to the battle.

For Kallias, time had all but stopped, he was one with his sword and the sword with him. Sounds muffled as if he were listening to birds from the bottom of a lake. The men could not keep up. The closer they came, the deadlier the dance became. Crowding him only worked against them.

A ball of fire exploded in the center of the courtyard next to Pekoe. She screamed and ducked but it swept around her and blew out. Dealla's breath had shielded her. "It's a protection spell!" the young woman called out. Guin looked up to see Yungir in a window of the tower as he cast another ball of fire towards them. Guin retaliated with a casting of the image of ice and the Rekinnder word Charlise had used. The fire ball froze, hit the ground and shattered. Yungir shouted from above, "Impossible! How did ya recover so quickly?"

Three men rushed out from the tower door. Dealla shot the middle man with an arrow of fire just as his pistol went off. The three men burst into flames, screamed and ran. One ran inside the tower. The blazes increased until they fell.

"It's clear!" shouted Guin. "Go! Go!" He moved his hands in a motion to shoo the women out as another spell was cast directly toward him. It tied his feet in place, recalling Guin's attention to Yungir.

Kallias ushered the women quickly through the archway. He glanced back the moment Guin was entangled and hesitated.

"Kallias come!" Jamila's voice beckoned him.

Leaving Guin to his own resources, Kallias followed a stone staircase, which led to a walkway, zigzagging down the southeast side towards the town. Over his shoulder, thick smoke billowed up from the fire in the courtyard. The tower peeked high above the plumes.

Guin counter-cast against another of Yungir's spells. Then suddenly his feet were released as Yungir disappeared inside the window. A flash of fire licked out of a window near Guin and smoke curled thick and black towards the night sky. He retrieved his pistols and trotted through the archway and down to join the others.

Roselana slowed as her eyes searched the scene behind her. "Glad you made it," she said as Guin caught up. She swept her hand in the air crossing the archway at the head of the staircase and murmured a few words. A solid rock wall appeared.

"You've learned quickly. I'm impressed," Guin crowed. Then they both hurried to catch up to the others. The toy-sized city below grew as they bounded with skips and hops down the long stone-carved switchback.

A crowd formed at the base of the staircase. They stood in formation, two wixxon in front, then a few akinn with a handful of longship men behind. The wixxon cast their webs which had previously tied Kallias and the women. This time though, the webs spun around the heroes as if creating the funnel of a tornado and blew away. Guin was missed as was Roselana since they had not caught up yet. The others stopped and drew their bows quickly showering the crowd with a hailstorm of imbued arrows. All but the longship men ran for cover or fell. The men aimed pistols and took their shots. Kallias charged head on, the sound of speeding lead so close it buzzed like mosquitoes in his ear. One of the longship men was caught off guard by the sudden charge and fumbled to reload his weapon. A flash of steel was all he saw as he fell, his companion dropped a pistol and fled toward the docks.

Kallias felt an odd sensation as akinn after akinn panicked and abandoned the fight at the mere sight of him. *Does everything I do, lend strength to their prophecy?* He had no time to think further on that but only to be glad it was not necessary to harm them.

Jamila and Zetrine were hot on Kallias' heels. Their training proved to be successful. They acted swiftly and deliberately chose their targets, making quick blade work of them. Charlise and Pekoe took up positions flanking the others and shooting past them at any akinn or wixxon flinging darts or any sailor with a pistol raised. Guin had not time to reload his pistols and instead drew his sword and fought at Roselana's side. The amazing effect of Pekoe's smoke arrows was that of confusion. She responded with great delight as they all saw she did not have to hit her target but only come close and the man would turn against his fellow longship man.

There came another sort of buzzing, the hum of the language of wixxon. From inside barred houses excited tones clamored with odd whistling. Dealla headed towards them. As she separated from the group, her form slipped down into that of wixxon. Now as wixxon, Dealla spoke the language. In a moment, she transformed from small wixxon to large, cumbersome kervplik and bashed in a door. The wixxon, who had been enslaved to Yungir, poured out of the houses with tooth and claw to fight against those who had imprisoned them including other wixxon, and taking up the slings and darts of the fallen to use at range.

Dealla returned to her rekinnder form as the freed wixxon released others. She cupped her hands to her mouth and blew through her thumbs into the hollow of her palms. The resulting sound was like a loud horn. Then she pulled out Roselana's bow again and took a place behind Guin and Roselana to fire upon anyone shooting in their direction.

Kallias, along with Jamila and Zetrine, took a defensive position around the others, guarding their front and flank against angry chargers. They kept them at bay as the archers engulfed man after man with elements of fire, smoke and ice. Inch by inch, footholds gained as the small group of warriors persevered and stood their ground, then crept eastward. Evading attackers, they delivered their own fatal and wounding blows with steel and magic arrow.

The wixxon females, recognized by the short red hair covering their heads and the edges of their ears, retreated with their young towards the woods surrounding the city. Just then a handful of kervplik hunters emerged from those woods. Dealla made herself the kervplik female Kallias had seen in the forest and shouted in the sloppy guttural language of theirs. The kervplik responded by ripping and digging boulders from around the hill to hurl at the fresh onslaught of longship men coming up from the docks.

Dealla returned to her form, but before she could aim bow back toward their attackers, her ears thrummed with the sound of a deep roar from above. The air around them was sucked upward causing all to pause and turn. There at the top of the mountainous staircase stood Yungir. Above him a great fire vortex formed.

"Fire flower!" someone cried out.

As the spiral spat its deadly missile towards them, Dealla lifted herself up to meet it, forming herself into a great monstrous fire giant. The fire ball struck her hard and splintered into shafts of sparks and molten rock. Some flew outward burning anyone and anything they touched. A splash of fire hit Charlise's leg and another, Pekoe's hair. They beat these out furiously.

As for the rest of the fire spiral, Dealla's form soaked it up, and she grew in size. As this burning creature roared, dozens of the attackers took to their heels. The kervplik rolled or hurled stones after them. The akinn abandoned the battle en masse, running for the city gates.

Yungir prepared another fire storm, pulling dust from the ground at his feet and igniting it. This larger one built up more slowly as it circled, and sapped strength from him.

Kallias braced against an overturned wagon. Charlise and Pekoe took cover with him. Their whimpers escaped as they tended to the wounds they endured. He gawked at Dealla's form and then to the tower and Yungir as the pyroclastic storm started to gain dimension. Flashes of his dream came to him. He felt a sudden relapse, as if he had been here before. "She is the mystic," he said with realization, though the two women were not paying attention to his words. "And I brought her here, for Asadia's sake. It's all coming true."

The time gave Dealla her chance. She regained her rekinnder form. Using her own abilities of elemental control, she shot three arrows succinctly up at Yungir. Each arrow hit its mark, smoke to his head, fire to his heart and ice in his torso. As he fell, the great magical tornado that had begun to build shattered and buried him in a heap of ash.

"Noooo!" shouted Guin and ran at Dealla sword in the air for a downward strike.

"Guin!" Roselana shouted but her voice was lost in the thundering din of battle. Kallias too had started in protest after Guin. He charged the mystic. Sounds began to deafen and time seemed to slow.

Dealla saw Guin's sword crest over her. She turned her head away. The blow came to her shoulder. But, it was not the sword which struck. Kallias' body hit against her, knocking her away as he intercepted Guin. A great ringing filled the city as the steel vibrated amid the chaos. Guin pushed forward. Kallias parried. Their bodies collided and a surprised look besieged Guin's eyes. His face went pale as he slipped to the ground, his hands gripping at Kallias' sleeves and streaking through splatters of his own blood. Guin's body and sword fell to the ground with a thud. Kallias turned in haste to help pull Dealla to her feet.

At Yungir's fall, all wixxon ceased fighting their own and unified against the men. The shamans ceased their casting of webs and blindness. The kervplik continued to hurl stones, logs and anything they could pick up in the city. The Bloodfish men, who had pushed them into wixxon territory by the numbers, were now backing away in retreat as they vainly shot their pistols or attacked with sword. Many buildings in the center of the city burned from the great splatter of magic fire. Zetrine, Pekoe and Jamila were caught in the onslaught of kervplik to kinnir and were swept out through the east gate. Kallias and the others fought with wixxon against tens of men, pressing them towards the docks and their ships. Few ships cast off before others were set ablaze.

Roselana saw the fallen Guin and ran to him. Kneeling at his side she took his sword away and placed her hand in his.

"Guin," she whispered softly, focusing on him as the destruction and battle continued around her.

"Roselana," his near whispered reply came followed by a harsh cough. "Roselana, forgive me."

"I do, Guin. I do." She squeezed his hand as a tear ran down her cheek.

"I truly ha-have loved ya, Roselana." His crystal gray eyes took her in. "Find the treasure. Please. I want...want ya to have everything...take...take my sword. My pistols—" He cough again and life left him. Roselana brought his hand to her lips and kissed the knuckles before resting it on his chest. She gathered up his weapons, tying his scabbard and sword to her waist beside her own and shoving the pistols into the back of her belt as he had always done. "I will never forget you, Guin." She knelt beside him again and wept.

The wixxon pressed the remaining men to the end of the piers or onto burning ships, save the few that escaped them. When the last longship man had left or perished, the wixxon halted and sent up a humming buzz like a swarm of bees in their victory.

Kallias returned to Guin's body and stood beside the weeping Roselana. "I'm sorry Roselana, he left me no choice. But we must see to it that this is over." When she hesitated, Kallias grabbed her elbow gently to help her up.

"Kallias," Dealla said with concern. "Sege d'Asadia?"

"Where is Zetrine and Pekoe," Charlise chimed in, then added, "and Jamila?"

"Let's check the pier." Kallias suggested.

They ran back through the city streets calling the names of their companions and searching in doors and around corners. Dealla slipped into her serlcat form and sniffed of the air and ground. She zigzagged about as if lost, for the women had not come south toward the docks. Then she bounded back toward the center of the city where they had all been together last. On her heels ran Kallias and the others. The cat continued faster to the bottom of the walkway and stopped at the feet of Asadia. The Baresian girl sat upon the bottom step-like rock, crying into her hands. When the great cat faced her, she jumped up, backed against the stone and lifted her sword ready to stab at the beast. This was the scene when Kallias caught up with Spiritdancer.

He ran and embraced his sister, putting a hand on her extended arm and pushing the sword down. "You're safe now. We have others to find," he said.

"That cat... it smells the blood, Kallias." Asadia motioned towards the serlcat, its lack of attack not recognized.

"This is Dealla, Sister. She helped us to find you," he said. He tapped his nose and pointed to the cat.

Asadia's eyes went wide. "There... I... I saw this giant fire pakao, Kallias. It stood right here. So big!" She began to move with him as he led her with an arm around her.

A short way into the center of the city, Roselana stood over Guin's body. "We can't just leave him like this."

Dealla slipped from serlcat to wixxon. Wixxon had come up from the docks and meandered through the city to survey the damages and collect bodies. Dealla buzzed to those in sight of the group. One came and stood next to Guin's body. With a quick nod at Dealla's odd wixxon sounds he began to wrap Guin's body into a cocoon. Dealla shifted to her rekinnder form. "Uvetol pakin von d'Guin uene juet elwa d'jaia nozonio. Tolukuez elwa d'zenupiir awo sege mile awis." She pointed to the east outside the city.

Roselana nodded and placed a hand once more onto the web-shrouded Guin. "The wixxon will keep him until we return. Our friends went toward the east." Roselana abbreviated Dealla's words.

"Lead the way," said Kallias as he held his sister under his arm. She continued to babble incoherently.

Dealla, Roselana and Charlise ran ahead through the streets. Crushed bodies and various buildings with large gaping holes, the evident destruction of the kervplik, cut a swath toward the east. Outside the gates, boulders used and reused for such carnage, were left behind. Dents from their impacts riddled the gald. Down the road as it rounded gradually to the south, craters and broken trees spotted the land.

"Asadia, please remain strong for me," said Kallias, pulling her along as they hurried after the others. She nodded, but slowed him down as her attention remained focused on all the destruction.

Dealla stopped when she saw that Kallias and Asadia did not keep up.

She spoke a few Rekinnder words to Roselana. When she received a nodded response from the girl, Dealla returned to the serlcat form and sped away, keeping to the road.

Chapter 33

A large humpbacked beast, something like a hairy cow, lumbered slowly beside Kallias and the women with Pekoe's small lifeless body strapped to its back. They moved quietly back toward Durgrinstar. The women had been found carrying Pekoe. Her body was shrouded in a white cloth they had taken from a satchel found on a longship man's body. Once they realized the others were not with them they had abandoned the fight, only not before a large stone had hit Pekoe's head, killing her. The kervplik made no distinction between friend and foe without Dealla.

Asadia had murmured constantly since they found her. Now she made one sane, matter of fact statement and then stopped. "I killed a man, Kallias."

He gave a knowing nod. "We all have." With one arm, he hugged her close to himself.

The weary troupe reached the rubble filled city. Where the city gates had been torn away a handful of wixxon barred their entrance, pointing spears at the great beast and looking questioningly at Kallias and the women. They buzzed.

Kallias halted alongside the others. The Spiritdancer beast huffed and snorted. "Speak to them, Dealla?"

The beast inclined her sizable head towards Kallias and huffed again. The wixxon eyed Kallias curiously as he spoke to the beast. He turned and began to speak to the wixxon. His approach slow and non-hostile with his hands held out palms open. They had no name for the bison in Baresi. "The creature will not harm you. It's carrying one of our own." He motioned back toward Pekoe's body. He then turned back to the smaller spear wielding creatures.

One from behind the few at the forefront clicked and buzzed, soft and low. He obviously recognized the warrior. The one closest to Kallias peeked at the body and nodded as they all dropped their spears. This one pointed to the one who buzzed and hummed. The other raised a hand indicating they should follow him. With their red, swollen eyes the mourning women regarded each other briefly.

The sad procession followed Kallias and Dealla, led by the wixxon, to an area at the north side of the city. There a clay and stone shrine of five pillars and a wide, winding staircase rose in a spiral. All along the sides were small cot like pallets of straw and wood, each with a web wrapped corpse. More of the little platforms were being constructed and more wixxon corpses were being wrapped. Each body had its own mourner who made a mark upon its forehead, perhaps a name, as each mark was different though some similar to others. At the preparation area was one large wrapped body, Guin. Kallias took Pekoe's body over his shoulder and resettled it upon one of the empty pallets, then said a silent farewell, his hand resting lightly on her forehead. Roselana ventured over to Guin's body. Her lips moved like Kallias'.

A female, with the gentle touch of a clawed hand, disturbed Kallias and pointed. When he did not appear to understand, she motioned to him to pick up Guin's body. Kallias pulled Guin over his shoulder with Roselana's aid. Then the wixxon walked them up to the center of the shrine. The cots, built as miniature pyres, lined the outer edge of this spiral. At the base one gigantic cot attested to the fact that at least one kervplik had either been shot or stabbed enough times to inflict a fatality. When they reached the center, in a large space stood a low, man-sized pallet. The tiny creature pointed to it and gave the soft hum. The two friends gently laid out Guin's body across the platform. Outside, Jamila, Zetrine and Charlise each placed Pekoe's bow, sword and an arrow at her sides as she lay in her permanent silence. After that they climbed up the wide, spiral steps. As they came to the center, they held each other in an embrace, hugging Roselana as well.

Dealla, in blue-eyed wixxon form, stepped up to Guin's body and spoke to some wixxon who had followed her. They quickly retreated and returned with hay and sticks for another pallet which they placed next to Guin's. Following them were a half dozen of their kind with Pekoe's body and all her belongings. These they placed on the pallet making sure to copy the placement of each item exactly. They looked to each of the women with their tiny lip-less smiles and bobbed their heads. Dealla pulled back the shroud to expose Pekoe's forehead and began to carve into it with the wixxon claws of her form. She put there the signs of Pekoe's bow. Then at Guin's body she sliced open the web exposing his forehead and face. Turning to Roselana and Kallias, she held a question in her eyes.

They both nodded but Roselana spoke. "He was a good man, torn between the love of his friends, and the kinship of his son. He had a good heart."

Dealla nodded and carved into his forehead some symbols, one of which Roselana could see was on her quiver and bow and another inscription partially of her own name that Dealla had burned into the leather of her cuirass. When Dealla had completed this she shifted to rekinnder. "Rezek," she began, placing a hand upon the forehead of the dear one. "Pee-koh, von masent d'awa haiaive." A tear fell as she spoke, and then she kissed the carved forehead and turned to Guin. "Essio d'Roselana. Padekoi azenu d'Guin." She paused and regarded Roselana again and then Kallias. "Tolu Guin d'essa wain." She completed her blessing and also kissed his forehead. Then she stepped aside and gave a single nod to the others. Charlise kissed Pekoe's forehead and then Guin's. She rested a hand on each of them and said, "I love you both." Finished with her blessing, she stepped aside towards Dealla.

Roselana spoke up quietly. "Dealla said something like, 'Pekoe stand with your head in the heavens.' And..." Roselana's voice quavered and she sniffed back her tears. "Of Guin, she said...she said he had a good heart." She cried quietly and wiped vainly at her tears while the others approached the bodies of their friends.

With a few words each, Jamila and Zetrine kissed Pekoe's forehead and Guin's. After which they took places beside Dealla. It was then Kallias' turn. The others watched him expectantly.

He stared at Pekoe's young, soft, golden features, her eyes closed as if she were asleep. "I failed you, little flower. Perhaps your spirit is with Sarad." He bent and his lips touched her cool skin. He approached Guin's side with glazed eyes. "I hope to understand some day. I forgive you. I'm sorry you won't be coming home with us." His lips softly touched the mystic's forehead and a single tear fell on Guin's cheek. Kallias settled between Roselana and Dealla.

Roselana stepped to Guin's side. Her long raven locks framed his face while her lips, wet with salty tears, touched his lips for a long moment. "You will always be in my heart, Guin," she said in hushed tones. She produced his longsword from his scabbard and placed it upon his covered chest. "I know you wanted me to have this, but you should keep it for honor until your body is consumed. I will look for it afterward." Into his scabbard, Roselana placed her sword, then removed her own from her belt. "You should have this too."

She ventured over to Pekoe. "My dearest, Pekoe. You always brought a smile to our lips and warmth to our hearts in these long hard treks. May you find peace." She kissed the younger girl's forehead. Wiping away her tears, she walked past the waiting Asadia. Roselana took a place next to Kallias and rested her head against his shoulder.

Asadia stood for a long moment such that they began to wonder if she were still in shock. Then she moved slowly to little Pekoe. "You're so small and dainty. I wish I had known you." She gave her a gentle kiss on the forehead and covered her head and face up again with the shroud. Then to Guin, she stood above his head noting first his body as if in disbelief. She put a nervous hand on each side of his white, lifeless face, then raised her head up, her expression distraught. "What was his name again?"

"Guin," Roselana said appreciatively.

Asadia nodded. "I didn't know Guin." She turned her eyes back to him. "But you were my hero. You kept me from violation and helped my brother. Thank you." She kissed his forehead. Asadia had not yet shed a single tear.

Two wixxon approached with buckets of a sweet-smelling oil and buzzed something to Dealla. She nodded. They splashed oil lightly over Guin's body and pyre and dribbled some across the floor to Pekoe's then repeated the splash and dribble to the first of the wixxon pyres in the spiral. Another wixxon came in holding a torch and with clawed hand pulled on Jamila's arm, indicating she should go, then motioned one at a time to the rest, but stopped Roselana and Kallias. Dealla also remained. The wixxon handed Kallias the torch and made a commanding sound.

Kallias took the torch with a sad smile imbued with honor and nodded his head to the little creature. The wixxon continued to spread the oil as the three friends waited silently. Soon a low hum began and then a higher note joined it. It was not long before the nearbeasts had created a beautiful harmony. Dealla put Roselana's hand in Kallias' and then took Roselana's other hand. She nodded to Kallias. Together they stepped forward to the pyres. Kallias lightly waved the torch under each platform and the oil took the flame and spread. The fire gave their faces a warm glow in the dark, moonless night.

"Bol," instructed Dealla nodding to the torch. Kallias dropped the torch as if knowing the word, and the oiled hay began to catch. Fire climbed and spread more quickly over the next pallet.

Dealla pulled on Roselana's hand, and she on Kallias', as Dealla led them swiftly around and around the spiral to the outside. They stopped and turned once they reached the crowd and the other women. The center of the spiral started with a billowing of dark smoke. Dealla took a handful of sand from the street and threw it then made a wind carry it to the smoke. It made the smoke glow with a blue green light amidst the plumes of gray. They continued to watch as the fire began to catch from one pyre to another. It appeared to be in a dance of its own as it followed the oil trail around the spiral.

The humming song rose and fell with the switching back and catching of the funeral fire's dance.

The wixxon who had led them from the gate, now bowed to Kallias and then asked something of Dealla. She touched Kallias to pull his attention from the spiral. With a look up to the manse butte, she brought his interest to the tower, which was still ablaze. Kallias then realized the wixxon was addressing him. He returned the creature's bow. It gestured to the rekinnder.

"Kallias," she said. After a thoughtful pause while she found the words, she asked, "Hand above d'pakin now? Mele awa tower d'Kallias?" Her broken Kinnir tongue was frank and her eyes said she was asking for the wixxon.

"It seems it'll be a ruin now. No more Mystic Manse, I'm afraid." Kallias smiled with amusement then went stone-faced realizing she was serious. He looked to the wixxon. "What do they want to know about the tower?"

"Hand above awis, longship men, d'pakin ven uene." She made a motion as if one hand was pressing down on the other. "Hand d'Kallias uez?"

"She means will you be their master now or something like that? Take over the tower," Roselana explained, coming up to his side.

"Tell them," he paused in thought then continued. "I'm grateful, but they are a free race now." He smiled.

"Free." She said the word and thought of its meaning a moment.

Kallias nodded once. "Free. Free of a tyrant, free of longship men, free to live life." He gestured with broad movements of his arms. "No one pressing down." He shook his head as he copied the hand sign Dealla had used.

Dealla smiled and nodded her understanding. She slipped into being the little wixxon with the bright blue eyes and began a long tirade in the humming, buzzing, clicking speech of theirs. First a few and then more and finally all of them turned from the funeral pyre and ceased their humming to listen to what she was telling them. Their dark shiny eyes blinked with their strange upper and lower eyelids. Some had renewed tears others began to take Kallias by one hand or the other and touch the back of it to their foreheads. Several of them scattered to buildings and houses which were not burning. These came back with stools and chairs which they placed in a semicircle and led each of the women and Kallias to sit.

"What's going on?" Roselana whispered to Kallias. He shrugged his not knowing.

As they all sat quietly in their company, wixxon came with bandages and ministered to each of the women, except Dealla. Kallias observed the dark bruise on Dealla's forehead and then the many nicks and scratches his little army had received without so much as a whimper from any of them. Then he looked to his own body and clothing. His shirt sleeves were riddled with holes and cuts. His cuirass had taken several hits as well. Miraculously, none of these had delivered so much as a scratch to his skin.

Then a wixxon brought a huge pot and built a fire in it over which he put a grating. This sat in the middle of their semicircle. Another came to the grating bearing a large forearm and hand. Before he could place it on the fire, the women screamed and turned their faces away. Dealla buzzed at him quickly and waved a hand. The abashed wixxon took the arm away and passed the buzzed words on to the others. Soon the female showed up with some vegetables. Some of these she placed on the grate for cooking. She looked askance at Dealla and Kallias. Kallias nodded. Dealla motioned to her. She put the rest of the vegetables on the fire.

Dealla spoke to the wixxon who seemed to be in the lead. They conversed for some time then she returned to rekinnder form. After awhile, another of the little creatures approached and handed Dealla her white bow and full quiver. She said something and bowed her head. The wixxon returned the nod and left. Then Dealla gave Roselana's bow and quiver, with a single arrow left in it, back to her.

"Vezam d'Mehanna," Roselana said, pulling her brows together as she took them. "Pik faleke ushen Asadia d'elwa." Then she stood and held the items out to Dealla.

Great affection shined in the rekinnder's eyes as she gently pushed them back to the Baresian woman. "Tolas hanatol d'awa awo Mehanna von ele."

"Uruan getheng," replied Roselana. "I'll treasure them always."

Kallias, stared blankly at the ground. "What is it Kallias?" Roselana asked as she returned to her stool.

"The prophecy has been fulfilled. But what now? We've no home to return to."

"We can't go home?" Asadia was horrified. "But why? Is there no one left?"

"We're the last, Sister."

"No! There are the inland tribes, Brother. Please." She pleaded and grasped his hand.

His thoughts turned to Dealla longingly, then to his sister. He felt his heart being stretch as if it were in a tug of war. He beheld the confused expressions of the other women. "It's only that—"

The wixxon handed each of them vegetables on a small platter. For most of the girls they were too hot to handle, but Dealla had no difficulty using her fingers to eat the roasted foods.

"You all wish to return to the Barrens?"

They looked at one another. Charlise was the first to speak. "There's no one for us here, is there? I mean. I like the forest and the water. There's so much of it. It is cooler here and smells pretty. But, they can't all be dead. Kallias, we have to find out if we still have families alive."

Zetrine spoke as she gingerly lifted and bit on a squash of some kind. "I think if we go back and there are no men, we'll be in some difficulty. But, as Asadia said, there are the inland tribes."

Kallias took his slab of vegetables but did not eat from them. His eyes took in all of Dealla, from her long slim finger's as they worked the strange steamed vegetables open, to her red lips and her blue eyes as she ate. "What was I thinking?" He emitted a nervous chuckle. "Of course, it's why I came, to bring you home. We'll leave tomorrow night."

Dealla froze. Her eyes met his.

"We can rebuild our village and take in-landers into our tribe." He spoke as if he wanted to leave. Perhaps he even did. But, when Dealla's eyes locked with his, he felt again the tugging within his chest. "Dealla, could come with?"

"I wish Guin were alive. He would come with us." Roselana fingered her untouched platter.

Eyes bright with unshed tears, Dealla spoke to Roselana. "Essio Roselana d'Guin?"

"Yes Dealla, I believe he loved me as much as I loved him," Roselana replied.

"Ushen elwa longship kindis. Zet pakin, uez." Dealla put her slab down and stood.

"Spare the men? What?" Roselana was puzzled.

Kallias stood as well.

She quickly took up her bow and quiver, hooking them over a shoulder and headed for the road at a run. Behind her one of the women whined, "We're not going to eat?" Dealla slipped into the serlcat and picked up speed.

"Wait!" Kallias cried and held out a hand expectantly. "Wait! Dealla!" The road beyond the fire was pitch black as she disappeared into its void. "Stay here," he commanded the others before running blindly down the road after her.

Chapter 34

Kallias' voice reached her sensitive serlcat ears in the darkness as Dealla sped along that southeast trail. She skidded to a stop and turned her night-glow blue eyes back over the road and waited, ears forward. Kallias appeared shortly after. His chest heaving and he took in a deep breath of the cool night air. He nodded to her. "I want to help."

Dealla changed form to speak to him. "Kallias good. Fear elwa d' pakin, no kill. Stop fight now. Spare kinnir."

"Right. Not kill. Spare the men. Then we haven't much time. Let's make haste."

"Kallias to ride?" Dealla asked.

"Dealla." He reached out and held her elbow gently as if to say something. He thought some and grinned. "A horse? Yes! You're much too fast for me to keep up."

She shook her head. "Ekuinoi." Dealla's expression became one of deep concentration as if trying to bring up a memory. Then she whirled the air in a soft cyan mist around her and there stood something like a stocky, thick legged horse with three toes on each foot and a back as tall as Kallias' head. She placed her front knees upon the ground so he could get upon her back. He grabbed hold around her neck and threw a leg over. Once mounted, he leaned forward and grasped her silvery mane. He spoke softly in the night breeze, his lips close to her perked ears. "Let's ride, Spiritdancer."

The equinoi spun about and galloped headlong down the road. As always, her eyes shined, making night vision easy for her. The power of the steed rippled through her muscles with every stride. Kallias used every muscle in his body to hold tight and to keep from being bounced off. He had ridden horses many times before but the equinoi proved to be broader and more powerful than any Baresian breed.

They rode through the night. Only when the sun rose behind the mountains, casting shadows across the road and lighting it with the soft white mists of morning, did the sound of shouts and gun fire reach them. Spiritdancer slowed to a stop and walked until the horrifying encounter came into view.

With boulders and tree trunks, the kervplik assaulted the tall earthen wall and wooden gates of an unfamiliar akinn village. Occasionally an akinn or longship man would appear at the top of the wall and shoot at one of the nearbeasts. The small bullets rarely hit anything vital and served only to anger the creatures further. At the base of the gate a group of the Bloodfish sailors pounded on it and pleaded to be let in, then scattered at the next onslaught. These were caught by occasional rocks and branches. The kervplik's single mindedness was now more apparent than in Durgrinstar as they focused much of their hostility upon those already fallen, burying them in stones and earthen debris. Those men outside of the gate who attempted to move away into the forests were stopped by a large boulder thrown or by the massive hand of a kervplik tossing them back toward the wall. Had there not been so many nearbeasts, the longship men would have had some fighting chance, but as it was, those outside the gates had no ammunition left. And it was quite impossible to get close enough to one of those beasts to strike with sword or knife.

Kallias stared at the massacre from Spiritdancer's back. He dismounted quickly. "How are we to save them without killing the beasts?"

Dealla returned to her form and pulled her bow. "Go." She pointed to the other side of the road in the shadows. She drew the pistol from his back and shoved it into his hand, then she took up a place across the road from him, also in the shadows. She drew her bow and let fly an arrow. The huge rock in a kervplik's hand suddenly blew apart. The near beast jumped and squealed.

Kallias waved to Dealla as she struck the blow and then remarked down to his pistol with disappointment. Keeping his voice low to avoid drawing attention, he asked, "What am I to do with this?" He surveyed the area, awaiting his moment. "I'll give myself away if I shoot it." He gestured to her again.

Dealla blinked and shook her head, not understanding. Then it occurred to her the limitation she had seen with the fire sticks. They could only shoot once before taking time to reload. She crossed the road quickly to Kallias. "Mele ele d'bow." She touched a branch, and as if growing, it gave her a good strong long stick which shaped itself. This bow she handed Kallias and took a hair from her head and touched one end of it to the top notch and another to the bottom to form the string. "Not fire omwa," she explained smiling. It was reminiscent of the fire bow and arrow she had made in the cave so long ago. Then she took from her quiver the un-barbed black fletched arrows and stuck them in the ground at Kallias' feet. She pantomimed pulling back the bowstring and said, "jin," just before releasing the imagined arrow. Dealla nodded, her eyes asking if he understood.

Kallias nodded with a smile and took the bow, he nocked an arrow. Pulling back, he waited, watching the carnage before him. "Ah ha!" In that instant, he saw a stack of logs bundled into a pyramid. A hunter had neared it at that moment. Kallias released the arrow and hit his mark. The rope binding the pile snapped and the large logs rolled just as the kervplik took a thunderous stride. The logs caught his legs and swept his feet from under him.

Dealla watched the logs roll. The commotion got the attention of two others who began to pick them up to use against the wall and men. Kallias shook his head as he only seemed to be helping the kervplik. Dealla turned to Kallias and handed him an arrow, then nocked one of her own. She drew back on the string, said, "Jin!" quietly enough not to be heard over the screams and crashes by anyone but Kallias. Then she let the arrow go. A line of electricity followed the arrow and a log blew apart in the kervplik's hand.

Kallias grinned as a dumbfounded look cascaded his visage. "I forgot to say the word," he took aim, picking his target, a hunter ready to hammer the door down. "'Jin!'" The arrow flew with a crackling sound and hit the end of the log, exploding and shattering it to pieces.

Dealla smiled and ran back across the road to her place in the shadows. However, she was seen by one of the kervplik, who turned away from the group and picked up a log. He moved cautiously up the road towards her peering into the shady forest as the sun continued to add light to it. Kallias saw this from his shelter as the lumbering giant made its way towards Dealla. He nocked another shaft and waited for the right moment. The kervplik caught sight of Dealla and raised the log above his head. Kallias let the arrow fly, expressed worry overcame his face as he forgot to say the enchantment again. His aim was also inaccurate, but it caught the beast in the armpit. The creature yelled and grabbed at the dangling shaft with the other hand, forgetting about the log, which plummeted stump end atop his head knocking him out cold.

The others heard the cry from the wounded one and turned all their attention up the road. They began galumphing quickly toward the unconscious creature. Dealla stepped out of the forest into the middle of the road between them and the fallen one. She dropped to one knee and placed her hands upon the ground with her head down for a long moment as they came at her. Kallias tensed as she brought herself out into the open. He waited. Every muscle in his body told him to run out there, but he had to believe she knew what she was doing.

As the kervplik approached and began lifting their chosen weapons up, the ground began to shake. It rippled out from beneath Dealla, pitching some of them to the ground. Their guttural shouts and instructions to one another added a cacophony of sound to the rumble of the gald. Those who could, began fleeing into the forest where trees rocked upon their roots. The rest crawled away as quickly as they could, like frightened children, leaving only the one on the road. Though some frightened cries went up from the village during the quake, the wall and gate on their side remained steady. Kallias clung to a tree, smiling in amazement. As the rumbling subsided, he peered about to see that all was clear, then strode towards Dealla.

She lifted her head to see the gates open and akinn men admitting the last few navy men into the town. The road cleared quickly. Only Kallias was left standing.

He took her hands in his and helped raise her to her feet. "You did it, Dealla. You spared the longship men."

Dealla smiled and shook her head. "Zet bosae ele. Mele awa et, d'kuita."

Kallias chuckled as he was lost with her language. Suddenly Dealla threw her arms around him. Caught in the sudden embrace, he froze for a moment but let his arms engulf her. Dealla rattled off some more of her language into his ear. She sounded happy and excited to tell him so much, but it was all a jumble he could not understand, nor did it really matter to him at the moment. Her joy brought him joy and he began slowly to draw his lips close to her chattering ones. The moment faded as the kervplik moaned.

He stopped and looked. Then Dealla led him by the hand into the forest to the west of the road where the nearbeast could not see them. Alone and wounded the kervplik had no heart left to pursue anything and shuffled off to the east.

Kallias watched the hulking creature leave in shame. He gazed into Dealla's adamant blue eyes a long moment while shadows danced on her face as the leaves swayed in the breeze. Then he kissed her. "Come home with me," he whispered.

Dealla's eyes lit up. Again she babbled something in Rekinnder but with Roselana's and Asadia's names in it.

"Roselana? Asadia?" Kallias presented a puzzled smile. "Why of course. We'll all go home."

She laughed and nodded then made her way back to the road with him in tow. Once there, she swirled herself into the great horse-like creature. Kallias could now see the equinoi had a shorter nose, was long haired all over and very squarely built for a horse. Still it resembled one. They loped northward back toward Durgrinstar and the ladies.

Kallias did not realized the splendor of the land until the ride back. With the burden of saving Asadia upon his shoulders, his surroundings never garnered his attention quite so much as it did at the present. This beauty was belied by the carnage brought upon it. He saw craters, where once large boulders had been sitting for centuries untouched, and broken trees with their branches strewn about. Scattered along the road were bodies of Bloodfish men and akinn. Each corpse told a tale of some cruel fate of bludgeoning. Side-by-side appeared the magnificence of the land and the repulsiveness of the conflict that had raked across it.

Spiritdancer slowed to a walk as she saw a group of figures at a distance up the road. Kallias held the edge of his palm to his forehead. He could not quite make out detail but he smiled knowingly when he realized the movements were those of familiar women. One of the women waved as she recognized Kallias atop the strange large horse.

"Kallias! Kallias!" the girls called excitedly.

Dealla's long strides soon caught up with them and she stopped to let Kallias down. Kallias hopped lightly to his feet. "Well, the longship men have been saved." Dealla returned to rekinnder form.

He was unsure if any of them heard him as they all chattered at once. "Did you feel it?" "The ground shook this morning." "—rocks rolling, walls falling—" "—creatures really sharp screams—" "Never had such a fright—" "Would you ever have believed it?" "—pyre fell, too—" "It's like we're in the old stories." "—coming true."

Kallias replied to the questions. "We did feel it," this with a chuckle and no explanation. "No, except for having been here. We've seen living proof our history is true."

"What a strange horse you make, Dealla," said Zetrine.

"Do you think they'll appreciate us now, because you've shown them mercy?" Jamila asked looking between Dealla and Kallias.

Kallias' eyes met hers. He gave her a gentle smile. "Jamila, we didn't come for revenge. We came to get Asadia."

"Are we going home now?" asked Asadia.

Dealla smiled. "Point of Gald, home."

Kallias felt a tug deep within his chest as everyone turned expectantly to him for a reply. "Well, I... uhm..."

"What? No," returned Asadia. "Baresi is home."

They passed glances amongst themselves. Then Roselana spoke up. "Kallias perhaps we should talk about it as we walk back to Durgrinstar. Because either way we are going to need the boat."

Kallias finally spoke. "We will need the boat. Good idea. Let's talk as we return."

They turned as a unit and headed down the road no one speaking at first. Dealla felt pushed to the outside as they spoke of this place they called their home.

Roselana's voice broke the silence as sweetly as birdsong. "I noticed that some of the wixxon were shot with the fire sticks, the guns, but didn't die. They went down and later others found them and took the ball out of their bodies. And now, they're awake and quite alive."

"I saw that too," said Charlise.

"That gives me hope that my brother perhaps isn't dead, though I saw him shot and fall," Roselana concluded.

"Perhaps so," Kallias gave Dealla short, longing glances.

It seemed to her as if they were going to be his last desirous gazes. That idea hurt, so Dealla walked eyes ahead or at her feet, as she dared not look Kallias' way.

"I think we shouldn't give up on our loved ones who may not be dead. We should go back and let them know we live, too." Roselana made a strong argument. The others chimed in and agreed that there needed to be rebuilding of their homes and a search for living relatives.

Kallias nodded with thoughts elsewhere but also added, "Let's hope I can sail." He smiled. "After all, I did crash here unexpectedly."

"Then we're all agreed upon returning to Baresi." Roselana made it a statement rather than a question though each answered in the affirmative and all stopped, expecting Kallias' confirmation.

He considered Dealla, whose eyes were fixed ahead, then affirmed the statement with a nod. "It's agreed. We go to Baresi."

Dealla turned betrayed eyes on him. Again she spoke quickly in her own tongue explaining much and pointing back the way they had come as if they had reached some agreement, the two of them.

They all stopped some few yards short of entering the city. Roselana turned around. "What? Isn't she coming with us?" Dealla then turned to Roselana and spoke rapidly. "Wait, wait, Dealla. It's too fast. I don't understand." Roselana shifted her attention to Kallias. "You did tell her to come, didn't you?"

"I asked. But I can't make her."

Dealla turned to Kallias and spoke again more slowly. "Mele jaia. Uvetol ka selendo elwa rekin kuita." Then waited for Roselana to translate.

Roselana shook her head slowly and gave a puzzled expression to Kallias. "This doesn't make much sense. She says she can't come until the new body wears off."

Dealla turned hopeful eyes to Kallias.

"What does she mean? Does she shed her skin, too, like a-a snake or like birds getting new feathers?"

Dealla saw the confusion on his face and knew something had gone wrong in the translation. She turned again to Roselana. "Tolu d'elwa rekin kuita."

"D'elwa rekin," Roselana repeated. "No, she said your new body."

"We—" Kallias motioned to the other Baresians then himself. "Have only but one body, Dealla."

"No, Kallias." Roselana paused. "She did not say your body as in just you. She said our new body. Not as in ours." Roselana motioned to all of them. "But our as in yours and hers. Kallias, I think—" Roselana hesitated to say more. Kallias remained in a silent frustration. Roselana pointed at Dealla and then put a hand on her own abdomen. "This new, Dealla? Is this kuita?" Dealla nodded and again turned hope filled eyes to Kallias as Roselana gave him a new translation. "She can't leave her nest until your baby is born, Kallias."

He gawked at her. "My... baby?" He paused, eyes and mouth broadening into a joyful expression. "Our baby?!" His shout caused Dealla to wince.

Dealla nodded eyes filled with uncertain gladness. All the women exchanged glances and then, almost at once, gathered around Dealla with hugs and chatter, which confused her at first.

"Congratulations, father," Roselana said with a soft smile.

"I'm going to be a father! I'm going to be a father!" His eyes began to get glassy. "This means, we... no, I can't leave yet. She's... I've..." he pleaded.

"Nine moons time though. That's so long," Asadia commented.

"Moon, ive," repeated Dealla, smiling toward Asadia.

Asadia nodded with a smirk and held up nine fingers. "Nine moon for that to be born." She punctuated her disappointment as she pointed to Dealla's belly.

Dealla shook her head. She took some time to find the words and said to Asadia, "Dõ season d'rekinnder, dõj moon gone, nij ive, lõj ive."

"No, it's faster for her, Asadia, only one season. She has but two moons left. We will stay until you and the little one are ready to travel," assured Roselana.

"Where will we live for so long?" asked Asadia.

Kallias smiled and held a finger towards the south. "Point of the Gald," he declared and embraced Dealla.

SELECTED TRANSLATIONS
of the REKINNDER

Selected Translations of the Rekinnder

Chapter 13

01 "Ak Mehanna! Atlo falke juet awa omwa da?"
Oh Mehanna! How did you come to this end?

02 "Palae mile awa von kinnir, shiive Rekinnder et awis?"
Why would you go with the kinnir, the killers of our people?

03 "Sege ala d'shrivez? Uene shrivez awo ala hol da!"
Where was he, your protector, when you needed protection from him?

04 "Zet jakala ka sega leot awa d'ala, von zet mahij pez leot ele awo awa. Atlo rivesh eot ele? Zon uez bosae ele."
You should not have followed him, and I should not have abandoned you. How could I listen to you then? Now I finally understand.

05 "Alle, alle d'awa, Mehanna! Tiiti juzaum kinnir! Shiive von gradin mis dö mis juzaum!"
I promise, my promise to you, Mehanna! I'll find the cowardly kinnir! I'll kill and mutilate that one, that coward.

06 "Uene uratol döj, waling kinnit."
When the first dies, others suffer.

Chapter 15

The Funeral Prayer of the Rekinnder
07 Amahal Mehanna. Essio d'ele.
Amahal ka vamase d'elwa lalipre.
Padekoi pez azenu d'Mahanna.
Rawnhaj Iasegald von rabnio d'ira.

Mahij ka lapret von lipret, wele zet gaio.
Iabriz owila olive d'awa.
Padekoi haiekala oliv enade.
Fri sel isa urume zon zonda.

Amahal ka azenua, ka selendo gald.
Amahal Mehanna. Mile owi urume.
Net fri iaowi ele d'olive awa gaio.
Rawnhaj Iasegald von rabnio d'ira.

Ele Dealla da, de-alle.

Return my beloved Mehanna,
Return to the wisdom of our ancestors.
Fly away, spirit of Mehanna,
As my eyes rain a flood upon Iasegald.

Leave to father and mother. who live no more.
I embrace your history within me.
Soar upward, remembered forever.
Let her breathe the sweet peace of the ultimate
existence.

Return to a spiritual state, to the birth of the world.
Return Mehanna. Go peacefully.
But allow me to keep your memories alive.
My eyes rain a flood upon Iasegald.

I am Dealla, the promise keeper.

08 Tolukuez azenu d'awa. Mahij rekin gald. Awo ma ka
   zonda.
   Grasp hold of your spirit. Leave the physical world.
   From ashes to ultimate freedom.

09 "Zet zon due d'elwa? Net d'elwa—zet...ele da."
   We are not the last, are we? But we are—no...I am.

10 "Zet due. Tiiti awis."

Not alone. I will find them.

***

REKINNDER LEXICON
and DICTIONARY

On the following pages you'll find the Rekinnder
Language divided into the following topics:

Lexicon
Dictionary
Numbers
Ordinals (Numerical Orders)

***

Rekinnder Lexicon

In this world of Iasegald, where the lands of Marisko, Baresi, Valandrea and others exist, what we in our world know as the English language is referred to as the Common language. The author of this book will be building upon the language of Rekinnder so long as there are books to write about them.

Pronunciation Key:

In Rekinnder, as in Spanish, Japanese and other languages of our world, vowels have but one sound each. Furthermore, in Rekinnder the consonants also have but one sound each. And, certain letters do not exist at all. G is always a hard sound as in get and NEVER sounds like j as in genius.

Letters of the Common that do not exist in Rekinnder are; c, q, x and y. There is also no ch sound in Rekinnder.

Vowels are a e i o and u only as the letter y does not exist in Rekinnder.

a = rounded ah as in father

e = like ay as in day

i = like ee as in feet

o = long o as in okay

u = like oo as in goose

Most other letters are pronounced as they are in the Common tongue.

Syntax and Markers:

As in many languages, Rekinnder does not use articles such as; a, an, and the.

States of being verbs, which are; is, am, are, was, were and be, do not exist. Replacing these is the marker; d', which appears before the word being emphasized. This marker, d', is also often used in place of the Common words of and to.

To state simply that a thing "is" or is in existence, the extended marker da is used. The marker, da, is placed independently at the end of a Rekinnder sentence. Da is

NOT USED AS A VERB in sentence construction, meaning it does not come first in a Rekinnder sentence.
Examples of using the marker d' and da:
The Common tongue: What do you know of this?
Rekinnder: Wetae bosae d'omwa? (Pronounced as: Way-tah-ay bo-sah-ay dohm-wah?)
Literally: What know (of) this? {... "do you" is understood.}

The Common tongue: What is this?
Rekinnder: Wetae omwa da? (Pronounced as: Way-tah-ay ohm-wah dah?)
Literally: What this exists?

Note: Negatives and positives may come at the beginning of a sentence. Colloquialisms exist as well, giving variety to the standard sentence constructions. Some syntax is as follows:
1. Verb, subject;
"Shiiv awis."
[(They burn.) Lit.: Burn they.]

2. Verb, subject, object/predicate phrase;
"Hanatol Mehana d'awa."
[(Mehanna gave it as a gift to you.) Lit.: A gift given (by) Mehanna to you.]

3. Verb, subject, adjective;
"Alaf olent d'Kallias."
[(I will/do dry Kallias' clothing.) Lit.: Dry (I) clothing (of)Kallias.]

4. Verb, subject, adjective modifiers, object;
"Piira ka kuite jaia."
[(Look at my new home.) Lit.: Look at new nest.]

5. Negative, Verb, subject, modifier da;
"Zet iajue ele da."

[(I have no one to comfort me.) Lit.: No solace mine exists.]

6. Colloquialisms with descriptive only and not complete sentences;
"Doisha d'vezj."
[(Arrows) Lit.: Wings of claws]
"Farnio ka vezam."
[(Weapon making table) Lit.: Table for weapons]

As in many languages a declarative sentence without a stated subject generally has an understood "you"/"awa" or "I"/"ele" as its subject. Content and situation can tell us which it is.
Interrogative pronouns begin questions and are followed by the verb and complete sentence.
"Sege d'Asadia?" [Where (is) Asadia?]
Plurals no longer exist as a form of word in Rekinnder. Singular words that by definition are representative of a multitude do exist; words such as many, crowd, herd, as well as pronouns such as; we, they and these.
Again, let content and situation be your guide where these peculiarities exist in the Rekinnder language.

Note: Guin's and Yungir's incantations: Arun fet shaun and shishakeen for example, are not Rekinnder. Therefore the meanings of these magic words will not be found in this lexicon word list.

Dictionary

Diction key:

Soft "ss" sounds like "ce" as in "once".

Single "s" connected to a syllable is hard "s" sound as in "goes".

The ending "zh" sounds like the "si" in the word "Asian".

Rekinnder - Diction key - Grammar - Common

A —

adint - (ah-deent) - n - tooth/teeth/dental

agos - (ah-goh-ss) - pn - which

akinn - (ah-keen-n) - n - humble being (race)

ala - (ah-la) - pn - he/him/his

alaf - (ah-lahf) - adj, v - dry/shed or leave the water

ali - (ah-lee) - pn - she/her/hers

alle - (ah-lay) - n, v - certain/promise/sure

amahal - (ah-mah-hahl) - n, v - return/go or come back

atlo - (aht-loh) - adv - how

awa - (ah-wah) - pn - you/your

awis - (ah-weese) - pn - they/them/their

awo - (ah-woh) - prep - from

azenu - (ah-zay-noo) - n - spirit/consciousness

azenua - (ah-zay-noo-ah) - n - spirit being/conscious being

B —

bol - (bohl) - n, prep - south/down

bolao - (boh-la-oh) - prep - below/under

bosae - (boh-sah-ay) - v - know/understand

brikar - (bree-kahr) - n - strength

brike - (bree-kay) - v - carry

briz - (breez) - n - arm(s)

D —

d' - (dh) - ~m~ - (to be)/of/by

da - (dah) - ~mv~ - exist(s) (to be)

Dealla - (day-ah-lah) - Pn - Promise Keeper
disu - (dee-soo) - n - mouth
diskus - (dee-skoo-ss) - v - say/said/speak
doisha - (doh-ee-shah) - n - wings
dolok - (doh-lohk) - n - shoulder
dolu - (doh-loo) - n, v - endure(ance)
due - (doo-ay) - adj - single/solitary/alone

E —
ekuine - (ay-koo-ee-nay) - n - ride/rideable/horse (equine)
ekuinoi - (ay-koo-ee-noh-ee) - n - a horse-like animal with
        three toes (equinoi)
ele - (ay-lay) - pn - I /me/my/mine
elwa - (ayl-wah) - pn - we/us/our(s)
enade - (ay-nah-day) - adv - always/forever/eternity
eot - (ay-oht) - v - can/would/could
essa - (ay-ssah) - n - heart
essio - (ayss-ee-oh) - adj, n, v - beloved/dear/love
et - (ayt) - pn - it
ete - (ay-tay) - pn - its
evia - (ay-vee-ah) - n - night

F —
faleke - (fah-lay-kay) - adj, v - done/finish
falke - (fall-kay) - v - do/did
farnio - (fahr-nee-oh) - n - table/still water
fet - (fayt) - prep - after/afterward
fobridis - (foh-bree-dee-ss) - v - command/shout
fri - (free) - v - allow/let/release
frusent - (froo-saynt) - v - confuse/daze

G —
gaffini - (gahf-fee-nee) - n - water animal/sea creature
gaio - (gah-ee-oh) - n - life/alive
gald - (gahld) - n - world
getheng - (gayth-ayng) - v - generous
goz - (gohz) - n - earth/ground
gozib - (goh-zeeb) - n - stone
gozibri - (goh-zee-bree) - v - turn to stone

gradin - (grah-deen) - v - bite/chew up
gragoz - (grah-gohz) - v - crush/grind/mutilate

H —

haiaive - (ha-ee-ah-ee-vay) - adj, n - highest/heavens(stars)
haiekala - (hah-ee-ay-kah-lah) - adv, n, prep - skyward/into
    the clouds
hanatol - (hah-nah-tohl) -n, v - give/gift/bless
hil - (heel) - n - air
hilio - (hee-lee-oh) - n, v - heat/hot
hilma - (heel-mah) - n - smoke
hol - (hol) - n, v - need

I —

ia - (ee-ah) - n, v - cradle/hold
iabriz - (ee-ah-breez) - n, v - embrace/cradle in arms
iajue - (ee-ah-joo-ay) - n, v - comfort/solace/turn to
iakin - (ee-ah-keen) - n - stomach/belly
iaowi - (ee-ah-oh-wee) - n - keep/maintain
Iasegald - (ee-ah-say-gahld) - Pn - Cradle of Living
    Things/the world name
io - (ee-oh) - n - fire/flame
ira - (ee-rah) - n - eyes
iris - (ee-ree-ss) - adj - visible
isa - (ee-sah) - adj, n - beauty(-iful)/sweet (ness)
ive - (ee-vay) - n - moon

J —

jaia - (jah-ee-ah) - n - nest/home
jakala - (jah-kah-lah) - v - follow
jalita - (jah-lee-tah) - n, v - roof/shelter
jez - (jayz) - adj - bad
jimio - (jee-mee-oh) - n, v - burn
jin - (jeen) - abbr - abbreviation of liojin (slang)
juet - (joo-et) - v - come/bring forth
juzaum - (joo-zah-oom) - n, v - betray/coward

K —

ka - (kah) - prep - as/to/for

kindis - (keen-dee-ss) - n - people/public/person
kinnir - (keen-neer) - n - estranged ones (human race)
kinnit - (keen-neet) - n - other/another
kuita - (koo-ee-tah) - n - baby
kuite - (koo-ee-tay) - adj - new

L —

laej - (lah-ayzh) - n - reason
lalipre - (lah-lee-pray) - n - ancestors
lapret - (lah-prayt) - n - father
leot - (lay-oht) - v - will/may/should
linist - (leen-eest) - n - stream/river
liojin - (lee-oh-jeen) - n - electric(-ity)
lipret - (lee-prayt) - n - mother
livo - (lee-voh) - n - moonlight

M —

ma - (mah) - n - dust/ashes
mahij - (mah-hee-zh) - v - leave/abandon/gone
maogra - (mah-oh-grah) - n - a sea monster
masent - (mah-saint) - n - head
Mehanna - (may-ha-nah) - Pn - Blessed Reward
mele - (may-lay) - v - make/made
mile - (mee-lay) - v - go
mis - (mee-ss) - pn - that
mrez - (mm-rayz) - n - shock/electric shock

N —

net - (nayt) - conj - but/however
nio - (nee-oh) - n - water
niolo - (nee-oh-loh) - n - ice
nozonio - (noh-zoh-nee-oh) - n - dark fire/funeral pyre
nust - (noost) - adj, n, pn - all/everything

O —

olef - (oh-layf) - n - fur/hair
olent - (oh-laynt) - n - clothing/removable fur
oliv - (oh-leev) - v - remember(ed)
olive - (oh-lee-vay) - n - memories/history

omwa - (ohm-wah) - pn - this
oni - (oh-nee) - n - story
owi - (oh-wee) - prep - in/into
owila - (oh-wee-lah) - prep - inside/within

P —
padekoi - (pah-day-koh-ee) - v - fly/soar
pak - (pahk) - n - animal/creature
pakao - (pah-kah-oh) - n - evil creature
pakeke - (pah-kay-kay) - n - rodent
pakin - (pah-keen) - n - all near beast races
palae - (pah-lah-ay) - adv - why
pez - (pays) - adv - far/away
piira - (pee-ee-rah) - v - see/watch
pik - (peek) - v - use/using
pressez - (pray-ssay-ez) - n, v - union/unite

R —
rab - (rahb) - v - fall
rabnio - (rahb-nee-oh) - n - rain/water fall
rarid - (rah-reed) - n, v - blind/cover eyes/hide
rawnhaj - (rahn-hah-zh) - n, v - flood/overwhelm/blanket
rekin - (ray-keen) - n - body/physical form
rekinnder - (ray-keen-n-dayr) - n - connected ones (race)
rezek - (ray-zayk) - v - stand/stand up
rivesh - (re-vaysh) - v - listen/hear

S —
sega - (say-gah) - adv - here
sege - (say-gay) - adv - where
sel - (sayl) - n, v - breath/breathe
sele - (say-lay) - n, v - cause
selendo - (say-layn-doh) - n, v - birth/child birth
shaiz - (shah-eez) - v - freeze
shiive - (shee-ee-vay) - v - kill/destroy/burn up
shrivej - (shree-vay-zh) - v - defend/protect

T —
tiau - (tee - ah - oo) - n - scent/smell

tiiti - (tee - ee - tee) - v - find/search/sniff-out
tol - (tohl) - n - hand(s)
tolas - (toh - la - ss) -v - take
tolu - (toh - loo) - v - have/has/grasp
tolukuez - (toh - loo - koo - ayz) - v - seize/grasp hold

U —
uene - (oo-ay-nay) - adv - when
uez - (oo-ays) - adv - now
uratol - (oo-rah-tohl) - n, v - death/die
uruan - (oo-roo-ahn) - n, v - accept/acceptance
urume- (oo-roo-may) - adj, n- peace (-ful)
ushen - (oo-shayn) - v - rescue/save
uvetol - (oo-vay-tohl) - v - remain/stay

V —
vamase - (vah-mah-say) - adj, n - wise/wisdom
ven - (vayn) - n -time
vezam - (vay-zahm) - n - weapon (any man-made weapon)
vezj - (vay-zh) - n - claw(s)
von - (vohn) - adv, conj, prep - and/with/also/too

W —
wain - (wah-een) - v - approve/like
waling - (wah-leeng) - n, v - pain/suffer
wele - (way-lay) - pn - who
wetae - (way-tah-ay) - pn - what
wopik - (woh-peek) - adj, n, v - purpose/use/useful

Z —
zenu - (zay-noo) - n - elements
zenupiir - (zay-noo-pee-eer) - n - friend/see into another
zefe - (zay-fay) - n - monkey
Zefebn - (zay-fayb-n) - Pn - marmoset (name given by Dealla)
zet - (zayt) - adv - no/not/negatives
zon - (zohn) - adj - (at) last/ultimate/final(ly)
zonda - (zohn-dah) - n - freedom/ultimate existence

Numbers and Counting

Rekinnder - Diction key - Digits - Word

dõ - (doh-oh) - 1 - One
ni - (nee) - 2 - Two
lõ - (loh-oh) - 3 - Three
mi - (mee) - 4 - Four
põn - (poh-ohn) - 5 - Five
ri - (ree) - 6 - Six
rõs - (roh-oh-ss) - 7 - Seven
fi - (fee) - 8 - Eight
gõt - (goh -oht) - 9 - Nine
vin - (veen) - 10 - Ten
vidõ - (vee-doh-oh) - 11 - Eleven
vini - (vee-nee) - 12 - Twelve
vilõ - (vee-loh-oh) - 13 - Thirteen
vimi - (vee-mee) - 14 - Fourteen
vipõn - (vee-poh-ohn) - 15 - Fifteen
viri - (vee-ree) - 16 - Sixteen
virõs - (vee-roh-oh-ss) - 17 - Seventeen
vifi - (vee-fee) - 18 - Eighteen
vigõt - (vee-goh-oht) - 19 - Nineteen
nivin - (nee-veen) - 20 - Twenty
lõvin - (loh-oh-veen) - 30 - Thirty
mivin - (mee-veen) - 40 - Forty
põnvin - (poh-ohn-veen) - 50 - Fifty
rivin - (ree-veen) - 60 - Sixty
rõsvin - (roh-oh-ss-veen) - 70 - Seventy
fivin - (fee-veen) - 80 - Eighty
gõtvin - (goh-oht-veen) - 90 - Ninety
hei - (hay-ee) - 100 - One hundred
hei nivin - (hay-ee nee-veen) - 120- One hundred-twenty
lõhei dõvin - (loh-oh-hay-ee doh-oh-veen) - 311 - Three
      hundred-eleven
mihei dõ - (mee-hay-ee doh-oh) - 401 - Four hundred-one
hei mivin dõ - (hay-ee mee-veen doh-oh) - 141 - One
      hundred-forty-one

Some ordinals:

When forming ordinals simply add a "j" to the tale end of the number no matter how long it is. This "j" is the extended sound represented by "zh" as mentioned above.

Rekinnder - Diction key - Digits - Word

dõj - (doh-oh-zh) - 1st - First
nij - (nee-zh) - 2nd - Second
lõj - (loh-oh-zh) - 3rd - Third
mij - (mee-zh) - 4th - Fourth
põnj - (poh-ohn-zh) - 5th - Fifth
nihei mivin nij - (nee-hay-ee mee-veen nee-zh) - Two
       hundred-forty-second

About the Author:
Luthie M West currently lives in Oregon with her husband. She has spent years exploring many of life's adventures and challenges, resulting in the discovery of a few wonderful passions. Among her passions are the creative endeavors of storytelling through her writing and stage acting.

Luthie recalls her first spark of storytelling inspiration when her mother had written a unique story just for her and her sisters. Soon after, when Luthie was barely 11, she acted on that inspiration and wrote her own unique story. Her family loved the story dearly, and Luthie has been developing original stories and telling them ever since.

Now, many years later, the stories are made available to a much wider family via her published books.

Other books by Luthie M West:
Visit Little Cabbagehead Books
For excerpts and links to your favorite online retailers:
https://LittleCabbageheadBooks.com

Children's Picture Books released in 2017;
Cat Soup
Tic Tac and the Raven
The Bully Frog
Laila's Magic Brush

Coming Next year, YA Fantasy;
Like an Owl in Moonlight

Like an Owl in Moonlight
by Luthie M West

ISBN: 978-1-7322514-5-8

***

Prologue

Elebrie galloped between the trees trying to catch up to the four unicorns ahead of her, laughing and leaping nimbly over bushes and logs. It wasn't fair to call a race and expect her to stay upon the ground just because ~they~ couldn't fly. She thought, *If they had wanted to come into the world with wings, why didn't they? Why torment her with their rules?* She leaped a log just as a rabbit popped its head up from a knot hole. Her wings spread reflexively and pulled her up out of the way, which slowed her down too. "Blast!"

They were headed toward Fern Feather Lake. If they turned south through the pixie grove toward Windswept Knoll she would not be able to keep her feet on the ground all the way to Marmoset Rock, because they would take the route over the fallen sycamore at the top of the slide. She'd jump that and be airborne. It was against her nature to keep her wings so tight to her body in all this rush of air and speed. They would accuse her of cheating like they always did if she went over their heads. But then again, they accused her even if she went around by the lake edge, too...if she won.

Elebrie leaped a berry-bush hedge. Her hooves clipped something and she stumbled but didn't fall. Behind her the plaintive "mawr" of a bear sounded. She stopped and turned. "Sorry!" she said in her best animal speak. She knew he couldn't be hurt by her as he was a native to the First Forever Forest, permitting her hooves to heal rather than harm him. But it was a rude interruption to his berry picking and required a politeness. Her apology was not remorse or regret, for like the unicorn, she did not have regrets. If the bear had no injuries from clumsy paws in the thorny bushes now, the healing power she just released would wait for the next time he pricked himself or got stung by a bee or had an acorn thrown at his sensitive nose by an angry squirrel. So it was nothing to Elebrie to have kicked him in her jump.

"Oh no!" She realized the time that her simple politeness and moment of thought cost her in the race. She ran again trying to keep her wings as close to her sides as possible.

Sure enough, the unicorns cut through the pixie grove. The tiny winged folk grabbed at her mane and tail. Small as they were, the swarm of them pulling on her, beating their many little wings against her forward thrust, slowed her just enough. They called out in their wee high pitched voices, "Where are you going, Elebrie?" and "Fly Elebrie" and "Use your wings!"

"You know where I'm going," she responded, zigzagging through towering evergreens. "It's a foot race, not a wing race. Let me go!" She jumped and stomped to try to shed them. "Why don't you ever stop them when they come through here?"

"They don't have wings," the little voices chimed.

One little pixie, Lakoima, flew backwards in front of Elebrie's face. "Why do you keep playing this racing? Why keep to your brother's rules? He's a bully." She perched herself between Elebrie's ears, grasping tiny handfuls of her forelock and bracing petite feet against her alicorn. "Let your sisters race him. You come fly with us."

That suggestion led them into another chorus; "Fly with us, Elebrie. Fly Elebrie, fly!"

"Lakoima! Let go!" Elebrie pleaded, "Everyone let go!"

"Take me up, Dear One. Fly me high into the blue!" The pixie yanked at the forelock.

"No. You stay to the trees or you'll pass out and fall again, Lako. Now let me go!" Finally, as always, she shook her head violently and let her body shudder all the way down to the tip of her tail, throwing the pixies every which way. As they tumbled over bushes and into treetops, their cries and shouts sounded like the whistling of the wind.

She focused again on catching up with her siblings. There it was, the split in the paths, one up one down. They slowed just enough so she could see their tails disappear up the incline towards the top of the knoll.

She was too late to make up for it. Her eyes filled with defiance. Who cared about their rules? She would go over the top and take their accusations. Holding herself more tightly together, Elebrie galloped with greater determination towards the eminent sycamore leap. And there it was with the dust of the unicorns rising on the other side. Her hooves pounded the earth in her final steps, preparing for the leap. It was this lowering that gave her a momentary traction that her physical lightness did not permit at a run. Her front legs first stretched and grabbed the ground as she lowered her head slightly bringing her neck and back into a straight line just before pulling her hind legs forward to push at the ground. The leap was an extraordinary feeling. The contact with the earth felt as if it had caught her weight firmly giving only enough to spring back and launch her into the air.

Elebrie watched the log sweep away beneath her, and as it did, she lifted her head and threw her wings open. This...this was the thrill she lived every day for. She lived for the times she would spring into the air like this, catch the wind and soar. Forget the race this time. Forget floating down over their heads to the rock and listening to them discount her magnificence. They were jealous is all.

Elebrie whooshed past the unicorns barely listening to their calls and protests. She flew.

That was the beginning, the day a single feather dropped from her wing. It would grow back, she knew. But the sadness was in the meaning.

It happened like this...

***

Part 1
The Villain

"An environment influenced by the living beings within it vibrates in harmony with those beings and can be said to take on a life of its own. Is it then any wonder that this be true even more so of a magical place whether made magical by claim or by creation?"
—Words of the Weave Scholar

***

Lack of Autumn

"Nowhere is the evidence of creatures of magic more pronounced than that in a forest of eternal springtime. Most specifically it is the evidence of at least one unicorn."
——*Words of the Weave*
Scholar

A tall, thin wizard stood staring out a window at a sparse and nearly dead stand of trees around the great edifice of his home and laboratory. His salt and pepper beard draped to the middle of his chest and scraggly bits of long threads of hair clung fitfully in a half-circle around his head at the level of his ears to droop around his collar or gather upon his shoulders.

"By gawds, I need a gardener," he mumbled.

"Master Zadok?" whined a voice behind him.

The mage turned. "What do you want slime? You reek and you've tracked your steps upon my carpet."

"Sorry Master," replied the goblin servant. "Slagspit has wet his self again. Is that student's tricks, Master. He..."

"What do you want?" The mage rubbed his temples, irritated.

"You sez remind you of new moon, Master. Is tonight, Master."

"And why did I tell you to remind me of the new moon?"

"Slagspit forgets, Master."

Zadok stepped away from the window and sat down in his great throne-like high-backed chair. He heaved a deep regretful sigh and said, "Oh Slagspit...life is miserable..." He ran his fingers through his steel-gray hair absently and then looked at it as it fell between them. "Oh damn it all, I've got only six hairs left on my head !" He cried.

"Oh no, Master. You has twenty and three that side alone!" Slagspit retorted gleefully, despite the fact that goblins know little about numbers.

Zadok gave him a narrow-eyed glare. "Remind me again. How is it you, a goblin, manage to speak the common tongue?"

Proudly Slagspit responded, "Oh, Master spells it on me! A wonderful gift!"

"Then shut up before I take it back."

"Yez, Master."

Zadok's eyes flashed and the goblin cowered. "Go collect some of the dog plants. And find my book! If one of your sniveling relatives has damaged it while cleaning up like you did with my crystal ball..."

The goblin raised both hands as if to calm the mage. "Oh no, Master. Slagspit does not let nasty relatives touches your book."

"Then find out where it went and who took it, and bring it back." His voice dripped saccharine though his face twisted into a threatening sneer.

"Yez, Master." Slagspit shuffled off.

Some time later, Zadok slumped in his chair. On his desk sat a large tome propped against a mountain of books. The pages turned with the casual lift of his gnarled index finger.

"Master." The rich tones of the handsome young mage apprentice, Mercet, reached Zadok's ears as if from near proximity. The word was commanded rather than asked though it was clearly a petition.

"Mercet." Zadok lowered his finger.

The brief moments passed that it took to cross the length of the laboratory but not a footfall was heard even when Mercet appeared from around the cluttered desk.

"Lesson time, Master."

"You're prompt."

"I don't wish to be transformed into a slug."

"Ah lesson learned."

"Yes, well. That was one of my first lessons. What will it be today? "

"You're arrogant. Bah! Well it suits you. How have you been doing on your translations?"

"Very good I would say. I've been able to read and memorize the scrolls of cold elements; frost and ice, by daggers and ray and by storm and spray. Hey there's a bit of a rhyme."

"Yes, yes. What else?"

"Oh charm spells, three kinds. Some healing spells strictly for personal use. Not to be wasted on the pathetic. Spells of aberration, emulation, transmogrification..."

"That reminds me." The younger mage stopped poised as he had been counting on his fingers. Zadok raised his eyes to him with little interest. "Stop popping into dragon form or whatever it is that's frightening Slagspit. He pisses himself and then tracks it onto my carpet."

Mercet's eyes filled with amusement. "Why I've done no such thing."

"Also stop lying to me until you know how to do it."

"Just practicing."

"Practice on the gullible." After a pause Zadok continued. "What do you know of magical forests?"

"The home of unicorns and other magical creatures?" Mercet asked smugly.

"Precisely."

"Nothing."

"Do you know if you lived in one you'd never die? You could do anything and everything you wanted...you would become young and stay that way. And like the unicorn, if you left you'd have some little time to effect some devastating influence and as soon as you returned home, return to your complete self, healthy, young...vital. You'd have forever to wield your magic..." He stopped, suddenly realizing something, and glowered at Mercet. "Don't get any ideas."

"But you would first have to know where there was an eternal forest of spring and what its borders were..." Mercet's words slowed as he recognized Zadok's expression. "You ~know~ of such a place?"

"I happened upon it one terrible winter. A place of eternal spring. A place where every living thing watches. Where every leaf and stem and root and petal heals and revitalizes."

Mercet's mouth hung open.

"But the damnable unicorn and its woods..." He paused, glanced sideways at the apprentice and back-tracked. "Unless one has the favor of a magical creature of that forest, the magic will push you out!" He made a shoving motion of his hands and a pile of books flew off of a bench across the room. "Any wounded thing can stay and convalesce. Can be, will be, trapped with enchantment and never want to leave. A forest like that rea-ches-to-the-heart..." Zadok moaned near to tears.

Mercet remained unmoved. "And you want back in."

"I will have it back!" He cried out with anger and frustration.

"But it would just push you out again. Do you mean to capture a unicorn.?"

"If a maiden is lured into the forest to bring one out, if one can be tricked, if distracted by the plaintive cries of her broken pure heart, if it does not protect itself from the magic...maybe an enchanted silver net will hold it."

"That's a lot of ifs."

"What else would you do?"

Mercet shrugged. "Drive the unicorn to the sea with a magical beast. Much easier."

"We're nowhere near the sea. Besides, I don't want to just look at unicorns. I don't even want one of the impudent things. I want..."

"Its forest." Mercet finished Zadok's sentence perfunctorily.

Zadok glared at him. "You think it's a small thing to want the forest and not the beast itself?"

"The unicorn itself can impart power and longevity maybe immortality. It's better used dead. You can't keep it forever alive against its will. You'll never have your forest. To be eternal the beast would have to live in it." Again Mercet's eyes held disdain.

"You said you knew nothing."

Mercet shrugged. "Well some insignificant amount."

"There is a way. I have found a way." Zadok's eyes burned with a fiery stare that unnerved Mercet. He scrutinized the younger mage as he regained his composure. "Handsome of face, dull of wit..."

Mercet scowled. "It's a wonder you bother with me," he said dryly.

"Mm, indeed." Zadok motioned for Mercet to turn around for his inspection. This Mercet did but kept his eyes upon his crafty old mentor. The young man stood almost six feet tall. Though most of his svelte form was obscured by his robe, his broad shoulders and chest filled in well. Dark eyes, a well trimmed goatee and shoulder length, wavy, black hair punctuated his smarmy good looks. Only the requisite dirt-brown robe of the apprentice seemed out of place on him. "But do you really have what it takes to be great? Have you the ability to keep focused on what is necessary and not be diverted by distraction and emotional attachments?"

"What sort of emotional attachments? I'm a dedicated and focused student, Master Zadok, completely at your service."

"Don't patronize me whelp. You're a self-serving leach who'd like nothing better than to see my entrails spilled upon the ground." Mercet stopped mid-turn and glared into Zadok's glaring eyes. Their matched expressions caused them to change in unison to one of amusement. "Yes. I believe you'll do the job nicely."

Mercet completed his turn and stood before Zadok with an air of importance. "I'm able to do any task you wish of me and of course to learn any magic necessary to accomplish it."

"It's why you've come to dear old master Zadok. To learn from the greatest wizard of Kryslis and blah, blah, blah."

Mercet clenched his teeth, returning to his former expression of loathing.

"Hate me all you want. You'll learn what you came for. In the meanwhile you serve my purposes. But this task should afford you some amusement. There's a particular woman you're to seduce."

Mercet smirked. "A woman? The wife of a baron or some rich widow?"

"No. You fool. I don't need riches. Do that on your own time. This woman is a virgin girl, the daughter of a grain farmer."

"What could you possibly gain from a grain farmer?"

"Nothing you idiot! It's the girl's innocence I want."

"Shouldn't you be seducing her then?" Mercet paused with a raised brow, examined Zadok slouched in his high-backed chair and tried to picture him seducing a young woman. The idea repulsed him and he laughed. But, the mocking had no effect upon the old man. Instead, Zadok murmured a few words and fanned his fingers before his face. Suddenly Mercet let his countenance drop as he stared into his own face. The indignity of Zadok's voice coming from his own likeness flared Mercet's ire toward the mage. "You'd do it with my face?"

"I could. But, I have other work to do." He waved away the transmogrification.

"How then am I to take a virgin for you? It makes no sense. If I seduce her, she'll give me her virginity...not you."

"No you nincompoop! I want to use her innocence not take it," the old man snapped. Mercet responded with a tight scowl. "All right, all right! Seduce may be too strong a word for now. How about beguile? Would it suit you better?"

"That's significantly different from seduction," the apprentice replied, "and less fun."

Zadok continued. "We'll take a short trip. On the way, I'll explain it to you."

"I'll have Slagspit prepare the wagon. How many days?"

"Not Slagspit or any other. You. I can't have the stench of goblin and gethim about us. We'll use horses only. Prepare for a ten-day."

Mercet eyed him curiously. "Yes, Master Zadok." With a curt nod, he left the room.

Late that afternoon, dust rose from the hard, dry earth behind Zadok's boot as he scuffled from the tower's door to the broad, rutted coach path circling before it. The goblin shuffled along behind him. Haloed by the circular drive was an area of yellowed grass spotted with an assortment of weeds. In the center of this sat the ruins of an old fountain. In its prime, the tower had seen many visitors and housed as many as a half-dozen students and servants, human servants, for its mage, whoever that was. It had been long abandoned when Zadok found it. Black vines clung to one side of the lower housing from the southeast corner and along the east wall reaching with its skeletal fingers around the tower base and upwards breaking into sparse, worm-like trails the higher up it went. Spiky thorns claimed it as the remnant of an ancient climbing rose. Formerly whitewashed stone was now splotched with weathered grays and greenish-yellow lichen. However strong or regal it once was, the stone now settled, the tower swayed so that the entire edifice mirrored its current mage, sagging front and back.

"No, you can't come. You must tend to the rooms. Find my book. Make sure none of your disgusting kin break anything or steal anything while I'm gone. And for gods sakes, all of you relieve yourselves outside and not in my commodes!"

"Yez, Master." Slagspit bobbed three times in lieu of a bow. "What if you does not returns, Master? Slagspit has never been left alone. Slagspit has never been master of the house."

Zadok cringed. "You are not master of the house even now. You are caretaker, so take care."

"But, Slagspit is boss over goblin fellows, yez?"

With a heavy sigh, Zadok nodded.

Mercet rode up from the stables with Zadok's horse and a pack horse in tow.

"Slagspit will not lets Master down!" He puffed himself up with pride and hot air, literally until his head and body were half again their normal size. Then he released the air with a wheeze that smelled of rotting fish. Zadok reeled. "But...but..." Slagspit sputtered.

"But what?" Zadok took the reins of his horse from Mercet.

"But what if something happens and master and Mercet does not return?"

"Then you're to round up all of your kinfolk into the tower. Tie them up with a rope in a big bundle. Get your bow and quiver ready. Then you must set fire to the tower and stand guard over your kin. Let none of them escape."

"When does Slagspit puts the fire out, Master?"

"You don't. You and your kin are to burn down with the tower. Nothing is to be left of you." Zadok fanned the air before his nose as a putrid odor arose from the goblin.

Slagspit looked down at the darkening spot of his trousers and tunic as a puddle formed at his feet. "Sorry, Master. Servant has wet his self again and also..."

"Yes, yes. Enough! You will carry out my command if I do not return after ten days."

"Yez, Master. Slagspit and his family will perishes in flame and glory for Master."

Zadok rolled his eyes and mounted his horse. "Don't go into the tower until you have cleaned yourself." He moved his horse into a walk then called out over his shoulder, "In the river! Not the drinking water!"

"Yez, Master!" Slagspit called after him and waved until the riders and their pack horse were out of sight.

They rode out quietly for two days. Mercet wondered all the while just when this explanation would come about. On the third day, as they cleared their morning camp the old man broke the silence. "What season is this?"

Mercet looked around at the colorful deciduous trees and blankets of fallen leaves. "We swept back two mountains of leaves for soft bedding and to clear up a place safe for our fire last night. We are bitten through with chill and rains but not snow, and you don't know what season it is?"

Zadok flung a palm out in Mercet's direction and the campfire instantly flared across five feet of air and set Mercet's pant leg aflame "Don't be impertinent!"

Mercet slapped at the fire and crushed the material to smother it out. "What are you doing? These are my only traveling clothes!"

Zadok flicked his wrist. "Shut up!"

Mercet's mouth clamped shut and he looked daggers at the master mage. It was at times like these he thought about the day when he would know all he needed to dispose of the old man.

Zadok looked away and released Mercet. "Remember who questions and who answers."

Mercet coughed and squawked a reply. "Yes, of course."

"Now what season is it?"

"Autumn," Mercet coughed again as he spoke and rubbed his throat. "What some call fall, as the leaves fall...for most trees, leaving them barren for winter." He motioned around himself as if to point out the obvious. "The uh...trees turn colors and the air cools considerably and uh..."

"That's enough. Remember that today."

Mercet nodded afraid to utter another word, but wore his thoughts on his countenance, working his jaw as he continued to break camp.

They rode into the day silent as before. The old mage stared at the road before them even as it entered a forest of dense conifers. Mercet followed pulling the pack horse along behind him. The archmage stopped his horse abruptly, rudely interrupting Mercet's reverie when his own horse pulled up to avoid the former's tail.

"Are we there?" Mercet asked.

Zadok ignored the question but urged his horse on and continued to look about expectantly. Mercet too, was alert, watching his instructor and following both the master's horse and his gaze. The density of the forest disbursed, giving way gradually to a forest of giant trees through which darkness was salted with the occasional glimpse of a green, sunlit glade or meadow. The effect was profoundly alluring.

"What season is it?" asked the old man.

"Autumn," Mercet said absently, reiterating the morning's answer without detail.

The old man's horse walked on as he scanned about.

They continued on the path for many long minutes as the windows to the meadows opened and closed between the trees more frequently, flourishing an assortment of brightly colored tapestries of nature.

"What season is it?"

"Autumn," Mercet answered dutifully remembering, though his face displayed the awe he felt.

After another long while, the master repeated his question yet again.

"Autumn, Master Zadok. We know it's autumn..."

Zadok stopped his horse three giant trees short of passing a bright glade of spring-green grass and wildflowers, where birds sang and water could be heard tumbling into a pool somewhere. His shoulders sank in despair, and he turned his horse about. For the first time since the morning, his eyes fell upon Mercet. They opened wide with recognition as he asked again with emphasis, "What season is it, Mercet?"

"Autumn. Master, you told me to remem..." As Mercet turned to meet his master's stare, the meaning of his questioning dawned upon the young mage. He scanned from Zadok to the trees to the glade just beyond their trail and back again. "You can't see it."

"You on the other hand, can." The archmage sneered but refrained from punishing the witless younger man. "How long?"

"I...you asked me to recall that it's autumn. I thought you meant..."

"HOW LONG?!" Zadok shouted.

Mercet shrugged and bowed his head apologetically. "Since you first asked. I could see small clearings between the great trees."

"I knew it!" Zadok shouted triumphantly.

"Do you wish to make camp here, Master?"

"No, no we mustn't disturb the forest. We'll use no wood or water nor leaf nor blade here. This place knows me, and if it should learn of you too, soon it will hide itself from you as well."

"Then we should go at once."

"We shall, but first go down there off the road," Zadok pointed between the trees to one side. "On foot, go down to where there is a large rock with the root of a giant tree curling over it, and from there, see if you can see the pool. There should be three stones over which the water falls from a spring down into it."

Mercet did as he was instructed and found the pool just as Zadok had described it. As he sat observing from behind the rock, many birds and animals came to have their drink of its water. Mercet watched for a while. Then Zadok's voice, like a close whisper in his ear, called him back. A psionic spell? Mercet wondered.

He returned to see the old man sitting at the side of the road upon a log, the three horses fettered in the middle of the road with their reins tied together at their muzzles to prevent them from eating even a stray blade of grass. "Did you see it?" Zadok asked.

"I saw an amazing number of animals of all kinds, the predator and its prey together, drinking from the pool, as if they were not mortal enemies. It was unbelievable how..."

Zadok held up a hand and without magic stopped the younger mage's ravings. "But no unicorn appeared to you."

Mercet shook his head. "I'm sorry no."

Zadok's expression became sympathetic, which was unusual enough that Mercet eyed him suspiciously. "It's alright the unicorn won't show herself. Didn't show herself to me either, but she's here somewhere." He cast his eyes about as if he would catch a glimpse of one.

"She? You know it is a female whose forest this is?"

"No. I say she, like we call cats she and dogs he, though the individual may not be of that gender."

"Ah, I see."

"Now we leave." Zadok set about unfettering the horses.

They camped outside the enchanted forest. At dawn Zadok chatted about herbs and runes and simple magic that Mercet had mastered and how and when best to apply them, which Mercet was not so aware of. He cautioned Mercet against using magic too freely or spontaneously, especially not while angered, which Mercet thought to be hypocritical of him.

That day as they moved away from the forest, Zadok took a road that meandered over some rolling farmland until a small village appeared in the near distance. He handed Mercet a small bag of coins and instructed him to go to the village and purchase a rapier. Then he set up the new camp just off the road at that spot. He was brewing tea when Mercet returned. "Did you know that there are elves in that town? I've never seen so many elves in one place." Mercet said, turning the handle of the weapon towards his master.

Zadok took the rapier and set it aside. "Mm yes," he replied. "This close to an enchanted forest, I'm not surprised." Zadok gestured for Mercet to get into their food supplies, meaning for him to get cooking a meal.

As they ate, they talked. "Your work will be to get the girl to go to the forest and bond with the unicorn there. You'll lay a trap using the girl to hold the unicorn's attention while you capture it with this." From a saddle bag resting by his foot, Zadok produced what appeared to be fine, loosely woven, shiny cloth.

"A cloth?" Mercet looked at his master as if the old man had lost his mind.

"A net, like I told you," the mage corrected. "Pure silver as finely woven as any elf could weave. Light as duck down but with the strength of a hundred centaurs. And it responds easily to magic. Lay it on the ground; say the words and..." Zadok snapped his fingers. "Got it!"

"Very nice!" Mercet held out a hand to take the net, but Zadok withheld the fey material.

"Not now. In time." He folded the net carefully and wrapped it in a burlap bag.

Mercet sipped at his tea attempting to hide his disappointment and contempt. He sat back and shivered with the cold. "How do I convince her to go to the forest?" The young man contemplated only as long as it took to wrap a blanket about his shoulders. His eyes narrowed. "Oh I know. Every maiden wants to meet a unicorn. 'Miss there is a forest right over there with a unicorn in it. Would you like to see?' 'Oh yes, kind sir, do show me.'" He made a display of play acting that caused Zadok's face to redden with ire. "And once there, what will ensure she meets a unicorn let alone bonds with it? Doesn't the unicorn have anything to say about it?"

"Shut up! There are forces of innate magic you're too stupid and ignorant to realize!"

"I am not stupid!" Mercet flinched, ready for a slap not with hands but of some painful magic. "But I'll admit to ignorance." He said meekly. The slap, oddly enough, was not delivered.

"It'll happen. Innocence is what draws the unicorn." Zadok hesitated, looking Mercet in the eyes. "If you can manage it, beguile her, remember?"

"I have a charm spell, I think. Works on animals for a short time. Should I use that?"

Zadok put on his benevolent teacher face and steepled his fingers. "No, she must go willingly to seek the unicorn for aid."

The apprentice gazed into the campfire. "Master, why would she need aid?"

Zadok rolled his eyes and waved the question away. He returned to his more malevolent self with a sneer.

He fished another object from the saddle bag as he tucked the net away. Then the mage handed an amulet to Mercet. "This is called the Dragon's Eye. It will allow me to keep track of your progress."

"Why not use your scrying pool?"

"I don't want to look at you, imbecile. I want to see what you're seeing."

Mercet looked it over. It was obviously a valuable piece. The chain was pure gold as was the setting. Five rubies surrounded a smooth, pale, gold-flecked-green disk. Mercet put it on. "Doesn't seem to do anything."

"Have you learned so little?" Zadok poured more tea for Mercet. Then, from a pocket in his waistcoat he pulled an object similar in appearance to the amulet. "Socroth viesay." With these words the disks both lit up, the amulet in gold light, the scrying device in a dull white. Soon Zadok showed the face of his magical device to Mercet. In the center was mirrored the image of Zadok displaying the device. At sight of the reflected image, Mercet raised the face of the amulet and peered into the shining eye. Zadok continued to hold the receiver as before. He didn't need to look into it to see his apprentice's face. He rolled his eyes again. "You can also call to me and hear me through the amulet."

His words were echoed in the amulet though not as loudly as Zadok's presence. "When she goes to the forest the first time, follow her. Tap it three times."

"Ah the strength of three." Mercet nodded sagely as if the lessons on triads and triunes was deep knowledge only seasoned mages knew rather than one of his very first lessons. Zadok pocketed the receptor and the eye closed.

"Whose insignia is inscribed on the back?" asked Mercet. He turned the back of it out toward Zadok. "It isn't yours. Got someone else's name under it too."

"Never you mind," snapped Zadok. "Just do what I said. And take it off until you need it."

"Yes, yes. Tap thrice to call you. I've got it." Mercet removed it, stuffing it into his bag beside his potion pack. He deliberately carried a variety of his favorite potions with him—just in case.

Long into the night Zadok talked about how the silver net was spun to capture a unicorn. All the while, he fed Mercet the tea and kept a pot boiling into which he continued to drop some herbs.

"What potion is this you are giving me?" Mercet asked without suspicion. "Something to cause me to be viewed as charming upon meeting this grain farmer's daughter? I assure you, no matter how ugly she is, I will be charming. Though by what you've been telling me, it'll take more than a few hours or mere days to accomplish what you ask. Won't the tea have worn off by then?"

Zadok grinned menacingly. "I have no doubt that you can be charming. The girl is quite beautiful, but I must rely upon your good judgment to not let her charms win you to her but to win her utterly with yours." He paused briefly. "Of course, you'll need some assistance to put you into a position that gains her undivided attention long enough for you to engage your charms and get her into the forest." Zadok poured out the rest of the tea, then dried and wrapped the pot in a rag. Mercet moved from the log he sat upon to the ground, preparing to settle in a comfortable place for the remainder of the night. Zadok took the younger man's cup and spoke as he put their dishes and supplies into the packs. "Harvest this year has not been generous for the farmer. Still, it was good enough that they have gone into Freefolk to get their winter supplies. By early morning, they should be coming right along this road. "

"How convenient," said Mercet with a smirk. "But, you have not yet told me what tea you've been feeding me all night. I smell and taste a bit of cinnamon."

"Indeed...and masterwort, touch of lobelia and generous mullein..." Zadok let his voice trail off.

"Mullein? Do you think I will lose courage as we sit talking? Or perhaps you expect me to fear the farmer's pitchfork?"

"No. I'll get him out of the way once you're there." Zadok looked up as the sun began to rise. "Let's pack up now."

Mercet scowled, as he felt quite tired and would like to have rested. Though he said so, the senior mage merely continued dismantling their camp, barking orders to Mercet. "It's good you added the lobelia," complained Mercet. "If I didn't despise you before I..."

"Good," interrupted Zadok as he secured the last of their loads. "Because then this won't hurt so badly." He drew out the rapier and plunged it through Mercet's torso just below his spleen. Before the startled young man could think to defend himself with spells or weapon, Zadok lunged at him again and again stabbing him in one shoulder and an upper arm. Then he wiped the rapier as the junior mage attempted to cast a harmful spell at his teacher.

Zadok thwarted the spell easily. "Don't waste your energy. The potion will keep you alive. But, don't use your healing magic either when I'm gone. You let her do the healing, and get her to go to the forest for the herbs." Mercet eyed him wildly. "Quit gawking. You'll figure it out. Now get up to the road. I'll let your horse go down the way a bit. You can happen on it there." With that Zadok mounted his own steed and led the other two horses away at a trot.

What is this diabolical plan? Will it succeed? Once you read this epic tale, you'll want to tell your friends about it.

https://littlecabbageheadbooks.com